# DEAD FALL

# DEAD FALL

## A THRILLER

## Brad Thor

**EMILY BESTLER BOOKS**

**ATRIA**

New York   London   Toronto   Sydney   New Delhi

ATRIA

An Imprint of Simon & Schuster, Inc.
1230 Avenue of the Americas
New York, NY 10020

First Emily Bestler Books/Atria Books hardcover edition July 2023

EMILY BESTLER BOOKS/ATRIA BOOKS and colophon
are trademarks of Simon & Schuster, Inc.

For information about special discounts for bulk purchases,
please contact Simon & Schuster Special Sales at
1-866-506-1949 or business@simonandschuster.com.

The Simon & Schuster Speakers Bureau can bring authors to your live event. For
more information or to book an event, contact the Simon & Schuster Speakers
Bureau at 1-866-248-3049 or visit our website at www.simonspeakers.com.

Manufactured in the United States of America

1   3   5   7   9   10   8   6   4   2

Library of Congress Cataloging-in-Publication Data has been applied for.

ISBN 978-1-9821-8219-9
ISBN 978-1-9821-8222-9 (ebook)

*For David Brown,*
*my longtime friend and publicist, who is an absolute mensch.*
*Thank you for helping me climb the mountain.*

There is no avoiding war; it can only be postponed to the advantage of others.

—Niccolò Machiavelli

# PROLOGUE

T he children ran for their lives. Those who could, fled into the woods. Those who couldn't—the smaller and the sickest among them—were forced to take up hiding places inside. The adults tried to convey calm, but it was wall-to-wall panic. And rightfully so. *The monsters were coming.*

In the basement of the abandoned Soviet-era tuberculosis hospital, via a decrepit passageway punctuated by broken light fixtures, rusted pipes, and puddles of fetid water, was the kitchen. And in that kitchen was the best answer the orphanage had been able to come up with for its most complicated problem.

An old pantry had been outfitted like a chicken coop. Its shelves had been taken over by wooden nesting boxes pre-staged with bedding. The few blankets that could be spared had been tacked to the walls to help deaden any sound. A run-down refrigerator with a false back hid the entrance of the pantry from view.

Each of the infants inside had been given an emergency ration of formula. The toddlers, many of whom were suffering from colds and flu, had been given small pieces of bread soaked in tea and dabbed with a little bit of honey. Anything to keep them quiet. It was imperative that they maintain absolute silence.

With all able-bodied men at the front, the entirety of the orphanage staff, save for its eighty-year-old custodian, was female. There was no one available to fight for them. They would have to look out for themselves.

Weeks' worth of discussions over what to do if this moment ever came had given birth to a plan. Everything about it—the running, the hiding, *all* of it—was extreme, but absolutely necessary. One of the evilest tendrils of the war was about to slither in and wrap itself around their throats.

The children had practiced taking deep, quiet breaths. Those with respiratory issues had been given pillows to cough into, but only as a last resort. Their hope for survival now rested not in their numbers, but in their ability to remain invisible.

Anna Royko, who had been at the orphanage for only a few months, had insisted on taking watch. She was an American of Ukrainian descent.

Born and raised in Chicago, the twenty-five-year-old had been deeply affected by the suffering she had seen coming out of Ukraine. When news broke that the Russians had bombed a children's hospital and maternity ward in Mariupol, she could no longer sit by. She had to do something.

After emailing her resignation to the law firm where she worked, she booked a one-way ticket to Poland, as martial law had been declared in Ukraine and commercial air traffic had been suspended.

She spent a week knocking on doors and visiting various aid organizations across Warsaw before one finally took her on board.

Though she had zero experience working for an NGO and even less experience operating in a war zone, it was her fluency in Ukrainian that proved too valuable to pass up.

The group that hired her was a small humanitarian organization focused on getting much-needed supplies to the hardest-hit orphanages throughout Ukraine. The position paid next to nothing, would require grueling hours, and was extremely dangerous. So much so that there were reams of waivers she was required to sign.

The good they were doing was unquestionable and so, keeping her inner lawyer in check, she moved rapidly through the paperwork. After signing and initialing where indicated, she started work the very same day.

What Anna saw on her first trip into Ukraine ripped her heart out. The misery, the desperation, the horrific conditions the children were living in . . . all of it. The only thing that gave her hope was the heroism of the adults who were risking everything to take care of them.

As the war ground on, the situations at the orphanages grew more dire. No matter how quickly she and her colleagues returned with supplies, there was never enough. It was like showing up as the *Titanic* was slipping under the icy water only to toss out pool noodles. Watching people slowly die, especially children, wasn't why she was there.

She had come to Ukraine to help ease people's suffering, if not to somehow reverse it. But when she and her team arrived at an orphanage for special needs children in the southern city of Mykolaiv—halfway between Odesa and Kherson—something inside her snapped. The building had been bombed and completely destroyed.

As badly as the supplies from Poland were needed, being a glorified delivery driver was no longer enough for her. She had to do more.

Remembering a dilapidated orphanage in an old tuberculosis hospital in eastern Ukraine, and the tirelessly dedicated women who ran it, she decided that was where she could make a difference. By focusing solely on that location and the children within it, she could have the greatest possible impact.

Once she got to Kharkiv and had finished distributing supplies, she bid her stunned NGO colleagues good-bye.

As she walked across Freedom Square and disappeared from view, she tuned out their voices, which were begging her to reconsider, as well as warning that she was making a grave and likely deadly mistake. Anna didn't care.

At that moment, she had no clue how she would reach her newly decided-upon destination, nor whether they would even accept her help. All she knew was that it was where she was being called to be.

When she finally made it to the orphanage's front doors, the pack with everything she owned slung across her back, everyone inside was shocked to see her.

Despite desperately needing an extra set of hands, they tried to discourage her from staying. They felt that by taking her in, they would somehow be depriving the other orphanages that had grown so dependent on her. Anna, however, would hear nothing of it.

Allowing her inner lawyer to come out, she informed the women that she knew they needed help and that she wouldn't take no for an answer.

The staff was stuck with her, whether they liked it or not. Truth be told, they were thrilled to have her.

She was a breath of fresh air. The children loved her. And as the youngest member of the staff by at least fifteen years, Anna had reservoirs of energy that none of them could match. With so many children, so few resources, and such an old building, there was always something that needed doing. No matter what the task, she was always the first to volunteer.

Which was what had brought her to the present moment—acting as the orphanage's official lookout.

In each of the designated hiding places, the children needed at least one adult with them. Since Anna knew the building like the back of her hand, was a runner who worked out daily, and could move from room to room and floor to floor quickly, everyone knew she was the best choice. She was also, the staff believed, fearless.

In their minds, based upon the characters they watched on TV, most American women were fiercely independent and didn't take shit from anyone. Throw in being an attorney, and it took Anna's badassery in their eyes to a whole different level.

But it was one particular incident that had cemented her reputation at the orphanage as someone that you didn't want to mess with.

Shortly after her arrival, a group of three men had shown up in the middle of the night attempting to "secure" the building's generator for the "war effort." Not only were they wearing tracksuits and gold jewelry, but they were also remarkably drunk.

The most likely explanation was that they were a mafia contingent roaming the region, stealing whatever would fetch a good price on the black market. Anna had been determined not to let that happen.

When one of them tried to intimidate her by pulling a knife and saying that he was going to rape her, she kneed him in the groin, grabbed a fistful of his hair, and pressed her own knife—one she had been carrying since arriving in Ukraine—against his throat.

His cohorts were shocked, knocked off balance by how quickly she had taken control. It only lasted for a moment. Soon enough, the duo had regained their composure and were gaming out their next move. The men didn't believe she would harm their associate.

When they advanced, however, Anna didn't waver. She pressed the blade deeper into the man's fleshy neck and kept going, even after she drew blood.

As the front of his shirt began to stain a deep red, the other men froze, once again unsure of how to proceed.

Anna told her captive to drop his knife, which he did, and she kicked it to the side.

There was only one message she wanted to get across to these scumbags—that this orphanage was more trouble than it was worth and that they shouldn't ever bother coming back.

Out of the corner of her eye, she saw that the custodian, who lived on the edge of the property, had shown up, shotgun in hand.

With backup on scene and her message delivered, Anna released her captive, giving the thug a shove in the direction of his comrades.

Watching them back off toward their vehicle, she offered one last piece of advice—that they find their man a hospital with a staff who knew what they were doing. None of the local butchers would be able to sew up the wound she had carved into the man's neck. If they didn't quickly head for one of the bigger cities and get him properly taken care of, the artery was going to rupture and he was going to bleed out.

It was a lie. Bluster. She hadn't cut him anywhere near his artery. But all that had mattered was that the would-be thieves believed it. And by the looks on their faces, they had. The men left and never came back.

Fast-forward to now and the orphanage was dealing with a whole new threat. Russian soldiers had been spotted on the outskirts of town.

They were moving from house to house. Scavenging. The stories of their looting were legion. Microwaves, winter clothing, washers and dryers . . . there had even been reports of the soldiers removing the ballistic plates from their tactical vests and inserting laptops and tablets they had stolen along the way. Their thievery, however, wasn't the worst of the conduct they had become known for.

Kidnap, rape, torture, and murder were what Ukrainians feared the most. Anyone was fair game for the Russians—not just women and girls, but men and little boys as well. They were barbaric.

The evil flowed straight from Moscow. Russian soldiers had not only been encouraged to commit sexual assaults, but they had even been issued Viagra.

The Russians were known to raid a village and stay for days, carrying out their horrors via around-the-clock shifts. The word *nightmare* didn't even begin to describe the abominations they so zealously perpetrated.

These terrors had become the orphanage staff's worst fear—that the children, whose care and protection had been entrusted to them, might be subject to such unspeakable crimes.

It was why they had worked so hard to develop their plan—the children who could run, would run. The rest would hide. And then everyone would pray. Everyone, that is, except Anna. She didn't have time for prayer.

Someone had suggested that they make the orphanage look deserted, as if it hadn't been occupied in years, but it simply wasn't feasible. The best they could hope to do was to make it look like everyone had fled. The final touches of that plan fell to Anna.

After making sure that the remaining children and adults were secreted away in their hiding places, she moved hastily through the building, ticking off her checklist.

All of the lights needed to be shut off, along with the boiler. Any remaining coats or boots near the front doors needed to be hidden. What little medicine and first aid supplies they had needed to be gathered up and tucked away for safekeeping.

Her sweep through the facility didn't have to be perfect, it just had to be convincing.

The Russians were used to people fleeing in advance of their arrival. As long as that appeared to be what had happened here, everything—the orphanage staff hoped—would be okay.

Moving from room to room, her heart pounding, Anna focused on what she had to do.

Contrary to how her colleagues saw her, she wasn't fearless. Only stupid people were fearless in the face of danger. She was, actually, quite afraid, but the orphanage had become her home and all of the souls within it her family.

She often thought of one of the quotes her sixth-grade teacher in Chicago had taped to the wall behind her desk. It was from Winston Churchill. "Fear is a reaction. Courage is a decision."

And so, as she had on the night of the attempted generator theft, Anna made a decision. Though she was scared, she would exhibit courage on behalf of the people and the place that she had grown to care so deeply about.

With the dark brown hair of her ponytail bouncing against the back of her neck, she hurriedly completed her check of the building and then moved to the window that would serve as her lookout position.

It killed her that they hadn't been able to hide all of the orphanage's food. Once the soldiers had discovered the kitchen, they were going to abscond with quite a bounty. There was no telling how the staff would ever replenish their stocks. So many of the items they depended on had gone from scarce to absolutely nonexistent. Even once everyday items like butter and eggs had become luxuries.

Peering out the window, Anna focused on the bare branches of the perfectly spaced trees that lined the driveway up to the former hospital. The contrast between the ugly, communist architecture and the facility's thoughtful grounds had fascinated her from her very first visit. Even under the brutal yoke of the Soviets, the Ukrainians had still found opportunities for artistic expression and ways to quietly nourish beauty.

Sadly, that was no longer the case. Ever since the Russian invasion, Ukrainians had been focused on one thing—survival.

Anna's thoughts were suddenly interrupted by bursts of machine-gun fire, which drew her attention toward the village.

Squinting through a pair of cracked binoculars that the custodian had scrounged, she could see a column of three military vehicles approaching. Each of them had been painted with a large, white *Z*.

Many Russian officials claimed that the letter was an abbreviation of the phrase "For victory," while others—with a straight face—said that it was meant to represent the expression "For peace." The Ukrainians, however, had their own definitions.

In Ukraine, the *Z* symbol was referred to either as the *Zwastika*—a reference to the Nazi swastika—or as the *Zieg*, a play on the Hitler salute, *Sieg Heil*.

As the column moved through the village, the men in the vehicles kept wildly firing their guns. What they were shooting at, Anna had no idea. She couldn't see a soul. Anyone in their right mind had either fled or was in hiding.

The hope at the orphanage was that the men would just keep moving, but as soon as Anna saw one of the vehicles peel off and head up the hospital's driveway, she knew that wasn't going to be the case. It was time to relay the situation to the others.

Moving rapidly through the halls, she used a wrench to tap on the pipes to transmit her message.

All of the staff, along with all of the children who were old enough to understand, now knew that the men had arrived and that no one must make a sound until Anna had given the all clear.

Slipping into her hiding spot, it was finally Anna's time to pray, which she did, fervently.

She asked God to protect everyone in the building, as well as the older children who had run off to hide in a cave deep within the woods.

Once her prayers were said, all she could do was wait and hold her breath. As it turned out, she didn't have to wait long.

Six horrifying men entered the building. Their heads were shaved and their faces had been painted to resemble skulls. They carried hatchets and long, curved knives that looked like something butchers might use.

Because the building had obviously been a hospital at one point, their first target was the dispensary. They wanted anything they could get their hands on—morphine, amphetamines, barbiturates, it didn't matter. The dispensary, however, turned out to be a dry hole. Every cabinet and every drawer had long been cleared out.

With no drugs to be found, they swept the offices, searching everywhere for bottles of alcohol or anything else of value. Once again, they came up empty.

Moving deeper into the building, they eventually discovered what the old hospital was currently being used for. Next to drugs and booze, their favorite spoils were women and children.

Running through the halls, the ghouls began squealing like little pigs and singing a Russian folk song, "Oysya, Ti Oysya."

"I won't touch you," the deviants sang, "don't worry. Oysya, you Oysya, don't be afraid of me."

From her hiding spot, Anna could hear them getting closer. Even though she didn't speak Russian, the singing made her blood run cold.

At some point, the pack decided to split up and fan out in different directions. A man coming toward her started howling like a wolf. He was either high or insane. Perhaps he was both. Anna didn't care. She just wanted them gone.

Frozen in place, she listened as he scuttled past. The body odor wafting off him was so rancid that she almost gagged and gave herself away. Thankfully, she kept it together.

Straining her ears, she waited for the man to turn down the next hallway, but he didn't. Instead, he came to a stop. She could feel that he was looking at something, studying it. Intuitively, she knew exactly what it was.

In front of the main staircase leading down to the kitchen, Anna had shoved a bookcase. Around it she had strewn trash and a few pieces of broken furniture. It was a less-than-optimal camouflage job, but it had been the only thing they could come up with.

A few seconds later, she heard the bookcase being scraped across the floor. *The fiend was pushing it away from the wall!*

It was followed by the sound of his footsteps bounding down the stairs two at a time. *He was headed for the kitchen.*

Soon enough, a series of loud crashing and banging sounds began. She could hear the invader overturning baker's racks and shelving units. It sounded like nothing more than wanton vandalism—destruction for destruction's sake. *Or was it?*

As another terrible thought entered her mind, her blood once again ran cold. *Could the bookcase at the top of the stairs have given him reason to believe that something else might be hidden in the kitchen?*

She had no way of knowing, but the fear gripped Anna so tightly that she could barely breathe. The bookcase had been *her* idea.

Regardless of what his motivation was, if this savage was intent on tearing the kitchen apart piece by piece, the odds were that he was going to uncover the infants and other children hiding in the pantry.

She couldn't let that happen. And while she knew it was insane—beyond insane, actually—she *had* to do something.

Against all the advice she had given her colleagues regarding *not* leaving their hiding places until after the threat had passed, she left hers.

Careful not to make any noise, she moved through the hallway and crept down the stairs, her knife clasped tightly in her hand. She had no idea how she was going to handle the situation, only that it needed to be handled and there was no one else but her.

With the sound of each broken dish or smashed cabinet, she flinched, but kept going. She had never been so terrified in all her life.

Drawing nearer to the kitchen, she took a deep breath and paused. *This was it.* Exhaling, she peered around the edge of the doorway into the kitchen. There, amid the destruction, she could see the Russian beast.

He had laid his hatchet on the counter and was focused on the old refrigerator, which was obscuring the entrance to the pantry. *Had he figured it out?*

If he hadn't yet, Anna was certain that he was about to. And once he had discovered the children and staff hiding on the other side, there was no telling what horrors he would unleash.

She had to come up with a plan—right now, right here—before any of the other monsters joined him in the basement. She was only going to get one chance.

She didn't want to tangle with the man, not physically, not if she didn't have to. There was no telling what kind of psychotic tricks he might have up his sleeve. She had heard the grisly tales of Russians carrying straight razors in order to disfigure their victims once they'd had their way with them. She had no intention of becoming a victim.

The key to successfully overcoming the soldier was to use the element of surprise to her advantage. At the same time, she needed to keep as much distance between them as possible. Doing a fast scan of the kitchen, she locked onto an idea.

The only question remaining was whether she could fully launch her attack before the ghoul had a chance to react. There was only one way to find out.

Taking a final, deep breath, she counted down from three, then slid through the doorway and into the kitchen.

What she wouldn't have given at this moment for a gun and the knowledge of how to use it. Instead she would have to rely on active-shooter training she had received at her law firm back in Chicago.

The instructor, an ex–Green Beret, had based his workshop on the *Run, Hide, Fight* formula and had spent most of his time focusing on the *Fight* component. As Anna crept toward the fire extinguisher, she was grateful for everything the Special Forces operative had taught her. She only wished she had heeded his advice about regularly checking to make sure the extinguisher was up to date.

Not that it would have mattered. With all the bombs and missiles that had been falling on Ukraine, fresh fire extinguishers were simply another unicorn of the war—something rumored to exist, but impossible to find.

With her heart thumping in her chest, she chose her steps as carefully, as quickly, and as quietly as she could. She made her way across the side of the kitchen and successfully removed the extinguisher from the wall. Pulling the pin, she headed toward the man who was still, thankfully, preoccupied with the fridge.

She was almost on top of him when something caused the Russian to spin. The moment he caught sight of her, he lunged for his hatchet.

Anna had no idea if she was close enough to blind him with the fog of the extinguisher, but she had no other choice. The moment had arrived and she squeezed the handle, deploying an enormous cloud.

Though the extinguisher was seriously out of date, there was just enough pressure to do the job.

While the demon couldn't see, Anna had pinpointed his location and knew exactly where he was standing.

Raising the extinguisher, she charged and used all of her strength to bring the cylinder crashing down against the man's head.

It was a death blow. Anna had succeeded in cracking open the ghoul's skull and spilling his brains onto the kitchen floor as his lifeless body collapsed.

The mixture of fear and adrenaline only made her heart pound harder in her chest. There was no time to catch her breath or reassess the situation. There was only time to act. At some point, which she had to assume would be sooner rather than later, the monster's colleagues would be looking for him. Eventually they would make their way to the basement. She now needed an entirely new plan.

But before she could react, she heard someone step into the kitchen and cock a pistol.

# CHAPTER 1

The hit, deep inside the Russian client state of Belarus, had required a tremendous amount of planning in a very short period of time. The target would be moving soon. Once the window had closed, no one knew when or where it would open again.

The final go/no-go call was left to the team leader, Scot Harvath. The opportunity was too juicy to pass up. Faisal Al-Masri was a big fish. Taking him off the board would have global repercussions. After reviewing all of the intel, Harvath had given the mission the green light.

Al-Masri was one of the highest-ranking members of the Islamic Revolutionary Guard Corps and the head of Iran's drone program. The fact that the Israelis, who were exceedingly good at what they did, had tried and failed—not once, but twice—to take him out wasn't lost on Harvath. The man was exceedingly smart when it came to his security. In other areas, however, he had been making nothing but bad decisions.

In Iraq and Syria, under his orders, IRGC drones had been targeting Americans. U.S. military members, diplomatic personnel, and civilian contractors had all come under attack. For that, Al-Masri had earned himself a VIP position on the CIA's kill list. But his problems didn't end there.

He and the IRGC had been selling their Shahed-136 drones to the Russians, who in turn had been using them against civilian sites and critical infrastructure across Ukraine. With winter approaching, Russian President Fedor Peshkov had stepped up his attacks on hospitals, schools, power stations, water treatment facilities, bus stations, train stations, and rail lines. His goal was to terrorize and demoralize the people of Ukraine, making them as miserable as possible. What he ended up doing, however, was pissing them off *more*.

When Ukrainian Intelligence learned that Al-Masri and a team of ten drone instructors were headed to Belarus to train Russian forces, they passed that information on to the CIA.

Knowing that they would likely be blamed for anything that happened to Al-Masri and his team, the Ukrainians had only one request—that the strike be audacious.

Harvath was happy to take it under advisement. America's hit a few years back on the head of the IRGC's Quds Force, Qasem Soleimani, hadn't exactly been low-key. They'd used a Hellfire missile on his motorcade and splattered him across four Baghdad neighborhoods.

As fitting as it would have been to also take Al-Masri via a drone-fired weapon, the United States didn't have anything in the skies above Belarus. Harvath and his group were going to have to be more creative. They were also going to have to assume a lot more risk.

Al-Masri and the IRGC instructors were being protected by the Russian National Guard and officers from the Federal Security Service, also known as the FSB, successor to the KGB. In theory, they would be alert, disciplined, and well practiced in close protection. But in reality, they were still Russians, which meant they were prone to being lazy, undisciplined, and assigned at the last minute to work they were unqualified for.

President Peshkov placed little value on the lives of his citizens. He had been feeding his people nonstop into the wood chipper that was the war in Ukraine. What kind of talent he had in reserve that he could assign to protect Al-Masri and his people was anyone's guess.

Not that the level of talent being fielded by the Russians would have any impact on his operation. He didn't plan on getting in a gunfight. There were too many of them. Instead, he was going to take them in transit.

Because of the sensitivity of this operation, the CIA didn't want any official fingerprints on it. They wanted the United States to maintain full deniability. That's why it had been given to Harvath and his team at the

Carlton Group—a private intelligence agency named after its founder, Reed Carlton.

A legendary maverick at the CIA, Carlton had come up with the vision for and had helped establish the Agency's famed Counterterrorism Center.

Unhappy with what he saw as the growing timidity of management, and choking to death on the bureaucracy and red tape, he decided to give retirement a whirl. While Mrs. Carlton had enjoyed riding off into the sunset, being out of the game drove Mr. Carlton insane. America's enemies were only growing more dangerous and more emboldened. Something needed to be done. And so he had done it. He started his own organization.

With the rise of private military corporations, Carlton had seen the next wave of opportunity as the creation of private intelligence agencies. He had made a big bet and it had paid off handsomely. Despite his violent passing, the organization he had founded not only lived on but was thriving, accepting some of the most dangerous assignments the CIA and the White House could throw at it. At the center of it all was a highly skilled team of former spies and ex–Special Forces operatives.

Harvath, who had distinguished himself as a U.S. Navy SEAL before being brought to the White House to help bolster their counterterrorism expertise, eventually caught the attention of Carlton. The "Old Man," as those who had known him best called him, had handpicked Harvath as his successor and had taught him everything he knew. He had taken an apex predator and had made Harvath even more cunning, more deadly, and more resolved to take the fight to America's enemies.

In essence, Carlton had enhanced an already exceptionally lethal weapon only to realize that he couldn't control it, at least not fully.

When Alzheimer's kicked in and his health began failing, he had asked Harvath to take over for him and run the organization. To everyone's surprise, including Carlton's, Harvath had said no. He wanted to remain in the field, to keep hunting bad guys, and to make sure that America's enemies had a constant reason to lose sleep at night. In short, he didn't think anyone could do better at his job than him.

To a certain degree, he was right. He had learned a lot of things over the years and had an impressive set of skills. He was very good at what he did. He was also getting older.

He was now working out twice as hard and taking a range of performance-enhancing drugs just to keep up. Bumps and bruises that he never used to feel often hurt like hell and were lingering much longer than they used to. Recovery time from serious injury was bordering on ridiculous.

The long and the short of it was that there was only so much more he could take. As his current superior, Gary Lawlor—the man who had been brought in to run the Carlton Group—was often heard to say, Harvath was a selfish prick who should have been spotting and developing the next generation of talent, not running around the globe kicking in doors and shooting bad guys in the face.

Harvath possessed a vast wealth of knowledge. To risk it by going downrange and constantly putting his life on the line was not only foolish, it also spoke to some sort of deep-seated issue that probably required professional help.

Having heard it all countless times, Harvath let it roll off his back—though the "prick" comment stung, just a little bit, coming from Lawlor, whom Harvath had known for a very long time.

Gary's choice of language notwithstanding, Scot wasn't going to step off the field and hang up his cleats until he was good and ready. And right now, he wasn't ready. Though he was beginning to think that he might be getting closer.

For the moment, however, the only thing that mattered was the Al-Masri operation. The plan was unconventional, right down to its code-name, and that was exactly what he had loved about it.

In an old thriller film called *Ronin*, a group of ex-spies and former Special Forces members are hired to conduct a dangerous assignment. Among them is a British man who lied about his background, claiming to have been with the SAS. An American who used to work for the CIA—played by Robert De Niro—pushes the Brit on his tactically unsound plan for an ambush. When the Brit starts to stammer, De Niro presses harder, demanding, "What color is the boathouse at Hereford?"—a reference to the training facility for the SAS. The imposter is unable to answer and exposes himself for the fraud that he is.

The film was a favorite around the Carlton Group offices. So, when it was proposed that the team structure a similar ambush to what the phony SAS character had suggested, "Operation Boathouse" was born. But instead of placing shooters across the road from each other, they were going to use explosives.

The Iranians were training their would-be Russian drone pilot students at a village in Belarus called Mykulichi. Iranians being Iranians, however, they wanted to take full advantage of being away from the watchful, disapproving eyes of the mullahs back in Tehran. They wanted to party. As such, they had said no to being housed with the Russians in Mykulichi and had demanded to be put up at a hotel in the much livelier city of Gomel.

This meant a daily back-and-forth commute. The Iranians still being Iranians, they wanted to be transported in style.

Drab, uncomfortable military vehicles were totally out of the question. They wanted climate-controlled, luxury SUVs with leather seats and onboard Wi-Fi. They were absolute prima donnas and it was going to be their downfall.

The only armored, nonmilitary luxury SUVs in the country belonged to the President and were at his residence in Minsk. There was no way he was going to give them up, and the Russians in charge of guarding the Iranians knew better than to ask. That meant that they would have to source locally available, thin-skinned vehicles.

The head of the protective detail, a grizzled FSB man who had been in some of the worst battles during the Soviet occupation of Afghanistan, had gone to work, putting together the best motorcade he could. Their marching orders had been crystal clear—protect the Iranians, but also do *everything* necessary to make them happy. They were expected to be half bodyguards and half camp counselors.

The FSB man was embarrassed by how far Russia had fallen. That the Iranians would be so technologically superior that the Kremlin would have to kiss their asses in order to defeat a country like Ukraine wasn't just a bitter pill to swallow, it was like drinking battery acid.

Everything he knew and understood about the superiority of the Russian people and their leadership was now in question. Nevertheless, he did his job to the best of his ability. He tracked down the vehicles.

The Russian National Guard troops were divided between two Chinese-made armored vehicles borrowed from the Belarusian military, Hummer knockoffs known as Dongfeng Mengshis. One had been designated as the lead vehicle and the other brought up the rear. In between were three Chevrolet Suburbans carrying Al-Masri, the Iranian drone instructors, and the FSB security agents.

The FSB man had mapped the most efficient routes. He had mapped alternatives. He had identified choke points and potential ambush areas—of which, unfortunately, there were many. Mykulichi was a remote village, which was why it had been chosen for the training. Because of its location, there were only so many ways in and out. It definitely hadn't been optimal, but he had continued to make the best of a bad situation.

He had pinpointed hospitals and had made detailed dossiers on each Iranian, including their blood types. He had then presented the information to his men and had made them drive the routes over and over, throwing them into different, highly unusual problems to see how they would react; challenging them to adjust.

*Train like you fight and fight like you train.* It was one of the oldest, truest maxims of combat. While decades ago his military instructors had been fond of quoting Chief of Staff of the Prussian Army Helmuth von Moltke, who had said that no battle plan survives after first contact with the enemy, he had preferred how American boxer Mike Tyson had phrased it—everyone has a plan until they get punched in the mouth.

The FSB man wanted his men to be able to take that punch, recalibrate, and stay in the fight. So he drilled them, relentlessly, near the point of mutiny, and then he treated them to a raucous night out. They had earned it.

His plan wasn't perfect, but given the circumstances and his limited resources, it was solid. He was confident that no matter what got thrown at them, his men would not only be able to handle it, but they would also react in a polished, professional manner. By the time the Iranians arrived, their Russian hosts were ready for them.

What they weren't ready for, however, was Harvath, his men, and the hell they were about to rain down.

On the last day of training, as the sun was slipping low toward the horizon, the Iranians and their Russian protectors clambered into their vehicles for the final drive from the testing range in Mykulichi to the hotel back in Gomel.

The Iranians were looking forward to a final night out before returning to Tehran. The Russians were looking forward to getting rid of the Iranians and completing their assignment. Neither group was going to get what they wanted.

On a narrow piece of road snaking through the thick woods, they came around a tight bend.

Once all of the vehicles were aligned, one of Harvath's teammates—an ex–Delta Force operative named Staelin—stepped out into the road. Balancing an RPG on his shoulder, he took aim and let it rip.

The weapon fired a high-explosive antitank "HEAT" munition, which was designed to penetrate the lead vehicle's armor, release a superheated jet that flaked off pieces of the metal called "spall," and send them racing through the interior in a tornado of shrapnel. It was the equivalent of having a big, very nasty fragmentation grenade dropped through an open sunroof. Those who weren't instantly killed would be badly wounded.

The driver of the lead vehicle had barely applied pressure to his brakes when the round tore into his Dongfeng.

At the back of the column, another one of Harvath's men, a former Force Recon Marine named Haney, stepped out with the same weapon and engaged the rear armored vehicle.

As soon as the Dongfengs were taken out and Staelin and Haney had retreated a safe distance in each direction, Harvath gave the command to two more teammates—Preisler, an ex-MARSOC Marine, and Johnson, an ex–Green Beret—to commence the next wave. This part of the attack was what had given Operation Boathouse its name.

Both sides of the road had been lined with M18A1 antipersonnel weapons known as claymores.

They were mines that, via a layer of C4 explosive, fired a shit ton of steel balls in a fan-shape pattern at almost four thousand feet per second. The force of the detonation deforms the balls into something similar to a .22 projectile.

The mines had been daisy-chained together, allowing Johnson to light up one side of the road and Preisler the other. The occupants of the unarmored, soft-skinned Suburbans never stood a chance.

Weapons up and at the ready, Harvath and his team went vehicle to vehicle, making sure there were no survivors.

When Harvath got to Al-Masri, he put several extra rounds in him. He wanted there to be no doubt who, specifically, they had come for.

Once that task was complete, the team took photos and collected evidence that would allow the CIA to confirm the identities of all the dead.

The final box that needed ticking was to add a little something special on behalf of the Ukrainians. Just as they had with the Operation Boathouse codename, they had decided to once again go Hollywood.

Since the beginning of the invasion, someone had taken a cue from the classic Cold War–era movie *Red Dawn* and had been spray-painting the word *Wolverines* on destroyed Russian vehicles across Ukraine.

Pulling out their own cans of spray paint, Harvath and his teammates did the same before packing up their gear and disappearing into the woods.

# CHAPTER 2

FBI supervisory special agent Joseph Carolan fumbled on the bedside table for his phone. The worst calls always came in the middle of the night.

He was a big man who stood six foot four and weighed in at two hundred and fifty pounds; a lifer who'd been at the Bureau longer than anyone could remember.

Carolan was known for his investigative skills, as well as for his zero-tolerance policy when it came to bullshit. People who wasted his time pissed him off. His coworkers referred to him as "Bear," both because of his size and because of his demeanor, which could swing anywhere from Gentle Ben to a rip-your-face-off grizzly, depending on how his day was going.

"Go for Carolan," he growled as he activated the call and pressed the phone to his ear.

The person on the other end had been well trained on how to deliver breaking news, especially to a superior whom you had just awakened. Make it quick, stick to the facts, don't speculate.

After listening for several moments, Carolan broke in, "Any press on scene yet?"

Once the question had been answered, he sat up in bed and began giving orders. "Have Metro PD fully tent the area around the body—no windows. Then have them push the perimeter out as far as they can. And if they haven't already begun canvassing the building, get it started. In the meantime, I want someone assigned to start pulling all the CCTV footage we can get our hands on. Got it? Good. Text me the address. I'll be there as soon as I can."

Disconnecting the call, Carolan placed the phone back on the nightstand and rubbed his stubbled face. Yet another morning he was going to have to skip his workout. At this rate, he was never going to shed the twenty-five pounds his doctor had been hounding him to lose.

"Coffee to go?" his wife, Margaret, offered. She had been a Bureau wife long enough to know not to ask questions. What's more, as a highly accomplished trial attorney who had known her husband since they'd both been in law school, she could read him better than anyone.

While he wouldn't publicly admit it, Joe was under tremendous stress. He had been promoted to his current position because the previous agent in his chair had suffered a massive heart attack. If there hadn't been an AED in the office, the woman would have crossed over right there.

She had gone on to flatline once more in the ambulance and then again upon arrival at the hospital. All of this in a fit, health-conscious forty-two-year-old with no underlying conditions, nor family history of heart disease, who ran four half-marathons a year.

Had it been brought on by the demands of the job? Or had something more nefarious been to blame? That's what headquarters was looking into.

So far, all of her toxicology screens had come back clean. That didn't mean, however, that there hadn't been an attempt on her life. What it meant was that nothing at this point was being ruled out. Carolan could be walking into the same set of crosshairs and had been told, in no uncertain terms, to watch his back.

The operation he had been put in charge of was codenamed "Quick Silver." It was housed in the FBI's Counterintelligence Division, specifically the Russia Operations section known in Bureau shorthand as CROS.

Operation Quick Silver had been created to root out Russian influence operations inside the United States that were designed to advance Russia's goals in Ukraine.

It was a broad purview that had the potential to reach into almost

every facet of American life—the military, the media, the government . . .
The possibilities were endless.

As such, the top brass at the FBI had been adamant that everything be
done by the book and follow the exact letter of the law. All effort was to
be taken to avoid embarrassing the Bureau. The last thing the FBI wanted
was to hand its enemies a propaganda victory. Agents, especially those directly involved in Operation Quick Silver, were to maintain the highest
levels of integrity at all times.

Carolan understood the solemnity of the situation. He didn't care
what Moscow's endgame was: he didn't like the Russians trying to manipulate America, its people, or its institutions.

The problem, however, was that the internet, coupled with a frac-
tured media landscape, made it all too possible for people to silo themselves. Too many citizens got their "news" and information only from
sources that supported their biases.

There was nothing the Russians loved more than injecting poison-
ous propaganda into the American cultural bloodstream. The return on
their investment—as Americans turned on each other and their own
institutions—was off the charts. And, despite all of Russia's economic
problems, it was the one area that the Kremlin was more than willing
to keep pumping ever-increasing piles of cash into. As long as Americans had a bottomless, and easy-to-influence, addiction to anger, Moscow would continue serving it to them.

All of this made Carolan's job exceedingly difficult. He not only had
to battle the Russians, but he also had to contend with some of his own
countrymen and -women—American taxpayers—of whom he was a
servant.

The fact that so many were acting as repeater stations for anti-
American propaganda was a difficult pill to swallow. These otherwise
good and patriotic people simply couldn't be bothered to do even a modicum of fact-checking.

While disheartening, there would always be a percentage of disen-
gaged citizens who didn't live up to their societal responsibilities. The
people who knew better, however, were the ones that really got his blood
boiling.

Next to corrupt politicians, the media grifters and digital con artists were the worst in his book. These people made their living not by telling people the truth, but by telling them anything and everything they wanted to hear. No lie was too outrageous. No conspiracy too corrosive. Collectively, there was no bottom with them, no line they wouldn't cross.

What was worse, the outrage they supplied was akin to hits of heroin. Like any addictive substance, it constantly needed to be delivered in stronger and stronger doses. The moment any grifter or con artist failed to provide an ever-more-potent product, the audience would migrate to someone else who did.

It was slow-motion cultural suicide; an arms race of weapons-grade stupid, which tens of millions of people were lapping up daily. Carolan worried for his grandchildren and what the country would look like by the time they reached adulthood.

He had always seen his duty as a citizen to be a steward of the Republic. No generation "owned" America. Instead, it was each generation's responsibility to do everything they could to make sure the next generation coming up was handed a freer, more prosperous, more secure United States than had been handed to them.

This was why Carolan had joined the FBI and had spent his life in service to his country. He believed in America and wanted to be of service to the nation that had given him, and his family, so much opportunity.

No other country on earth empowered the individual the way America did. Nowhere were the rights and liberties of citizens so well protected. There were times he shuddered to think about what his life might have been like had he been born in another country, especially one not nearly so free.

That thought was playing out in his mind as he pulled up behind a row of squad cars double-parked in front of a luxury condo building in the popular Washington, D.C., neighborhood known as the West End.

Getting out of his vehicle, he made sure his credentials were visible and headed toward the "LZ."

The term was short for "Landing Zone," a macabre law enforcement reference used to designate the spot where a body had come to rest after falling off a roof, from a balcony, or out of a window. Since Carolan could see the tent he had requested, as well as a bunch of Metro cops standing around, he didn't need anyone to point him in the right direction.

After signing the perimeter log, he stepped inside the tent and made eye contact with the young FBI agent who had called and woken him up.

Jennifer Fields was one of the youngest and most accomplished agents at CROS. When Carolan had inherited Quick Silver, she was the first person he wanted transferred to his team.

Fields had been born and raised in Harlem. Her dad had been a cop and her mother a nurse. They had worked their asses off to give their daughter an exceptional education. She attended Penn and graduated with a double major in criminology and finance. She was a remarkable student who sat atop the dean's list every semester, and the FBI had made her an offer before she'd even been fitted for her cap and gown.

She impressed all of her instructors at Quantico. On top of being smart as hell, she was a natural athlete who blew away many of her male classmates during physical training.

Known for crushing a second, unrequired workout at the end of the day, she caught the attention of some of the hard-core members of the Hostage Rescue Team, who invited her to participate in extra training with them. Suffice it to say she left the FBI Academy with a rather special set of skills.

Having spent her high school and college summers working in the Brighton Beach neighborhood of Brooklyn, she had learned a lot about its Russian immigrant community. And while she had to fight her way up through the ranks at the Bureau to get there, CROS was a perfect fit for her.

What's more, Carolan was the perfect boss—or at least he was proving to be. As soon as he had been installed as the new director of Quick Silver, he had made her his number two. And it wasn't some bullshit, politically correct promotion because he needed a woman or a person of color. Joe made it clear that he not only believed in her, but also, in entrusting her with such responsibility, he expected a hell of a lot from her. Fields had assured him that she was up to the task.

As he walked up to her under the tent, she handed him a Styrofoam to-go cup. "Iced Caramel Macchiato. Seven pumps of syrup. Just the way you like it," she said, loud enough for the cops standing nearby to hear.

"Even has my name on it," he replied, accepting the cup. Across the front, written in black Sharpie and massive caps, was the word BOSS with a heart drawn around it.

While Carolan could be a detail-oriented hard-ass, he appreciated a good sense of humor. The darker, the better, as it was a sign of high intelligence.

The ability to make light of tough situations was a necessary trait in law enforcement. If you couldn't make jokes to let off some of the pressure, you were going to lose your mind.

Fields had nothing to worry about in that area. She had a great sense of humor and could go dark with the best of them. It was just one of a long list of reasons Carolan had selected her for the team.

Taking a sip of the hot black coffee she had handed him, he nodded at the tarp covering the body and said, "Okay, take me through it."

Fields removed the notepad from her back pocket and began reading: "Dimitri Burman. Forty-eight. Estonian-born U.S. citizen. Software guy. Made a fortune in Moscow and St. Petersburg before moving back to the U.S. about seven years ago."

"Married? Divorced?"

"Single," she answered. "No kids. Lived in the penthouse on the eleventh floor."

"Let's look at the body."

Fields followed him over, then bent down and pulled back the tarp.

Carolan set down his coffee, accepted a pair of latex gloves, and took his time studying the corpse.

"What personal items did he have on him?" he asked, looking at the man's shoes before continuing his examination.

"Let's see," Fields replied, looking through several evidence bags that had been placed in a clear plastic tub on a nearby folding table. "One Rolex watch, one cracked cell phone, one key chain with various keys, and approximately eleven hundred dollars cash."

"No wallet?"

Fields double-checked the bin, as well as the evidence log. "Nope, no wallet."

A missing wallet, if in fact it had completely vanished, was an important detail. But there was another reason the wallet's absence was salient, something that was gnawing at the back of Carolan's mind. He just couldn't remember what it was.

He decided to shift to another topic. "Have you been up to his condo yet?"

"Not yet. Metro was still processing it when I got here."

Carolan stood, covered the body back up with the tarp, and peeled off his gloves. Motioning to a spot away from the cops, he began walking and signaled for her to follow.

Once they were out of earshot, he said, "Over the phone, you stated that Burman was a critic of the Russian government."

"And then some," Fields responded. "He was particularly outspoken about President Peshkov and the war in Ukraine."

"Enough to get him noticed by Moscow?"

Fields nodded. "Lots of posts on social media and several interviews that have gone viral. That's why I wanted you here to assess the scene."

"So, we may be looking at a case of Sudden Russian Death Syndrome."

Once again, Fields nodded. "Gravity does seem to be the number one killer of Peshkov's critics."

"And even more so since he invaded Ukraine."

The Russians weren't shy about political assassinations. It had been a favorite tool in their bag of tricks dating all the way back to the Bolshevik Revolution.

Russians killing Russians was one thing. Russians killing an American citizen, however, was something entirely different.

Not to mention the fact that Burman, if he had been murdered and this wasn't a suicide, had been killed in the capital of the United States, only a mile from the White House.

A hit like that would have taken gigantic balls, even by Russian standards. Moscow would have known that there'd be hell to pay for such a move.

What form that hell would take was above Carolan's pay grade. His job right now was to gather the facts, find any loose threads, and start pulling on them.

"So, what's next?" Fields asked. "Want to head up to the condo?"

"Have you seen the building's CCTV footage yet?"

"I did. Our guy can be seen entering via the front door, walking through the lobby, and getting on the elevator, all of it alone, about an hour ago."

"What about exterior cameras?" Carolan replied.

"The camera in front is working. The one in back has been out for about two days. They're waiting on a replacement from the security company. Supply chain issues."

"Was our guy dropped off or on foot?"

"On foot."

"Anyone else in the vicinity? Same side of the street? Opposite side? Following him via a slow-moving vehicle?"

"Not that I could see," stated Fields. "I've got to tell you, if Russian Intelligence is behind this, they did a good job staying out of sight. That said, I've had a copy sent to our office and we've got agents out combing the neighborhood for all additional footage."

"I don't like that the rear camera was down. If he had unannounced visitors upstairs waiting for him, that's the most likely point of entry." Almost as an afterthought, he added, "Do we know if our guy kept a vehicle here in the building?"

Fields nodded. "Bought a new Tesla a few months ago. I already went down to the garage looking for it. His parking space is empty."

*Interesting*, Carolan thought to himself. *Maybe it's in the shop.*

On the edge of the perimeter a handful of people loitered, drawn like curious bugs to the flashing red and blue lights of the D.C. police vehicles. And, as was his habit, the FBI man scanned their faces.

It wouldn't have been the first time a killer had stood outside a crime scene watching. He also wouldn't have put it past the Russians to send someone along to observe how Burman's death was being handled and which agencies had been activated.

Had he been thinking further ahead, he might have tasked a plainclothes agent to mingle with bystanders and capture their images. Hindsight was always twenty-twenty.

Carolan paid attention for any telltale signs—cheap suits, bad haircuts, and/or known staffers from the Russian Embassy. Thus far, nothing screamed Kremlin spy.

The only person who did capture his attention was an unkempt, red-headed man in his early thirties with a bushy beard. There was something about him that seemed off.

Frankly, he looked like a weirdo, but considering the hour, that shouldn't have been surprising. Not many normal people were out prowling the streets at this time.

That wasn't completely it, however. There was something else. The guy didn't fit the fashionable neighborhood and gave off a very sketchy vibe.

*What are you doing here?* Carolan was wondering to himself when the man broke eye contact, raised a camera with a long lens, and began snapping photos.

He could be a stringer; a freelance photographer. Regardless, Carolan didn't like him.

The only thing he liked less right now was getting his photo taken. Turning to Fields, he said, "Let's head upstairs."

On the eleventh floor, at the door to Burman's penthouse, the patrol officer standing guard called for the lead Metro detective, a guy named Greer, to come out and give a thumbs-up or -down on allowing the two FBI agents entry.

"Remind me again why the Bureau is here?" the detective asked.

"National security," said Fields.

"Same reason you gave downstairs for having my officers push the perimeter back. If you want to get inside the deceased's dwelling, I'm going to need more than just *national security*, which frankly sounds like an all-purpose, bullshit, Christmas tree phrase that you can put anything underneath that you want."

"National. Security," Fields repeated, drawing the words out.

"Fuck. Off," Detective Greer responded, using the exact same cadence.

Normally, D.C. Metro cops and the FBI got along better than this, but it took all kinds of people to make up an organization. What's more, the overnight shift was sometimes a place where departments parked the assholes nobody on the day shift wanted to deal with.

Unfortunately, right now Carolan didn't have the luxury of bouncing to another detective. While he certainly could have had his office call the guy's superior, that would have only wasted time and cemented the man's animosity. Better to have the detective on his side.

What's more, this wasn't the first time an FBI agent had encountered resistance from local law enforcement. They could be very protective of their turf, which was understandable. Not many cops liked the idea of the government coming in and bigfooting their cases.

Carolan knew from experience that the best thing he could do was to immediately shoot the elephant in the middle of the room. "You're right. This isn't about national security. And if it stays that way, you won't see either of us ever again. I just want to be able to go back to the office and tell my boss that he was wrong."

That last part was a lie. Carolan's superiors had no idea he was here. In fact, they wouldn't know for several hours still that Burman was even dead. But suggesting that he might be able to return to headquarters and proverbially spit in his boss's eye was a good way to attempt to bond with the detective. After all, it was probably a safe bet that a cop this disagreeable didn't have a good relationship with his higher-ups.

"What's your interest in the deceased?" Greer asked.

"The Russian government is not too fond of him," Carolan replied.

"And so, you think maybe Humpty Dumpty was pushed?"

"It'd be a lot easier for me if he wasn't."

"That makes two of us," the detective stated.

"Listen, I'm being honest. I don't want anything to do with your case. The best possible outcome here is that this guy jumped. And I don't say that flippantly. Suicide is a serious issue. I say it as someone who can't even see his desk for all the open files I have on it."

"That also makes two of us."

"Okay," said Carolan, sensing progress, "then let us help you. The sooner we rule out homicide, the sooner you and I can get back to all of our other cases."

"Booties and gloves," Detective Greer said, relenting. "Anything you uncover, you share with me."

"And vice versa," replied Carolan, removing a business card and handing it to the man.

Greer handed over his card and once Carolan and Fields had donned the requisite protective gear, they were given free roam of the condo.

"Nice job with bad cop," said Fields as they stepped inside, scanned the rather sparse evidence log, and began looking around.

"Believe it or not, some of the biggest pains in the ass on the way in can end up being your best allies overall. The key is to remember that everybody has a job to do and nobody wants to be told how to do it."

"I'll make sure to remind you of that at my next performance review," Fields responded with a smile.

Carolan shook his head and smiled back. "Let's check out the terrace first."

The incredible living room had floor-to-ceiling, lanai-style sliding glass walls that could be retracted to connect the space to the outdoors. Careful not to disturb anything, they stepped through the one glass panel that had been left open.

The fancy terrace reminded him of something you would have seen at a Ritz-Carlton or a Four Seasons. Three-foot-by-three-foot concrete tiles were spaced a couple of inches apart and had precisely manicured, perfectly uniform strips of grass growing between. The plush, all-weather furniture was nicer than anything Carolan had on the inside of his house, much less what was on his back deck.

He and Fields walked the terrace back and forth, finally coming to a stop at the spot from which Burman either jumped or was pushed, and looked over the glass railing to the street below. Eleven floors were indeed a long way down.

After bending down to examine several of the concrete tiles, Carolan motioned for them to return inside.

"You go that way," he said, pointing down the hall, "and I'll go this way. We'll meet back here in twenty minutes."

Burman's large, modern condo was tastefully and expensively

decorated. The floors were clad in marble and the walls were hung with pop art pieces by the likes of Roy Lichtenstein and Keith Haring. For the cost of the furniture alone, Carolan figured that he could have sent all four of his kids to college and then on to graduate school.

He searched two guest rooms with en suite baths, as well as a home gym and sauna at his end of the condo. There was nothing of interest to be found. He hoped Fields was having better luck and decided to join her.

She was looking through what appeared to be Burman's home office when he found her. "Anything good?" he asked.

"He's got great taste," she said, picking up a rich, leatherbound notebook from the desk and fanning the pages. "Right down to his Hermès daily planner, which appears to be only for looks, as all of the pages are blank."

"Did you try his computer?"

Fields nodded. "Locked with a biometric scanner."

"Fingerprint or iris?"

"Does it matter?"

"If it unlocks via a fingerprint, we could bring the body up before the medical examiner gets here," Carolan replied.

"No such luck. Iris."

"Then we're screwed. Dead men not only tell no tales, but lifeless eyeballs can't fool artificial intelligence. With his money, he'd have top-of-the-line. What about any credit card or bank statements?"

"Look at this place," she said with a sweep of her hand. "All this glass and chrome. Our guy's a minimalist. Even more important, he's a techie. He doesn't do paper."

Carolan didn't like it, but she was right. The odds that they were going to find some shoe box or accordion file stuffed with receipts for Burman's accountant were next to nothing.

"How about his bedroom and master bath?" he asked.

"I may have found something the police overlooked," Fields responded as she held up a small stub.

"What's that?"

"A valet ticket."

"From where?"

"The pocket of a suit jacket in his closet."

"Very funny. Try again."

"The Commodore Yacht Club."

Carolan took a deep breath and then, exhaling, replied, "Fuck."

Fields had rarely heard him curse. "What's wrong with the Commodore Yacht Club?"

"Pocket that ticket and don't let Detective Greer know you have it. I'll explain once we're outside."

"You're asking me to remove evidence from a crime scene. It'd be nice to know why before I do."

"We now have a bona fide national security issue on our hands. Burman didn't die by suicide."

# CHAPTER 3

Harvath had thought it a fitting tribute to Reed Carlton that he and his team had used the same family of smugglers to get them into and out of Belarus that the Old Man had used back in the days of the Iron Curtain.

Two more of Harvath's teammates—another ex–Delta Force operative named Palmer and the team's only female member, a former Army soldier named Ashby—had been held in reserve to act as a quick reaction force if anything had gone wrong.

Thankfully, nothing had, which was rare. It had been a good, clean operation and Al-Masri's death had already made the news. Harvath hoped it would win him a few brownie points back at the office. Lately, it felt like he had been in the penalty box.

Over the course of the last month, he had been assigned to operations in four different countries—Tajikistan, Afghanistan, India, and Romania. He was overdue to rotate home. Yet the powers that be back in Northern Virginia had told him to stay put, in Bucharest of all places.

It wasn't that Bucharest was a bad city. It actually had quite a lot going for it. He'd made a couple of good contacts in the Romanian Intelligence community and had been keeping his skills sharp cross-training with their Special Forces. But it wasn't like being home. And that, he suspected, was the point.

The phrase *be careful what you wish for* had kept pinging in his head. Because he had made it clear that he didn't want to stop doing fieldwork, his employer appeared to be giving him exactly what he said he wanted. They were keeping him overseas and keeping him busy with mission after mission.

Was it a punishment? Some sort of twisted tactic meant to grind him down and get him to tap out? Or was the Carlton Group just that busy? Despite pushing for clarification, none had been forthcoming.

Compounding his frustration was the fact that he was engaged to a woman who lived in Oslo and two months had passed since they had last seen each other.

Part of the problem was the demands of his job. The other part was that her position with Norwegian Intelligence was equally demanding.

Unlike Harvath, Sølvi Kolstad had recently accepted a promotion that almost entirely removed her from field operations. She had been put in charge of one of Norway's most clandestine programs. If the Russians ever invaded, it would be up to her department to mount a shadow intelligence service and coordinate resistance. She now practically lived at her office. But she missed him and needed a break as well, so Harvath had made an executive decision.

When the smugglers got them safely across the border from Belarus into Poland, Harvath and the team had driven the rest of the way to Warsaw, dropping their SUV off at the airport. His teammates had boarded a flight back to the United States and he was supposed to catch a flight back to Bucharest, but he opted to pull the plug.

Warsaw was only an hour-and-forty-five-minute flight from both Bucharest and Oslo. It was a physical representation of what he and Sølvi had been trying to do throughout their long-distance relationship: meeting in the middle.

As soon as his operation was over and he was safely across the border, he had texted Sølvi. She had jumped at the chance for them to see each other.

Figuring he would probably be denied, Harvath hadn't requested the days off; he had simply taken them. A weekend in Warsaw with Sølvi would be more restorative than going back to Bucharest and staring at the walls of his hotel room. And even if the Carlton Group ended up calling and needing something done in Romania, he could be back before anyone ever knew that he hadn't yet returned.

The hardest part of his plan ended up being finding a room in the Polish capital. He had arrived on the country's National Independence Day. All of the rooms were booked. Thankfully, he had a contact at the U.S. Embassy who was able to pull a few strings and get him a reservation.

In the heart of Warsaw's Old Town, his suite at the Mondrian overlooked the cobbled streets and pastel-colored buildings of Market Square. Since Sølvi wouldn't be getting in until later, he had taken a cab in from the airport alone.

It was hard to believe that the last time he had entered Poland it had been in a rigid inflatable boat, under machine-gun fire, as he had sped across Goldfarb—the lake Poland shared with the Russian exclave of Kaliningrad. All things being equal, a rented car from the border and then a taxi from the airport was a lot more civilized.

After checking in, he spent the afternoon exploring. Warsaw was an amazing city, steeped in history, which was one of Harvath's favorite subjects.

The excitement for Independence Day was palpable. The cafés were overflowing, anyone who wasn't drinking was singing, and Polish flags were flying everywhere. The country had come a long way and had much to be proud of.

As Harvath moved about the capital, there was a certain piece of Poland's past that he was particularly interested in visiting and, as a warrior, to which he wanted to pay his respects.

In the summer of 1944, the Polish underground launched the largest operation of any European resistance movement of World War II, known as the Warsaw Uprising. The Poles battled Nazi troops for sixty-three days. They received little to no outside help.

The Soviet Red Army had halted their advance on the outskirts of the city, which allowed the Nazis to turn their attention to crushing the Polish Home Army, known as the "Armia Krajowa," or AK for short.

Despite early successes, which saw the AK make clever use of the city's sewer system and take large portions of the city, the Germans launched a series of absolutely monstrous counterattacks. Goaded on by Heinrich Himmler, the sadistic head of the SS, Hitler ordered that Warsaw, and its inhabitants, be completely destroyed and wiped from the face of the earth.

Tanks, dive-bombers, and artillery were unleashed on the Polish capital, along with some of the most ruthless units of the SS. Chief among those units was the notorious Dirlewanger Brigade.

The brigade, filled with violent criminals, mental asylum patients, and even concentration camp inmates, was named after an SS *Oberführer* and personal friend of Himmler's—Oskar Dirlewanger.

Dirlewanger was a convicted rapist, known for being a barbaric, mentally unstable alcoholic, child molester, and devotee of sadism and necrophilia.

Few in history had ever matched Dirlewanger's cruelty. He was reviled by most of the Nazi high command. Hitler and Himmler, however, were quite taken with his methods.

Under his command, citizens were rounded up en masse and massacred regardless of age or sex. Hospitals, with patients still inside, were burned to the ground, while nurses were whipped, gang-raped, and hung naked alongside the doctors outside. As it was happening, depraved Nazi soldiers sang a popular German drinking ballad called "There's a Hofbräuhaus in Munich." Thousands more victims across the city, including many wounded resistance fighters recovering in field hospitals, were shot and set on fire with flamethrowers.

Winston Churchill pleaded with President Franklin Delano Roosevelt for help, but was refused.

By the time America did eventually come around it was too little, too late. Adding to the horror of it all, most of the supplies airdropped to the Poles, including desperately needed ammunition, ended up being recovered and used by the Nazis.

Once the revolution had been smashed, the Germans looted anything of value and then razed most of what few buildings had been left standing. Warsaw was reduced to rubble.

The atrocities committed by Dirlewanger and the Nazis were some of the worst of World War II. When all was said and done, 20,000 members of the AK had been killed and more than 200,000 of Warsaw's citizens had been slaughtered.

Harvath visited multiple locations of the resistance and ended his tour at the Warsaw Rising Museum. It was a solemn experience, particularly the "little insurgent" room, dedicated to the youngest members of the uprising. By the time he got back to the Old Town, he was ready for a drink.

As the Mondrian was a collection of suites and apartments spread across a series of separate, historic buildings, there was no traditional "lobby bar" that he could drop in on.

Instead, he found an excellent place nearby called Podwale Bar and Books. Complete with dark wood paneling, a fireplace, and shelves of leatherbound books, the place had a true British colonial feel to it.

He found a table, away from the piano player, with a view of the front door. The thought of sitting upstairs in the cigar bar and enjoying a Cuban, or one of the establishment's exclusive, hand-rolled cigars, had crossed his mind, but he decided to save that experience as something he and Sølvi might do together later.

Instead, he focused on Podwale's extensive whiskey selection. After studying the list, he ordered a Laphroaig, checked his watch, and settled back. Sølvi's flight wouldn't land for a few more hours still.

It felt good to relax. *Really* relax. The whole time he had been in Bucharest, there'd been an underlying tension. It was like purgatory. He was on the bubble and could be called up at any moment and sent into action, yet no call ever came.

But now, here in Warsaw and waiting for Sølvi to show up, it felt like he was on a vacation of sorts. He could let his guard down, just a little bit, and think of things other than work. It was healthy and, despite whatever consequences might await him once the weekend was over, he was glad to have orchestrated this little personal, covert operation.

When the waitress delivered his drink, he thanked her and took a sip. It had a smokey taste with a nice, long finish. The warmth of it going down only served to put him deeper into relaxation mode.

He was taking his second sip when the app on his phone pinged with an encrypted text. It was from one of his colleagues in Northern Virginia, except the man didn't appear to be back in the U.S. The text read: **Just arrived. We need to meet.**

*Fuck* was the first word that popped into Harvath's mind. Setting his whiskey down, he typed back: **Where are you?**

**Not far.**

If the guy was standing around waiting for him to touch down in Bucharest, he'd better have a comfortable place to sit. It was going to be a long wait.

Harvath was about to explain that he had taken off for the weekend, when another text came in. It was a map of Warsaw with a digital pin placed near the zoo on the other side of the Vistula River.

Harvath didn't know why the office had come looking for him, but they had found him. Whatever was going on, sending someone in person meant that it was serious.

Downing his drink, he left some cash on the table and exited the bar. He had a bad feeling that his vacation was about to come to an abrupt end and an even worse feeling about what was to follow.

# CHAPTER 4

Making certain that he wasn't being followed, Harvath hopped the tram and rode across the Slasko-Dabrowski Bridge. At Praski Park, he got off and walked the rest of the way to No. 8 Florianska Street on foot.

It was a tasteful, French-style apartment building of creamy white stone, topped with a copper roof that had weathered to a fine verdigris. Finding the name on the directory he had been instructed to look for, he pressed the corresponding button. Seconds later a buzzer sounded and the door unlocked.

A fully exposed, ornate, wrought-iron elevator anchored the lobby of polished marble. Its cage was inset with stained glass panels and reminded Harvath of the Grand Hotel in Mexico City.

As attractive as it was, he opted for the stairs. Elevators could be death traps—especially if the wrong people knew you were coming.

On the fourth floor, he made his way down the hall to a pair of large, oak doors and knocked. A scurry of noises from the other side told him that the man he was here to see wasn't alone.

There was the sound of heavy breathing as the lock was turned. Then, as soon as the door was opened, the two enormous, white dogs were upon him.

Harvath smiled as he scratched the animals along their throats and behind their ears.

The little man who owned them allowed it to go on for a few more minutes before calling his Caucasian Ovcharkas—Argos and Draco—back into the apartment.

Harvath followed, closing and locking the door behind him. The two men then warmly shook hands. "It's good to see you, Nick."

"You too," the little man replied.

Standing under three feet tall, he had a condition known as primordial dwarfism. The dogs were not only constant, loyal companions, but also his protectors who zealously guarded him.

Known to intelligence agencies around the world simply as the "Troll," to his friends the little man was known as Nicholas. He had started out as one of Harvath's greatest foes, but over time, as he had backed away from trafficking in the purchase and sale of highly classified and sensitive information, he and Harvath had developed both a deep personal and professional relationship.

Harvath had personally brought Nicholas on board at the Carlton Group, vouching for him and giving him a fresh start; a chance to be part of something good, something bigger than himself. And while there had rightly been suspicion over the little man's loyalties, he had more than proven his worth to the organization and to the United States government.

Now, here he was, in Warsaw. Harvath had more than a few questions. Pointing at the ceiling and other places as they walked into the living room, he asked, "Is it safe to talk?"

Nicholas nodded. "This is one of the few local safe houses the Russians *don't* know about. The CIA swept it this morning. Let me start out by saying, good job on Operation Boathouse. It was a solid hit. Everyone back home is pleased."

"Glad to hear it," he replied, then changed gears. "Since I'm using my own cell phone, credit cards, and rescheduled my flight back to Bucharest, I'm not going to ask how you found me, but I am going to ask what you're doing here. We could have debriefed over secure video."

"True," the little man replied as he approached a brass liquor cart, "but I wanted to talk in person. Drink?"

"Why? Am I going to need one?"

Nicholas nodded. "I think so," he said, opening a bottle of Polish brandy for himself and pouring some into a snifter.

Harvath was uncomfortable with where this might be headed, but accepted his advice, filled a glass with two fingers of bourbon, and took a seat on the couch.

The apartment smelled like stale cigarettes and too many warm days with the windows never having been opened.

After giving the dogs the command to lie down, Nicholas joined him. Placing two folders on the coffee table, he climbed up onto the couch.

"Cheers," he said, raising his snifter.

"What are we drinking to?"

The little man thought for a moment and replied, "To a strong stomach."

Harvath didn't like the sound of that, either, but clinked glasses with his friend anyway. "Cheers."

Once they each had taken a sip, he returned to asking questions. "Let's not pull any more punches. Why are you here? What do we need to talk about in person?"

"We need to talk about what's in those," said Nicholas, pointing at the folders.

"Do they have anything to do with why I've been cooling my heels in Bucharest?"

The little man nodded.

*Okay,* Harvath thought. *At least we are getting somewhere.* "Which one should I open first?"

Nicholas pointed to the one on the left.

Setting down his drink, Harvath picked up the folder, opened it, and began reading.

As he read, Nicholas filled in some background. "Since Russia's invasion of Ukraine, twenty-six American citizens have been killed. Fourteen of them have died fighting alongside Ukrainian forces, four have died of non-combat-related injuries, and the remaining eight—six aid workers, plus two journalists—were either tortured to death or summarily executed by Russian forces."

The little man had been right to suggest they toast to strong stomachs. The photographs, especially those of the aid workers who had been tortured to death, were particularly hard to look at. Nicholas seemed to be reading his mind.

"*Horrific* doesn't even begin to cover it. That's the reason you've been on hold in Romania," he said. "The White House has been chomping at the bit to respond, but gathering any sort of actionable intelligence inside Ukraine has been next to impossible. An even greater problem are the diplomatic and political ramifications of putting any sort of boots on the ground.

"Contributing weapons systems, ammunition, and other types of matériel is one thing. If, however, the U.S. sends in troops, we'll be in a hot war with Russia that'll suck in our NATO allies and go global within weeks, if not days. The Pentagon believes China would use it as an opportunity to take Taiwan, Iran will move against Israel and possibly Saudi Arabia, while a multitude of other simmering conflicts would flare and the likelihood of nuclear weapons being unleashed would rise to levels not even seen during the height of the Cold War."

"So, the answer is we do nothing else?" Harvath replied. "We wait until it's over, hope Ukraine wins, and only then launch a global manhunt for those responsible and drag them to The Hague for war crimes tribunals? It took the Israelis almost fifteen years to hunt down Adolf Eichmann."

Nicholas shook his head. "That's not what we're talking about. You need to keep in mind that there are not only international factors at stake here, but domestic ones as well. Sixty-eight percent of American voters still believe it's important for Congress to keep aid flowing to Ukraine."

"That's a great number," Harvath interjected. "When's the last time seven out of ten Americans agreed on anything?"

"I'm with you, but that's not the only number the White House is watching. In the spring, only twelve percent of voters thought the U.S. was doing too much to help Ukraine. In the eight months since, that number has doubled to twenty-four percent and it has got Washington worried."

"Russia, *unprovoked*, invaded a sovereign nation."

Nicholas put up his hands. "Moscow claims it was in response to Ukraine getting too cozy with NATO."

"The Russian President loves to blame everything on NATO expansion," Harvath responded. "Finland and Sweden have both now decided to join NATO *because* of Russia's invasion of Ukraine. But we haven't heard so much as a peep out of the Kremlin. If Peshkov was so concerned about NATO invading Russia, why hasn't he reinforced his border with Finland? In fact, he's done just the opposite. He pulled Russian troops away from the border with Finland, as well as with the other Baltic NATO member states, in order to reinforce his operations in Ukraine.

"And what makes his NATO excuse even more ridiculous is the fact that the Ukrainians informed Moscow that they were willing to rule out any future NATO membership in order to prevent a war. You know what President Peshkov did? He turned them down cold. The man is insane. He thinks he's the reincarnation of Peter the Great. His invasion of Ukraine is about one thing and one thing only—imperial conquest and his desire to go down in history as the person who put the old Russian Empire back together again. Fuck that guy."

"Considering your history with him," Nicholas replied, "I'm sure the feeling is mutual."

"I should have killed him when I had the chance. If I had known this was coming, I wouldn't have thought twice about it. The Ukrainian people have a right to decide their own destiny. The Russians don't have a right to decide it for them. The Russians also don't have a right to invade Ukraine and rape, maim, torture, and kill their way across the country. And torturing and killing noncombatant Americans, aid workers and journalists no less, is way beyond the pale. Somebody needs to send Peshkov and his thugs in Moscow a message."

As someone who had grown up in Soviet Georgia, Nicholas shared Harvath's hatred of Russian brutality. He also had a clear-eyed view of what was going on.

In his estimation, no one had summed it up better than the political scientist and former counselor of the U.S. Department of State Eliot A. Cohen.

What was happening between Russia and Ukraine was a war not only of will and resilience, but also of vitality. Russian President Peshkov was in his seventies, and his Chief of the General Staff—in charge of the war in Ukraine—was only months away from his seventieth birthday.

Ukraine's President and Chief of Staff, on the other hand, were both in their forties.

In Russia, the largest and strongest support for the war was among those old enough to remember, and pine for, the old Soviet Union. On the contrary, in Ukraine support for the war was overwhelming across all age groups. To put it bluntly, it was a Russian invasion led by the aging men of Peshkov's inner circle against a generation of Ukrainians in their prime.

Among a host of excellent insights, Cohen had one line in particular that had resonated and stuck with Nicholas. What was happening in Ukraine was a war between a calcified society lost in its brutal past and a free society looking toward a decent future. Nicholas couldn't have said it any better himself.

In hindsight, perhaps he and Harvath shouldn't have toasted to strong stomachs, but rather to independence—the independence being celebrated outside the windows of the safe house at this very moment by the free people of Poland, as well as the independence that hopefully every man, woman, and child in Ukraine would soon know.

Like Harvath, he also wanted to see more get done, especially when it came to putting the largest dent possible in Russia's war crimes, which was why he had flown more than four thousand miles to hand Harvath his next mission in person.

Pointing at the second folder on the table, Nicholas said, "Now let's talk about the rest of the reason I'm here."

If folder number two was anything like folder number one, Harvath wanted a bit more fortification before diving in.

Picking up his glass, he took another sip of bourbon and then opened the file. He skipped over the reports and went straight to the photos. The impact was like being punched in the face.

It wasn't the blood that bothered him. He'd seen plenty of blood over his career. It was the bodies. The tiny bodies. Children. All slaughtered. It was gruesome. Harvath felt a tidal wave of rage building inside him.

He had a thing about targeting the defenseless, especially children. People and societies should always be judged by how they treat the weakest among them.

Slowly, he asked, "What happened? Who did this?"

"The photographs were taken at an orphanage in eastern Ukraine. It was attacked by a unit of Russian mercenaries."

"Wagner?" Harvath replied.

Nicholas nodded.

Harvath had tangled with the Wagner Group before and almost hadn't survived to tell the tale. They were exceedingly aggressive and absolutely ruthless. But the butchery of women and children? This was beyond barbaric, even for them.

"We believe they're behind the murder of the six American aid workers," the little man explained, "as well as the two American journalists."

"To what end? These guys are all ex–Russian Special Forces. There's always been at least a little discipline in their ranks."

"Not anymore. The war has upended everything. Just like the Russian military, Wagner has burned through a ton of men. It's gotten so bad that they've been reduced to recruiting from prisons and insane asylums. Rapists, serial killers, drug addicts—Wagner is taking anyone they can get and promising full pardons in return."

Harvath was instantly reminded of the Nazis' Dirlewanger Brigade and all the atrocities that unit committed during the Warsaw Uprising.

"How do we know these are Wagner mercs and not Russian soldiers?"

Nicholas pointed to several of the reports Harvath had flipped past and replied, "As you know, Wagner mercenaries wear a patch on their uniform, usually along their right shoulder, that identifies them as being part of the organization. It depicts a skull, inside a set of crosshairs, with the words 'Wagner Group' written in English above and Russian below. In each of our cases, someone recounted seeing the patch."

"But Wagner makes up, what, at least ten percent of Russian forces fighting in Ukraine? You're going to need a lot more than that patch to ID the people responsible."

"What if I told you that we've also identified a unit patch?" Nicholas asked.

"I'd say you've successfully narrowed down your search to a needle in a field of needle stacks."

The little man was accustomed to his friend's occasional sarcasm.

Humor, tinged with cynicism, was a sine qua non of maintaining sanity in their business.

"The unit," he continued, "goes by the name the 'Ravens' and uses the bird as their symbol. Its members were initially comprised of prisoners from Russia's notorious penal colony Number Six, built along the border with Kazakhstan, which dates back to the 1700s.

"Every criminal at Number Six is considered the worst of the worst. From murderers and terrorists to cannibals and child molesters, all are serving life sentences without the possibility of parole.

"Upon arrival, before they even enter the prison, they're blindfolded so that they can't make any mental maps that might help facilitate a breakout.

"They're kept in isolation, each behind three steel doors, and only allowed out for ninety minutes a day to exercise inside a large, iron cage.

"A 'Raven' was the nickname given to anyone cunning enough to have ever risked escape and to have successfully broken free."

"You said the unit was *initially* comprised of prisoners from penal colony Number Six," Harvath stated. "What about now?"

"Our intelligence is somewhat limited. From what we've been able to pick up, only a few of the original Ravens are still around. Like the rest of the Wagner Group, they have reached deep into other prisons, and even mental asylums."

"What a fucking nightmare."

Nicholas gestured toward the folders. "The nightmare would be in letting them continue."

Harvath didn't disagree. He held up one of the orphanage photos. "Why show me this? You already had my attention with six dead American aid workers and two dead American journalists."

"Because there was also an American at the orphanage," he replied, activating his phone and showing him a picture. "Anna Royko. A twenty-five-year-old attorney from Chicago. She had given up her job to go help in Ukraine."

"I don't recognize her," Harvath said, flipping back through the grisly photos, surprised that he had missed her. "Was she one of the victims?"

"We're not sure. Her body hasn't been found. We think they may have taken her."

If that was true, Harvath didn't even want to begin thinking about the horrors she was probably suffering. Shaking his head, he exhaled and said, "You and I both know that if she was taken, it wasn't as a hostage to be ransomed back. These guys aren't going to pop up in a few days looking to negotiate."

"No, they're not," Nicholas responded. "That's why I'm here."

"So, what's the plan?"

"We want you to confirm what happened to her. If she's alive, you get her out."

"And if she's dead?"

"You kill every single person associated with that unit."

Harvath paused and studied his friend as he ran down a list. "Active war zone. Wagner mercenaries. Zero actionable intelligence. How am I doing so far?"

"So far, so good," the little man replied.

"I'm glad we both appreciate the job. That said, as far as manpower is concerned, I'm going to need my entire team to turn around and fly back, plus a contingent of local guys, weapons, ammo, vehicles—"

Nicholas held up his hand and cut him off. "Nope. Just you."

"Very funny. I also want at least a dozen Javelins for Haney and Staelin, as many claymores as you can get your hands on for Preisler and Johnson, full demo packages with C-4, det cord, timers, and breaching charges for Palmer and Ashby—"

Once again, his friend cut him off. "I wasn't joking. We can't send you with your team."

"Why not?"

"It's complicated."

Harvath took another sip of bourbon and sat back on the couch. "Explain."

Nicholas exhaled and asked, "Do you remember when the Chinese hacked the OPM?"

"The Office of Personnel Management? The agency that processes the SF86 paperwork for top-secret clearances?"

"That's the one," the little man replied. "It happened around the same time that the Chinese hacked major health insurance companies like Anthem and Blue Cross Blue Shield. What wasn't reported was that the Chinese also succeeded in a significant hack of the IRS. They were able to pull not only the names and Social Security numbers of those who had applied for clearances, but also their employment and health insurance histories."

"Meaning they can cross-reference everything."

Nicholas nodded. "That's our problem. With enough digging, the Chinese can conceivably connect you and your teammates."

"Why is that a problem?"

"Because it's exactly the kind of information they'd be likely to share with the Russians."

"And that causes trouble for us how?" Harvath asked.

"Not us. The White House. One former American Special Operations soldier choosing to go fight in Ukraine is deniable. A whole team, one that can be traced back to a private intelligence company rumored to conduct off-the-books black ops for the U.S. government, is a ticket to disaster. The Kremlin would claim the United States had officially put troops into the conflict and, as such, had declared war on Russia."

"And thanks to China, they'd have plenty of receipts to prove it."

"Correct," Nicholas responded. "We obviously don't want that and neither do the Ukrainians. They don't want to give the Russians a reason to dramatically overreact."

"Meaning tactical nukes."

"Or worse."

Harvath was familiar with the Russian strategic doctrine of "escalate to deescalate." Essentially, it was a deadly form of brinksmanship. It meant detonating one or more lower-yield, likely battlefield nukes in order to push the world to the edge of global thermonuclear warfare.

Moscow believed that once it had done so, its enemies would capitulate and back down, rather than push their luck and risk further escalation. Though widely discussed, it had never been tried. Harvath more than understood the risks and most definitely didn't want to see it attempted. The loss of life and attendant destruction from the smaller nuclear devices would be bad enough. If, however, ICBMs started flying, it would be game over for everyone.

"So, it'd be just me. No support," he stated.

"Actually," said Nicholas, "the Ukrainians offered up a potential solution."

Harvath leaned forward. "I'm listening."

"Like us, they want this Wagner unit dealt with. The problem for them is that they can't afford to assemble a proper hunting party. They need their best, most highly skilled people focused on the front lines."

"It's a war. I get that. But they can't spare anyone?"

The little man held up his hand yet again. "This is where the potential solution comes in. If you agree, they're going to provide you with a team."

"From where?"

"The Ukrainian International Legion. English speakers with significant, in-country combat experience. They know the terrain; they know the enemy and they know the enemy's capabilities."

"How many guys?"

"Four."

Harvath looked at him. "*Four?* You've got to be kidding me. That's all they're willing to put up?"

"That's all they can part with. And believe me, it took some work. But these are good soldiers. They're tough, they're committed, and they know what they're doing."

"Have you seen their jackets?"

"I have. In a SCIF at the Pentagon," said Nicholas, referring to a sensitive compartmented information facility. "Operational security for the Ukrainians is paramount and they're beyond protective when it comes to the identities and backgrounds of their fighters. They don't want the Russians being able to track down and harass their families."

"Understandable. But if I agree to do this, when do I get to see their files?" Harvath asked.

"Presumably, when we get to Ukraine."

"*We?* I thought I was going in alone."

"I'll be lending my expertise to their Defense Ministry's Directorate of Intelligence, the GUR, in Kyiv."

"In a personal or professional capacity?"

"Technically, personal. But let's be clear, the U.S. and its allies want to see that Ukraine continues to be given every possible advantage. Devastating Russia's military, without a single drop of NATO blood being spilled, is a win-win for the West."

Harvath couldn't have agreed more. His only wish was that he was being offered a greater role in hastening Russia's defeat.

The entire time he had been in Bucharest, it had felt like sitting on the bench during the Super Bowl. Just over the border in Ukraine, the largest land war since World War II was taking place. A valiant population was fighting for its very survival against one of America's oldest and most despised adversaries.

While Harvath enjoyed, and was quite skilled at, eliminating Islamic terrorists, there was nothing he took greater pleasure in than killing Russian operatives, whether they be spies, soldiers, or Wagner mercenaries. The Russians had, after all, been behind the brutal murder of his mentor, one of his closest colleagues, and most importantly, the love of his life before Sølvi, his deceased wife, Lara.

There was no length he wouldn't go to in order to further exact revenge and inflict as much pain as possible on Moscow and its goons. Throw in innocent Americans who had been executed at the hands of Russian forces, as well as one who might have been kidnapped and could currently be in need of rescue, and it made for an assignment that Harvath would have great difficulty turning down—no matter how poorly staffed, supplied, or supported it was.

The only problem was that he hadn't come to Warsaw for a mission briefing. He had come to spend a long-overdue weekend with Sølvi. That said, he knew that if Anna Royko was still alive, time was of the essence.

"When do we leave?" he asked.

"It's a forty-five-minute hop from here to the airport in Rzeszów. Then it's a long, slow grind by overnight train. A detachment from the GUR has been assigned to accompany us. The sooner we get going, the better."

Harvath looked at his watch. Sølvi would be boarding her flight any minute. "I need to make a call."

# CHAPTER 5

Special Agent Jennifer Fields poked her boss when she saw that the valet for the Commodore Yacht Club had come on duty.

"We're on," she said, watching as the young man opened his stand.

Carolan looked up from his phone and replied, "Let's give it a few minutes. We don't want to be the first ones in."

Fields readjusted her sidearm and settled back in her seat. "Just so we're clear," she stated, watching the valet, "I think everything you told me about this place is next-level lunatic."

"Too bad your opinion doesn't matter. Which goes double for mine."

"Are people that stupid?"

Carolan shrugged. He was in a mood.

"So, you're telling me," she continued, "that I could start a conspiracy tomorrow, in which Martin Luther King, Coolio, and Flip Wilson weren't dead, but had been put into suspended animation, just waiting for the right moment to be brought back in order to convince the Black community to support something crazy, like the U.S. government going back on the gold standard?"

"I think you'd have better luck with Tupac and Bernie Mac over Coolio and Flip Wilson, but yes, with the right resources, that's what I'm telling you."

Fields shook her head. "That's insane."

"Life is complicated. People want a sense of control over the uncontrollable. They want easy answers, and conspiracy theories fill that need."

"There's no way the answer is that simple."

"Of course it is. People see themselves as the heroes of their own stories. Nobody wants to live in a boring timeline. Conspiracy theories offer a heroic adventure; a sense of excitement, the feeling that you're privy to some sort of secret knowledge that no one else sees."

"That's ridiculous."

"*And*," he pressed on, "the more people ridicule you, the more you revel in your superiority over them. To you, the uninitiated are sheep. They're sleepwalking while you're fully awake—aware of the 'real' world and everything that's happening within it. No matter how many actual facts get launched at you, no matter how much data gets presented demonstrating how wrong you are, it doesn't matter."

"Why not?"

"Because conspiracies, by their very nature, are unfalsifiable. That's what makes them so dangerous and why the Russians love them so much. They're experts at weaponizing them against the U.S. and derive a huge return on an incredibly small investment. It's like injecting the population with an aggressive form of societal cancer. Once it's in the body politic, all the Russians have to do is sit back and watch as our country eats away at itself and gets weaker and weaker."

"Which is what you think the Russians are attempting to do with Burman's death."

Carolan nodded. "An old Soviet disinformation specialist dubbed it the 'Potter's Wheel.' You pick a central point for your audience to focus on and then start things spinning. Once you've captured their attention and have them mesmerized, all you have to do is drop a lump of wet clay onto it and you can shape it into anything you want."

"Meaning any sort of conspiracy."

Carolan nodded again. "In this case, the wheel is the yacht club. It's the perfect jumping-off point for a Russian conspiracy. It's members-only, which means the general public is not going to be able to get inside and there's only so much information people can dig up about it online. The club itself would be completely naïve when it comes to information warfare, so they'd have no clue as to how to fight back once they found themselves in the conspiracy crosshairs."

"Hold up. How do you know the Russians even have an interest in it?"

"Because we keep a close eye on several of their most prolific troll farms. Over the last six months, we watched one of those farms gathering information about the club, its employees, and its membership."

Fields shook her head. "The Russians must vacuum up a ton of information, on a ton of weird subjects, every day. Why would you care about this one?"

"You're right. There's a lot of stuff we don't have the time or manpower to follow up on. The Commodore Yacht Club, however, is different. Among its membership are six Senators, fifteen members of the House, a Supreme Court Justice, and multiple other prominent D.C. personalities. It's no accident that the Russians have been looking at it."

"Agreed. But how do you go from them looking at it to assuming they're building some kind of information operation around it?"

"It helps to know where to look."

"Meaning?"

"The troll farms divide up the work. No single operation is conducted under the same roof. While a farm in St. Petersburg may be doing the initial research, another in Rostov-on-Don will be creating and populating blogs with disinformation, while a third farm in Kazan or Vladivostok will be pushing bots and fake accounts out onto social media to amplify whatever messaging has been decided upon. As much as they try to mix things up and cover their tracks, there's still a pattern to their behavior. Although this time, it was a bit harder to catch.

"Three years ago in Tampa, a homeless man named Alejandro Diaz, naked and high on bath salts, was found in the act of eating another homeless man's face off. Tampa PD shot him eight times, at which point he turned and charged them. The responding officers fired seventeen more rounds, stopping Diaz and dropping him to the ground. They described it like something out of a zombie movie.

"As you can imagine, it made for pretty spectacular headlines, which were picked up across the country. Then, the story faded.

"A couple of weeks later, the *Tampa Bay Times* had a short follow-up piece. Diaz had an aunt all the way up in Pensacola who came down to claim the body. There was just one problem. The corpse that was presented to her wasn't that of her nephew. Someone had screwed up. Alejandro Diaz's body had mistakenly been cremated.

"Thankfully for all involved, the aunt didn't want to make a big deal out of it. She was deeply ashamed of what her nephew had done, but as his only living relative had felt obliged to see to his remains. She left Tampa with his ashes and a stream of apologies."

"That's a horrible story," said Fields, "but what does it have to do with a D.C. yacht club and Russian troll farms?"

"In the last two months, a blog popped up—allegedly based in Florida—called *The Public Truth*, which was looking into what 'really happened' to Alejandro Diaz. It was posing a lot of outlandish questions, like, if there was no body, how can anyone be sure he's really dead? Did Diaz wear the face of his victim in order to escape just like Hannibal Lecter in *The Silence of the Lambs*? Could the killer cannibal still be on the loose? And on and on with that kind of absurd nonsense. Not long after *The Public Truth* went live, the Commodore Yacht Club was raided by Immigration and Customs Enforcement."

Fields's eyes widened. "They got hit by ICE?" she asked. "What for?"

"Apparently, the club was using a *lot* of undocumented labor."

"How come I never heard any of this?"

"With six Senators, fifteen members of the House, a Supreme Court Justice, and a host of other D.C. muckety-mucks on the membership roster, I'm going to go out on a limb and suggest someone called in a favor to keep it quiet. The story did, however, break on one blog in particular."

"Lemme guess. *The Public Truth* blog; the one dedicated to Alejandro Diaz."

"Bingo," Carolan replied. "But you're going to love this because it goes even further. One of the employees rounded up that day is named Gustavo Alejandro Diaz."

"Any relation to the cannibal from Tampa?"

"Nope. The man had never even set foot in the state of Florida. Not that it mattered. All *The Public Truth* blog needed to do was insinuate that it was the same person and the fuse was then lit.

"Adding fuel to the fire was the fact that one of the other employees taken into custody—a dishwasher—had multiple outstanding felony warrants, one of which was for child molestation."

"Jesus," she exclaimed.

"The blog ran with that, too. It published a totally bogus 'report' that the pair came from the same South American country, had been smuggled into the United States by the same coyote, and that there were wire transfers—washed through an account in the Caymans—that traced back to a powerful group of club members, none of which is true."

"This was all the Russian troll farms at work?"

Carolan nodded. "As you can imagine, with a small collection of bots and fake social media accounts, a story this juicy was able to start gaining purchase in some of the darker corners of the internet. Because of the club's location and membership, it played right into people's growing distrust of government and institutions. But to keep the fire spreading, it had to be stoked even further with more outrageous kindling. This is where the conspiracy really takes off.

"They took the myth of the cannibal and mashed it together with the outstanding warrant for child molestation. The next thing you know, the club is home to a child-trafficking cabal of pedophiles who feast on their victims' flesh."

"Like I said," Fields replied. "Next-level lunacy."

"Even better, they allegedly keep scores of children locked up in the club's basement."

"*Basement?* There aren't any basements along this part of the Potomac. The water table's too high. Half that club, if not more," she said, pointing out the window, "is built on pylons."

"You don't think a cabal of evil, child-trafficking politicians and elite power brokers can't figure out how to sink a secret basement beneath their yacht club? Could they have ordered the Army Corps of Engineers to build a top-secret, backup fallout shelter for Congress there? Better yet, maybe the club is constructed over an abandoned D.C. metro stop that has been erased from all modern maps. Perhaps the basement is actually an old vault that Abraham Lincoln used to hide the Union's gold in case the Confederacy ever stormed the capital. How can anyone really be sure?"

Fields smiled. "We're back to all that stuff about conspiracy theories being unfalsifiable, aren't we?"

"We are," Carolan responded.

"So why do you think this connects to Burman and how are you so convinced we're looking at his murder and not a suicide?"

"I'll take those in reverse order, starting with his shoes. He was wearing pristine, white leather sneakers. The toes, however, were noticeably scuffed. Unless he drags his feet around town like a petulant six-year-old, somebody—likely a person on each arm—dragged him out onto the terrace and tossed him over. I'm guessing that he was heavily under the influence of something and probably wasn't even conscious."

"What makes you say that?"

"Because if you're dragging me anywhere against my will, I'm digging in my heels, not my toes."

"Good point," Fields admitted.

"Another reason I'm leaning toward murder is the fact that his wallet is missing. It wasn't on the evidence log for the personal effects found on his body and it wasn't on the list up in his apartment."

"Could it have been a robbery gone bad?"

"They take his wallet but leave his Rolex, eleven hundred bucks in cash, and all the art and everything else in his penthouse? No way. Plus, how many robberies have you ever heard of where they throw the victim off a roof? It would have been much easier to kill him inside the building. This is all about creating a public spectacle. That's what they wanted. And it's quintessential Moscow."

"You and I both know," said Fields, "that people get tossed out of windows and off of rooftops in Russia all of the time, but here? In the United States?"

"I had trouble remembering earlier, but there was one. Four years ago. A Russian media figure who had run afoul of Peshkov fell out the window of his hotel in Manhattan. He had been seen drinking heavily in the bar that evening and, with no evidence to the contrary, the cause of his death was ruled accidental.

"But what triggered my recollection was that—like Burman—his wallet was never found. Afterward, someone told me a rumor that Russian wet-work teams have been known to keep the wallets of their targets as a kind of scalp, proving to their superiors that they were the cause of death and not some well-timed accident."

"Okay, I'm willing to go with both—that Burman was killed by the Russians and that Moscow wants to build some sort of conspiracy theory around the Commodore Yacht Club. What I don't get is, what's the connective tissue? What ties the two together?"

Carolan spread his hands as if he were revealing a table loaded with food and replied, "Like everything else in this town—politics. And more to our purposes, *geopolitics*. The Commodore has a certain slant, which makes absolutely no difference to me, but it does to the Russians.

"To a person, the Senators and Congressmen who are members here are decidedly pro-Ukraine. Not only are they some of Kyiv's biggest backers, but there's also more than one defense contractor who moors a boat here, as well as a handful of lobbyists who are getting their beaks pretty wet via the war."

"But why tie Burman into all of this?" Fields asked. "Was he even a member of the club?"

"I don't recall seeing his name on the roster. Not that it matters. Killing a Peshkov critic could serve more than one agenda. It sends a message to all the other critics, particularly those who think they're beyond the reach of Moscow, that none of them are safe—not even steps away from the White House.

"Also, a high-profile death makes the conspiracy surrounding the club even more salacious and draws in exponentially more eyeballs. A dead body stinks in more ways than one, and some of that stink risks sticking to members in ways that none of them deserve."

"So, the Kremlin gets a potential twofer in bumping off Burman. That still doesn't give us enough proof to make our case."

"True," Carolan responded as he turned off the engine and reached into the backseat for his jacket. "For that, we're going to need to do a little more legwork. Let's see what the Commodore's staff can tell us about Burman and what may have happened last night."

Glad to be getting out of the car and taking some action, Fields was first to open her door and step into the parking lot.

As she did, the heavyset, redheaded man from earlier raised his camera and began snapping more photos.

It was no coincidence that he was there at the same time. Someone had sent him. The question was, who and why?

# CHAPTER 6

From his polished wingtips to his manicured hands, Leonid Grechko was one of the more interesting men in Russian Intelligence. He was a gentleman's spy—well-educated, urbane, and a keen observer of human behavior. He was also ruthless.

He had held all of the plumb Western assignments—London, Paris, Berlin, Rome, Madrid, and eventually Washington.

Not only could he speak like his counterparts, but he could also think like them, which made him particularly useful to his superiors.

Upon returning to Moscow, he had been summoned to the Director's office, promoted, and tasked with assembling a department with the goal of conducting a "heart transplant."

In 1923, Joseph Stalin had established an effort known as the Special Disinformation Office, which eventually became known as the Active Measures Department. His goal was to shape world events via political warfare and it allowed for everything from espionage and propaganda to sabotage, assassination, and beyond.

Active measures were looked upon as an art form. They had been rhapsodized as the heart and soul of Soviet, and then Russian, intelligence. Its foremost practitioners were lavished in espionage circles with the types of praise reserved for poets and composers.

As the masters of these dark arts began to die and fade away after the Cold War, it sent the value of operatives like Leonid Grechko soaring.

The Kremlin was willing to make the next stage of his career very worth his while.

He was provided with a generous increase in pay, a substantial budget, and, as he wanted to break from the existing groupthink of the Foreign Intelligence Service, also known as the SVR, he was allowed to set up shop "off campus."

Grechko chose a narrow, three-story building west of Red Square in the Arbat District. Its location provided easy access to the Kremlin, the Ministry of Foreign Affairs, and a range of other organizations that he needed to call upon from time to time. Even better, the neighborhood was popular with tourists.

It played host to an array of Western eateries including Brisket BBQ, Ulysses Pub, and even a Hard Rock Cafe—all of which Grechko encouraged his staff to eat and drink in as often as possible. He wanted them marinating in the tastes, sounds, and smells of the cultures they were working to influence. The better they knew the enemy, the more successful their efforts would be.

Unlike his subordinates, Grechko already knew the enemy. What's more, he had sacrificed almost his entire adult life in service to his country. While he believed in the cause, he also believed in enjoying the perks of his position. As a result, he had no problem flexing his expense account at Arbat's more elegant bars and restaurants. The glamourous White Rabbit, with its never-ending city views and world-renowned chef, as well as the sleek, wildly trendy Sakhalin, were two of his favorites.

This evening, however, he was at a hole-in-the-wall called Nazhrat'sya—Russian slang for "shit-faced." It was in the basement of a building just off Pushkin Square, a couple of blocks from the Chekhovskaya metro station.

Grechko ignored the hundred-plus bras hanging from the ceiling, laid a five-thousand-ruble note on the bar, and told the bartender exactly what he wanted.

A "Revolver" was essentially a Manhattan, but with a twist. Grechko preferred Bulleit rye, something extremely hard to come by since sanctions had been imposed. Most shifty Moscow establishments, a club to which this one appeared to belong, often refilled their higher-end liquor bottles with inferior product, figuring their unsophisticated patrons wouldn't know the difference. Grechko assured the bartender that he *would* know the difference and warned him against trying to rip him off.

Uncomfortable with the man's vibe, and unsure of whether this well-dressed customer was a government official or an organized crime figure, the bartender handed his keys to a colleague and sent him to retrieve an unopened bottle of the American bourbon from the office.

When the employee returned, the bartender presented the bottle to Grechko and, once the man nodded his approval, began making the cocktail.

Instead of the sweet vermouth found in the Manhattan, coffee liqueur is used, followed by a few dashes of orange bitters. The bartender withdrew a lighter and was about to flame the orange peel garnish, but Grechko waved him away. The only thing he liked less than cocktail umbrellas were cocktail pyrotechnics. *Shake it, serve it, and fuck off.* That was his mantra.

Once again, the bartender seemed to be able to pick up on the man's vibe and disappeared to deal with another customer.

Grechko sipped his drink. Despite the peeling paint, the floor that stuck to his shoes with every step, and the women's lingerie hanging from the light fixtures like pennants strung across a Himalayan base camp, the staff could mix a decent cocktail. As he drank, he took a look around.

This early in the evening, the clientele was thin—a few Russian students mixed with some tourists who were either lost or traveling on next to no money.

The intelligence operative checked his watch. His contact was late. Grechko didn't like that. Being punctual was a sign of respect. So was choosing a meeting location commensurate with the standing of the participants. As a former diplomat turned full-time presidential advisor, Oleg Beglov knew better. Being a member of the Kremlin's most inner circle, however, meant that he didn't have to care.

Providing reports directly to Beglov had become routine. The war had been a disaster from the start—both from a military and a PR standpoint. President Peshkov detested the comparison to Hitler's invasion of

Czechoslovakia's Sudetenland. This, despite the fact that he was voicing his own version of one of Hitler's key justifications—that he was stepping in to defend ethnic Russians who were being unfairly treated.

It was bullshit when Hitler tried to justify his actions on behalf of "ethnic Germans" and it was bullshit now as Peshkov engaged in a similar lie.

Of particular importance was that Europe and its Western allies had learned their lesson eighty-plus years ago with Hitler. This time there was no feckless Neville Chamberlain happy to stand aside in exchange for a bogus promise of peace and an end to any further territorial ambition.

The West had made it crystal clear that it wasn't going to give the Russian President an inch. Peshkov had woefully underestimated their response. But his decision to invade hadn't been made in a vacuum. He'd had good reason to think he might not meet serious resistance.

Less than ten years earlier, the Russian President had successfully rolled his battalion tactical groups into eastern Ukraine and sliced off a nice chunk of the country. The rest of the world had done nothing. Worse still, the United States—a key signatory to the Budapest Memorandum, an agreement promising to protect the territorial integrity of Ukraine in the aftermath of the implosion of the USSR in exchange for Ukraine giving up its nuclear weapon stockpiles—did little more than shrug.

Next to some light sanctions and a few strongly worded letters, the only serious thing that happened to the Russians in the wake of their first invasion was that they got kicked out of the G8, which then became the G7.

As far as Peshkov was concerned, it had all been worth it. He had taken another step toward his ultimate goal of reconstituting Imperial Russia. As the old saying went, "There can be no Russian Empire without Ukraine." He was on his way.

But when he went to take his next step, his lightning-fast invasion was stopped dead in its tracks. The undertrained, underequipped Ukrainians put up a fierce defense. What should have only taken the Russians a matter of days, weeks tops, had turned into a meat-grinding stalemate. No matter how much the Russians threw at Ukraine, the Ukrainians fought back twice as hard. They simply refused to be defeated. Their obstinance enraged Peshkov.

The Russian President doubled down and pulled out all the stops. Absolutely nothing was off the table. It didn't matter if he smashed every building and killed every last Ukrainian civilian in the process. Russia was a global power. He would not be embarrassed by a bunch of peasant farmers from a country known as the breadbasket of Europe. Not only *would* Russia conquer them, but these people *deserved* to be conquered. Better yet, they deserved to be *crushed* and to have their culture wiped from the face of the earth and forgotten by history.

The biggest problem for Peshkov was that the crushing and wiping from the face of the earth wasn't happening fast enough. That was why Leonid Grechko and Oleg Beglov were meeting.

Pulling out his cell phone to check for any updates, the intelligence operative looked toward the door and saw the presidential advisor enter. *It was about time*.

"Sorry I'm late," said Beglov as he approached the bar and signaled for the barman.

He was a good fifteen years younger than Grechko, in his mid to late forties. Easily the youngest of Peshkov's confidants. He was tall and trim, with a head of thick, somewhat damp hair. His mustache and detached, pointy beard, as well as his narrow, brown eyes, were reminiscent of Lenin's.

Moscow gossip had him pegged as Peshkov's protégé, the man who would one day replace him and lead all of Russia.

Grechko wasn't sure how much of that to believe. As the saying went, those who know don't talk, and those who talk don't know. Russians loved to speculate. It was practically a national pastime. That was especially true inside the intelligence services.

After ordering a gin and tonic, Beglov tilted his head toward an empty table in the corner. "Shall we take a seat over there?"

Grechko scooped up his change from the bar and walked over while the advisor waited for his drink. There were only two chairs and the intelligence operative took the one that gave him the best view of the room.

A few moments later, Beglov, cocktail in hand, joined him. He threw his overcoat over the back of the other chair and set his briefcase on the floor by his feet. "To your health," he offered, raising his glass.

"Vashe zdarovye," Grechko repeated, lifting his in return.

There was a rowdy chant from the other side of the room as a group of students recited a drinking poem and downed a round of shots. The intelligence operative rolled his eyes. Not overdramatically, but enough for his colleague to notice.

"Not your type of place?" Beglov asked.

Grechko smiled. "I'm just sorry there isn't any karaoke tonight."

"That's only on Wednesdays," the advisor said, smiling back.

"So, you're a regular?"

"I'm in the neighborhood from time to time," he responded, adjusting his wedding band. "I have a friend who lives nearby."

The intelligence officer knew a thing or two about his counterpart. One of them was that in addition to a wife and two grown children, Beglov had a mistress—a younger and very attractive associate curator at the State Tretyakov Gallery, the leading collection of Russian fine art in the world. Grechko assumed that this was the "friend" who lived nearby and also the reason why Beglov had arrived late with wet hair.

Enough of Grechko's time had already been wasted and so he pivoted to work. "I have news from Turtle Bay."

Turtle Bay was the New York City neighborhood where the United Nations was located.

Beglov leaned in.

"The contraband seized in the Gulf of Oman is going to Kyiv."

American warships from the Fifth Fleet, along with vessels of the British and French navies, had interdicted multiple fishing trawlers attempting to smuggle Iranian weapons to Tehran-backed Houthi rebels in Yemen. Thousands of Russian-style battle rifles, machine guns, antitank missiles, surface-to-air missiles, engines for land-attack cruise missiles, and over a million rounds of ammunition had been seized.

Normally, such illicit lethal cargo—evidence of Iran's violations of UN Security Council resolution 2624—would remain stored at U.S. bases across the region until official proceedings could be undertaken.

"Damn it," the advisor responded. "That should have been tied up in red tape for at least another year. We were assured that we had enough votes to keep it stalled."

"Our special military operation," Grechko replied, using the carefully crafted term concocted by the Kremlin, "remains unpopular even among some of our friends. I'm told Beijing was unwilling to block the transfer."

At the mention of China, Beglov grew angry. "The goddamn Chinese are not our friends. And don't let anyone tell you that they are. They're ravenous for resources. They want our coal, our gas, and our aluminum. All of it. And they want it as cheap as possible. The more we suffer, the further prices fall. Believe me, they're not crying any tears for us."

Grechko knew that the relationship between Moscow and Beijing was eroding. It wasn't frosty, not yet, but it was heading in that direction.

The Chinese had been supplying Russia with certain military technology such as navigation and jamming equipment, as well as fighter jet parts. But what Moscow really needed was more, *lots more*, lethal aid—things like bombs and missiles, rifles and ammunition.

Beijing had been warned by the Americans not to send any; that it was a bright red line with enormous consequences if they crossed it. But the Chinese being the Chinese, they had crossed it.

China, however, hadn't done so in order to help Russia win the war in Ukraine, but rather to keep the Russians bogged down in it. They wanted to see it dragged out. The longer the war ground on, the further America would deplete its military stockpiles.

If they could sufficiently bleed the United States, they would have a once-in-a-lifetime opportunity—the ability to take Taiwan without the American military being able to mount an effective and sustained response.

Thus, the war in Ukraine was a proxy war for the Chinese. They didn't give two fucks about Russia's well-being.

Grechko didn't blame Beglov for being unhappy with them. In advance of their own invasion of Taiwan, China was getting free lessons on everything from keeping a battered, heavily sanctioned economy afloat to how President Peshkov had managed to hold on to power.

Grechko had wondered as well. Considering how badly things had been going, he was stunned that the Russian leader hadn't been toppled and replaced, much less assassinated. The man was either the most skilled politician in Russian history or its luckiest.

The extent to which the oligarchs around him had suffered—the freezing of bank accounts, the seizure of real estate, yachts, and private jets—it was enough to make the Pope himself think about hiring an assassin. Peshkov was living on borrowed time. At some point, his luck or his skill was going to run dry. Then the real struggle for power would begin.

While, as the heir apparent, he might entertain such thoughts, Beglov was far too wise to ever discuss such things—much less in public, and lesser still with someone he had only recently begun a professional relationship with.

For his part, Grechko was both smart enough and experienced enough not to raise such questions. To do so would have been an act of treason. If there was one thing he knew, it was that in Russia, *everyone* was replaceable. Even him.

Having vented about the Chinese, Beglov got back to business. "Unfortunately, I am taking my wife for dinner shortly. It's her birthday, so we'll need to be brief. The President has been concerned about the Americans, particularly their support for Ukraine. What can I tell him about your efforts?"

The advisor was a real piece of work—cutting an intelligence meeting short in order to have a tryst with his mistress, on his wife's birthday. It was a wonder that the entire country hadn't yet risen up against the political class and hanged them from lampposts.

"The software problem has been fixed," he said, referring to Burman's death in D.C.

"Excellent. And our internet source will make sure it is documented?"

"It has already been added to the site," Grechko replied. "Complete with photographs from the scene. A follow-up story is in the works."

"Make sure I get links to everything."

The intelligence operative didn't know why that should be his problem, but he nodded anyway.

"What about Dasher?"

Grechko couldn't believe the advisor was using an actual operational codename in public, but especially one like Dasher. The American was one of the best assets the SVR had ever recruited. He quickly scanned the room to make sure no one had overheard them.

"Everything is on track."

"The President wants your efforts accelerated."

This was exactly what Grechko had worried about. As the war ground on, Peshkov was going to get more desperate. Having established a direct line of contact via Beglov, the Russian President was able to assert his will without any pushback from FSB headquarters.

He was a man who despised being compared to Hitler, so it was odd to see him taking this kind of micromanagement right out of the Führer's playbook. Regardless, Grechko was stuck.

Even though it meant taking on more risk, and on American soil no less, he would have to do as Peshkov had ordered. His activities would be moved up.

His superiors were going to be pissed and his operatives on the ground in the United States jumpy. But without missing a beat, he replied, "I'll make it happen."

Beglov was pleased. "Your professionalism has not gone unnoticed by the Kremlin. We need more men like you. Especially now. Keep it up."

Grechko watched as the advisor knocked back the remainder of his cocktail, stood up, and gathered his things to leave.

"Don't forget those links," Beglov reminded him.

The pair shook hands and the intelligence operative followed him with his eyes as the advisor exited the shitty little bar.

Though he could have pointed it out to him, Grechko decided not to warn the man that he had lipstick on the back of his collar.

Carelessness, both personal and professional, had a way of catching up with everyone. In times of war, the Fates had a way of accelerating those reckonings.

Grechko made a mental note not to be standing anywhere near Peshkov or Beglov when theirs arrived. Both men were very likely headed for violent, bloody ends.

In the meantime, all the intelligence operative could do was his job. If the Fates had something bloody and violent planned for him, he would never see it coming. His enemies were that good—even the Americans—and he was now about to turn the heat up on them.

# CHAPTER 7

A crusty operative from Polish Intelligence met Harvath and Nicholas at Poland's baroque Przemysl Glowny station. He spirited them, along with Argos, Draco, and three porters, past the passport control line, over to the platform, and onto the overnight train to Kyiv.

They were being given exclusive access to the private car used to ferry dignitaries, heads of state, and other VIPs across the border and on to Kyiv.

In addition to several staterooms, there was a narrow conference room with a long, polished table and a living room area with a suite of leather club chairs.

The wood-paneled interior reminded Harvath of the Compiègne Wagon, where the Germans were forced to sign the armistice ending World War I, and in which Hitler, reveling in the irony, forced the French to sign their surrender in World War II.

After a quick tour, the Polish Intelligence operative ran through the rules of the road. "All of the curtains are to remain fully closed and all passengers are expected to practice strict light discipline. The train isn't armored; however, the windows in this car have been covered with ballistic film."

Harvath was familiar with the product. It was used on a lot of government buildings and, while it offered some blast mitigation, it was best known for reducing the amount of flying glass after an explosion.

That said, he was also familiar with what mortar rounds, RPGs, and other assorted munitions were capable of. The train was headed into a war zone. If they took a direct hit, window film was going to be about as helpful as rearranging the deck chairs on the *Lusitania*.

When the man was done speaking, Harvath thanked him.

"You're welcome," the intelligence officer replied as he checked his watch. "If you want something from the catering car, I'd go now. They'll be letting the other passengers board soon."

"We're all set," Nicholas answered as he tipped the porters, removed a bottle of wine from one of his bags, and pulled out some of the food he had packed.

"Then I'll leave you to it," the man said, stepping out of the conference room into the passageway.

As he did, he paused at the door and added, "I'm not supposed to ask why you're going to Ukraine. But if it involves killing Russians, I hope you kill as many of those motherfuckers as possible."

Before Harvath or Nicholas could respond, the man had turned and exited the train.

"That's an interesting way to say good-bye," Harvath remarked.

"Not if you're a Pole," said Nicholas. "These people have long memories. They remember what it was like living under the Soviets. They know all too well that if the Russians win in Ukraine, they could come for Poland next."

"Which, as a NATO member, would absolutely trigger World War III."

"Let's hope we never have to find out," the little man replied. "Hungry?"

"Sure," Harvath replied, walking over to the assortment of hard-sided, olive-drab Storm cases Nicholas had brought from the United States. The ones meant for him had been tagged with his call sign—*Norseman*. He opened the rifle case first.

Inside was an all-black, Gen II, Galil ACE chambered in 7.62. It had been tricked out with a suppressor, a holographic sight, a magnifier, and a side-folding, telescoping stock. Nestled in the gray foam next to it was a sling and a bunch of thirty-round polymer PMAGs.

"Who chose this rifle?" he asked. Picking it up, he cycled the bolt to make sure it was unloaded and then gauged the Galil's balance. It was lighter than he had expected, which was important, considering how much the ammo weighed.

"Gage," said Nicholas, identifying the member of Harvath's team back in the States who had been put in charge of assembling the weapons package. "At a glance, it looks like an AK, so he figured it would help you blend in. It's also compatible with AK and AKM mags, which are all over the place in Ukraine, so you won't have trouble finding extras if you need them."

Harvath set the rifle back in its case and inspected the rest of the gear. Gage made an excellent quartermaster. He had thought of practically everything.

In addition to a Glock pistol, which Harvath knew Ukrainian Special Forces carried and which would stand up to a lot of punishment on the battlefield, there was a helmet, night-vision goggles, a thermal scope, a handheld drone, encrypted radios, a land navigation kit, an individual first aid kit (also known as an IFAK or blowout kit), a SERE—survival, evasion, resistance, and escape—kit, a plate carrier with plates and multiple pouches, a battle belt with a holster for the Glock and additional pouches, tactical gloves, chem lights, an envelope filled with cash, multiple cartons of cigarettes, which in war could be even better than cash, and a host of other smart and very useful items.

He was still organizing everything when the train, like some giant beast, shuddered angrily awake and began lumbering forward, crawling out of the station into the darkness.

As they crept out of Przemysl, Nicholas uncorked the wine and invited Harvath to join him for a toast. "A farewell to civilization," he offered.

Standing at the window, they clinked glasses and, with all the lights in the carriage extinguished, pulled back the curtains enough to see outside.

It didn't take long to put the city of less than sixty thousand behind them. Twenty-five minutes more and they'd be at the border crossing. Then, after the bogies had been adjusted to accommodate the wider, Russian-gauge tracks, they'd be in Ukraine and "unofficially" at war.

There was something odd about heading into battle via train. It had an antiquated, kind of time-warp feeling to it, like arriving via steamship or on horseback. It was definitely worlds away from parachuting out of a C-130 or being flown in via helicopter. But no matter how you got there, war was still war—and that was very much at the forefront of Harvath's mind.

There had only been so much that he could tell Sølvi. While she was disappointed that he needed to cancel their weekend, she understood. He wouldn't have done it unless something critical had popped up. And critical things did often pop up. Such was the nature of their business.

At the same time, she had an uncanny ability to read Harvath and often picked up on what he *wasn't* saying. It was one of the many attributes that made her so good at her job.

She knew that he was going into harm's way and that this assignment was going to be particularly dangerous. She could feel in her bones that it had something to do with Ukraine. "Get in. Do what you have to do. And then get out—as quickly as you can."

They told each other "I love you" and then ended their encrypted video call. It didn't make any sense to draw things out. It would have only made it harder for each of them.

Harvath had been concerned about canceling their plans. Just as she could read him, he could also read her. Her job had been weighing on her.

In the wake of Finland's formal application to join NATO, that country had recently begun the construction of a barrier wall along their border with Russia.

If Moscow decided to get scrappy with the Finns, the Norwegians would be the closest NATO ally called to action. A significant portion of that work would flow through Sølvi's office. It would be enough to keep anyone on edge, even someone as icy cool as she was.

He had hoped to talk it all out while they were in Warsaw, to make some solid, long-term plans. He wanted them to have something concrete to look forward to. They couldn't be a couple yet apart from each other forever. Where should they aim to be in one year? Two? What would things look like for them five years from now?

On his last visit to Norway, he had met an ex-CIA operative—an

American—who still did contract work for the Agency. He had married a beautiful Norwegian woman and had set up house in northern Norway.

By all outward appearances, the man was retired. Langley, however, gave him enough to keep him busy—especially with Russia's northern fleet in his backyard along with an enormous state-of-the-art American/Norwegian radar installation.

Harvath could see himself getting used to something like that, provided there was enough action going on. He wasn't about to toddle off into the sunset and begin bird-watching. Not now. In fact, not ever.

However, if dialing down his op tempo—just a smidge—meant that he might be able to live in the same place with Sølvi, he was willing to consider it.

Right now, though, he had to compartmentalize all of that. Thoughts of Sølvi and their future had to be locked in that steel box he kept in the attic of his mind and shoved into its farthest corner. From this moment forward, his entire focus needed to be on the mission. Thinking of anything else would only end up getting him killed.

Stepping away from the window, he turned his attention back to the gear while Nicholas assembled something for them to eat.

As the train neared Lviv, the first major Ukrainian city since crossing the border, the PA system crackled to life. Passengers were warned to keep their window curtains drawn and to continue practicing light discipline. They were further notified that the train would be making a brief stop in Lviv to pick up Ukrainian Border Control officers and that under no circumstances should anyone attempt to disembark.

"I once knew a woman from Lviv," Nicholas said, after the announcement had ended. "She had the bluest eyes I have ever seen. Like glaciers. Absolutely remarkable."

No doubt there was a story behind this woman, and, to be honest, considering the little man's past, Harvath probably didn't want to hear it. So instead of taking the bait, he changed the subject. "Is this where we meet our escort?"

Nicholas nodded. "It's not too late to turn back."

Harvath smiled. "And let somebody else have all the fun? Not a chance."

They rode the last few kilometers in silence, each man attending to his own thoughts. With the arrival of the GUR team, things were about to get very real, right down to Harvath swearing an oath to Ukraine's International Legion—something he had been instructed was integral to his assignment.

Once the train had pulled into the Lviv station and come to a stop, Border Control officers entered the first public compartment up near the locomotive, while two more entered the dining car.

As this was happening, four men from Ukrainian Intelligence quietly slipped aboard the private carriage and knocked on the conference room door. Nicholas brought his dogs to obedience at his side while Harvath opened it.

The leader of the team, a man named Kozar, introduced himself and then had his teammates step forward and shake hands.

All in their thirties, the men were wearing dark jeans, leather jackets, and hiking boots. It looked as if it had been several days since any of them had shaved. Despite the stubble, the men were clean and professional.

"May I?" Kozar asked, pointing at Argos and Draco as the train began moving again. "I haven't seen my dogs since the war started."

"What kind of dogs?" Nicholas asked, having Kozar stand still as he brought Draco over first and then Argos to familiarize themselves with him.

"Anatolian shepherds."

"Those are beautiful animals. Independent, yet very loyal. Large as well."

Kozar scratched Nicholas's dogs under their chins and replied, "Mine are not nearly as large as yours. Ovcharkas, correct?"

"You know your breeds."

"We're fielding a special K9 unit that will employ them."

"Out of Ukrainian Intelligence?" the little man asked. "For what purpose?"

"The Soviets used Ovcharkas for years and they still have a fearsome reputation across the Russian military. Bottom line, they scare the shit out of the Russians. We believe they will be useful in certain interrogation settings."

Nicholas liked the way the Ukrainians thought. "I agree. My dogs have been fantastic. I cannot say enough good things about the breed. My friend Scot has one as well."

"Had," Harvath corrected him.

"Oh, that's right," the little man stated. "I forgot. I gave you one as a puppy and you gave it away."

Kozar looked at Harvath. "How could you give a dog like that away?"

"He knows damn well why," Harvath responded, pointing at his friend. "He also knows that the dog is living a much better life up in the wilds of Maine than at my house with me gone all the time."

"The dog also has a much better owner now, too," Nicholas conceded. "Calmer. Much gentler and considerably more relaxed."

Harvath rubbed his nose with his middle finger.

"She's also much more attractive, which is important, as many pets end up looking like their owners."

"Where are yours?" Harvath asked Kozar, ignoring the additional jibe.

"My wife and children went to stay with her parents, who live outside of Ukraine. They took the dogs with them."

"It must be tough to be without them," said Nicholas.

"My teenagers," Kozar responded wryly, "or my dogs?"

"No, your in-laws."

The intelligence operative laughed. "Very funny," he said. Turning to his men he added, "I like this guy."

"Trust me," Harvath offered. "It'll fade."

This time it was Nicholas who subtly gave his friend the finger.

"Okay," said Kozar, doling out a final pat to the dogs and directing everyone to the conference table. "Let's get down to business."

One of the men placed a small LED lamp on the table and activated its red-light feature. Another man produced a stack of folders from a briefcase he was carrying. Removing a document from the stack, he flipped to the signature page and slid it across the table to Harvath.

Kozar handed him a pen and said, "This is your contract. It states that you are joining Ukraine's International Legion of your own free will, that in volunteering, you understand the inherent risks, that you are combat-qualified, and that you will abide by all the terms and conditions hereto—including all relevant international laws governing warfare, including both the Geneva and Hague Conventions.

"You will, at all times on the battlefield, distinguish yourself from the civilian population by visibly identifying yourself as a member of the Ukrainian Armed Forces. If you do not, and if you are captured by the enemy, you understand that you run the risk of not enjoying certain protections, including prisoner-of-war status. Do you have any questions?"

Harvath shook his head. Nicholas had fully briefed him on the trip down. The Russians were labeling all foreign fighters assisting Ukraine, particularly those from the West, as mercenaries and "unlawful combatants." As such, in Russia's opinion, they could be tried as criminals and immediately sentenced to death. It was not only incorrect, but it was also a blatant war crime. The Russians were beyond the point of caring. No matter how many civilians they killed, no matter how many international laws and conventions they broke, they were committed to victory.

"This contract," Kozar continued, "shall be in effect for the entirety of the martial law, but you may sever it and leave your voluntary service to the Ukrainian Armed Forces at any time."

Taking the pen, Harvath signed the document.

Kozar witnessed it with his signature, then passed it back to the man with the briefcase, who inked it with a large, round, official rubber stamp and placed the document back in the folder from whence it came.

"On behalf of the Defense Ministry of Ukraine," said Kozar, extending his hand, "I want to thank you for volunteering and welcome you to the Ukrainian International Legion, Captain Harvath."

Harvath shook his hand and watched as the man with the briefcase slid another document across the table.

After reviewing it, Kozar passed it to Harvath. "These are your orders. You have been assigned to the Legionnaires Special Services Group—our Special Forces wing."

"And what about my team?"

"They've been drawn from the regular International Legion."

"So, not SF soldiers?"

"No," the intelligence operative admitted, "but they're battle-tested and have solid experience. These are the best of the men we can spare."

It wasn't exactly a ringing endorsement, but Harvath knew a decision like this wasn't being made by Kozar. It was coming from much higher up on the food chain.

The man with the briefcase handed over four folders, each containing a service record. Harvath scanned them.

There were two Americans, a Brit, and a Canadian. They had all done tours in Afghanistan, and everyone, except for the Canadian, who was too young and whose country didn't "officially" participate in the war, had done at least one tour in Iraq.

To cut down on confusion and streamline communications, call signs were standard across the Ukrainian forces, including the legion. The Americans—a former Army Staff Sergeant and a no-longer-active Marine Lance Corporal—were known respectively as *Hookah* and *Krueger*. The former British Army Second Lieutenant was referred to as *Jacks* and the former Canadian Army Corporal had the call sign *Biscuit*.

Stapled to the inside of each folder was a photograph.

Hookah had some of the biggest ears Harvath had ever seen and he wondered how the man had avoided getting the call sign *Dumbo*. He also had a large, flat boxer's nose that made him look like he'd been hit in the face with a shovel. Other than these unusual features, he had jet-black hair and dark and narrow eyes that gave off a mean-as-hell vibe. He was forty-two years old.

Krueger looked like he could have been working at an investment bank or running a movie studio. He had short blond hair and a chiseled face with a dent in his chin. Even from his photo, it was obvious that he had taken the Marine Corps maxim of "fitness for life" seriously. He was thirty-four.

Jacks had a thick neck and a big head with receding, messy brown hair. He looked like an assistant high school football coach, not yet carrying a massive paunch, who had just rolled out of bed. It was hard to tell if the scowl in his photo was intentional or if that was how the thirty-eight-year-old always looked. Harvath figured he'd find out soon enough.

Biscuit was a short, skinny kid with a shaved head and dark circles under his eyes. For someone his age, he didn't appear to possess any of the vitality of youth. He looked like a drug addict who had been given the option of either going to prison or fighting in Ukraine. It wouldn't have surprised Harvath at all to be told the twenty-seven-year-old had tracks up and down his arms and was missing a bunch of teeth.

Knowing he wasn't allowed to keep the folders, Harvath slid them back to the man with the briefcase and asked Kozar, "And what about vehicles, munitions, communications gear, and the rest of what we'll need?"

"Your team has already been sourcing those supplies. They should have everything assembled by the time you reach them."

"Which will be when?"

"When we get to Kyiv, you'll transfer trains. Two of my men will accompany you farther east to Kharkiv. There you'll be met by a GUR liaison from the legion who will facilitate getting you the rest of the way to your team."

"And my colleague?" Harvath asked, nodding at Nicholas.

"He and the dogs get off with us in Kyiv," Kozar replied, conveying that "us" meant him and the man with the briefcase. "The GUR has a special, fortified command facility not far from the station. That's where we'll be based."

"In the meantime," the man with the briefcase stated, "we need to give you a final briefing on the people you're going after. Some new intelligence has come to our attention."

Harvath waited for another folder to be handed to him, but the man with the briefcase seemed reluctant to proceed.

The man looked at his boss. Only when Kozar nodded his permission did he proceed. "First, I need to remind you that, per our agreement, this information must remain classified and none of it may leave this room."

That was the deal the United States had agreed to and so Harvath nodded his assent.

"Good," the man replied. "Second, I need to warn you. What I am about to show you is quite inhuman. Even by Russian standards."

# CHAPTER 8

If Harvath never saw the inside of another train again—Ukrainian or otherwise—it would be too soon.

He had seen Nicholas and the dogs off at the Kyiv-Pasazhyrskyi railway station with the help of Kozar's men, Artem and Symon, who were accompanying him to Kharkiv and had unloaded his gear onto a luggage cart and tracked down the platform for their next train.

With a few minutes to spare before departure, they had grabbed coffees and something to eat. Then they had boarded the train.

Even though they didn't have a private carriage, they did have a small, albeit musty, compartment all to themselves. Not that it made much difference. The train was practically empty. Very few people were headed east toward the front lines of the war.

Pulling out of the station, there was a definite mood change. Instead of leaving their tactical gear packed away, Artem and Symon got everything out and had it staged in the compartment—rifles, chest rigs, helmets, all of it. They suggested Harvath do the same.

Once he had pre-positioned his most necessary gear, he turned his attention out the window and drank what remained of his coffee.

Unlike the overnight trip from Poland, which took place with the shades drawn, they were now traveling in daylight and able to do so with the window curtains open.

Outside, they passed farm after farm. There were fields as far as the eye could see. It reminded him a lot of driving through Wisconsin or Iowa.

The pastoral scenery was so peaceful, it was hard to process that the war was on this region's doorstep—that the tractors and livestock he was looking at now could be tanks and Russian troops within hours or days. The fragility of civilization couldn't have been depicted in greater relief.

Yet, as the farmers, their families, and various other villagers and townspeople proved, life persisted. It carried on, despite the circumstances.

In some cases, life carried on with a greater, renewed vigor *because of* the circumstances.

Living, he saw as the train passed and people went about their business, could become the ultimate act of courage, of pride, and the ultimate act of defiance.

It reminded him of the line spoken decades ago by Ronald Reagan, "There's no argument over the choice between peace and war, but there's only one guaranteed way you can have peace—and you can have it in the next second—surrender."

That kind of peace, however, wasn't true peace. As was made evident by the balance of the speech, it was an invitation to forgo freedom and live in slavery.

Everywhere Harvath looked, it was obvious which decision the Ukrainians had made. There would be no peace as long as the Russians occupied their country. He respected them for that. Immensely.

Eventually he got tired of watching the Ukrainian countryside pass by. As Artem was reading a newspaper he had miraculously found and Symon was quietly rewatching a video his wife sent of their kids, he decided to close his eyes for a while. After what he'd learned about the Raven unit, he hadn't slept well last night and there was no telling when he'd get a chance to catch up on his rest.

With his eyes closed, the train rocking gently side to side, and his mind forcing out all thoughts, it wasn't difficult for him to fall asleep.

They were nearing Kharkiv when he was jerked awake by the train's rapid deceleration and the sound of squealing brakes.

Opening his eyes, he saw that Artem was already up and exiting the compartment. "What's going on?"

Symon took a look out the window. "There must be something wrong up ahead. Grab your kit."

Harvath did as the man suggested, quickly putting on his plate carrier and battle belt, then slinging his rifle. He was grateful to Gage for also including ammunition in his care package.

He followed Symon into the gangway and toward the vestibule. As they moved, a voice delivered a message over the public address system.

"There's something wrong with the tracks," Symon explained. "The engineer is going to investigate. Want to stretch your legs?"

"How do you know it's not an ambush?"

"Russian sabotage is practically a daily occurrence. All around the country, they strike different pieces of track. That's why the trains travel at reduced speed. Welcome to life in Ukraine."

Harvath was about to respond when they arrived at the vestibule and Symon, helmet in hand, pointed at the doors on both sides and asked, "Port or starboard?"

Tactically, Harvath could come up with good reasons against both. They were in the middle of the Ukrainian countryside. There was nothing but fields outside and very little cover or concealment along the tracks.

Symon walked over to the door on the right and peered through the glass, assessing the situation. He then stepped over to the door on the left.

After taking a look, he turned to Harvath and said, "We're going out this door. Put your helmet on." Smiling, he added, "Just in case."

No sooner had the man uttered those words than a high-caliber sniper's bullet pierced the glass and went through his skull, just above his right temple.

As blood, bone, and bits of brain showered the vestibule, Harvath hit the deck. He had no idea where Artem was, though he assumed the man had moved through the train up to the first carriage to figure out what was going on. They didn't have radios or any other means by which to communicate.

Harvath thought about hitting the opposite door and dropping down under the train, but he knew that as crude as the Russians were, if they wanted to kill as many passengers as possible, they'd have hitters on that side, too.

By the same token, the train was almost empty. If they'd done any reconnaissance whatsoever, they'd know that. This couldn't be about flushing out passengers just so they could gun them down, could it?

Then Harvath, who hated wearing helmets, heard a telltale whistle through the broken window and couldn't get his on fast enough.

They weren't shooting people as they got off the train, they were shooting people to keep them *on* the train. At least to keep them on the train for the incoming mortar rounds to do their work.

Scrambling to his feet, but keeping below the window line, Harvath sprinted for the rear of the train.

As he moved, mortar round after mortar round landed behind him. The Russians had sabotaged the tracks not just to interfere with this particular route, but to bring one of its trains to a standstill so that they could effectively shell a stationary target.

There was no time to grab the rest of his gear and he sped right past his compartment. The sounds of the explosions were deafening.

His back was burning; absolutely on fucking fire. He couldn't tell if it was from the heat of the mortars detonating, or if he'd been riddled with shrapnel and his brain hadn't yet had time to connect the dots.

All he knew was that movement was life. *Get off the X. Move.* And that was exactly what he continued to do. Still crouching low, he ran as fast as he could to the back of the train. What he would do once he got there, he still hadn't figured out. There were two more cars to go.

In the next vestibule, there was a young woman facedown on the floor. The broken window above her and the amount of blood pooled around her told him all he needed to know. There was no point in stopping to check on her or render aid. She was dead.

He noted that she had been shot on the opposite side of the train from Symon. That meant that he had assessed the situation correctly. There were shooters on both sides. The question remaining was, how many?

Was it a single sniper—one left, one right—with enough setback to be able to target the length of all the cars? Or were there teams positioned up and down the tracks?

This was one of the worst parts of what he was called to do—making life-or-death decisions with little to no reliable information. And just like right now, there never seemed to be enough time in which to make them. But he had no choice. The explosions were chewing up the train, the mortars landing closer and closer to his position. The only way out of this was via the rear door at the back of the train.

There was just one problem. The final carriage was a dining car with even bigger windows and they lined both sides. Unless Harvath planned on crawling, which there was not enough time to do, he was going to have to risk exposure—unless.

At the head of the car was a fire extinguisher. Ripping it off the wall, he pulled the pin and clamped down on the handle, filling the carriage with retardant fog. It wasn't perfect, but it would at least add a little camouflage to his movements. Putting his head down, he charged.

Instantly as he entered the carriage, the windows began shattering from sniper fire. They had no idea who he was or where he was, just that someone was very likely attempting an escape. In order to compensate for the poor visibility, they were throwing rounds everywhere. Harvath knew that if he didn't make it to that door in the next three seconds, one of those bullets was going to find him. He ran as fast as he could, his ears already ringing from the explosions.

Hitting the door, he tried to open it, but it was locked. The mechanism was foreign to him and he couldn't see well enough to unlock it.

As he struggled with the handle, the sniper fire intensified. The bullets were not only coming through the windows, but also through the walls. The glasses, dishes, and ceramic coffee cups were shattering across the shelves just behind him.

Harvath fought to maintain his cool. In the back of his mind, however, he was aware that not only were the odds of getting hit by one of the bullets increasing exponentially, but so were the chances that the final mortar, meant to destroy the carriage he was standing in, had already been loosed. At any moment, he would hear its shrill, unmistakable, inbound whistle. Then he did. The mortar was headed straight for him.

Feeling along the doorframe, he found what he was looking for—an emergency release. He punched it and the lock released. Throwing the door open, he didn't have time to weigh his options. All he could do was jump—and that's what he did.

As he jumped, the last and final mortar hit the carriage. The force of the blast sent Harvath flying beyond the tracks and into the field.

He landed hard, taking the brutal brunt of the fall on his left side. But at least he was alive. For the moment.

Around him clods of dirt began jumping into the air. At least one of the snipers had him in his sights.

Out of the corner of his eye, he noticed a shallow culvert several feet away and lunged for it, hoping to escape their crosshairs. Off in the distance, air raid sirens wailed.

The Russian sabotage team had achieved their goal. The train was destroyed. He didn't hold out much hope for additional survivors. It had been all too easy for the snipers to pick off their targets.

The only reason Harvath wasn't dead too was that he had known to keep moving. He'd also been lucky as hell. If the other people on that train had received half the training that he'd had, maybe some of them would have survived as well. He was reminded for the umpteenth time that life was often not only unfair, but also exceedingly cruel, especially in times of war.

He thought about engaging the snipers but realized that it would be a waste of his ammo. He had no idea where they were specifically. He would be firing blind.

The question then became, who could hold out the longest? Unless they still had a mortar team out there and were willing to waste shells trying to dial them in on his location, he figured he had the advantage. He could simply wait them out. At some point, a local response team was going to show up and then the shooters would have to break off. *But what if that wasn't their plan?*

What if the snipers planned to continue to lie in wait to take out anyone and everyone who arrived to render assistance? *The bloodbath*, Harvath realized, *would only get worse*. He couldn't let that happen. He needed to act.

From the limited amount he could see, without raising his head too high up and getting it blown off, farther back in the field was a small copse of trees. If Harvath was a sniper and had responsibility for staking out the train from this side of the tracks, that's where he would be.

What he needed was a way to confirm his supposition. He needed some means by which to flush the sniper out, to make him reveal himself. As it turned out, someone else was about to do that for him. That someone was Artem.

The Ukrainian Intelligence operative was alive. But by the way he was moving, he looked to be seriously injured. Even so, he had risked opening himself up to attack to reach another, injured passenger and pull her to safety behind a piece of nearby wreckage. It was an act of pure selflessness and courage.

As soon as he had gotten to the woman, he was fully in the open and visible to the Russian sniper who began firing from within the copse of trees. It was all the confirmation Harvath needed. With his magnifier engaged, he began putting rounds on the target.

He strafed the copse like he was sweeping a well-oiled Weedwacker through soft summer grass.

The sniper on the opposite side of the tracks tried to engage him, but the wind was pushing the smoke from the bombed-out train carriages right at him, making it very difficult to see.

Harvath emptied an entire mag of 7.62, reloaded the Galil, and continued to fire. He didn't stop shooting until he saw that Artem and the woman were out of the line of fire and had made it back behind cover.

Harvath waited to see if the sniper would readjust and attack his position, but no attack came. The only gunfire was from the sniper on the other side. His rounds were so poorly placed that they didn't come anywhere near the culvert Harvath was taking cover in. He decided he wasn't going to get a better chance than right now to make his move.

Using the heavy, black smoke from the burning train to mask his advance, he headed for the copse of trees, rifle up and at the ready.

Once he was twenty yards out, he kicked it into high gear and rushed the sniper's position.

Stepping through the trees, he found the Russian, in his bloodstained ghillie suit, with multiple rounds to his head, neck, and torso. Harvath didn't bother to reach down and check for a pulse. The man was definitely dead. One down and, he hoped, only one more to go.

Shutting out the pain he was in, Harvath let the Galil hang from its sling, grabbed the sniper's rifle—an older, yet still highly effective Lobaev SVL—plus an extra magazine, and hauled ass toward the wreckage.

As he did, he prayed the breeze would hold and allow the smoke to continue to obscure his movements.

Nearing the train, he called out to make sure Artem knew there was a "friendly" coming in. Harvath hadn't traveled all the way to Ukraine to get shot by somebody on the same side of the conflict.

The intelligence operative responded and directed Harvath to where he and the female passenger he had rescued were taking cover.

The first thing Harvath noticed was what bad shape Artem was in. It was more serious than he had thought. His left thigh had been shredded and he had lost a lot of blood. He was about to ask why the fuck the man hadn't applied a tourniquet when he looked over at the female passenger. She was in even worse shape, *and* she was pregnant.

Artem had sacrificed his tourniquet for her. In doing so, he had very likely saved her life. But he had also put his own in great danger.

Setting down the sniper rifle, Harvath pulled his tourniquet from his chest rig and expertly applied it to the man's wound.

"Symon?" the intelligence officer asked.

Harvath shook his head. "I'm sorry," he said, marking the time on his watch. He needed to get them both to a hospital immediately. Before he could do that, however, there was the issue of the other sniper to deal with.

Several minutes had gone by without any shooting from that direction. Had the man fled? Or was he still out there, dug in, and simply biding his time?

He knew where the smart money was. Snipers were nothing if not the most patient of predators.

There was also the persistent rumor that any Russian who attempted to retreat or who fell short of their mission was being shot on sight. That kind of policy was never going to be good for morale, but it undoubtedly boosted soldiers' interest in getting the job done, which only added to the pile of smart money pointing to at least one more sniper still being out there.

In grabbing the dead Russian's rifle, Harvath had hoped that he could use Artem to flush out the other shooter and finish him off, but the Ukrainian man was on the verge of passing out. He was out of the fight. Harvath was going to have to come up with another idea.

He pulled his cell phone from his pocket, wanting to warn local authorities and prevent them from falling for the ambush. For all he knew, in addition to the sniper, there still might be a mortar team out there.

He tried to get a signal, but his device showed no bars. Quickly turning to the others, he asked, "Do either of you have your cell phone?"

Artem could barely keep his eyes open, but pointed to where a pocket must have been on his left side. That meant he was a *no*.

Harvath, who spoke a little Russian, addressed the woman, hoping that she might understand his question. She did, but shook her head and said something about her purse or her bag being somewhere on the train.

As the train was nothing but twisted, burning steel, that meant she too was a no. It also meant that there was no way to warn the local authorities. He needed to figure something else out.

The smoke was the only advantage he had. All of the other counterattack methods he might employ—calling in fire support, rushing the sniper, or conducting some sort of pincer movement—were out of the question. That left him with just one option, to evacuate his wounded and retreat.

Laying aside the sniper rifle, he looked around for anything in the wreckage that could function as an improvised stretcher. They'd be able to move a lot faster if he could drag Artem rather than having to carry him. *Where*, precisely, he was going to drag him was the next question, which really didn't matter at this second. He just wanted to get as far away from the train, and the remaining sniper, as quickly as possible.

Moving through the debris, he was hoping to find a blanket or a tarp of some sort that he could lay Artem on top of. The female passenger's injury was to her arm. And while she might have to move slowly because of how far along she was, he hoped she'd be able to do so without his assistance. What the hell she was doing this close to the front lines in her advanced state of pregnancy was anyone's guess. He didn't have the time or the desire to learn her story. The wind could shift at any moment and all three of them would be sitting ducks.

He found some webbing connected to a couple of short, dented poles that might do the trick, but worried that the thin nylon wouldn't hold up to being dragged across the ground, and so kept on looking.

Seconds later, he found exactly what he needed—some passenger's heavy canvas duffle, complete with shoulder straps. Unzipping it, he dumped the contents and rushed with it back to the Ukrainian Intelligence officer.

Repositioning his Galil so that it hung off to his side, he drew his fixed-blade knife, sliced through the seams until he had one flat piece of material, and then laid it on the ground next to Artem. Then he bent down and helped move the man over and place him on top of it.

He had almost finished the process when he felt Artem's entire body stiffen. The guy was about to have a seizure or, because they were both facing different directions, he had opened his eyes long enough to see something that Harvath couldn't. A quick intake of breath from the pregnant woman, set back behind the piece of the train they had been using for cover, told him they were in trouble.

"Don't move," a male voice said in Russian.

The man then repeated the phrase in Ukrainian. Harvath didn't need to turn around to know who it was. The sniper had chosen to climb out of his hole and close ranks. For the life of him, Harvath couldn't understand why.

"Turn," the man ordered. "Face me."

Harvath slowly lowered Artem the rest of the way to the canvas before doing what the man asked. As he did, he felt Artem remove the Glock from the holster on his battle belt.

Harvath turned, but in such a way as to use his body as a screen, so that the Russian wouldn't see that the Ukrainian Intelligence officer was now armed.

Looking at the sniper, Harvath had a pretty good idea why he had broken cover and approached the train.

The man, who was pointing his rifle right at him, had a bandolier full of grenades—just like the other sniper. It was an unusual item for them to have been outfitted with. Normally, snipers didn't get in close enough to use grenades. Then, suddenly, it hit him.

Whenever the Russians were involved, the maxim was always: *Anything worth doing is worth overdoing.* It wouldn't have been enough to have sabotaged the tracks and destroyed the train. Survivors needed to be killed and then booby traps needed to be set. That way, any first responders unlucky enough to roll over one of the bodies would have the very unpleasant and likely deadly experience of a grenade going off in their face. The Russians really were animals. This particular Russian animal, however, was about to be culled.

Artem had taken the Glock with his right hand, which meant that Harvath was going to have to step to his left to give him a clean shot. The only question was exactly when to make his move. With his back to the intel officer, there was no way to get any sort of cue.

"Hands up," the sniper ordered, repeating the command in Ukrainian.

Very slowly, Harvath complied. He knew the Russian would be expecting Artem to do the same. It was now or never.

Harvath didn't waste the moment. He pivoted hard to his left, clearing the way for the Ukrainian Intelligence officer to take out the sniper. But so weakened by blood loss, Artem couldn't lift the pistol and take the shot.

"Po'shyol na hui," the sniper sneered, aiming his rifle at Artem and applying pressure to the trigger. *Fuck you*.

The sound of a Lobaev SVL rifle going off was like the gods hurling lightning bolts. In this particular case, it looked like the Russian sniper had been their target. One minute his head was there; the next it had been turned to hamburger and his body dropped to the ground.

Harvath kicked the weapon away from the dead man—just in case—after which he made sure Artem was okay. Then he checked on the pregnant woman.

"Khoroshaya rabota," he said, gently taking the other sniper's rifle from her. *Good job*. He was in awe of both her courage and her skill.

"You're welcome," she replied in English, wincing from the pain she was in, but managing a small smile.

He was about to ask her if she was able to walk, when he saw a group of military and police vehicles arriving. Behind them were several ambulances.

Bending down, he took his Glock back and told Artem to hang on. He was going to make it. Help was here.

Harvath wished he could have said the same to Symon and everyone else who had been on that train, but that wasn't possible.

Looking over at the corpse of the dead sniper, he knew that things were going to get much worse and much uglier before they got any better. Such was the nature of war. You had to fight in it in order to win it.

If this was the kind of war the Russians wanted to wage, Harvath couldn't wait to bring the fight to them. He could be more brutal and more cunning than they could ever imagine.

These barbarians were about to learn what barbarism really tasted like.

# CHAPTER 9

Anna Royko had been beaten so savagely that, in addition to cuts, cigarette burns, and multiple broken bones, both of her eyes had swollen shut.

It was a blessing, of sorts, not being able to see. Her captors were monsters. Just looking at them for the first time, up close, face-to-ghoulishly-painted-face, had made her want to die. Without them saying a word, she had known what was going to happen to her, what *they* were going to do to her. Then they had given her a preview by committing unspeakable atrocities at the orphanage before tying her hands and feet, putting a bag over her head, and spiriting her away.

After four days of torture, she had prayed for her life to end—right there, at that very moment. Though not terribly religious, she had found God in that moment and had asked Him to take her, to end her life. And as the pain and the abuse were compounded and wore on, she had turned from asking God to end her suffering, to begging Him, and finally challenging Him to prove that He existed by striking her dead.

But no matter how fervently she prayed, no matter how badly she begged, and no matter how bitterly she challenged Him, God did not answer.

It was the lowest, darkest place Anna had ever been in. It was a black, bottomless pit of unimaginable anguish and sorrow. Had she not been restrained and had the means, she would have done the job God refused to do. She would have taken her own life.

The only thing worse than the suffocating despair was the flicker of ridiculous hope that ignited itself from time to time and for no reason.

Like a pilot light suddenly visible in a darkened basement, it would show itself, tempting her to envision a bold escape and a life outside wherever she was being held captive. She knew all too well, however, that often in bad situations, it was the hope that killed you.

Hope, Anna had convinced herself, was something she couldn't afford. Hope would only help give her the will to continue to live one more day. And living was the last thing she wanted to do. She wanted to die.

If she could just go to sleep and never wake up again, that would be an amazing gift. She no longer believed in God. And if there was no God, how could there be any heaven? Not that any of it mattered. Even if there was nothing other than empty, cold darkness, she would take it in exchange for what she was suffering through.

These foul-smelling, feral animals who beat her and forced themselves upon her had seen to it that she no longer even saw herself as a person, a human being.

What life could she possibly have after this horror? Who could possibly relate to what she had been through? How could she ever form a loving, tender partnership in which she trusted and gave herself to someone else? She had been taken, tortured, and broken by evil, wild things and could never go back to life among civilized people again.

To go on living was now a curse and the only way to break that curse was through death. But how?

She was chained to a bed, which was bolted to the floor. She was not allowed to use a bathroom. There was an old paint can under the bed that she was expected to use as a chamber pot.

Ten minutes before the men wanted to use her, they would bring in a bucket of freezing-cold water—likely drawn from some well outside—and hand her the same dirty rag she had been using over and over again.

The room itself was made out of stone. There was one small window at the far end. It was up high, which made her think she was being kept in a basement of some sort. The window had been covered with newspaper, so even during the day, not much sunlight filtered through.

On the occasions when the door to her room had been opened and she could see into the hallway, it appeared to be lined with all sorts of art—paintings in gilded frames, old statues, large altarpieces, and various sorts of religious icons.

She had no idea where the trove had come from, but assumed that it must have been looted. The men who were holding her were most definitely not a cabal of secret preservationists.

These Russian pigs were not different from countless invaders throughout history. Art and artifacts were stolen for two predominant reasons—profit, and as a means of cultural genocide; the complete and utter destruction of a nation's heritage.

How and why the men had ended up at the orphanage, she hadn't a clue. Based on the amount of substance abuse she had noticed among her captors, she assumed they had been drawn to the building because it had once been a hospital and they had entered in hopes of finding drugs. It must have been a daily, full-time job finding enough narcotics and alcohol to keep all of the men as numbed up as they were.

She assumed that was what they were doing when she heard them pile into their vehicles and drive off every morning. That, and stealing more art, as the mountains of it in the hallway only continued to grow.

From conversations she had overheard, she had learned that the men were not conventional soldiers. They were mercenaries. Many had been recruited from prisons and mental asylums. It explained their brutality, heavily tattooed bodies, and some extremely frightening mental health issues.

As best she could tell, the men were not engaged in any combat operations. The only resistance they discussed was that put up by the inhabitants of the villages they passed through—usually women and seniors.

The only authority she had seen in the organization was wielded by a bald, muscle-bound gorilla of a man referred to as the "Colonel."

The Colonel had never touched her. He was a sadist who enjoyed sitting in the room, watching his most brutal men—the ones he called his "war dogs"—have their way with her.

Once she realized that he got off on her pain, she stopped giving him what he wanted. She stopped resisting. She stopped crying. She just lay there. After that, he lost interest and she hadn't seen him since.

It was an infinitesimally small victory, but a victory nonetheless. The Colonel, however, seemed to be able to read her mind and had known what she had done because immediately thereafter, the amount of food they gave her was scaled way back. She didn't think it was a coincidence.

If they intended to starve her to death, that was fine by her. She just wished they would hurry it up.

Of course, that wasn't going to happen. They would keep her alive for as long as she served their purposes. Once that had happened, or once they had found a fresh replacement for her, then they would kill her. As far as Anna was concerned, the end couldn't come soon enough.

In the moments when she was left alone and she was not plagued by nightmares or despair, she dreamed of revenge.

She envisioned locking the doors of the building, setting it on fire, and burning the men alive. It was the worst torture she could think of— for the monsters to know that they were going to die and for their deaths to be racked with as much fear and pain as possible.

Once or twice, she wondered what she might do with the art—how she would go about burning the building to the ground but save the artifacts from destruction. In a way, they were her fellow hostages. If she could escape, didn't she have an obligation to them as well?

She was losing her mind. Seeing the stolen pieces of art as anything other than inanimate objects without agency was the rambling of a madwoman. Yet she hadn't been able to shake the thought. And the more she tried to expunge it from her mind, the more firmly it took root.

It began to give her something more powerful than hope; it began to give her purpose. Purpose was a reason to stay alive. She didn't know that she wanted one.

In fact, she was quite certain that what she truly wanted was for her life to be over. But the more she struggled to push the sense of purpose from her mind, the more insistent it became. It took on a life and a voice all its own and began speaking to her, pushing her, arguing with her.

In her moments of clarity, which were happening less and less often, she grasped that she was having a complete and utter psychotic break, but she had neither the energy nor the will to fight to hold on to what was left of her mind.

Maybe to escape the trauma of her captivity, it was better to go crazy. If she couldn't escape in body, then why not escape inward, into the boundless expanse of her own mind? There, she could be safe. There, no one could touch her. No one could hurt her. Not anymore.

And so, with her eyes swollen shut, she severed her mental tether to reality and allowed herself to let go.

# CHAPTER 10

The FBI was an around-the-clock operation. Its personnel worked twenty-four hours a day, seven days a week, three hundred and sixty-five days a year.

That said, Carolan preferred coming in off hours. He wasn't a big people person and office politics had always bothered him.

The Bureau's Counterintelligence Division was relatively quiet on the weekends, which was just the way he liked it.

Even better, the Russia Operations section was all but empty. That meant no ringing phones. No useless meetings that could have been handled via email. Nobody popping their head in the door wanting to chat. No distractions.

He needed the silence because he had to get his head wrapped around this case and shake something loose.

The trip to the Commodore Yacht Club hadn't produced a ton of fruit. The manager, the bartender, and a waitress all confirmed that Burman had been there the previous evening. He had been the guest of one of the members—a former Senator turned lobbyist named Greg Wilson.

Thursdays in D.C. were popular nights to go out and there had also been a junior members' social function going on. The club had been packed.

Burman and Wilson had had drinks and dinner together. But when Wilson left, Burman stayed behind and had a few more drinks in the bar, chatting up several of the women.

Once he was ready to call it a night, he was way too drunk to drive. He decided instead to call an Uber and left his car behind. The Uber, Carolan learned after reaching out to a contact at the company and arranging to meet the driver, had dropped him at some late-night gyro place a few blocks from his apartment building. He made small talk during the drive, was pretty wasted, and gave the driver a big tip.

The owners of the gyro shop confirmed that he had been there, alone, and had ordered food to go, which he started eating before he had even stepped outside. They didn't remember anyone hanging around outside, nor did they notice anyone following him.

The CCTV footage the FBI had sourced from buildings in the area showed him walking by himself, eating his food. They had him on camera all the way up to the moment he had entered his apartment building. There was nothing weird. Nothing nefarious.

Carolan was starting to worry that maybe he was trying to hammer a square Russian peg into a totally unrelated round hole.

Burman, according to multiple sources, had unquestionably been drunk. Not only had witnesses served him and seen him consuming alcohol, but he'd also had trouble with his balance and had been slurring his words. Who's to say he hadn't gone out onto the terrace of his own accord and, while there, done something stupid like lean too far back against the railing while taking a selfie? Drunk people did dumb stuff every day and every night. Trying to guess what someone in an impaired state was thinking was an exercise in futility.

But what if that was exactly what the Russians had wanted everyone to think? That Burman—whom lots of people had seen drinking—had been drunk and must have either accidentally fallen, or been suffering from suicidal ideation, which, in his stupor, had resulted in his deciding to take his own life by jumping off his rooftop terrace.

Barring some overzealous investigator, it would be an open-and-shut case. While Carolan's logical brain might have been warning him that he was chasing smoke, his gut was telling him that there was fire. And if there was one thing he had learned over the course of his career, it was that his gut was always right—even if his brain took longer to fit the pieces together and catch up.

Leading with your gut wasn't always the best way to handle things. Emotions cloud your judgment. Carolan had seen plenty of good agents step in it by not thinking things through. From time to time, even he was guilty of it. The trip to the yacht club was a perfect example.

He didn't need to take Fields inside with him. Experience had taught him that hanging back and waiting for some members to show up for lunch was the wise play. Hoity-toity places like the Commodore didn't like it when law enforcement of any kind came sniffing around, especially when there were guests on the premises. They preferred to keep that stuff out of the customers' view.

As good a tool as it was to put pressure on the manager to elicit fuller and more rapid cooperation, it had cost them time. Once the interviews were over and they had stepped outside, about to hand Burman's ticket to the valet in order to search his car, they saw D.C. Metro Homicide Detective Greer at the other end of the parking lot with a tow truck. He had served the Tesla dealership with a warrant and they had helped him electronically locate the vehicle.

That's where Carolan had screwed up. If he had divided the workload with Fields, she could have already gone through the car from top to bottom. She was good and there was no telling what she would have found. Now he was going to have to depend upon professional courtesy from the D.C. Metro police to fill him in.

Any hope he'd had of driving off without an encounter was dashed when Greer noticed the pair and waved them over.

"Let me do the talking," Carolan had instructed Fields.

When the three met in the center of the parking lot, the detective remarked, "What a coincidence."

"Half-price oysters," the FBI man stated. "We never miss Fridays at the Commodore."

"Bullshit. Even at half price, neither of you could afford this place. What are you doing here?"

"We got a tip."

"From who?"

"It doesn't matter. Burman was seen having dinner inside last night. We came to check it out."

"And when were you going to tell me?" the cop asked.

"Right after we checked it out. I was going to text you from the car."

Greer wasn't buying it, but he played along. "And?"

"Burman had a lot to drink. According to the staff, he was pretty intoxicated. Definitely too drunk to drive. He left his car here and took an Uber instead."

"Who was he the guest of?" Greer asked. "You can't get in that place unless you're with a member."

"Former Senator Greg Wilson."

"Greg 'Grab Ass' Wilson? *That* former United States Senator?"

Carolan didn't care for the language, especially in front of Fields, but he nodded anyway. They were talking about the same person.

"Why was Burman having dinner with him?"

The FBI agent shrugged. "Who knows? Wilson's a lobbyist now. Burman was a rich businessman. They could have been talking about anything."

"Have you talked to Wilson yet?"

"He wasn't even on my radar until ten minutes ago."

"Who do you think the ex-Senator is likely to be more forthcoming with," Greer asked, "the Bureau or D.C. Homicide?"

Carolan didn't even need to think about it. "The Bureau," he replied. "No question."

"Why?"

"Before he lost his seat, he was assigned to the Select Committee on Intelligence. He's always had a pretty good relationship with the FBI."

"I want to know the minute you're done interviewing him. I also want to be cc'd on your notes."

"No problem," said Carolan, who then pointed at the tow truck leaving the lot and asked, "Is that Burman's vehicle?"

The detective nodded. "We'll see if there's any physical evidence inside or if the GPS turns up anything of interest."

"When were you going to tell me that you had located his vehicle?"

Greer smiled. "Right after we hooked it up. I was just going to text you from my car."

*Touché*, the FBI man had thought. This process might end up being collaborative in the end, but there was going to be a lot of push/pull before then. Neither of them was going to hand over leads or evidence without fully kicking the tires on them first. It was unfortunate, but it was just the nature of the game—especially when two different organizations were competing for first prize.

He and Fields had left Greer and the Commodore parking lot to piece together the rest of Burman's evening.

From the Uber ride, to the gyro restaurant, and finally back to his penthouse, all of his movements were accounted for. Nothing was out of place or unusual, except for the broken CCTV camera at the rear of his building, which could have simply been a coincidence.

Carolan, however, didn't like coincidences. Without sufficient proof to the contrary, his position would remain that the rear camera had been sabotaged.

Despite a thorough canvassing of the area, there were no additional CCTV cameras with a clear view of the back of Burman's building. If he had, in fact, been the victim of foul play, his killers couldn't have hoped for a more favorable scenario.

The missing wallet, the scuffed-up toes of the man's shoes, the very public nature of his death, his criticisms of the Russian President, and, most importantly, Carolan's gut, told him that they were looking at a murder. He just needed more proof.

D.C. Metro police had gotten a warrant for Burman's phone and had turned it over to the FBI in hopes that they could crack the encryption and unlock it. There was no telling how long that would take. The Bureau's team was excellent, but it was a painstaking process. Too many unsuccessful attempts at unlocking and the phone could self-destruct, destroying any evidence that it might contain.

Carolan wasn't at a dead end, yet, but he was quickly running out of alleys he could head down. It was the reason he had come into the office this morning. When he got to a point like this in a case, he wasn't fun to be around. He could be a real short-tempered prick. His wife didn't deserve that.

He was also a big believer in the old saying that getting things done is a matter of applying the seat of one's pants to the seat of one's chair. Being successful in any endeavor, even in the world of criminal investigations, was all about perseverance.

As former Senator Greg Wilson was the only potential lead they had, he had decided to spend the morning digging further into him.

He had hoped to interview Wilson in person yesterday, but when he had called Wilson's office, he had been informed that Wilson was out of town on business and wouldn't be available until Monday.

The fact that the former Senator had eaten dinner with the victim the night before and then had left town shortly after the body had been discovered wasn't exactly a mark in the plus column for him.

Nevertheless, Wilson's assistant had willingly volunteered that her boss was seeing a client up in New England and that the trip had been on the books for some time. *Yet another "coincidence,"* Carolan thought to himself, displeased.

Booting up his computer, ready to do a nice, deep dive on the previously embattled Senator, his phone rang.

"Special Agent Carolan," he said, picking it up.

It was Fields. "Boss, you're going to want to hop online."

"Why?" he asked, opening a browser tab.

"That blog in Florida—the one with all the coverage about the supposed killer cannibal Alejandro Diaz."

"*The Public Truth*. What about it?"

"Just take a look at the site," she replied. "I'll hold on."

Carolan punched in the address and waited for it to load. Once it had, he was shocked to see photos of himself all over it.

The 50-point headline, bracketed by flashing red sirens, read: MANGLED BODY FOUND ON D.C. SIDEWALK. DIAZ STRIKES AGAIN? FBI LAUNCHES MANHUNT.

The photos ranged from wide shots of the crime scene at Burman's building to tighter shots of him arriving, stepping into the tent covering the body, and then going upstairs with Fields. They were followed by multiple photos of the Commodore Yacht Club, including Carolan entering and leaving with Fields, as well as standing in the parking lot with Detective Greer while Burman's black Tesla was being towed away.

Carolan knew, without a doubt, who had taken the photos. It was that dumpy, redheaded guy he had seen outside Burman's carrying the camera with the long lens.

D.C. Metro's radio traffic was encrypted, so the man must have had a source inside the department.

A leak inside a law enforcement organization was never a good thing, but one so close to an investigation with massive national security implications was downright dangerous.

He thanked Fields for the tip and told her he would call her back. He wanted to read what *The Public Truth* was "reporting" about Burman's death and to see what he could learn, if anything, about the redheaded man with the camera.

His deep dive into Greg Wilson would have to wait.

# CHAPTER 11

Kyle Paulsen stepped into the kitchen and reached around his wife for the coffeepot. He was a tall, fit man in his mid-seventies. "Is Shit-Kickers here yet?"

"*Kyle*," she chastised. "I wish you wouldn't call Senator Wilson that."

"First of all, it's *ex*-Senator Wilson, and secondly, he works for me. I get to call him whatever I want."

"If I live to be a hundred, I don't think I'll ever understand the pleasure you take in torturing that man."

"He's a swamp creature, Elaine. From the moment he emerged from his mother's womb, he's had one hand reaching out for payoffs, the other for power, and all the while crying for attention."

"But still."

"But *nothing*. During his two terms in the Senate, did things in this country get better or worse?"

Elaine Paulsen rolled her eyes. "I know a rhetorical question when I hear one."

"Yes or no?"

"Don't be ridiculous. You know exactly where I stand on all of this. Morally and culturally, I think we've slipped—a lot. That being the case, Gregory Wilson is just one man. He was one out of a hundred Senators. The blame doesn't rest squarely with him."

"No, but he's a good place to start."

"The voters are another," she replied. "People get the government they deserve."

"True," said Kyle Paulsen. "His replacement is a considerable improvement."

"Why did you hire Senator Wilson, then?"

"Because swamp creatures prefer to work with their own. If I go down to Capitol Hill, all they see is a big, fat checkbook. They'll mind their manners, put on an air of false piety, and tell me whatever they think it'll take to get their hands on my money.

"But when Shit-Kickers goes to the Hill, his fellow Congresscritters see one of their own. Wilson speaks their language. Even out of office, he's still a comrade in arms to them, a coconspirator who isn't afraid of getting his hands, or anything else, dirty."

Elaine paused, trying to come up with something positive about the former Senator. "You have to admit, he has always been quite conversant in the Constitution."

"That's always been an act. Boob bait for his rube voters. He used to carry a pocket version with him just in case there was a camera and then, faster than you could say 'Slick Willy Wilson,' he'd whip it out. It's a wonder he never developed a permanent case of bullshit elbow from it. Most transparent person in the Senate. Ever."

"And yet here he is, pulling into our driveway," Mrs. Paulsen observed, pointing out the kitchen window.

"I'll be in my study," said Mr. Paulsen as he splashed some creamer into his coffee. "Don't let him talk your ear off at the front door. He thinks he's a real charmer, that one."

"I will speak with the Senator for as long as I please. He traveled all the way up here. There should be at least one bright spot in his visit."

"That's always been your problem, Elaine. You're too nice. Especially to the help."

"And your problem is that you're never happy unless you're complaining about something. Now, take your coffee and get out of my kitchen," she teased. "I'll show the Senator in."

•     •     •

True to her word, Mrs. Paulsen took her time visiting with former Senator Wilson, who insisted, as he always did, that she call him "Greg." By the time she delivered him to her husband's study, Kyle Paulsen was convinced that his wife had been dragging out the small talk with Wilson just to piss him off.

When the man finally entered his study, Paulsen remained behind his desk and let Wilson come to him.

"Good to see you again, Kyle," said Wilson as he stepped into the richly appointed room.

Rolling ladders with shiny brass fittings fronted mahogany bookcases stuffed with leatherbound editions. Oil paintings depicting scenes of whaling and other eighteenth-century seafaring life hung in heavy, gilded frames. The floors were covered with insanely expensive Persian carpets fit for a sheikh.

But the room's focal point, the feature that most took visitors' breath away, was the gigantic picture window overlooking Frenchman Bay. From it, you could see everything from the Egg Rock Lighthouse to the Porcupine Islands and beyond.

In front of the window was an antique telescope and next to it a collection of navigation equipment—sextants and compasses, many of them hundreds of years old.

Pictures of the couple's children and grandchildren were everywhere. They had a large family.

"Greg," said Paulsen, accepting the man's hand.

"I've said it before, but I'll say it again," Wilson remarked. "You have the best office I have ever seen."

The older man ignored the compliment. He also ignored the former southern Senator's ever-present cowboy boots, which he despised and normally took a shot at. Right now, something else had totally gripped his attention. "What the hell happened to your teeth?"

"My *teeth*?" replied Wilson, his hand self-consciously rising to cover his mouth before he caught himself, lowered it back down, and smiled. "I had them whitened. What do you think? They say it knocks ten years off your appearance."

"I don't know who *they* are, but whatever you were charged, you got ripped off."

Wilson fought to keep his temper under control. He couldn't stand this cantankerous motherfucker. The man never had a single kind word to say about anything. If he wasn't bitching about Wilson's boots, it was about his beard—and now he'd found a new target: his teeth.

Whoever said that money couldn't buy happiness was one hundred percent correct. Despite his vast fortune, Kyle Paulsen was one of the unhappiest people he had ever met.

Like most Americans who had built generational wealth, Paulsen's story was about being in the right place at the right time, with the right idea—even if it was in an incredibly boring business.

Paulsen had come up with a formula for asphalt paving that was resistant to cracking and allowed for a much-lengthened life span. The only people who didn't think his product was absolutely brilliant were the state and local crews paid to fill potholes. Everyone else loved it.

As was typical with a good chunk of the uberwealthy, the more money they had, the smarter they thought they were, which invariably led them to want to play in the ultimate competitor sport—politics.

Some strapped the armor on, climbed into the arena, and ran for elected office. Others accepted a government position based upon how much money they had helped an administration raise. The rest poured money in from the sidelines hoping to influence policy and legislation. Kyle Paulsen was a member of the third category of political players.

He had a long list of initiatives he wanted to see achieved in the next session of Congress, which was why Wilson had flown up to sit down with him. It was an aggressive agenda. As the man in Washington responsible for helping Paulsen achieve his goals, he wanted to make sure that they were on the same page and setting realistic expectations.

Having learned a long time ago that he wouldn't be offered a seat, Wilson sat himself down in one of the leather chairs in front of Paulsen's desk, removed a thick binder from his briefcase, and pulled a pen from his suitcoat pocket.

"There's going to be a narrow majority in the House," he said, flipping to a page of recent notes and getting right to business. "The Senate is up for grabs, but I think it'll break in our direction. With that in mind, my recommendation would be that we pick three major items and focus on them like a laser. What did you have in mind?"

Paulsen leaned forward, fists on his desk. "Ukraine. Ukraine. Ukraine. How about that for three major items?"

It wasn't exactly what Wilson meant, but it was a start. "Can you be more specific?"

"No more weapons. No more money. And we criminalize the actions of any American who goes over there to fight. I don't care if they've got a Bronze Star, a Silver Star, a Purple Heart, or the yellow rose of fucking Texas between their teeth: our tax dollars went to train them so that they could defend the United States, not some corrupt nation halfway around the world that most Americans can't even find on a goddamn map.

"That *war*, if you even want to call it that, is between Ukraine and Russia—not us. We didn't start it and it's not our responsibility to stop it. It's a quagmire. We learned nothing in Vietnam and even less in Afghanistan. With every day that passes, we're getting sucked deeper and deeper into the mess. Very soon, we're going to wake up to find ourselves in an all-out hot war with Russia. It'll be World War III and the fact that I can say 'I told you so' won't make a damn bit of difference to my children and my grandchildren. This insanity has to stop. Right fucking now."

The old man was on a tear this morning, which was fine by Wilson. The more fired up he was, the easier he was to manipulate. "So, no China initiatives? No farm subsidies or border policy issues?"

"In case you've suddenly been struck deaf, I want you to read my lips," the old man snarled. "Our focus is going to be Ukraine, Ukraine, Ukraine. Everything else is on the back burner. Understand me?"

"I hear you loud and clear," Wilson replied, making a few notes in his binder. "Let's talk about practicality. The bulk of the lethal aid getting ready to ship was passed by the last Congress. We're not going to be able to claw that back. Financing is a different issue. There's some room there for us to have a significant impact.

"Where I really think you're onto something, however, is this idea of U.S. citizens being legally prohibited from fighting. The United

Kingdom has legislation making it illegal for British nationals to fight over there as well as to assist others who are engaged in the conflict."

"And we need to stop sending over current and prior U.S. military members to help train the Ukrainians," Paulsen added. "I don't care if those morons in Washington have committed new weapons systems or not. Let the Ukrainians learn how to read the fucking manuals. With every American that enters that country, we are one step closer to war with Russia."

"We definitely do not want war with Russia," said Wilson. "I think that's an excellent place from which to build common ground up on the hill."

Paulsen shook his head. "Fuck common ground. I want you to go scorched earth on anyone who gets in your way. Opposition research, blackmail . . . you practice whatever dark arts you need to make this happen."

"That could get pretty expensive."

"I don't care. I have more money than my family will ever be able to spend. This is about the safety and future of our country."

Wilson loved where this was going. He had spent a lot of time getting Paulsen to this point and it was turning out to be worth every insult he had been suffered to endure.

"And something else," the old man added. "I want a list of everyone on our side who attempts to get in the way."

"What for?"

"We're going to set up a new PAC, stuffed to the rafters with money, to field challengers and to make sure that they lose their next primary."

It just kept getting better—like hitting the lottery over and over again in the same day. Paulsen was a diamond-encrusted bulldozer and Wilson was in the driver's seat. He couldn't wait to get back to D.C. and get started.

But he couldn't leave, not just yet. He needed to make sure Paulsen felt he had gotten his money's worth from the visit.

There were also a few more items on his hidden agenda, the things his handler had specifically asked for, that he needed to secure before leaving. Once he had those tasks completed, he could head back to D.C. and maybe even do a little celebrating.

# CHAPTER 12

The only gear Harvath possessed was what he had been carrying on his person when he had jumped out of the train. Everything else had been incinerated. Poking through the wreckage would have been pointless. His carriage had been destroyed.

He indicated to rescuers where he had last seen Symon and then hopped into the ambulance with Artem, the pregnant woman having already been taken away in a separate ambulance.

It was a fast but bumpy ride to the hospital in Kharkiv—Ukraine's second-largest city.

As they got closer into town, he was able to get cell service. Opening his encrypted messaging app, he texted Nicholas an update.

By the time they arrived, word of the attack on the train had already spread. Personnel congregated at the emergency room entrance, ready to receive the wounded.

Sadly, only a handful of people had survived. Most of the train's staff and passengers had been killed. Efforts would very soon move from rescue to recovery.

The burning sensation Harvath had felt during the attack turned out to be a superheated piece of plastic that had fused to the back of his shirt and melted through to his skin. The wound was red and painful, but mercifully there were no blisters. A nurse treated his injury and helped find him a new shirt. Then she took him to see Artem.

His leg would need surgery, but he had been stabilized and was expected to make it. The doctors agreed to give him a few moments alone to speak with Harvath.

Without wasting any time, he provided the name, a rough description, and the location of the GUR operative waiting for Harvath at the main railway station. He also conveyed the passwords that were to be used. Then he thanked Harvath for what he had done and told him to be careful. He wished him a successful outcome for his mission.

Harvath thanked the man in return and once again extended his condolences over the loss of Symon. He told the intelligence officer to get well soon and then stood back as the medical team came back into the room and wheeled Artem out for surgery.

At the emergency entrance, he found the ambulance driver who had brought them in from the train attack. He was loading his vehicle with body bags, preparing to go back. Harvath asked if he could drop him at the station on his way and the man told him to get in.

They made small talk, mostly in Russian, which most of the residents this close to the border spoke. The driver figured Harvath was in-country to fight for the International Legion and thanked him for his service. He explained that it was unusual to see foreign fighters arrive with their own weapons. Harvath told him that he had been training soldiers in Lviv before deciding to join troops at the front. It wasn't the best lie, but it seemed to satisfy the man.

When they pulled up to the station, the driver opened his glove box, removed a yellow-and-blue armband, and handed it to him. "As long as you're carrying weapons, you'll want to wear this," he said. "At least until they issue you a uniform."

Harvath slipped the band over his arm, thanked the man, and climbed out of the ambulance.

Standing on the curb, he watched as the man drove away, back to the horror of the train attack. He knew all too well what sifting through the wreckage for human remains was going to be like.

Whether or not the phrase was uttered by Plato, Santayana, or General Sherman, war truly was hell. It burned and blistered and ripped and scarred everyone it touched. As was so often said, only the dead know the end of war.

Entering the "Stalin's empire"–style, yellow-and-white railway station, Harvath observed the trickle of people making their way through. Pre-conflict, it would have been a lively location bustling with travelers. These days it was a dangerous place to linger. The station had been targeted repeatedly by the Russians.

The tinge of history, that feeling of having romantically traveled back in time, that he had experienced when boarding the overnight train in Poland was gone. Now, looking at the stacks of charred sandbags, the walls pockmarked by shrapnel, and the gaping holes blasted through the roof above, it felt as if he were approaching the gates of hell themselves.

He found his new contact, a tall, blond woman in her twenties, standing at the counter in an empty café just off the arrivals hall.

She was attractive and had taken the time to do her makeup. He couldn't tell if it was out of pride, defiance, or because she was shuttling an American to the front and saw it as a reason to get done up. On the counter next to her was an old Ken Follett paperback.

Harvath stood nearby and ordered an espresso. Looking down at her book, he spoke the phrase Artem had given him: "*The Pillars of the Earth* is his best book."

"I prefer his more contemporary novels," she replied. "*Eye of the Needle* is the best."

With the sign and countersign delivered and their bona fides established, he extended his hand. "Harvath."

"Zira," she said, shaking it. "I heard about the attack. What happened to your escort?"

"One didn't make it and the other is in the hospital."

"I'm very sorry to hear that."

"Did you know them?" he asked.

She shook her head. "The GUR is a large organization. But regardless, I am saddened every time I hear someone has been killed or injured. The operative in the hospital, is he expected to make it?"

"He is," Harvath replied.

"Good," said Zira, removing some money and paying for their coffees. "We should get moving. Do you have any bags?"

With his Galil slung across his shoulder, Harvath patted the rest of the gear he was carrying and said, "This is all I have."

The GUR woman gathered up her change and asked, "What about your papers? You won't get very far without them."

Knowing that if he had to hurriedly grab his equipment he might not be coming back, Harvath had wisely tucked his important documents, as well as the cash and some other items, into the zippered compartment of his chest rig. Removing his orders, he showed them to her.

Satisfied, she folded the papers and handed them back to him. "I'm parked outside," she said. "Follow me."

Her vehicle was a beat-up, forest-green Toyota Land Cruiser from the late 1990s. It had been outfitted with a snorkel, a bully bar, and a roof rack, as well as a dual jerry can holder, which at the moment only had one gas can in it.

The interior wasn't much to look at, either. Rips in the stained cloth seats had been mended with different colors and types of tape. The header was torn and the rear left passenger door panel cover was missing. It smelled like stale cigarettes and spilled diesel. Letting his rifle hang in front of him, Harvath cracked the window as soon as he got in and shut his door.

"Hungry?" she asked as she pulled out of the lot and reached behind her seat for a greasy paper bag.

"What is it?"

"Varenyky," she replied. "Dumplings. They're probably not very warm, but they're still good. There's also bottled water in back."

Harvath thanked her, grabbed a bottle of water, and helped himself to a couple of the dumplings.

The filling tasted like it was made from liver and fried onions. He had eaten much, much worse in his career and was grateful for the sustenance.

. 'hev left the city center, he noticed that they were headed to the n₀_____ .ve were supposed to head east to meet the team."

... .ccii a change of plans," she replied. "The base where they were waiting has taken heavy shelling. We believe it's still under observation and not safe. They're going to meet us at a safe house outside the city instead."

The woman exhibited a small facial cue that he had been taught to pick up on. Under duress, such as when lying, people revealed certain microexpressions. *Was she lying?*

He couldn't be sure. In war, *everyone* was under duress. And that duress often lived on as PTSD. Nevertheless, his Spidey sense was awake and tingling. As they drove, he remained on guard.

What he saw through the windshield was unbelievable. The amount of destruction Kharkiv had suffered was next level. Peshkov had thrown everything he had at the city. From hypersonic missiles to flesh-melting "thermite rain" bombs, he hadn't held anything back.

Building after building had been reduced to rubble and the streets were lined with the blackened husks of burned-out cars. It looked like something out of a postapocalyptic zombie movie.

But then, for every razed apartment block or those with their façades sheared away, exposing the dwellings inside like some macabre, life-sized dollhouse, there were other structures that had survived without a scratch, completely intact. There was absolutely no rhyme or reason to it. Just pure luck.

And as bad as the inside of the Land Cruiser smelled, the outside—through Harvath's open window—was even worse. The air smelled like fire and death and despair. In short, it smelled like war.

As they got to the outskirts of the city, the ruins of Russian tanks and armored personnel carriers could be seen, reminders of Moscow's countless attempts to take the city. Ukraine's ability to repel the invaders again and again was a testament to both their spirit and the Kremlin's pathological hubris.

Though Kharkiv boasted one and a half million inhabitants, it went from urban to rural very quickly.

Before Harvath knew it, they had left the paved city behind and were driving down a forested dirt road. The breeze coming through his window was much cleaner, fresher.

The woman hadn't said much. She didn't use her phone, nor had she turned on the radio. Despite the current front lines being less than a hundred miles away, there were no checkpoints, no stepped-up security presence, at least nothing that was visible. The city and its environs seemed to be experiencing a respite. How long it would last was anyone's guess. They rode in silence.

Eventually, tiny Soviet-era houses began to appear in the woods—country houses, or dachas as they were known. They were weekend and summer places, normally passed from generation to generation, that allowed citizens to escape from the city and get back to nature. These dwellings, however, had seen much better days.

This area had seen heavy fighting. Many of the tall pines had been snapped like Popsicle sticks. Of those that hadn't, many bore scars along their trunks of bullets that had come whizzing past. Here and there, as on the outskirts of Kharkiv, lay tanks, APCs, and other rusting military vehicles that had been destroyed in battle.

It was hard to imagine this as a vacation area, a place where children laughed and rode their bikes while adults sat outside eating and sharing homemade wine with their friends and neighbors.

They had passed four dachas so far and he had yet to see one that was either unblemished or had all of its windows still intact.

At a narrow turnoff, the woman pulled onto a short, gravel drive and headed toward what he assumed was the safe house. Harvath scanned their surroundings as they drove. Signs of heavy combat could still be seen all over. He could only imagine how many troops the Russians had poured through here and what kind of response the Ukrainians had mounted to meet them. It had a real Ardennes Forest, World War II feeling to it.

Soon enough a small house appeared, and they rolled to a stop in front of it. "Here we are," she said, putting the Land Cruiser in park and turning off the ignition. "It's not much, but for the moment it's home."

The woods around the house were quiet. *Too* quiet for Harvath's liking. There were no birds, no insects. It was as if it was some kind of dead zone—a place living things actively avoided. The animals' instincts were keeping them away.

Harvath's instincts were sending him very much the same message. They were telling him to go, and to go *now*.

But he didn't have that luxury. He couldn't just fly away to someplace else. He had a mission to accomplish and that was what he was going to do. Adjusting his rifle, he exited the vehicle.

This dacha, even more so than the others, had gotten the shit knocked out of it. Many of the windows were broken and the wood siding had been riddled with bullet holes. The chimney was cracked and half of it had fallen down. Part of the second story was singed, as if it had been on fire at one point.

Whatever had taken place here, it looked like it had been one hell of a fight. The home appeared barely habitable, which might have been why it was chosen as a safe house. Who would have thought of being holed up in a place like this? Gathering her gear, the woman headed inside. Harvath followed.

The bullets that had been flying outside had ripped right through the home's interior. Signs of entry and exit were evident everywhere. While someone had taken time to spackle the holes, the white putty stood in sharp contrast to the mellow color of the aged, wood-clad walls.

Any artwork that might have once adorned the cottage was gone. Some fishing poles, which had escaped the gunfire, hung on a couple of the walls, as well as a few pieces of taxidermy. The living room, Harvath noticed upon entering, held a couch, two chairs, and a trio of footstools.

From where he stood, he could see a table and a few mismatched chairs in the dining room. Beyond that was a rustic kitchen, some other room around the corner—probably a bedroom—and a narrow staircase leading up to the second story.

Minus the bullet holes and plastic sheeting covering the broken windows, it reminded him of his grandparents' cabin in Wisconsin. It even had the same musty odor mixed with the scent of mothballs and fireplace.

"If you want a hot shower," the woman said, laying her things on the dining room table, "you'll have to stoke the boiler out back."

Considering the burns to his back, a hot shower was about the last thing he wanted right now. What's more, there was no way he was going to strip off all his gear, let his guard down, and give her any advantage over him.

She had bought him a coffee and had given him a ride out to the middle of nowhere—that's all. The fact that she had been carrying the

Ken Follett book and had known the location and the countersign didn't mean that she was who she said she was.

"Thank you," he replied. "I'll pass on the shower for now. How long until the team gets here?"

"Not for a couple more hours. They're en route, but were delayed by a minesweeping operation on one of the roads."

There it was—another excuse for why things were not going according to plan *and* another microexpression. His Spidey sense jumped into the red zone. She *was* lying to him. He was positive. But to what end?

Whether or not she really was a GUR operative didn't matter. If she was working for the Russians, she'd be after information. The easiest—and usually the fastest—way to do that was to convince him that she was on his side, that she was one of the "good guys."

"I saw from your papers," she continued, "that they made you a captain in the legion. That's pretty impressive. What was your background before coming to Ukraine?"

Harvath had a pretty good idea of how things might unfold if she suspected that he was onto her, so he needed to be very careful. "I was a schoolteacher," he replied.

"What do you teach?"

"Idiots."

The woman chuckled. Even though English was not her first language, she spoke it and, more importantly, understood it quite well. "What subject?"

"Physical fitness."

"And for this they made you a captain? What will you be doing at the front? Improving their jumping jacks?"

Joining the woman in the dining room, he took a slow look around. If this was an interrogation, even a soft one, there'd be some sort of recording device. Probably more than one. But considering the size of fiber-optic cameras and subminiature microphones, you could be looking right at them and never even know they were there.

"In another life, I was in the military," he stated.

"What was your specialty?"

"I broke things."

"Like what?"

Harvath pulled out a chair at the opposite end of the table, set his rifle next to him, and sat down. "Usually very big, very expensive things."

"You were a saboteur."

"I prefer the term *deconstructionist* or *reverse engineer*."

She smiled. "You must have been *very* good at it. The GUR made you a captain and assigned you to the Special Services Group."

"Is that good?" he asked, smiling back. "The Special Services Group? It sounds like it could be a lot of work."

"I suppose that depends on what you'll be *deconstructing*. Any ideas?"

She was totally milking him for intel. Whoever this woman was, she was definitely not one of the good guys and definitely not on his side.

"Could be anything. Bridges. Tunnels. Ships. Aircraft. Maybe even the Sayano-Shushenskaya Dam."

Harvath was enjoying screwing with her. Sayano-Shushenskaya was the largest power plant in Russia. The way her eyes widened confirmed that she was familiar with it.

"So, your expertise involves penetrating far into enemy territory."

"They wouldn't have made me a captain if all I was going to do was blow up stuff on this side."

"I wouldn't think so," she agreed, then probed further. "I would imagine there's a lot of reconnaissance that goes into your assignments."

"Not really. Most of it I just do on my phone. Google Earth and some of the other sites. You know?"

In addition to being certain that she was playing for the bad guys, he was also certain that his team was not en route to the dacha.

Very soon, one of two things was going to happen. Either she was going to get wise that he was stringing her along, or she was going to conclude that under the present circumstances, he had reached the limit of what he was willing to reveal. Both situations would end badly for him. He needed to make sure that didn't happen.

But first, he needed the answer to one crucial question—*were they alone?*

Immediately after the thought popped into his head, he received an answer in the form of a heavy thud from upstairs.

The woman turned to look over her shoulder and up the staircase.

"What was that?" he asked.

"I don't know," she replied, turning back around. "A few of the beams upstairs are damaged. Something must have fallen. It's nothing."

*Once again, she was lying.*

"Who else is here?"

"No one," she stated. "It's just us."

It was time to end this. With his left hand, Harvath began reaching for his rifle. "I'm going to have a look."

"No, you're not," she said, drawing an RPC FORT-20 pistol and pointing it at him. "You're going to stay where you are."

Slowly, Harvath drew his hand back and abandoned his reach for the rifle.

All pretense of charm having been thrown out the window the second her gun came out, the woman now glowered at him as she spoke. "Enough games. I want to know why you're here and what your targets are. For every lie you tell me, I will put a bullet in one of your extremities. Who sent you? You have three seconds to answer me. Three. Two—"

"One," said Harvath as he pressed the trigger of his Glock, which he had drawn when she had turned to look up the stairs, and which he had placed in his lap, out of her sight under the table.

The bullet struck her just below the stomach, shattering her pelvis. Simultaneously, she fired her weapon and missed Harvath by only a couple of inches.

As she screamed in agony, he dropped to the floor and continued firing round after round into her.

From what was probably a bedroom just off the kitchen, a man appeared with an AK-47. Snapping his pistol to the right, Harvath adjusted his aim and let loose with a controlled pair. One bullet went through the man's lower jaw and through the roof of his mouth. The other hit just above the bridge of his nose and drilled right into the control box of his brain. He was dead before he even hit the floor.

Jumping to his feet, he checked on the woman. She was wheezing, with blood running from her nose and mouth. She wasn't dead yet, but she would be soon. Raising his pistol, he delivered a head shot, putting her out of her misery.

Dumping his current magazine, he slammed in a fresh one and swept the downstairs. He had no idea how many others might be in the house, but figured there had to be at least one more. That sound they had heard upstairs hadn't come from something falling. Someone was up there.

With the downstairs cleared, he made ready to take the stairs. He hated stairs of all kinds. In his experience, the best way to handle stairs was to let somebody else do it. They were death traps.

Staying to the outside of the woven cotton runner, he focused on the edge of the stairs, which he hoped would be less squeaky. Raising his pistol, he began climbing.

He moved slowly, testing each step before fully committing his weight lest he give his position and progress away. After all the shooting, whoever was left in the house knew that they weren't alone. There was no reason to help them paint a better picture.

Keeping pressure on his trigger, he reached the top of the stairs, but instead of peering around the corner—and very likely getting his head blown off—he bent down into a crouch and then risked a quick peek.

As he did, he was shocked to come almost face-to-face with a woman. She was blond, like the dead one downstairs, and had been badly roughed up. She was bound, gagged, and had been tied to a chair that had tipped over. He figured that was where the thud had come from.

Her eyes were wide. Frantic. She was trying to signal something. Harvath didn't wait to formulate a precise interpretation. There was a closet with its door partially ajar. Aiming his Glock, he lit it up.

As the weapon bucked in his hands and spat out a torrent of hot shell casings, the captive woman became even more agitated. Rocking and fighting against her restraints, she screamed from behind her gag.

Harvath couldn't figure out what the hell was going on, until he saw a flash of motion up near the ceiling. The trapdoor pull-chain from a retractable attic ladder was swaying ever so slightly.

Looking down at the woman, he motioned toward the ladder, and she began nodding emphatically.

With standard-issue mags, which was what he was carrying, his

Glock could hold a total of eighteen rounds. He had dumped close to half of them into the closet. It was now time to dump the rest into the attic.

Not knowing precisely where the threat was, he put rounds in and around the trapdoor, hoping to take the person out.

When his slide locked back, he punched the mag release, flicked the pistol to the side, and shot the spent magazine out the bottom of the weapon. He drove home a new one before the empty mag had even hit the floor and then thumbed the slide release, ready to reengage. Then he waited. There was no return fire.

Keeping one eye on the trapdoor, he reached down and released the woman's gag. "Do you speak English?" he whispered.

She nodded.

"How many of them are in the house?"

"Three," she replied. "Two men. One woman."

Harvath slid his blade from its sheath and freed her from her re-straints. "Are you injured?" he asked, putting the knife back.

She shook her head.

"Good. When I say *move*, I want you to get down those stairs as quickly and as quietly as you can, but don't go outside. Do you understand?"

Once again, the woman nodded.

Harvath had no idea if the person in the attic had been neutralized or not. He also didn't know if there was a vent or an opening of any sort up there, which could turn it into the perfect sniper's nest once he and the woman left the dacha and were exposed out in the open.

Fixing her with his eyes, he whispered the command, "*Move.*"

The moment she hit the stairs he was right behind her, covering her and urging her forward.

Arriving at the ground floor, he thought that maybe the person in the attic had been killed. He was about to exhale when the ceiling erupted in a hail of automatic weapons fire and everything around them began exploding.

Harvath pointed at the fireplace, yelled for her to take cover, and lunged for his rifle as he dove under the table and the bullets kept coming.

So much for the question of whether the guy in the attic had been neutralized. Now it was all about who could take out whom first.

In any interior fight, Harvath would always take the ground floor over being higher up. On the ground floor, he had that advantage because he controlled the house. He was going to use it to force the shooter's hand. He was going to try to smoke the guy out. Literally.

Using his rifle to extend his reach, he hooked the AK-47 belonging to the first man he had killed and pulled it to him under the table.

"Know how to use this?" he yelled to the woman.

She nodded and Harvath slid it to her.

"When I tell you to begin, I want you to shoot back and forth across the ceiling. Short bursts. Keep him pinned down. Okay?"

The woman checked the bolt carrier to make sure the weapon was charged, flipped off the safety, and nodded.

Harvath counted backward from three in his head and then ordered, "Now!"

Exactly as she had been told, the woman strafed the ceiling with short, controlled bursts.

With the AK-47 booming behind him and providing cover fire, Harvath raced into the kitchen.

He didn't know exactly what he would find. He only prayed that the ingredients he needed would be there.

Dish soap was a slam dunk. There were also rags and glass bottles. What there weren't, were any sort of flammable liquids. That meant that Molotov cocktails were out of the question. But it didn't mean that getting one hell of a fire going was off the table.

There was a roll of paper towels, a large bag of mothballs, flour, and a box of kitchen matches. Along with a frying pan, he had everything he needed.

Pulling a rifle magazine from his chest rig, he set it on the floor and kicked it over to the woman so she could continue laying down cover fire. He then quickly lined the frying pan with paper towels and then assembled a mountain of mothballs on top.

As soon that was done, he struck several matches, ignited the paper towels, and dropped the others into the pan.

He knew that when mothballs got hot, they underwent a chemical process called sublimation in which they went right from being a solid into a vapor. And those vapors were flammable as hell. They stank to high heaven, but they were the ultimate fire starters, especially those made of naphthalene.

Within seconds an enormous flame was leaping out of the pan. Careful not to drop it, he hurried over to the stairwell, cocked it back, and launched the flaming mass onto the stairs covered with the cotton runner.

Tossing the pan into the sink, he snatched the bag of flour and raced back to the stairwell. Flour, powdered nondairy creamer, spices, or dried milk were some of the nastiest, most flammable food items you could find in a kitchen.

Packed densely in a bag, it was relatively benign. But when Harvath tore open the top of that bag and threw the highly flammable flour into the oxygen-rich air over burning mothballs, it created a huge column of fire.

By the time he had picked his rifle back up, the cotton runner was completely on fire and the walls of the stairwell were alight as well.

He rushed to the fireplace and handed the woman another magazine.

"What now?" she asked, reloading.

No sooner had she stopped firing than the man in the attic began shooting down on them again.

At any moment, he was going to realize that the cottage was on fire. Considering its age, and the fact that it was built entirely from wood, it wouldn't take long for it to be entirely engulfed. Only a madman would remain in the attic hoping to take a shot at a couple of people as they fled. The man in the attic would need to make his escape, too.

The challenge for Harvath was in timing their exit. But he had something the man in the attic didn't—a partner. He also had a plan.

After Harvath told the woman what he wanted to do, they awaited a pause from the shooting upstairs. As soon as it came, she raised her weapon and began firing.

Harvath rushed over to the two dead bodies, grabbed what he needed, and then moved with the woman to one of the broken windows on the far side of the living room, where he ripped down the plastic.

Based on the dacha's design, if there was a vent of some sort up in the attic that the shooter might use, he expected it to overlook the front, or the back, of the structure. That made bailing out on the side their best option.

His rifle primed and ready, Harvath leaned out the window and scanned for threats. Not seeing any, he took care to avoid the bits of broken glass and rusty nail heads along the sill, swung his legs out, and jumped down.

The moment his feet touched the ground, he moved for cover and took up a defensive firing position. Then, covering her, he signaled for the woman to join him. The little building was going up like a tinderbox.

He watched as she balanced on the sill and hung one leg out the window and then attempted to swing the other. But something happened.

"I'm stuck," she exclaimed. "I'm caught on something."

"Jump," Harvath told her.

"I can't."

Behind her, he could see bright orange flames licking the dining room and headed in her direction. "Jump," he repeated.

Throwing the AK-47 down onto the ground, she used both hands to pull at the part of her pants that was caught.

With the flames continuing to get closer, Harvath noticed something even more dangerous behind her.

"Get down!" he yelled.

Without a moment's hesitation, she bent over, threw all of her weight toward her outside leg, and forced herself to tumble out of the window.

She hit the ground hard and landed on top of her rifle as Harvath let loose with a furious barrage of rounds from his Galil. He kept firing until he could no longer see the man inside.

Swapping magazines, he motioned for the woman to come to him and kept his rifle trained on the house.

The woman's pants were torn and she was bleeding from a pretty good gash, but it wasn't anything life-threatening.

"We need to move," he said. "Now, while we know he's still in the house. Are you good?"

She nodded and readied her rifle.

"We're going to go for the Land Cruiser. Stay behind me and stay close. Understand?"

Once more, she nodded.

Getting up, Harvath led her around the rear of the dacha. There were more trees and brush that way and therefore more cover. The last thing he intended to do was loop around the front.

The building was completely enveloped in flames at this point. Thick pillars of smoke could be seen billowing up into the sky. The pops and crackle from the fire were almost as loud as gunshots.

Having witnessed the state of Kharkiv, he doubted any of the local fire services had the capacity to come put water on a tiny cottage out in the forest. Besides, by the time they got here, it would only be a pile of embers.

Coming around the back of the dacha, he saw a traditional sauna, or banya as it was known. They were such a custom in Ukraine that Harvath remembered having read about soldiers building fortified versions in the trenches along the front lines.

Just beyond it was the Land Cruiser, fully intact, but a little too close to the burning building for his taste. He picked up the pace, anxious to get the hell out of there.

As they drew even with the SUV, Harvath pulled out the keys he had taken off the dead woman and stood guard as the woman he had just saved climbed into the passenger seat.

Closing her door, he was about to move around the front of the vehicle and get behind the wheel when one of the dacha's unbroken windows exploded.

He spun, expecting it to have been caused by the heat from fire. Instead what he saw was the man from the attic, bleeding and engulfed by flames, stand up and hobble toward him.

Gone was his rifle. How and where he had lost it was no concern of Harvath's. In its place, the man now carried a knife.

Raising his own rifle, Harvath seated the stock against his shoulder and took careful aim. As the man was moving, it was a difficult shot to make.

Convinced he had a good sight picture, he pressed the trigger. Then, for good measure, he fired again.

He watched as the man went down, a bullet through each of his knees.

Tossing his rifle into the Land Cruiser, Harvath got in, turned over the engine, and, putting it into gear, left the man from the attic—the third member of the Kharkiv ambush party—to burn to death, alone on the ground, screaming.

# CHAPTER 13

Nicholas stood watching as his dogs enjoyed a few moments of fresh air. Though the breeze was cold, he was enjoying it as well. The sun, when it poked out from behind the clouds, felt good on his skin.

The GUR had made it clear that because of the clandestine nature of his work and the constant threat of Russian attack, the amount of time he could stand out in the open needed to be limited.

Closing his eyes, he turned his face up to the sky. He had read enough history of war, especially about the Brits during the Blitz, to know to be grateful for moments like this.

As he enjoyed his few minutes outside, he and the dogs were surrounded by hard, well-trained men with guns. Even though they were relatively safe, his mind was troubled by the most recent text he had received from Harvath.

Targeting civilians and civilian infrastructure, though against international law, was nothing new for the Russians. As such, Ukraine had experienced multiple train attacks. What bothered him, however, was what had followed—the imposter who had been waiting at the station in Kharkiv. The Russians had known Harvath was coming.

Actually, that wasn't true. The Russians had known *someone* was coming. If they had been aware that it was Harvath, there would have been a kill team the size of a battalion waiting for him.

But even if they didn't have a name, how did they know that anyone of note was arriving in the first place? Which begged another question—why attack the train *and* post a fake GUR agent at the station? Based on the initial reports Nicholas had read, it was amazing that any of the passengers had survived.

Perhaps the Russians didn't know what train Harvath was coming in on and only had a general time frame in which the fake agent needed to be at the station. As thoroughly as Nicholas understood the Russian mindset, there were times when trying to think like them made his head hurt. But that wasn't the worst of it.

Outside of a small group in Ukraine, the only other people who knew of Harvath's assignment was an even smaller group back in Washington. In one of those circles, the Russians had managed to place a mole.

Compounding the situation, if the Russians knew about Harvath, they very likely knew about him, too. Both he and Scot had plenty of enemies in Moscow and now that they had stepped into a war zone, they were even more enticing targets. If the mole was inside the GUR, it was hard to say who was now the most vulnerable.

Once Harvath had linked up with his team from the legion, he would be in the wind and free of any interface with Ukrainian Intelligence.

Nicholas, on the other hand, was literally eating the GUR's food and sleeping under their roof. If the mole *was* in their agency, he wouldn't be truly safe until his work for them was done and he was back across the border in Poland.

That realization made part of him want to pack up and get the hell out of there right now. Ukrainian Intelligence had gotten plenty far without him. The country wasn't going to lose the war just because he decided to pull the plug. In all fairness, he could still assist them with a lot of operational issues from afar.

But there was another part of him—the part that had stood up and said *yes* to the assignment in the first place. He believed in what this fight represented and why the Ukrainians needed to win it. His contribution would be to help teach the GUR how to better hack the Russians and how to best exploit the fruits of those labors.

Much of it couldn't be taught. It was an art form of sorts—driven by instinct and a feeling for how certain pieces of intelligence fit together. To really take them to the next level, he needed to be in the same room, shoulder to shoulder, carrying out operations with them in real time.

There was no one more qualified for this assignment. He had grown up speaking Russian and was a savant when it came to identifying, sifting, and leveraging intelligence.

He also had a deeply personal reason for being here. He wanted to be in the best possible position to assist Harvath.

Wars could be chaotic, bureaucratic, and very, very messy. Harvath and his team would be in the field alone, without a reliable cavalry and with almost zero air support. Accessing prime, grade-A intelligence was going to be critical if Harvath was to be successful. And, as his best friend, Nicholas wanted that more than he wanted anything else—even more than the Ukrainians winning the war.

Harvath was getting married soon. Nicholas had a new baby about to be christened. Harvath was going to be her godfather. The two friends had many important moments yet to be shared and many good years ahead. He was determined that they stick around long enough to enjoy each and every one of them.

From where he stood, he could see the bronze statue of St. Michael the Archangel, brandishing a sword and shield as he towered over the Lach Gates in Independence Square. St. Michael was the patron saint of Kyiv and the divine protector of all of Ukraine.

Though not a particularly religious person, Nicholas offered up a prayer for Harvath's safety. He also entreated the saint for help in finding the mole.

As he was finishing his silent appeal, he noticed a bird as it landed upon the tip of one of the Archangel's golden wings. It appeared to be a raven. Was it a sign? An omen of some sort?

Nicholas had no idea. All he knew was that upon seeing it, the breeze turned even colder and his chest tightened. It felt as if someone were walking across his grave.

Argos and Draco had noticed it, too. Both dogs raised their heads, cocked their ears, and stood frozen in place.

But as soon as the ill wind began to blow, it was gone. And with it, so too did the bird disappear.

The dogs lowered their heads and went back to what they were doing. The muscles of Nicholas's chest relaxed.

Up above, in a window obscured by draperies, a figure stepped back from the glass. Their next move had been confirmed.

# CHAPTER 14

H arvath couldn't drive and properly question the woman at the same time. So, as soon as they were a safe distance away from the burning dacha, he pulled over.

The first thing he did was a medical evaluation. Despite all of the rounds that had been flying, neither of them had been shot. He examined her leg and, pulling a bandage from his IFAK, dressed her wound. Then she filled him in on who she was and what, to the best of her knowledge, had happened.

She was the real Zira—the GUR operative who worked with the International Legion and was supposed to meet Harvath at the train station. Her orders were to transport him to a Ukrainian military base near Staryi Saltiv. There he would be issued his uniform, ID card, and other items before being linked up with his team.

Before dawn this morning, the two men from the dacha had broken into her apartment. They kidnapped her and took her to the dacha. In addition to roughing her up, they had information and photographs of several of her family members whom they threatened to harm. She was embarrassed for having broken and apologized to Harvath for not having held out longer. He told her that she had nothing to be ashamed of.

He put her through a full battery of questions—all of which she answered. There was nothing about her responses that suggested she was being anything but honest and forthright. As far as he was concerned, she was telling him the truth.

She had no idea who her tormentors had been other than that they were "filthy Russians." She assumed they were operatives from Russian Military Intelligence, as those tended to be the people who carried out these sorts of operations inside Ukraine. Harvath agreed that they were the most likely culprit.

Unfortunately, she had no idea how they had known about her assignment. The most logical explanation was that they had a source somewhere inside Ukrainian Intelligence. It pained her to say that, but even legendary agencies like the CIA and MI6 had known their share of traitors. The fact that it had happened during wartime, when the country was enduring an invasion, and the information had been given to the enemy, only made the act that much more evil and reprehensible.

Harvath agreed with that as well. He was a big believer that treason should be dealt with in the harshest terms. It established a bright line and made it crystal clear what would happen to those who aided a nation's enemies.

After having all of his questions answered, he inventoried his gear and gave her a chance to take herself off this assignment. She had been through a lot. No one would blame her if she wanted to tap out. He could drop her off in the next town or village and see himself the rest of the way to the forward operating base at Staryi Saltiv.

Zira, however, refused his offer. She wouldn't give Ukraine's enemies the satisfaction. She would see her mission through. And once she had gotten him to the base, she would return to Kharkiv and file a full and accurate report with her superiors. They needed to know what had happened. If there was a mole in their organization, they needed to start the hunt immediately.

She was a fighter. Harvath liked that. She was also a professional. Since she knew the roads and it was her responsibility to get him to the base, she insisted on driving. He turned over the keys and climbed into the passenger seat.

He preferred riding shotgun, especially this close to the front. If anything bad happened, he wanted to be able to get on his weapon right away.

He was also exhausted. It would feel good to dial it down a couple of notches and not have to worry about being behind the wheel. Sitting back in his seat, he allowed himself to close his eyes and to slip into a medita-tive state.

When he felt the Land Cruiser slow down a little while later, he had flashbacks of the train coming to a stop and his eyes snapped open. There was a checkpoint up ahead. At this point, as far as he was concerned, he suspected everyone and gripped his weapon a little tighter.

Zira noticed. "Don't worry," she said, rolling down her window. "Everything is okay."

Arriving at the checkpoint, she put the SUV in park and it was in-stantly surrounded by men with guns. As she chatted with the officer at her door, the conversation quickly became heated.

Harvath didn't speak a word of Ukrainian, but he was getting the gist of it, including her insulting the Russians who had beaten her and taken her identification. She then pantomimed the firefight and did a zombie-like impression of the man who had burst through the window, com-pletely on fire, and walked toward them, at which point Harvath had shot him in the knees.

Upon hearing this detail, the stunned officer's eyebrows shot up in bemused surprise and he called his men over to hear Zira's story for themselves.

When she got to the part about kneecapping the flaming Russian zom-bie, Harvath received smiles all around and a thumbs-up from several of the Ukrainian soldiers.

The officer gestured toward Harvath and asked a question, which Zira translated. "He wants to know if you have any identification. Mine is back at my apartment. He wouldn't be doing his job if he didn't ask."

"Of course," Harvath replied, fishing the paperwork out of the pocket in his plate carrier and handing it to her.

Zira passed it along to the officer, who gave it a quick once-over and handed it back, saying to Harvath in English, "Thank you, Captain."

The man then looked at Zira and delivered a cheerful "Palianytsia!" to which she laughed and replied just as cheerfully, "Palianytsia!"

He then stood back and waved them through.

Rolling up her window, Zira put the car in gear and drove on, the smile lingering on her face.

Considering what she had been through today, it was a tribute to her resilience that she could muster up any sort of good cheer. He wondered what had caused it.

"That word you just spoke," he began.

"*Palianytsia?*"

"Yes. I heard you say it to each other in the beginning, too. Although it didn't sound as nice. What is it? Some sort of greeting or a way to wish someone well?"

Zira laughed. "It's a type of Ukrainian peasant bread. We make it in our fireplaces."

"I don't get it."

"The only people who can't pronounce it correctly are the Russians. When we meet someone we don't know, we challenge them to say *palianytsia*. If they can pronounce it, we know they're okay; they aren't Russian. Then, as a joke when we part, we ask them say it one more time. Just to make sure."

Harvath smiled back. It was a good joke. He liked the Ukrainians' sense of humor. "Will you teach me how to pronounce it correctly?" he asked.

Zira winked at him and said, "Da. Of course, comrade."

.   .   .

By the time they reached the base, Zira had really grown on him and he was sorry to have to say good-bye. Though he had only met a handful of Ukrainians so far, his admiration for their spirit had continued to expand. They had that magic ingredient, that zest, that was necessary for any underdog to face down a bigger, stronger enemy and emerge victorious.

After handing him off to an efficient yet very busy Supply Sergeant, she turned to head back to her Land Cruiser.

"Palianytsia," he said as she walked away.

"Palianytsia!" she replied with a wave and another laugh.

Steering Harvath in the other direction, the Sergeant gave him the rundown of what they needed to accomplish and the time within which they had to do it.

"First, you get your uniform and other personal items from the quartermaster. Next, we will get you an ID. Then, finally, we will make a stop at the armory. You already have a rifle and a sidearm, so those won't be necessary. But if you wish to pick up extra ammunition, magazines, and some grenades, you can do so then."

"What about Javelins?"

The Sergeant chuckled. "*Everybody* wants Javelins. Nobody wants to go through the training."

"I'm trained on Javelins."

The Sergeant looked at Harvath's paperwork, which was clipped to his clipboard. "I don't see any certification here."

"Trust me."

"I trust God. Anyone else must make the request through their company commander."

"Did you happen to see in my paperwork that I'm with Special Services Group?"

"Yes," the man replied. "Which means your request will get fulfilled faster than most. I'm guessing one week. Two weeks tops."

"Terrific," Harvath replied, shaking his head. He was disappointed but not surprised by the bureaucracy. There wasn't a military on the planet that didn't suffer from some form of it. "What about the rest of the gear and equipment I requested?"

The Sergeant began looking through the paperwork once more, but Harvath stopped. He already knew that there was nothing there. "I'll take it up with my team. Where are they?"

"At the front."

"When will they get here?"

"They're not coming to you. You're going to them. There's a transport departing in half an hour. If you move quickly enough, you can get a meal in you before you leave."

"They were supposed to already be here waiting for me."

"I don't know what to tell you," the man stated. "Fighters were needed at the front. This is a war. We don't have the luxury of allowing people to sit around."

Harvath was transitioning from disappointment in the bureaucracy to being actively pissed off. His team was supposed to have been pulled from the line and returned to the base to do mission prep.

"Listen," he said to the Ukrainian soldier, "I have my orders and they don't include me going to the front just to collect my guys and bring them back here."

"You aren't coming back here," the man responded. "According to your orders, you're headed to a village called Kolodyazne. Once you rendezvous with your men, you're more than halfway there. It would be a waste of time to come all the way back."

"Then we compromise. Give me the gear my men requisitioned, and a vehicle, and I'll be out of your hair."

The harried Sergeant was growing frustrated as well. "Captain, there is no gear other than what I have offered you. If there was, it would have had to go through me. I apologize. I don't know what you were told."

*Typical SNAFU*, Harvath thought to himself. *Situation normal, all fucked up.* It wasn't, however, this particular soldier's fault. "How about just a vehicle, then?"

"The only vehicle leaving this base for the front departs in less than thirty minutes. If you want to get to your men today, you need to be on it."

Zira, whose cell phone was sitting with her ID back at her apartment in Kharkiv, had already driven off the base. There was no way of letting her know that he needed her to return so that he could "borrow" her Land Cruiser.

Even if he had the Sergeant radio the soldiers at the earlier checkpoint, it would take her more than a half hour to get there. And what if she took a different route? By the time they had figured out that Zira couldn't be recalled, the transport to the front would have already left. Harvath needed to make a decision.

"One final question," he said. "How am I supposed to get my team from the front to Kolodyazne?"

The Supply Sergeant smiled and replied wryly, "As you pointed out, you're with Special Services Group. I'm sure you'll think of something."

# CHAPTER 15

Of all the forward operating bases Harvath could have launched from, he ended up at one that housed some of the oldest armored personnel carriers, or APCs for short, he had ever seen. The M113 waiting to take him, along with a group of infantrymen and supplies, up to the front looked like it had rolled on its treads straight out of the Vietnam War. It was equipped with a .50-caliber Browning M2 heavy machine gun known as a "Ma Deuce," which wasn't as desirable as an autocannon, but was a fine enough weapon.

For some reason, though, the gun shields—meant to protect the operator of the .50-cal—had been removed. Maybe they had been cannibalized for use on another vehicle. Maybe they had been stripped on a prior operation where every ounce of weight had been critical. There was no telling, although he would have been willing to bet that, somewhere, it involved more bureaucracy.

All Harvath knew was that whoever was standing in that hatch, running that gun, was going to be doing so with more exposure to enemy fire than should have been necessary. But as a former U.S. Secretary of Defense once said, "You go to war with the Army you have, not the Army you might want or wish you had at a later time." That included equipment. Some armor was better than none.

He waited for the supplies to be loaded and then walked up the rear ramp into the belly of the vehicle and took a seat. He was joined by a group of eight soldiers and their party was rounded out by two crew members—a driver and the commander, who also served as the gunner—who would be transporting them.

Within seconds, the hydraulic ramp had been raised, the turbocharged Detroit Diesel engine had roared to life, and they were moving.

The vehicle had a range of three hundred miles thanks to its twin armored fuel tanks, and could reach a top speed of forty miles per hour. It had been a long time since Harvath had ridden in one of these and he didn't miss it. Even though this APC was probably from the 1980s or early 1990s, the U.S. military had developed a lot of other vehicles that were safer and much more comfortable.

One of the biggest things he disliked about the M113 was the lack of exterior visibility. He would have much preferred to be traveling in an MRAP or an armored Humvee. At least then he'd be able to see what was going on outside.

But since there was nothing he could do about it, he leaned back and tried to enjoy the ride.

Everything began to slow down—his thoughts, his breathing, his heart rate, even his perception of time itself. It was an enforced calm before the storm.

A lot of energy, as well as a lot of adrenaline, could be used up in anticipation of arriving at a battle. A little bit of fear was natural, even healthy, helping to sharpen your edge. If, however, you allowed it to eat you up and deplete your reserves, it was like showing up to combat with only half your ammunition.

Looking at the soldiers who were traveling with him, he saw a range of ages—from teenagers all the way to men in their fifties. None of them looked like this was their first trip to the front. They weren't engaged in nervous chatter or cracking crude jokes. Each of them was every inch the professional soldier. Even the youngest among them had a seasoned, competent air. That said, they also looked tired. *Really* tired.

Ukraine had stunned the world with its ability to combat Russia's invasion and push Moscow's forces back. But as determined as the Ukrainians were to defend their homeland, war exacted a steep and heavy toll. You could see it on the faces of every man in the APC.

They had experienced the horrors of combat firsthand and were returning to the front, not because they wanted to—no sane person, given the choice, wanted war—but because it was a necessary requirement for them to secure freedom for themselves, their families, and the future generations of their country.

Yet again, Harvath couldn't help but wonder how different things would have been had the West simply stood up to Peshkov when he had first sliced off a piece of Ukraine just under a decade ago. But it hadn't.

There was nothing as provocative as weakness. Inaction *was* action. Autocrats, strongmen, and dictators could all smell weakness from miles away. It was an aphrodisiac to them; an open invitation to come and take what they wanted, a promise that there would be no consequences for their actions. Only when civilized nations drew a bright line and followed through with heavy consequences for crossing that line could those dictators, autocrats, and strongmen be kept in check.

The opportunity to administer an ounce of prevention in Ukraine had been ignored. Now the inevitable, bloody, costly cure was being delivered.

Harvath hoped that the world would pay attention this time, and lock the suffering and the carnage into their memory banks, but he had his doubts. He was constantly astounded by how many people either forgot history or chose to willfully ignore it.

Pay now or pay later. It was one of life's most frequent propositions. Far too many chose to kick the can and pay later. Perhaps they were hoping someone else would pick up the bill and pay for them. But regardless of who paid, doing so later always came at a greater cost. The butchery happening across Ukraine was a perfect example.

Harvath worked on pushing the thought from his mind. He had a job to do. That needed to remain his focus.

He held little hope that Anna Royko was still alive. By all accounts, the men who had attacked the orphanage were evil personified. Had Nicholas not had photos to back up what had happened there, it would have been incredibly difficult to believe.

Difficult, but not impossible.

The world was full of incredibly malign individuals. Rarely, however, did you see them banded together in such a grotesque confederation.

The parallels between the Wagner Group's Ravens and the Nazi

Dirlewanger Brigade still struck him as uncanny. It was as if the SS unit had been brought back to life some eighty years later.

Man's inhumanity to man was a tale as old as time, but the Ravens were taking it to the next level.

The updated intelligence that the GUR man with the briefcase had shared was the stuff of nightmares. It had also provided a possible lead. That was why Harvath and his new team were going to Kolodyazne first.

The danger of the assignment—both in relation to the men they were hunting and how they would be operating within the shadow of the front lines—had not been lost on him. They weren't looking for a needle in a haystack; they were looking for a live hand grenade under a mountain of rusty razor blades surrounded by a sea of molten lava.

If there was one thing he knew, it was that as bad as things had started, this mission could get exponentially worse. Even the best-planned operations were subject to Murphy's Law. And there were few places Murphy liked more to come out and play than an active war zone. It was his playground and the combatants his playthings.

Feeling his heart rate climbing, Harvath admonished himself for allowing his thoughts to get away from him. He closed his eyes and worked on his breathing. There was nothing he could do until he arrived at the front. He had to make the best of it. He was going to be stuck inside this tin can for the next two hours.

Aside from some intermittent radio traffic and the occasional communication between the driver and the gunner, the ride was long and boring. A few of the soldiers chatted quietly. Some slept. Others listened to music or played cards. One read a book.

If Harvath could have had anything, in addition to all of the burned-up equipment he had lost, he would have loved to have had a book. He'd always been a big reader, especially on deployments. Books helped take his mind off things and pass the time.

In Belarus, he had read a great thriller called *Wolf Trap* by an author named Connor Sullivan. He would have loved to have picked up another, but the Ukraine operation had gone into motion so quickly, he hadn't had the time.

Listening to the treads of the APC rumbling over the road, he tried to keep his mind in a quiet, meditative state. The only thing that pulled him out of it was when the driver abruptly slowed or changed course to avoid something in their path. Russian land mines, like Russian sabotage of the Ukrainian rail lines, were a constant threat. All in all, their journey had been uneventful.

•     •     •

Passing through an abandoned, battle-scarred village about a half hour from the front, Harvath was rocked awake by the sound of gunfire. It was soon joined by the M113's driver yelling something in Ukrainian.

Shaking off the fog of the trancelike state he had been in, he instantly realized what had happened. He didn't need for the driver to yell his command again. Harvath was closest, which meant that he needed to be the one to act.

As bullets pinged off the steel skin of the APC, he reached up, pulled the dead gunner out of the hatch, and took his place.

When the driver shouted a new order in Ukrainian, Harvath yelled back for him to speak English or Russian.

"The church!" the driver yelled in English, speeding forward. "Shoot the church!"

Harvath swung the Browning M2 heavy machine gun hard left and opened up on the bell tower.

The .50-caliber rounds thundered out of the Ma Deuce and punched hole after hole in the structure.

Every fifth round was a tracer, and Harvath used them to fine-tune his fire. He tore the wooden tower to shreds and even rang the bell, *twice*.

He then paused his shooting, his thumbs ready to reengage the trigger, waiting for some sort of response, but there was no return fire. Either he had taken him out or the sniper had fled.

Nearing the edge of the village, Harvath could see a bridge up ahead over a small river. The driver brought the APC to a halt and seemed to be weighing what to do next.

Harvath took advantage of the pause to call for more ammo. As the men below scrambled to grab him a can, he scanned the town for additional threats. Where there was one sniper, there were likely more hostile actors. Whether it was a squad, or an entire platoon, was unknowable. They were close enough to the front that it could be anything.

Reloading the .50-cal, Harvath charged the weapon and called out to the driver, "We can't sit out in the open like this all day. We need to get moving."

"I know," the Ukrainian shouted back. "I am not sure about the bridge. It could be rigged."

Harvath gave it a quick glance. There was no way to be certain. Not without getting underneath and thoroughly checking it out, section by section. The man was right to be uneasy. Harvath was growing uneasy as well.

The sniper, or more likely one of his comrades, could be waiting for the APC to roll across before blowing whatever explosives they had hidden beneath.

Harvath assumed that the driver knew his route and that not only had he made this run before, but there had been no recent reports of enemy activity in the area.

"Forget the bridge," said Harvath. "We'll take a different route."

The driver was about to respond, when he detected motion near the edge of one of the buildings. As a Russian soldier stepped into the open and the driver saw what he was carrying, he yelled, "RPG!"

Harvath swung the machine gun and began firing before he had even gotten a full sight picture. In so doing, he tore a racing stripe down the side of the building before sawing the Russian in half, just as the soldier managed to launch his weapon.

The rocket ripped through the air and sizzled right past them, missing the APC by less than two feet.

Harvath didn't want to see what might be coming next. Thankfully, he didn't need to tell the driver to get them to cover. The man was already moving.

He pulled down a narrow side street and stopped. Staying on the .50-cal, Harvath yelled down below for the rest of the soldiers to grab what they needed and to dismount.

Making a run for the bridge was totally out of the question. Even if it was safe to cross and hadn't been rigged with explosives, the Russians were armed with RPGs. The APC couldn't outrun those. What's more, Harvath knew damn well that they had just gotten very lucky. The next Russian to materialize with an RPG wasn't going to miss. Which meant that being anywhere near the APC right now was a bad idea.

They needed to find a good, defensible position and get their arms around what they were dealing with. How many Russian soldiers were out there? What kind of weapons and equipment did they have? And, if necessary, how quickly could the Ukrainians get reinforcements to them?

The first thing that they needed to settle was who was in charge. As the only officer, Harvath didn't plan on holding a vote. These soldiers were under his command.

Giving a rapid series of orders, he then dropped down into the APC to grab his gear. The supplies they were being forced to leave behind, partic- ularly the rockets, grenades, and ammunition, turned his stomach. It was destined for the men at the front. He would be damned if he was going to let the Russians have any of it. But by the same token, he thought it might make pretty good bait.

Working as quickly as he could, he manufactured a very guerrilla- style, down-and-dirty set of booby traps. Exiting the rear of the APC, he made sure the driver saw what he had done, just in case he didn't make it back and someone else needed to disable them.

Loaded down with gear, not knowing what kind of a fight they had just driven into, Harvath directed the soldiers toward one of the nearest concrete buildings—the village school.

In addition, he wanted a sniper of their own on a roof nearby and one of the Ukrainian soldiers immediately volunteered.

After agreeing on the best location, the man performed a quick radio check and then took off as two of his colleagues covered him.

That left positioning the remaining soldiers inside the school so that they didn't provide any weak spots that the enemy might exploit.

From a weapons standpoint, all of the men were outfitted with rifles as well as sidearms and a few grenades each. Harvath's biggest hope had been to find a tripod for the .50-cal somewhere in the APC. Unfortunately, he hadn't seen one and neither had the driver. They would have to do without the heavy machine gun.

The other issue Harvath had to contend with was exactly when, and how, to engage the Russian soldiers. He and the Ukrainians might be able to leverage the element of surprise, but once that was gone, they would be at the mercy of whatever the Russians threw at them. If Russians decided to rain down RPGs, or worse, Harvath was going to need a very good Plan B.

That was why he was intent on quickly gathering as much intelligence as possible.

He decided he'd be the one to conduct reconnaissance, taking one other soldier with him. The best English speaker was a tall, blond-haired twenty-two-year-old from Odesa named Oleh. Harvath told him to load up on extra grenades and ammo and then went to speak to the APC driver. He was leaving him in charge of everything until he got back.

Certain that the driver knew what he wanted him to do, Harvath grabbed a few extra items and then slipped out the back of the school with Oleh.

Weapons up and at the ready, they stuck to backyards, moving swiftly but carefully from the ruins of one building to the next.

However many Russians there were in the village, it wasn't going to take them long to locate the APC. Once they had found it abandoned, there'd be a house-to-house search for its occupants. Harvath wanted to be back at the school before that happened.

His plan was to push to the town square, loop behind it, and come up the other side. That would put him in the vicinity of where the church sniper and the Russian with the RPG had been.

Like the forest with its dachas outside of Kharkiv, this area had seen some pretty heavy fighting at some point. If not for the bullet holes and bomb craters, it might have been easy to imagine that a massive tornado had swept through, flattening almost everything in its path.

Surveying the destruction, particularly the downed power lines, torn-up streets, and uninhabitable houses, Harvath couldn't help but wonder what had become of all the inhabitants. How many had survived? Where had they gone? How would they start over?

These had not been wealthy people. Many would have had children and grandparents and pets. Judging by the debris, they had left many of their possessions behind, probably fleeing with whatever they could carry or cram into a vehicle.

He was reminded, yet again, of images of World War II—civilians fleeing the Nazis with everything they owned in a suitcase, or piled high on a wagon, maybe balanced on the back of a bicycle. It was almost surreal thinking about this happening today—in the era of smartphones, high-speed internet, and artificial intelligence. No matter how many leaps forward we took in technology and modern conveniences, war didn't disappear. Many human beings were still nothing more than animals at their core.

It was reality, but it still pissed Harvath off. Oleh should have been at university, dreaming of graduation, and maybe thinking of a more serious commitment with his girlfriend. Instead he was carrying a rifle, picking his way through some rubble-strewn village he had probably never heard of, risking his life to push foreign invaders out of his country. Had you told him a year ago that this was where he was going to be, he might never have believed you.

But maybe he would have. The Ukrainians knew that they had a revanchist Russia on their doorstep. When nothing happened to Peshkov after his first incursion, back when Oleh was just in grade school, why wouldn't the young man have expected the Russians to be back?

The death. The destruction. The gruesome barbarity. It was difficult to find words for. It was even tougher to wrap your head around—especially in the twenty-first century.

Harvath's heart broke for these people. No matter how this war ended, things were never going to be the same for them.

He felt even worse for their children. No adult, much less a child, should ever be exposed to what so many of them had been forced to suffer. He had no idea how you ever fully healed from that kind of psychological and sometimes even physical trauma.

The cost of this war would continue far beyond any hoped-for cessation of hostilities. The bill would be revisited upon many of the survivors for the rest of their lives. War, without question, absolutely was hell. The Russians deserved every bad thing that was coming to them.

Pausing near the square, Harvath had Oleh radio their sniper for a SITREP. For the moment, everything was still quiet, and so they kept moving.

Scrambling over splintered timbers, piles of broken bricks, and jagged pieces of metal roofing panels, Harvath was careful where he placed his footholds. The last thing he needed was to suffer some stupid, preventable injury that would slow him down or, worse, knock him out of the fight. He had come too far and had already been through too much to allow that to happen.

Completing their hook behind the square, they were coming up along the other side of the village when Harvath spotted something up ahead and gave Oleh the signal to halt.

Adjusting the magnifier atop his suppressed rifle, Harvath peered through his optic and assessed the situation.

"What do you see?" Oleh whispered.

"Four Russian soldiers," Harvath replied. "And they're headed right toward us."

The young Ukrainian was confused. "Toward us? That doesn't make any sense. Unless—"

"Unless they're a flanking element and the rest of their team is already headed for our APC."

At that moment, almost in answer to their question, the sniper's quiet voice came over the radio and Oleh translated, "Multiple Russian soldiers, moving fast, approaching from the east."

"How many?" asked Harvath.

"Ten, maybe twelve. At least two are carrying RPGs. What do you want to do?"

Harvath would have loved to have waited until the Ukrainians back at the school had as many fish in the barrel as possible. Then, with their shots all lined up, let them be the first to fire. But that wasn't in the cards.

Directing Oleh behind some rubble, he told him to take up a firing position and to radio two orders to the others. First, the sniper's primary targets were the men with the RPGs. Second, neither the sniper, nor anyone else, was allowed to shoot until Harvath gave the command.

Oleh relayed the message and then confirmed that it had been received by the others. "Now what?" the young Ukrainian asked.

Preparing his magnifier for closer combat, Harvath replied, "We get ready for one hell of a gunfight."

# CHAPTER 16

There were a lot of things Harvath would have preferred—more guns, more men, a better-prepared trap—but in warfare, having the element of surprise was an advantage you never squandered. That was why he had seized the moment.

As the four Russian soldiers approached, he made ready. They were moving exactly as he and Oleh had—carefully, from building to building, optimizing their cover and concealment. There was an area coming up, an open piece of uneven ground, where they were going to be in the open and exposed. That's where they would take them.

At the same instant, on the other side of the village, their sniper would take out the two Russian soldiers who were carrying the RPGs. Once those soldiers were down, the sniper had permission to take out any other Russians at will.

It was Harvath's hope that the sniper fire would drive the remaining Russians toward the school, where the balance of the Ukrainian soldiers would be waiting to finish them off. A lot was going to have to go right for his plan to be successful.

Looking through his holographic sight, he gauged the distance of the four Russians closing in on them. He had no idea how good a shooter Oleh was. Because of that, he wanted to wait until they were within a hundred yards before engaging them. The only downside was that they'd mostly be through the open space and almost to cover by then.

If Harvath was lucky and if nothing went wrong, he figured he could take out two of the men. The other two were Oleh's responsibility. He was about to see what they both were made of.

"Ready?" he asked.

Oleh nodded and snugged the butt of his weapon in tighter against his shoulder. Like his colleagues' rifles, it was an older, Russian AK-74 with no fancy optics or attachments—just iron sights and heavily worn, wood furniture. It looked like it had been liberated from some Cold War museum.

When the AK-74 had entered service via Soviet forces in Afghanistan sometime around 1979, the CIA had been anxious to study it and had allegedly offered a $5,000 bounty for the first one captured by Afghan mujahideen forces.

Judging by the condition of Oleh's weapon, it might have been the very same rifle. Harvath's concern about the young Ukrainian's ability to make not one but both of his shots was growing. That said, it was too late to change the plan. The Russians were almost in range.

They had agreed that Harvath would take the first two targets and Oleh would take the remainders.

Though the soldiers were wearing plate carriers, there was no guarantee that they had any ballistic plates inserted. Nevertheless, Harvath would be targeting vulnerable areas other than center mass. He had encouraged Oleh to take the best shots he could. The object was to take these men out of the fight by any means possible.

With the first of the Russians coming into range, Harvath waited for the second and then sent two squelch clicks over the radio, which began their five-second countdown. Applying pressure to his trigger, he exhaled and lined up his shot.

*Three. Two. One.* Harvath, Oleh, and the sniper on the rooftop on the other side of the village all fired at the same time.

Harvath didn't bother waiting until his first target had hit the ground. Moving the suppressed muzzle of his weapon a fraction of an inch to the right, he exhaled and pressed the trigger again.

A couple of feet to his left, Oleh had already fired four rounds in an attempt to double-tap each of his targets.

Staying calm, Harvath inhaled and scanned the open area. Both of the targets he had engaged were down. Oleh's targets were not only still up, but were running for cover.

Harvath sighted in on the slower of the two men, pressed his trigger, and sent a round through the base of the man's neck, dropping him like a stone. He then canted his rifle to the side, ready to shoot the other soldier, but that Russian had already disappeared. *Fuck.*

"I'm sorry," said Oleh as he and Harvath leapt to their feet. "I thought I had both of them."

There were a million things Harvath could have said to buoy the young Ukrainian's confidence, but now wasn't the time.

Off in the distance, he could already hear a gun battle beginning to rage. They needed to take out their fourth Russian and then get to the school.

"Let's go," Harvath ordered as he signaled for Oleh to fall in behind him and began maneuvering toward the building their target had escaped into.

The young Ukrainian followed Harvath's command, intent not to let the American down again. He made sure to keep his eyes and ears open, constantly checking their six o'clock to make sure no one was coming up on them from the rear.

Entering what must have originally been some sort of repair shop, Harvath buttonhooked left while Oleh went right. The *clack, clack, clack* of gunfire outside echoed through the shop's broken windows up front and bounced off the walls.

Bits of old, rusted junk hung from the ceiling and the rough-hewn lumber shelves had been all but stripped bare. Harvath motioned for Oleh to crouch down as they each took an aisle and moved forward.

He had no idea what the Ukrainian was seeing, but the first thing that Harvath noticed in his aisle was a stream of blood. *Fresh* blood. Perhaps at least one of Oleh's shots had been better placed than he had thought.

Keeping one eye on where he was going and another on the blood, Harvath advanced. Either their missing Russian had hauled ass through the shop and was already outside and on his way to reuniting with his team, or he was still inside and close. *Very* close.

As the hairs stood up on the back of Harvath's neck, he was certain he had his answer.

Coming around the endcap of his aisle, he saw Oleh with a pistol to his head and the missing Russian standing right behind him.

"Drop your weapon," the Russian ordered.

Harvath tightened his grip and began applying pressure to his trigger. He could see that the Russian's fatigues were stained a deep crimson and that he was losing a lot of blood.

"Drop your weapon," the Russian repeated, "or I *will* kill him."

As the Russian pressed the barrel of his Vektor pistol harder against Oleh's temple, Harvath locked in his sight picture and exhaled.

"I am not going to say it again. If you do not drop your—"

Harvath, still in a semi-crouch as he had come around the endcap, applied full pressure to his trigger and sent a round right through the cleft in the Russian's upper lip, which exited out the top of the man's skull. His pistol hit the shop floor only a second before his lifeless body did.

"Are you injured?" Harvath asked.

Too stunned to speak, Oleh merely shook his head.

"Good. We need to cross back over to the other side of the village. Are you with me?"

Slowly, the young man nodded.

"Okay," said Harvath. "I'll lead. You stay behind me. Stay close. Understand?"

Once again, Oleh slowly nodded.

Harvath snapped his fingers in the Ukrainian's face to get his attention. "Are you all right? We good?"

The young man nodded. More with-it this time.

"On me," Harvath ordered as he moved toward the front of the shop. Oleh followed.

Harvath opened the door, waited, and then carefully peered out. The gun battle was still going hard in the direction of the school and the APC.

As no rounds had been fired at him, he stepped fully into the open and took a wider look. All clear.

Satisfied that they were good to go, he signaled Oleh to ready his rifle and tighten up.

Once the young Ukrainian indicated that he was ready to move, Harvath gave the command and they slipped out of the shop and hustled to their first piece of cover.

They were sacrificing a little safety for a lot of speed, but it was a necessary trade-off. Harvath had no idea how many, if any, of the Russians the Ukrainian sniper had been able to pick off. What's more, he had no idea if the rest of the Ukrainians back at the school had entered the fight, though by the sound of the gunfire, they were all fully engaged.

Moving from building to building, Harvath and Oleh arrived at an open space just before the town square. It would get them back to the school faster. With no Russians in sight, Harvath was willing to risk it.

There were two pieces of cover as they made their way across—a burned-out old Russian tank and an equally obliterated Russian APC. Their first objective was the tank.

Counting to three, Harvath sent Oleh running toward it while he covered him. Then he had the young Ukrainian return the favor. They both made it successfully to their first objective. Next was their run to the APC.

As he had before, Harvath told Oleh that he was going to count to three and cover him as he ran to the APC, at which point the young man would cover him. Oleh nodded, but seemed out of it.

Harvath snapped his fingers to get his attention once more and ordered him to focus. The Ukrainian shook it off and appeared to focus.

Using his rifle to scan for any threats, Harvath then counted to three and sent the young man running for the cover of the destroyed APC.

He waited for several seconds for Oleh to get his rifle up and to start scanning for threats. There was definitely something not right with the kid.

He finally got the young Ukrainian's attention; Oleh signaled back that he was okay and that Harvath could make the dash to the APC.

Ready to return fire if any should come his way, Harvath ran his ass off, not exactly confident that Oleh's head was fully in the game. He made it to the APC, however, in one piece.

"Oleh, seriously," he said. "You need to snap out of it. We're almost there. Can you do that for me?"

The young Ukrainian nodded, but it was another of those halfhearted nods. Harvath was worried that he wasn't going to make it.

"We're almost there," he informed him. "You've got this. Okay?"

Once more, the Ukrainian nodded.

Harvath studied the distance from the APC to their next piece of cover. It was the longest they were going to have to be out in the open. He wasn't exactly crazy about it, but as long as they moved fast, they should be okay.

"See where the front of that building has collapsed?" Harvath asked, pointing at their next objective. "I want you to run toward where the roof has caved in. Okay? Stay away from the window openings. Do you understand?"

The young man nodded, but that wasn't good enough for Harvath. "Repeat it back to me."

"Roof. Not windows," Oleh mumbled.

It wasn't the committed, emphatic response Harvath would have preferred, but at least he knew the kid had heard him.

"Move fast, keep your head down, and wait for me to get there," said Harvath. This part was almost over. Once they had fully made it across, if Oleh couldn't get his shit together, Harvath would park him someplace safe and come back for him once the dust had settled. The only thing he'd be in a firefight was a liability.

After a quick scan, Harvath reminded him to move fast and keep his head down, then counted to three and sent him running.

To his credit, the young Ukrainian moved fast. Not world-record fast, but fast enough. Just as important, he took cover where he had been told to. Now it was Harvath's turn to cross.

But once again, Oleh wasn't ready.

In almost any other circumstance, Harvath might have allowed him a moment to catch his breath, but they didn't have a single second to spare. The kid needed to pull it together. Harvath signaled the Ukrainian to get his rifle up and cover him.

Readying his own rifle, Harvath was about to charge out from behind the APC when a shot rang out, kicking up a cloud of debris as it landed just next to Oleh.

Reflexively, the young man rolled away from where the bullet had landed, right toward the place Harvath had told him not to—the ruins of the open windows.

Harvath tried to signal him to go back to where he was, to retreat into the wreckage of the collapsed roof, but Oleh wasn't paying attention.

"Get back!" Harvath shouted, giving himself away to the sniper. "Get back to where I told you to be."

As he yelled at Oleh to return under the collapsed roof, he scanned the other buildings with his rifle, trying to find the sniper.

All the while, he was wondering why the Russians would have put a sniper here in the first place. Then it hit him. Wherever the shooter was, he had a view of this location, as well as where the fighting was up by the school and the APC. That narrowed things down considerably.

But what it didn't do was throw a big, bright spotlight on the sniper's precise perch.

There were a couple of locations where a shooter could be hiding that would allow him to fire in both directions. But short of a means by which to flush him out, the act of pinpointing his nest was going to be next to impossible. That was when Oleh adjusted his position again.

Propping his gun up on the sill of one of the shattered windows, he signaled Harvath to run and began firing in the direction of where he believed the sniper to be. But he was off. *Way* off.

Because of his position behind the APC, Harvath had a different vantage point than Oleh. When the sniper fired again, he saw a faint muzzle flash and now knew where the shooter was hiding.

He pumped round after round into the window and kept doing so as he ran toward Oleh.

Skidding to a stop at the pile of rubble, he lunged for cover under the collapsed roof. In doing so, he clipped a beam and sent a searing, white-hot bolt of pain down his hip.

"Motherfucker," he growled, kicking it with his boot.

Suddenly, the debris above him shifted and he instantly regretted his hotheadedness. Rolling hard to his right, he barely escaped being hit by an even bigger, heavier beam that had broken loose from the second story. The sniper notwithstanding, this was a tremendously dangerous place to be holed up.

As he looked over at Oleh, he noticed that the man's weapon had fallen silent and that he wasn't moving. Harvath called out, but the young Ukrainian didn't respond.

Careful to stay close to the wall and out of the sniper's line of fire, he crawled to where Oleh was slumped, his back to him, just beneath the window.

Turning him over, he saw the kid's lifeless eyes and knew that he was dead. The sniper's bullet had entered just above his body armor and had likely traveled down to his heart, killing him almost instantly.

Harvath closed Oleh's eyelids. There was nothing else he could do. The war had claimed another victim; one with his entire life in front of him. There would be no returning to university, no going back to Odesa, no wife, no family. Everything he'd had was now over—cut entirely too short.

As the battle raged back near the school and around the Ukrainian APC, Harvath inserted a fresh magazine into his rifle and prepared to return to the fight.

He had been wrong in believing that there was nothing he could do for Oleh. There actually was something. He could kill every last Russian in the village. And he would start by making sure the sniper who had shot him was dead.

Since putting all of those rounds into the window where he had seen the muzzle flash, Harvath hadn't noticed any further activity. But if this was the same shooter who had been in the bell tower earlier, he might be quite practiced at fleeing the moment his nest was pinpointed. There was only one way to be certain.

Doing a wide enough loop to avoid the sniper's crosshairs was not an option. There wasn't time. What's more, there was no telling what kind of damage the man could do in the meantime.

The shortest distance between Harvath and the shooter was a straight line, and, as batshit crazy as it was, that was Harvath's plan.

Creeping to the edge of the wall, he made sure his weapon was hot, took a deep breath, and then, ignoring the pain in his hip, came out firing.

He did as he had done before—running as fast as he could while putting rounds on the sniper's location, hoping to keep the man pinned down and preventing him from shooting back.

His plan seemed to have worked. He made it all the way to the building without being shot at.

The thought of charging into another, unfamiliar Ukrainian house in order to deal with a Russian shooter on the second floor didn't exactly appeal to him, but Harvath had something much better going for him this time. Instead of mothballs and flour, he had fragmentation grenades.

He also had two perfect targets—the broken window the sniper had been shooting out of and a huge hole in the roof.

Using the wreckage of a bombed-out car for cover, Harvath changed magazines. Then, removing the grenades from his pouch, he pulled their pins and let them fly.

The moment they detonated, he was on his feet.

Charging up to the house, he kicked in the front door, made entry, and swept for threats.

With the downstairs secure, he took the stairs two at a time, vigilant and ready for any danger.

Arriving at the second story, he found the sniper exactly where he had expected him to be. The man was alive, but just barely.

Several of Harvath's rounds had found their mark, though from which volley, he couldn't be sure. The bullets alone would have ended his life, but the shrapnel from the fragmentation grenades had definitely accelerated the process. Just to be safe, he kicked the man's rifle out of reach.

The sniper was guppy breathing. Adjusting his aim, Harvath applied pressure to the trigger of his Galil and put a round through the man's head for Oleh, finishing him off.

He stepped to one of the other windows, where he had a direct line of sight to the Russians and the Ukrainians battling it out. The dead Russian's radio was chirping with desperate pleas from his comrades.

Setting his weapon aside, he bent down and picked up the sniper's old SVD rifle. He ejected the curved, ten-round box magazine and saw that there were several shots left.

He got himself into a comfortable position and then radioed the Ukrainians, letting them know where he was and what he was about to do.

As soon as he received confirmation, he peered through the telescopic sight, flipped off the safety, and aligned the crosshairs with his first target. Exhaling, he pressed the SVD's trigger and let a round fly.

*Hit.*

The Russian soldier dropped.

Before the man's colleagues could figure out what had happened, Harvath readjusted his sight picture and had acquired a new target. Exhaling, he pressed the trigger again. *Hit.*

The Russian soldiers had no idea where the rounds were coming from, only that someone had gotten the drop on them and that they were dangerously exposed. The men bolted for cover.

Harvath waited, his gaze focused through the telescopic sight, but he didn't see so much as the toe of a single Russian boot. He had helped take two more pieces off the board. To remove any others, which he fully intended to do, he was going to have to get moving. Switching back to his Galil, he headed downstairs and exited the house.

Based on the way the fight was unfolding, he figured his best opportunity to pick off one or two more Russians was near the APC, so that was where he headed.

Using every piece of available cover, he zigzagged through the village, letting the sound of gunfire be his guide.

While the Ukrainians were doing what they needed to do to repel the attack, the Russians were dumping withering amounts of ammo on the school. They seemed hell-bent on victory and taking control of the village.

Harvath had no idea if the town was of any strategic importance or why the Russians would want it. All he knew was that he and the Ukrainians were going to make sure that they didn't get it.

Getting closer to the fight, he radioed their sniper, only to discover that the soldier had come under heavy fire and had been forced to retreat back to the school. There was no longer a shooter running overwatch. If Harvath did decide to work the edges of the fray, knocking off any Russians he could find, he'd be doing it without backup.

It wasn't Harvath's preferred method of operation, but he was no stranger to going it alone. The sun was beginning to set. He didn't know about the Ukrainians, but he didn't have any night-vision goggles. If the Russians had come fully equipped, it could end up being a very long and bloody night. That was reason enough for Harvath to risk going it alone. They needed to end this thing before it got dark.

Nearing the school, it was harder to conceal his movements. Each time he changed cover, he was forced to expose himself for longer periods of time. There just weren't enough places to hide. He was going to have to make a very difficult decision.

From this angle of approach, the Russians were going to be able to see him at any moment. If he got lucky, he'd be able to get off one, maybe two shots. If he didn't get lucky, he'd get off zero and they'd be focusing a lot of lead in his direction. Adding to their advantage, they'd have much better cover than he did.

Net-net, it wasn't worth it. If he wanted the most effective strike, he would have to come at them from a better approach. It was a no-brainer. His best choice was to loop around and hope to use the Ukrainian APC for cover.

The only drawback was that once he stirred the hornet's nest, if the Russians decided to break off from the school and come after him, he was going to be in massive trouble. But as an old SEAL instructor of his liked to say, Don't ever be part of the problem. Be the *entire* problem. If the Russians decided to come for him, he was going to make it as costly for them as possible.

Breaking off, he slipped between two ruined houses and moved backyard to backyard, as rapidly as he could.

Arriving at the side street where they had ditched the APC, he took a second to survey the scene. Everything appeared the same. The vehicle was still there, its gunner's hatch ajar, just as he had left it. That meant all the booby traps were still in place, too. Suddenly, having the Russians chasing him didn't seem like such a bad idea.

Staying hidden, he removed one of his partially loaded magazines and transferred the rounds into another mag. It was time to put his plan into action.

Approaching the back of the APC, he laid the empty magazine on the ground and partially cracked the door cut into the rear ramp. With the trap baited, he went to draw the Russians into an old-fashioned game of chicken.

Sticking close to the jagged façades of the buildings on the opposite side of the street, he crept toward the Russian position. They were still laying down obscene amounts of fire on the school.

Two of their dead were lying in the road and Harvath was glad to see that they were the ones with RPGs that his Ukrainian sniper had taken out.

Finding a good piece of cover, he steadied himself against the wall, established his sight picture, and, as he exhaled, began firing.

There was so much noise, the Russians didn't realize another gun had joined the fight until they saw another of their men go down.

When the first Russian turned to engage, Harvath shot him square in the chest, knocking him over backward. It was the last shot he was able to visually confirm hitting its target.

As several of the soldiers began shooting at him, Harvath had to duck back behind cover. With the rounds falling on his position like a hailstorm, all he could do was point the muzzle of his Galil in their direction and blindly fire.

He ran his magazine dry and, pulling his weapon back in, swapped it out for a fresh one. The Russians took advantage of his pause to unload on him.

The bullets popped and whizzed all around him—high, low, and wide. Whoever these soldiers were, they were not terribly good marksmen. Their aim and their discipline sucked.

Based on how many Russians Peshkov had fed into the wood chipper of Ukraine, Harvath could only figure that a good chunk of the soldiers now seeing combat had very little experience and even less training.

The moment they stopped firing, Harvath went at them again—this time risking a peek to better direct his fire. He needed to be a big enough pain in the ass that they couldn't help but come after him. What he saw made him pull his head *and* his rifle in and start to retreat—the bullets pinging around him were cover fire for a group of soldiers headed to take him out.

The Russians had likely figured out that this was the guy who had been thinning their ranks. Now that they had a fix on him, they weren't going to let him get away, which was exactly what he wanted.

Running as fast as he could, Harvath raced back past the APC and around the corner. He kept going until he found a pile of rubble large enough to safely take refuge behind.

Tucking in, he radioed the Ukrainians to get ready. Half of the Russians attacking their position had just broken off and were about to hit the APC.

Not knowing what kind of training they'd had, Harvath figured one of two things was going to happen. The Russians were either going to drop a grenade down the open gunner's hatch, or they were going to line up in a stack, yank open the rear door, and fill the belly of the APC with automatic weapons fire. For all he knew, they might even do both. The result, however, would be the same. All that mattered was that they took the bait.

By now, they should be coming around the corner and have full view of the large, armor-plated vehicle. As they got closer, eventually even the least observant among them was going to discover the empty magazine near the rear hatch.

If they only sent one soldier forward to investigate, he'd see all this, plus notice that the gunner's hatch was ajar. It would only be a matter of seconds now as they settled on a plan and put it into action.

Harvath wished the Ukrainians still had the sniper in place. He would have killed for a play-by-play. As it was, he had to settle for waiting and decided to count backward in his head from thirty. That would have to be more than enough time for them to orient and act.

He counted all the way down yet arrived at zero and still nothing had happened. Back at the school, the gun battle was still raging. *What the hell was the delay?*

Had the Russians smelled a trap? Had they bypassed the APC altogether? Had he miscalculated and now they were only steps away from being right on top of him?

The noise from the gunfight was perfect auditory camouflage. He wouldn't have known they were there until one of the Russians stuck a weapon in his face and pulled the trigger. The thought of the Russians turning the tables on him like that was nuts, but it would be the ultimate irony. Murphy pulling one last cruel trick before Harvath got his ticket punched. He had to risk peering out from behind the rubble.

Leading with his Galil, he crawled to the edge of the pile and then rolled onto his side to take a look. As he did, there was an enormous explosion.

All of the wooden buildings around the APC were flattened and a gigantic, roiling orange fireball shot up into the sky.

The shock wave pelted Harvath with hot pieces of flying rock, glass, and other debris. Moving as fast as he could, he rolled back behind his pile of rubble.

As soon as the rain of detritus had subsided, Harvath leapt to his feet and ran back toward the blast zone. If any of the Russian soldiers had survived, he needed to make sure that they couldn't return to the fight.

Arriving at the flaming APC, he saw nothing but dead bodies and body parts. His ears were ringing, and he strained to hear any sounds of gunfire coming from the school.

Slowly, his hearing started to come back. After a lull in the fighting, probably due to the shock of the explosion, the battle was back on.

Gripping his weapon a little tighter, Harvath headed toward the school to finish the job and mop up the remaining Russians.

This had been an expensive detour. He needed to get to the front and link up with his team. Every minute they weren't chasing the Ravens was one more minute in which those psychopaths were free to inflict their terror.

# CHAPTER 17

The Colonel loved to watch his war dogs work. The men from the asylums were always the first ones in. They were fearless. And with their faces painted like skulls—terrifying.

As long as their drug of choice was available—narcotics, alcohol, or women—they were easy to keep in line. The hard-core criminals—the rapists, gangsters, and thieves—were more difficult. They had a level of functional intelligence, as well as street smarts, that seemed to be lacking in the insane. The criminals were able to think beyond their immediate gratification. And while they also gorged on a steady diet of drugs, women, and alcohol, they additionally wanted money. The war wouldn't go on forever. At some point it would end, and when it did they wanted to have a nice chest of riches to show for it and from which to retire, or finance their next endeavor.

The Colonel didn't blame them. Yes, by joining the war and agreeing to fight they had secured their freedom, but that agreement with the Russian state had ended the minute they had all gone AWOL.

Even the Colonel was a wanted man, marked by Moscow for death. He had not only stopped fighting for Russia, but was actively stealing from Peshkov and his cronies inside the Kremlin.

He had been a mercenary for over two decades, rising to become one of the top battlefield commanders in the Wagner Group. All of his life, he had watched as the oligarchs in Russia enriched themselves by pillaging his country's wealth and resources. He had seen high-ranking Wagner men, including the company's founder, do the same.

He had come from a poor family with an overbearing, overweight beast of an alcoholic father and a frail, idealistic mother who, despite an unhappy and frequently abusive marriage, had higher hopes for her only child.

Disillusioned with the inability of the state, especially in the realm of education, to help her son advance, she had encouraged him to take control of his life. Her advice was that he never depend on anyone but himself. If he saw something he wanted, he should take it. The world was rough, and cruel, and cheap, and disappointing. The sooner he realized this, the sooner he could figure out what he wanted and then go get it.

On his sixteenth birthday, his mother died by suicide.

His father blamed him. He said that his mother had always felt inadequate and that having a child had only made her insecurities worse. She had developed what the doctors call postpartum depression and had never fully recovered.

Having a son who received terrible marks and showed so little promise had been an immense burden on her. According to his father, he was an embarrassment to their family. They couldn't show their faces anywhere. In constant trouble at school and with the police, he made them ashamed. His mother had taken her life to finally be rid of the indignity of it all.

He knew his father had been lying. That it was his drinking and the subsequent beatings his mother had to endure that had worsened any depression she may have had, and that finally drove her to take her own life. His father was a horrific human being and even worse when drunk. He was also very large—too large for a boy of only sixteen to deal with. Until one night, when he had passed out on the toilet after consuming two bottles of vodka, which happened a couple of times a year, and the opportunity presented itself.

The decision had not been hard. He had been fantasizing about murdering his father for as long as he could remember. The question was not what to do, but what *not* to do.

He had wanted to pick up a hammer and to take out every ounce of his rage. He had wanted to make the man pay for all the pain he and his mother had suffered.

But even at sixteen, he had been smart enough to know that if it looked like a murder, especially a violent act of passion, all suspicion would fall on him. Therefore, it had to look like an accident.

The benefit of spending years fantasizing about killing your father was that you tried countless scenarios on for size in your mind. He had done his homework and knew which kinds of murders the police solved, which went unsolved, and what types they didn't even bother investigating. His plan was to have his father's death fall into the very last category. Knowing that the man was dead and that he had caused it would be incredibly unsatisfying, but it would have to be enough.

Not knowing how long his father would remain passed out, he had needed to act quickly.

He had a friend whose family had a food packaging facility. Often, they would sneak into the warehouse and steal blocks of dry ice to use to make fog at parties. He knew how to get inside, exactly where it was kept, and how to get precisely the right amount back to his apartment without anyone knowing.

After placing it in the bathroom sink, he sealed the air vent and the bathroom door. When he returned to check on his father two hours later, the man was dead.

Technically, he had died from hypercapnia—a buildup of carbon dioxide in the bloodstream that pushes out the oxygen—brought about by the gas given off as the dry ice melted.

The police had chalked it up to a fat guy who'd had too much to drink and ended up choking himself to death after he had passed out. No obvious signs of foul play meant no investigation. The boy was sent to live with an aunt in another city.

His problems at school and with the police only continued to grow. He was a bully, which extended well beyond the schoolyard.

A growth spurt had kicked in. He had inherited his father's large frame, though not yet the man's paunch. Not satisfied with simply terrorizing his schoolmates, he had begun strong-arming shop owners, taking things and refusing to pay. The police delivered his aunt an ultimatum—either the young thug cleaned up his act, or they planned to send him off to a youth detention facility.

A month later, he had run away from his aunt's home and, falsifying his age, had joined the Russian military.

For a time, the Army felt like the perfect place for him. He was a brute who even intimidated some of his superiors. His aggression and cold-heartedness were encouraged. He built his body to an impressive size through weight lifting and by injecting himself with steroids and human growth hormone.

He fought in underground, no-holds-barred fight competitions on the weekends and was unstoppable.

But as his body and his impressive list of wins continued to grow, so too did his ego. He had believed himself untouchable. Right up until the extremely toxic relationship he was in crossed over into abhorrent physical abuse.

The young woman had been keeping the relationship secret from her parents, especially her father—the base commander. When her nose and jaw were broken there were no more secrets.

Her father had had the boyfriend beaten with bats and lead pipes. He was kept in solitary confinement and given the bare minimum of medical care until he could walk. Then, in the middle of winter, he was dishonorably discharged and thrown off the base in only his underwear—no money, no ID, no jacket, no shoes, no socks, nothing.

Between his still incompletely healed injuries and a crippling case of hypothermia, he had almost died. But for an old farmer who had seen him collapse into a snowbank along the road, he would have.

Unable to lift the man, the farmer had used his tractor to drag him back to his barn, where he and his wife had tended to him. It took a full two months to recover.

When he was ready to leave, he did so in the middle of the night, having helped himself to the old couple's car, a firearm, and a tea tin in which they had hidden their emergency savings. He never said good-bye. He never thanked them. They were disposable to him.

He spent a year beating around, working odd jobs, fighting in bouts when he could find them, drinking, abusing women, and being an all-around asshole, until he started hearing rumors about a new, clandestine paramilitary organization called the Wagner Group.

Wagner was looking for men with prior military experience. Even better, they were not averse to accepting men who had been dishonorably discharged.

Making his way to St. Petersburg, he identified and then mercilessly harassed a recruiter until he received an interview. As it turned out, the recruiter had also done some no-holds-barred fighting and put in a good word. Within a week, he had been hired.

From that point forward, he saw action in multiple civil wars, including Mali, Libya, Syria, and the Central African Republic.

As a member of Peshkov's private army, or the "little green men," as they became known, he'd also spent a lot of time waging war in the Donbas region of eastern Ukraine.

Once Peshkov had decided that his annexation of the east wasn't enough and that he intended to take the entire country, the man—now an incredibly seasoned mercenary—had been called to battle yet again.

The Colonel, as his men called him, had learned to love war. He loved it more than anything he had ever loved in his life. The power. The destruction. The pain. The pleasures. It was lived at full volume, in full vivid color, at its most brutal and intense. One was never as alive as when one was at war.

This most recent war, however, had taken a heavy toll. In his decades of combat, he had never seen anything like it. For every Ukrainian that was killed, the Ukrainians killed two Russians. Both the Russian Army and Wagner had run out of fresh recruits, which was why the Colonel had come up with the idea for his unit of Ravens.

The way Wagner had chosen to use the men had angered him. Instead of taking the time and expense to properly train and equip them so that they could strategically maneuver and leverage opportunities on the battlefield, they were thrown at fortified Ukrainian positions in high-attrition human waves.

He understood that because they had come from the worst prisons and mental asylums, Wagner had considered them to be expendable and nothing more than cannon fodder. But that wasn't how you won wars. That was how you lost them. Eventually there'd be no more meat to feed into the grinder.

The writing was on the wall. No matter what happened, the policy wasn't going to change. The elites back in Moscow and St. Petersburg had their minds made up. With that being the case, the Colonel knew that he needed to make his mind up, too.

It wasn't easy. After losing his boyhood home, he had gone on to lose his home in the Russian Army. Now he was weighing whether or not to leave Wagner, which had been his home longer than anything else. But then the opportunity of a lifetime had dropped into his lap.

He and his Ravens had been involved in a ferocious, three-day battle with Ukrainian forces. They had no food or water and were almost out of ammunition.

Moving to a more defensible position, they had come across a small, extremely well-equipped detachment of Russian Army soldiers. Certainly they could share some of their supplies to help his beleaguered Ravens achieve their objective and secure the entire sector.

But the soldiers were rude and arrogant. They claimed to be on a much more important assignment. Not one ration nor one bottle of water would be shared with the Wagner mercenaries.

There was something odd about these men. They were not down-and-dirty soldiers. From their uniforms to their hands, they were too clean; several of them too soft.

Many of the Ravens were, by nature, unstable. Under even the best of situations, they could be difficult to control. The tone and posture of the recalcitrant soldiers pissed them off. Things got very heated, very quickly.

For his part, the Colonel liked what he was seeing. His men were asserting their dominance. The Russian Army soldiers had been given a chance to be cooperative and they had chosen not to be. Now the Ravens were no longer asking for help. They were going to take what they needed. And once the violence switch had been flipped, things escalated exponentially. The bloodbath happened so fast, the soldiers didn't even know what had hit them.

By the time the gunfire had subsided, the Colonel was already sitting on the hood and helping himself to food and water from one of the officers' vehicles. There would be some work to do, dressing up the scene to look like an ambush by the Ukrainians, but he was confident that it could all be taken care of, and they could be on their way within the hour.

He was taking a long pull of water when one of his closest subordinates approached.

"You should see this," the man said, holding out an accordion file he had removed from one of the other vehicles.

"What is it?"

"The details of their assignment."

Setting down the water bottle, he motioned for the man to hand him the file. The first thing he pulled out was a map. More specifically, it was a map of the Kharkiv region. On it, different locations had been numbered and marked. None of it made any sense until, in another pocket, he found a list, complete with descriptions that corresponded to the numbers. These men weren't soldiers after all.

They were looters. *Professional* looters. In fact, they were treasure hunters sent by the Kremlin to scoop up some of Ukraine's most valuable and culturally significant pieces of art.

In his hands, the Colonel was holding a treasure map. He knew nothing about art, but that didn't bother him. He knew people who knew people. If he could get his hands on any of the items on the list, much less all of them, the battle would be half won. He could find buyers or, at the very least, someone to act as a middleman, a seller.

It was an incredible stroke of good fortune. Something that came along very seldom, especially during war. He had heard of Wagner mercenaries who had gotten rich looting and smuggling antiquities out of Libya and Syria. A bounty of this proportion could be worth millions of dollars, maybe even tens or hundreds of millions of dollars.

Remaining with the Wagner Group was no longer a question. His mind was made up. He and his men would carve their own path. They were done taking orders from the elites. From that moment forward, they were the masters of their own destiny.

That was what had brought them to a small, shuttered winery outside yet another tiny village and set amid rows of wild, untended vines.

According to his map, there was a treasure hidden here. No matter what symbolic resistance the occupants might put up, he was going to find it. He and his war dogs always found what they came looking for. Torturing people in the process only made the experience more enjoyable.

As he heard the howls from his men inside, he knew that they had found something.

He hoped that it was a fresh, attractive young woman. The one that they had taken from the orphanage and were keeping back at their outpost was on her last legs.

He was looking forward to killing her himself. But not until they had found a replacement.

This close to the front, however, replacements were few and far between. They might be stuck with the one they had for a little longer. The question was, could she hang on? Hearing his men howl once more, he decided to go inside and see what they had found.

As he walked, he smiled. He knew the American woman wasn't going to survive, but prolonging her life might very well make for an exquisitely painful and entertaining game.

# CHAPTER 18

Greg Wilson was nervous. The last thing he wanted to do was to speak to the FBI before he had spoken with his handler. Should he have a lawyer present for the interview? Would they believe his story about why he and Burman were having dinner at the yacht club? What if they didn't? What if they pressed for more information? He needed answers and until he got them, he planned to stay out of D.C. and to give the FBI the widest berth possible.

That's why his handler had suggested Boston. It was an hour-and-twenty-minute flight for both of them. Halfway between Hancock County–Bar Harbor Airport in Maine and Reagan National in D.C. They settled on Come A Casa, a tiny hole-in-the-wall restaurant off Prince Street in the city's Little Italy neighborhood, known to locals as the North End.

The handler had suggested that Wilson take the ferry from Logan International Airport across the bay to the Hyatt and catch a cab to a small bookstore a few blocks down from the restaurant.

Upon his recruitment, the former Senator had been taught the basics about tradecraft. It was important that he knew how to move, meet, and communicate without tipping off U.S. Intelligence. While many American politicians weren't very bright and were about as deep as a puddle, Wilson was different. He showed promise.

But to hear him speak, Wilson believed his value was limited, that he had a very short "shelf life."

The scandal that had engulfed him had been humiliating. He had been outed for having had multiple extramarital affairs. One had been with his pastor's wife, another with a porn actress, and the third with a staffer in his Senate office.

All of the relationships had been consensual. None of the women had accused him of forcing himself on them. The one considered the most potentially damaging had been the affair with his staffer and she had gone public claiming that she had pursued him and not vice versa.

The timing of the revelations couldn't have been worse. They had come, drip, drip, drip—one after another—in the closing days of a bruising primary battle. There was no time to knock them all down, to get his rebuttals properly circulating. His constituents saw him as a liar and a hypocrite.

They had no idea how dirty the laundry was that hung in every congressional office closet on Capitol Hill. Nor were they aware of the forest of skeletons you had to battle through just to get to it.

He wasn't a "dirty" politician. He was merely a weak man who had succumbed to his passions. Power was the ultimate aphrodisiac and he had been unable to say no to the women who had wanted to bask in it.

He had known it was wrong. He knew he should have shown character and stopped things before they went too far, but he didn't. The fact that he could have these women was as far as his thought process had gone. Character, and all the other virtues, had left the building. And because of his weakness, he had been made to suffer.

In addition to losing his primary, he had lost his wife—the only woman to ever love him for who he really was. She had loved him before he had ever dreamed of running for office and would have stayed with him long after he had decided to retire from politics.

As a wise person, most probably a woman, once said, God gave men two heads, and they often do their most important thinking with the wrong one. That was Greg Wilson in a nutshell.

But instead of allowing the experience to humble him and forge a better man, Wilson blamed everyone else and allowed his heart to be hardened.

He blamed the pastor's wife, who couldn't keep her guilt-ridden mouth shut and confessed the affair to her husband. He blamed the money-grubbing porn star, who wanted to make a quick buck and was shopping her story to the tabloids. He blamed the staffer in his office, who was dumb enough to admit the relationship to a gossipy friend, who in turn hinted at it over lunch with a reporter from the *Washington Post*.

Finally, he blamed his opponent, his opponent's campaign manager, and their opposition research person. None of these stories had yet seen the full light of day. Someone had toiled in the shadows to source and secure them before perfectly orchestrating their release. It had taken a lot of skill, a lot of money, or both to make that happen and it had ruined Greg Wilson's political career.

The only saving grace had been that while voters wanted nothing further to do with him, his former colleagues were more than happy to take meetings with him as long as it furthered their interests. It wasn't lost on a single one of them that, but for the grace of God, the same thing could have happened to them. Because of this, Wilson was able to remain among the powerful in D.C. and earn a lucrative living.

That living, however, was not lucrative enough. He had a target in mind—$10 million. Enough to disappear and be comfortable on.

His constituents and, in his opinion, his country had not only turned their backs on him, but they also never deserved him in the first place. They could all go screw themselves. As soon as he had amassed his ten million, he would be gone.

There was a small Caribbean nation that, in exchange for making a large deposit in their national bank, would fast-track him to citizenship. Their passport was accepted worldwide by all the countries he would ever want to visit. The country also didn't have an extradition treaty with the United States.

While that hadn't been something he was originally looking for, it did become an added benefit once he went to work for the Russians.

The kicker for Wilson, the real knife through the heart, had been when his children had stopped talking to him. They silenced his calls, ignored his texts, and refused to see him. They even sent back the birthday and Christmas gifts he had sent them. As far as he was concerned, there was nothing left worth living for. That was when the Russians had made their move.

Wilson had been caught a bit flat-footed, unaware that he was being softened up. He had wrongly believed that he had a new client on the hook and that all he had to do was reel him into the boat. Then his would-be handler had laid everything out on the table.

It wasn't an obscene pitch—not even for an ex–U.S. Senator who was being asked to work against the interests of his country on behalf of a hostile foreign power. It came down to a question of ideology, of the path that could best secure a peaceful and prosperous future for both countries.

At one point in his life, the first thing Wilson would have done after such a recruitment attempt was to immediately reach out to the FBI. But not now. These were different times, he told himself. He was a different man. And as far as he was concerned, the United States was a different country. He was ready to cash in. He accepted Russia's offer.

His handler's name was Joe Nistal. He was a handsome man in his early forties—tall, with broad shoulders and a thick head of wavy brown hair. He wasn't exactly the picture that sprang to mind when one thought of a Russian Intelligence officer.

Nistal spoke perfect English and was up on everything American. From sports and politics to literature and pop culture, this guy was a Fourth of July baseball game, baked in an apple pie, wrapped in an American flag. There wasn't a single cell in this guy's body that suggested he worked for Moscow.

Topping it all off, he was smooth and exceedingly charming. There were moments when Wilson could absolutely forget who the man was and what his objectives were.

When Wilson arrived, Nistal was already at a small table, covered with a well-worn red-and-white-checked tablecloth, at the back of the restaurant. The Russian stood as his asset approached.

"It's good to see you," said Nistal, extending his hand. "Thanks for meeting with me."

"Thanks for making the time," Wilson replied, shaking the man's hand and accepting the seat across from him.

The Russian studied him for a moment. "Something's different about you."

"Like what?"

"I don't know. That's what I'm trying to figure out. Are you running? Lifting weights?"

"I am doing a little more walking," Wilson admitted, somewhat flattered.

"How many pounds have you lost?"

"None yet."

His handler kept looking at him. "New haircut?"

"Nope."

Nistal dropped the volume of his voice and leaned in. "Botox?"

The ex-Senator laughed. "No. No Botox."

"Please tell me your secret isn't that you've quit drinking."

"God, no," said Wilson, as he laughed again. "You really can't tell?"

The Russian shook his head.

"I had my teeth whitened," he stated, flashing a broad smile.

"That's it," Nistal replied with a snap of his fingers. "They look great. Shaved at least ten years off."

"Thank you," said Wilson, who was suddenly smarting a little less from Kyle Paulsen's barbs that morning.

"As long as neither of us has quit drinking, how about some Chianti?"

The former Senator pointed at his teeth and shook his head. "No red wine, no tea, and coffee only in moderation."

"And only then through a straw, right?"

"I hadn't thought of that," said Wilson, thinking it was a good idea.

The waitress had arrived at the table, and holding up two fingers, Nistal said, "Two Morettis, please."

The young woman left to go get their beers as the Russian continued. "Everything okay with your flight in?"

Wilson nodded. "No problem. Half-empty. Even landed a few minutes ahead of schedule."

"Good. By the way, don't let the simple décor fool you. The food here is fantastic. I highly recommend the linguini alle vongole. It's the best in all of Boston."

"What are we going to do?" the ex-Senator asked, trying to steer the conversation toward why they were meeting.

Nistal handed him a menu. "First, we're going to order lunch. Then we'll talk. Everything is going to be okay. Trust me."

"Glasses?" the waitress asked as she set the ice-cold bottles of Italian beer down on the table.

"Yes, please," Wilson replied.

The waitress produced two glasses, took their orders, and then headed off toward the kitchen.

Once she was gone, the Russian held up his bottle and said, "Cheers."

"Cheers," Wilson replied as he clinked his glass against it.

"America makes excellent beer," Nistal remarked after taking a sip, "but I do love an Italian beer every once in a while."

"Can we talk now?"

"Of course. You have my complete and undivided attention. I'll even set my beer down."

Wilson looked at him. "Why do I get the feeling that you're not taking this seriously?"

"I am," the handler admitted. "Just not as seriously as you."

"Why not?"

"Because you didn't do anything."

"What do you mean I 'didn't do anything'?" I've done a ton. Enough for them to lock me up for a very long time. I wouldn't do well in prison, Joe. I'm not built for that."

"You need to calm down," the Russian responded. "You're not going to prison."

"How do you know that?"

"Because, like I said, *you* didn't do anything. You didn't kill Burman."

"So, he *was* murdered. Did you do it?"

"Me?" Nistal asked. "Personally?"

"You, or your people?"

"Greg, we don't go around killing people. That's not what we do."

Wilson chuckled. "You seem to forget that I was on the Intelligence Committee. I know all too well what your people do. And have done."

The Russian needed to get control of his asset. Wilson's anxiety was getting the better of him. "Nobody knows what happened to Burman. It's possible he may have died by suicide."

"Give me a fucking break. I was with him Thursday night. The guy was riding high. He didn't have a care in the world. That's not somebody who goes home and ends it all."

Nistal shrugged. "Anthony Bourdain. Kate Spade. Depression is a terrible thing. Even fabulously wealthy, incredibly successful people can get worn down and choose suicide as the only way to escape their pain. Dimitri Burman is no exception."

Wilson didn't have a rebuttal for that. He had heard that depression could be so bad that even people who seemed to have everything to live for might see it as the only way out. "So what am I supposed to tell the FBI?"

"The truth."

"That dinner with Burman, at my club, was your idea?"

"Not the *whole* truth," the Russian clarified. "You stick with the broad brushstrokes. The less you lie, the less you need to remember. Burman wanted to hire your firm. Technology policy isn't really your thing, so you were ambivalent. The money was hard to say no to, so you had agreed to dinner to discuss things a bit more."

"That's it?"

"That's it. Again, tell the truth. Just not the whole truth."

"Okay," Wilson relented. "But as long as we're on the subject, why don't you tell *me* the truth. Why did you really want me to meet with Burman? And why at the Commodore?"

"First, you were very clear that once you hit ten million dollars, you were out. I thought Burman might make a pretty good client for you. Second, I wanted to make sure neither of you were under surveillance."

"You were there?"

Nistal nodded. "The best thing about your yacht club is that unless you have a boat at the dock, the only way in or out is via the front door."

"Or the service entrance."

"Which is practically attached to the front door. The point is that I could see everything from outside in the parking lot."

"And why would either of us be under surveillance?" Wilson asked.

"I'm good at what I do and that's because I take nothing for granted. As long as you and I are working together, I will always have your back. I protect my assets. Full stop.

"As for Burman, he made a lot of money in Russia. He still has a few investments there. In the current climate, that automatically raises eyebrows in the United States—particularly when it comes to sanctions. I wanted to see if the FBI had thought enough about it to have put a tail on him. The good news is that neither of you were being followed."

Wilson seemed relieved. "So the interview is just routine. The FBI is simply doing their due diligence."

"Exactly," said Nistal. "Burman was a critic of President Peshkov who met an untimely demise. Because it happened on American soil, it's only natural that the FBI would get involved. You're going to get a few boring questions, they'll thank you, and that will be that."

"Are you sure?"

"I'm positive. You had drinks and dinner, right?"

Wilson nodded.

"What did you talk about?"

"Local sports, a little bit about art, and then he wanted to sound me out on the new congressional majority and what their legislative agenda was likely to be. He wanted to know where they were headed on both foreign and domestic policy."

"And what did you tell him?"

Wilson laughed. "How much time do you have? Politics *is* my baseball. Once I get started, you pretty much need a binding UN resolution just to get me to shut up. I explained that I believed the U.S. was entering a deeper phase of isolationism.

"I told him they'd be focusing almost exclusively on key domestic policy issues like border security, manufacturing, education, and illicit drugs. Foreign policy items would absolutely not be front and center, unless they could be used in such a way as to draw attention to the majority's domestic policy agenda."

"And what did he have to say about your thoughts?"

"As you said," Wilson replied, "the man was no fan of Peshkov or anyone else at the Kremlin. He was quite clear that he believed America was shirking its responsibilities by not stepping up sanctions and bolstering support to Ukraine."

The Russian nodded. "Make sure to share that with the FBI."

"You're not worried about how that will look?"

"All I'm concerned about is you. And *you* have nothing to worry about. In fact, I find it fascinating that even though Burman was interested in hiring your firm to lobby for him on tech issues, all he talked about at dinner was Russia and Ukraine."

Wilson nodded. "Good point."

"What happened after dinner?"

"I went home. He went to the bar."

"Is that normal at your club, for a member to leave a guest? Is something like that allowed?"

"With all the money I spend there?" the ex-Senator asked. "Who cares? What's more, who's going to enforce a rule like that?"

Nistal put up his hands in mock surrender. "Don't shoot the messenger. I'm just asking for our friends at the FBI."

Wilson smiled and dialed it down. "The bar was rocking. Burman had been eyeing several women. He asked if I minded if he stayed for a nightcap. I told him to have a good time and to put any drinks on my tab."

"That was it?"

"That was it. I never saw or heard from him again."

The Russian smiled. "You're going to be fine. Wait until Monday morning and then call the FBI. Not too early. Don't do it first thing. Make them come to you at your office. Don't go to them. And meet in your actual office, not the conference room. You want them to see all the plaques and awards and framed American flags that'll remind them of your status as a former United States Senator."

"Should I have my lawyer there?"

Nistal shook his head. "Absolutely not. You were on the Intelligence Committee. You were a friend to the FBI. This is a family-style sit-down. You have nothing to fear or to hide."

"What if they ask me a question I can't answer?"

"How much did you and Burman have to drink?"

"We went through a couple of bottles of damn good wine."

"All charged to your account?"

Wilson nodded.

"There you go," the handler said. "You had a couple of martinis before you left your house for dinner and then you and Burman really tied one on at the club. You were entertaining a prospective client. All you have to say is 'I'm sorry, Agent So-and-so. I wish I could answer that question, but I just don't remember.'"

The ex-Senator smiled. "Thank you. I feel much better."

"Good. Now, I need a favor."

Wilson tightened up. "What is it?"

"Relax," the handler said. "Your boots. I want to get a pair just like them for my boss."

"Really?"

"Yes, really. The exact same. U.S. size ten. Can you make that happen?"

"Of course. I'd be happy to."

The Russian smiled. "Thank you. Gift giving is a thing back home. It goes a long way."

"I understand," said Wilson, taking a long sip of beer. Then, excusing himself, he stood up and asked where the restroom was.

Nistal pointed it out to him and joked, "There's a gun taped behind the toilet tank. I need that for my next meeting. Leave it, and you can take some cannoli with you."

Wilson smirked at the *Godfather* reference. Pressing his index finger to the side of his nose, he then slid it away and pointed at his handler, employing a movie reference of his own.

By the time he returned to the table, their lunch had been served. Business complete, they ate and made amiable conversation.

When the bill came, Nistal paid and, as was their custom, allowed Wilson to leave the restaurant alone.

Across the street, several buildings up, was a Boston Department of Public Works van. In the back, working an unrelated case, were a pair of FBI agents.

They were investigating a local organized crime syndicate and had been assigned to conduct surveillance on a pair of capos who happened to be eating lunch in the adjacent restaurant.

Looking through his camera, the junior agent asked, "Isn't that former Senator Greg Wilson?"

The senior agent raised his own camera. "It certainly is," he replied as he clicked away.

"What's he doing in Boston?"

"Hell if I know. Maybe he's banging a local porn star."

The junior agent laughed. "If he is, good for him. The talent in Boston is much better than in D.C."

That made the senior agent chuckle. "Funny to see him walk out all by himself. He doesn't strike me as the kind of guy who lunches alone. Politicians crave an audience. It's like oxygen to them."

"Let's keep our eyes peeled," the junior agent replied. "Who knows? Maybe he's seeing another married woman and she's going to slip out on her own."

Glad for a little excitement in their otherwise boring stakeout, the agents settled back and waited.

A few minutes later, a tall man in his forties with wavy brown hair exited the restaurant. Pretending to be searching for a cab, he looked up and down the block before turning to his right and heading south.

"Doesn't look like a porn star or a married woman to me," the junior agent said, peering through his camera.

"Me neither," the senior agent responded as he nevertheless, once again, clicked away.

# CHAPTER 19

"Excuse me?" Jenny Fields said, turning her attention back to her boss. "You tracked down his personal information *how*?"

"Don't give me any crap," Carolan said. "You know how I got it."

"Did a judge give it to you?" she pressed. "Did you receive it courtesy of a legally obtained warrant, tied with a pretty pink bow? Pretty pink bows are awesome. Almost as awesome as legally obtained warrants."

"For the record, you're still giving me crap, which I believe I requested you not to."

"Well, too fucking bad, Chief. What the hell are you doing?"

"You don't have to be here," Carolan responded.

"And miss being witness to you losing your job and getting the Bureau sued? Aw, hell no. I'm absolutely here for that."

"Nobody's going to get sued."

Fields laughed out loud. "Says the guy *with* a fucking law degree."

"Easy on the language, okay? I know you're upset, but let's lay off the cuss words."

"Out of everything that's going on here, it's the F-word that bothers you the most? We need to discuss your priorities."

"You want to discuss my priorities?" Carolan asked. "Here they are—we nail the Russians. Period."

Fields looked at him. "Did you ever play Monopoly as a kid?"

"Sure. Why?"

"Because you just skipped over *Constitution* Avenue, which has a Supreme Court's worth of hotels, and you're going to go straight to jail without collecting two hundred dollars or your FBI pension. You're breaking the damn law. We don't do that. *You* don't do that."

She was right. "Okay, fine. Yes. I've cut a couple of corners," he admitted. "But—"

Fields held up her hand and stopped him. "There is no *but* in our business. We are law enforcement officers. We *enforce* the law."

"In any other situation, yes, but—"

"In *every* situation," she declared. "That's what sets us apart. That's what makes the United States that shining city on the hill. We are the world's last greatest hope, because we do the right thing. And the right thing is *always* hard. If it wasn't, everyone would do it."

"You're right," he said. "I admit it."

"*But*," she replied, knowing he was going to offer some sort of justification.

"No buts. The Russians are waging a disinformation campaign against us. They're counting on the fact that we'll obey every one of our own laws. They're expecting us not to color outside the lines, even if it means doing so would save our country and put them in the fucking ground."

Fields's eyes went wide. "Now look who's using the F-word."

"Marquess of Queensberry Rules, the Geneva and Hague Conventions," he said, plowing forward, "what people never talk about is that those guidelines, those rulebooks, only matter when both sides agree to be bound by them."

"So, holding ourselves, and thereby America, to a higher standard doesn't matter?"

"Of course it matters," Carolan responded. "But only if we win."

"I'm sorry?"

"No one is going to care, especially not the citizens we're responsible for protecting, if we lose, but we did so honorably. A code of conduct is a wonderful thing to have, right up to the moment the enemy is burning our houses down and slaughtering our children. We're fighting with our arms and our legs tied behind our backs."

"If you don't like the rules," said Fields, "maybe it's time to find another game."

"Maybe you're right," the man agreed. "Maybe it is time for me to find another game. To be honest, there are days where I just don't know anymore. But I can tell you this with full certainty: today isn't one of those days."

"So, because you believe we're 'at war,' you're going to get your yippee-ki-yay on and violate the civil liberties of an American citizen, a journalist no less. Is that about right?"

"This guy," said Carolan as he pointed to the folder he was holding, "Mike Taylor, has a rap sheet. Three priors."

"All misdemeanors."

"He's also a white nationalist."

"Allegedly."

"That doesn't bother you?"

Fields looked at him. "Why? Because I'm Black? I don't care if the guy's an armband-wearing Nazi. If he's a law-abiding citizen, he's entitled to his rights. In fact, even if he breaks the law, he's still entitled to his applicable rights."

"What about the order of protection against him on behalf of a White House staffer?"

"That's serious, I will grant you that, but her job shouldn't play into this. She's his ex-fiancée. By all accounts, they had a volatile relationship."

"Which ended in the order of protection, which he violated the night of Burman's death."

"Because she happens to live in the same neighborhood as Burman and he came within five hundred feet of her apartment building? That's pretty weak sauce. A technicality at best."

Carolan raised an eyebrow. "What are laws if not a series of technicalities?"

"So, you want to use the supposed violation of the protection order to shake his tree and to see if anything falls out?"

"Yup."

"And the FBI's jurisdiction in this versus Metro PD is what?"

"The ex-fiancée is a federal employee. That gives us jurisdiction."

Fields shook her head. "You're stretching that one so thin, I can actually see through it. Next, you—"

"Like I said, you don't have to be here."

Holding up her hand, she said, "I'm not done yet."

Carolan quieted down and let her speak.

"Next, you used your contacts at his cell phone and email providers to give you a sneak peek into his records. Did you have to write up an exigent-threat letter on Bureau letterhead, or did they just hand you what you wanted?"

"No comment."

"All because this guy was at two scenes from our investigation and then posted photos of you on some whacko blog site? Is that about right?"

"Every piece of this is interconnected," he said. "Trust me."

"I trust you, *personally*. It's your judgment I'm really starting to worry about."

"How'd the guy know about the murder scene and the Commodore Yacht Club?"

"You said it yourself," she replied. "He's probably got a source inside D.C. Metro. Even so, that's what journalists do. They cultivate sources. If Metro has a problem with it, let them sort it out."

"What if his source isn't inside D.C. Metro? What if he's getting his information from somewhere else?"

"Like where? The Russians?"

Once again, Carolan raised an eyebrow.

"Even if he did, he's never going to admit that to you," Fields stated. "What's more, I'm guessing that if it was the Russians, they're smart enough not to have left a trail that the FBI could pick up just doing a search of phone and email records. Correct?"

Her boss nodded. "I only looked back over the last couple of days, but there wasn't anything there that looked suspicious."

"Yet here we are," she replied, nodding at the outside of the chubby, redheaded photographer's building. "You know it's not too late to pull the plug on this. I'll forget you ever told me about the phone and email records and we'll put this Mike Taylor character in our rearview mirror. That would be the smart thing to do."

"We're not doing that," Carolan stated. "This is just going to be a nice knock-and-talk."

"Which he'll be recording. You know that, right? I can already see the next headline on *The Public Truth*—FRUSTRATED FEDS FISH AS FRESH LEADS FIZZLE."

"That's not half-bad. If this crime-fighting job doesn't work out, you may have a career as a writer."

"Don't tempt me," Fields replied. "And just so we're *crystal* clear, I was against this from the jump, okay? I'm here solely to back you up."

"Duly noted," said Carolan as he put the car in park and turned off the ignition. "Let's go pay Internet Adolf a visit."

Fields rolled her eyes, got out of the vehicle, and walked up to the building with her boss.

A woman with a child in a stroller was on her way out and Carolan held the door for her. Savvy city person that she was, the woman paused to make sure the strangers weren't taking advantage of the situation to access the building announced.

When it became obvious that she wasn't going to move until she got some more information, Carolan flashed her his FBI credentials, along with a smile.

"Whoever it is, I hope you brought a warrant," the woman stated.

"Nothing like that," Fields offered. "We're here to transport a witness to court."

"On a Saturday," said the woman. "Right."

"Special session."

"Whatever," the woman replied, no longer interested. Adjusting the diaper bag over her shoulder, she pushed the stroller and walked away.

"She was fun," said Carolan, once the woman was out of earshot.

"Just be grateful she let us in," Fields replied. "I'm guessing you didn't have a plan beyond ringing Taylor's buzzer."

"I always have a plan," the man responded, tapping his jacket pocket. "Brought my picks. Just in case."

"Of course. Because what's breaking and entering at this point?"

Carolan pointed to the stairs. "After you. Third floor."

The stairwell smelled like a dirty, wet dog, which, unless there was one in residence, usually meant a building had a rodent problem. Carolan tried not to breathe too deeply. He hated rodents, especially rats.

At the third floor, they stepped into the dingy hallway and walked three doors down to Taylor's. Pausing, Carolan and Fields listened.

There was a TV on inside. The high-pitched whine suggested some sort of motor sport. In addition, there was a faint odor of weed. Carolan knocked.

It took a second to get a response. "Who is it?"

"FBI," Carolan responded. "Open up, Mr. Taylor."

"Hold on a moment," the voice responded, a bit shaken.

Fields looked at her boss and, imitating what she figured Taylor was doing inside, pantomimed spraying a ton of air freshener.

A good two minutes later, the chain was unlatched, the dead bolt was unlocked, and a rumpled Taylor opened the door.

He was wearing tattered sweatpants and a vintage Doobie Brothers T-shirt. The living room windows were open wide, the ceiling fan was on full blast, and a big hit of air freshener had just been dispersed. Nevertheless, it still smelled like marijuana.

The TV, though now muted, was tuned to the São Paolo Grand Prix from Brazil. Above a faux-leather couch hung a pair of mismatched duck hunting prints. On the opposite wall was a neon beer sign. There was an empty pizza box on the coffee table and an oversized aluminum water bottle with a rainbow-colored unicorn proclaiming, *I Hate People.*

If not for the odor, and a bit of redness to his eyes, you wouldn't have known that Taylor had been smoking pot. "What do you want?" the red-headed man asked.

"We'd like to have a chat," Carolan replied. "May we come in?"

"A chat about what?"

"I think you know what."

"If this is about publishing photos of you," said Taylor, "I was completely within my rights. Public place. Freedom of the press. You're not going to intimidate me."

"That's not why we're here. We just want to talk."

"You keep saying that, but you refuse to identify what you want to talk about. I'm not interested. Have a nice day."

When Taylor went to close the door, Carolan leaned in and put his considerable bulk against it, preventing it from budging.

"What's your interest in Dimitri Burman?" the FBI man asked.

"Same as yours," Taylor replied. "Now, would you mind moving away from my door?"

"What were you doing outside Burman's building two nights ago?"

"You know what I was doing. You saw me. I was taking photos."

"How'd you know something worth photographing was going on?"

"I got a tip."

"A tip from who?" Fields asked.

"None of your business."

"And at the Commodore Yacht Club?" Carolan asked.

"I got another tip."

"Look at you," said Fields. "You're piling up more tips than a hooker at a leper colony."

Taylor ignored her and kept his focus on Carolan. "I'm done talking. Now get away from my door before I call the cops."

"I don't think you want to call the cops, Mr. Taylor."

"And why's that?"

Carolan removed a copy of the order of protection from his jacket pocket and asked, "Do you know what this is?"

Slowly, Taylor nodded.

"Part of the investigation into Dimitri Burman's death required that we examine security camera footage from other buildings in the neighborhood. Your former fiancée lives not too far from Burman's place, doesn't she?"

Once again, Taylor nodded.

"After you got done taking pictures at Mr. Burman's, did you happen to walk past your ex's building? Did you maybe use that long lens of yours to try to see if she was home? If she was upstairs alone or with someone?"

Taylor didn't respond.

"Because you know," Carolan continued, "that would be a violation of the protective order. You could be in some serious trouble."

"Look," said the redheaded man, "I don't want to go back to court."

"You wouldn't just be going to court. You'd be going to jail."

"But on the bright side," interjected Fields, "a guy like you would be on the receiving end of a lot of tips. If you know what I mean."

This time, Taylor did look at her. Then he quickly shifted his nervous gaze back to Carolan. "Can we talk? Off the record?"

The FBI man nodded. "If it's truly off the record—no recordings and none of this gets published—then yes."

Taylor pulled his iPhone from his sweatpants pocket. Holding it up for both agents to see, he stopped the recording and then fully deleted the file.

# CHAPTER 20

With Harvath's help, the Ukrainians back at the school were victorious, defeating the last of the Russians who had been attacking their position.

In the immediate aftermath, they topped up their ammo and assessed their situation. The news about Oleh's death hit hard. He had been well-liked among his comrades. He was one of the youngest in their group, and they had seen it as their duty to watch over him. They understood that there had been nothing that Harvath could do. They didn't blame him. More to the point, they appreciated that Harvath had finished the sniper off on Oleh's behalf. A small team prepared to retrieve Oleh's body.

The bulk of the soldiers carried out the task of sweeping the village, searching for any Russian soldiers who might still be alive.

They found an old barn where the Russians had set up camp. There were a few supplies there, enough to hold them over until they could be reinforced, which wasn't going to happen until the day after tomorrow at the earliest.

"What do you mean 'reinforced'?" Harvath asked.

"Our orders are to hold the bridge," replied Givi, their APC driver, who had managed to raise superiors via his field radio.

"Not to get these men to the front?"

Givi pointed at all the dead Russian soldiers in the street and said, "This is the front now."

While not happy with the change of plans, Harvath understood the situation. It was the nature of war. Bridges were valuable. If any others in the area had fallen under enemy control or had been destroyed, this bridge might be the only one left connecting the Ukrainians with the larger battlefield. They couldn't let the Russians have it. But that left Harvath with a problem.

"I can't wait for your reinforcements to get here," he said. "How do I get to my men? It needs to be tonight."

Givi thought for a minute. "Obviously, our APC is not available because you blew it up."

Harvath held up his hand to stop the man. "Technically, it was the Russians."

"*Technically*, you are correct."

"So, what are my other options?"

"There are two Russian vehicles inside the barn."

"Tell me one is a tank," said Harvath.

"No. There are no tanks. Only a cargo truck and a small, off-road utility vehicle."

"I'll take it."

"You can't take it," said Givi. "I need both here. But I will make you a deal."

"What is it?"

"Since you are Special Services Group, I assume you have experience blowing things up."

Harvath nodded. "I've blown up a few things over my career."

"Any bridges?"

"One or two. Why?"

"Then you know what you're doing. None of us have that kind of experience."

"I don't understand," said Harvath. "You're supposed to protect this bridge, not blow it up."

"Exactly. We're going to need to use it. And as I said when we first arrived, I need to make sure that it hasn't been rigged. If we can find a boat and get some flashlights, would you be willing to go underneath and check it out?"

Harvath wasn't crazy about yet another delay. Glancing at his watch, he tried to estimate how much time this new task would take.

"If you do this," the Ukrainian added, "I will personally drive you to your men. What do you think? Do we have a deal?"

"For Oleh," said Harvath, sticking out his hand.

"For Oleh," Givi replied, shaking it.

.    .    .

The Ukrainians found an old, aluminum fishing boat, painted puke green, from a bombed-out garage at the edge of the village that somehow had escaped damage. In the fading light, it looked seaworthy, but Harvath couldn't be positive until he got it in the water.

Accompanying him was one of the larger soldiers, whose job was to man the oars and keep the boat steady against the river's current.

They unfastened the soft top of the off-road utility vehicle—a jeep-like, Soviet-era UAZ-469, laid the boat across the back, and drove it down to the water, upstream from the bridge.

Once satisfied that it would stay afloat, Harvath and his oarsman shoved off.

Despite being in a hurry, Harvath forced himself to slow down and take his time. He, after all, was going to be one of the first people to cross this bridge. It was in his literal best interest to make sure it was safe.

Coming to that conclusion, however, was a colossal pain in the ass. The amount of wiring that ran beneath the structure was mind-boggling. There were years' worth of electrical lines, telephone lines, and what looked like an old telegraph cable. What there wasn't, were explosives.

After having worked his way across the river and back, Harvath was confident that the bridge was safe.

Dragging the boat ashore, he discovered that they had another problem to deal with.

"We can't find any paint," said Givi.

"For what?"

"The UAZ. When we capture Russian vehicles, we repaint them—at least partially, so people know they belong to the good guys."

"Don't you have a Ukrainian flag or something we can drape over the hood?"

"We did," said Givi, mimicking the explosion of the APC, then adding, "But not anymore."

"Not my fault," Harvath reminded him.

"I know. The Russians did it. And they're continuing to be an additional part of our problem."

"In what way?"

"As we saw, our intelligence about this area was not as fresh as it should be. We don't know if there are more Russians between us and the battlefield."

"Which means," said Harvath, "driving a Russian vehicle could be a good thing."

"Or a very bad thing. As the reports of what happened here circulate, everyone's going to be on edge. It's getting dark. And nighttime is the worst. You're tired and your mind starts playing tricks. You begin to see and hear Russians everywhere. We could be mistaken for the enemy."

"Which, with us rolling around in one of their vehicles, could also happen in broad daylight," said Harvath. "What's Plan B?"

Givi, again, thought for a moment and then said, "In the Kherson region, our soldiers have been painting a white cross on their vehicles. But we don't have any white paint, either."

"I'll handle the paint," Harvath replied. "You radio forward and let them know we're coming. Tell them the type of vehicle we are driving and that ours will have white crosses on the hood and doors. Make sure that they know any patrols or checkpoints need to let us pass."

As Givi got on his radio, Harvath hopped in the UAZ and drove it back to the school.

In the past, there had been some small, tradecraft-style elements he had used to identify his vehicles—things like a ballcap or a certain colored folder on the dash, a chem light behind the grille, or a special LED in the corner of the windshield. But those had been civilian vehicles and they hadn't been in a war zone. He wanted something as unmistakable as possible.

Back at the school, it took him several minutes to track down everything he was looking for. There was neither an art classroom nor an art supplies cabinet. While he had held out hope that there might be some children's paint lying around, it was only a slim hope. Finding some, especially under these circumstances, would have been like hitting the lottery.

On the other hand, there was one item that was in good supply— chalk. Gathering up every piece he could find, he placed them in a plastic bag and pulverized them with the butt of his pistol, creating a fine dust.

In a bucket, he mixed what appeared to be some sort of talcum powder with water and glue. Then he added the chalk and adjusted the mix of ingredients as he stirred and came to the consistency he wanted.

While he allowed it to rest, he searched out something he could use to apply the paint to the vehicle. He found an old sponge in the school's bathroom. It would have to do.

After painting the symbol on the hood, doors, and canvas roof of the vehicle, he drove over to the barn to meet up with Givi.

There was one additional item he wanted. By the time he got there, the Ukrainian soldier already had it waiting.

"That's it?" Harvath asked, looking at the aged device sitting on a table.

"Be grateful," Givi replied. "Most Russian units don't have any night-vision capability at all."

To help them avoid enemy detection, Harvath wanted to do as much of the drive as they could with the lights off. The only way that would be possible was with night vision.

"How are you going to hold that device, steer the vehicle, and shift gears?"

"You're going to shift for me," said Givi.

"And on your way back?"

"I'll figure something out."

Harvath didn't like it, but Givi was a soldier. He knew the risks.

After confirming a handful of important points on the map, they loaded their gear into the UAZ.

"Good job on the crosses," the Ukrainian said, admiring Harvath's work. "Where'd you find the paint?"

"I didn't find it. I made it."

"You *made* paint?"

Harvath nodded. "After demolition, the most important instruction at Special Services Group is art class. You should see my sculptures."

Givi laughed and they headed out.

Driving across the bridge, neither man said a word until they got to the other side. Then it was Harvath who broke the silence. "Like I said, totally safe."

"I never doubted it," Givi responded, peering through his night-vision device. "Third gear, please."

Harvath helped shift and soon enough they had left the bridge and the village behind. They were in the open countryside. As the road straightened out, Givi asked Harvath to shift into fourth, the UAZ's highest gear. Once that was complete, his assistance would not be needed for a while.

Using the red beam feature on his flashlight, Harvath followed along on a map Givi had taken off one of the dead Russians. Only the bridge had been marked. Other than that, there was no useful Russian intelligence on it.

During daylight hours, the drive would have taken about a half hour. Driving under low-light conditions, however, especially once they got into the windy portions in the hills, meant the trip would take almost an hour. Harvath had slung his rifle in front of him, at the ready.

Givi didn't mind small talk and so Harvath engaged the man. He had a wife and three kids back home in western Ukraine. He was a truck driver by profession. The day the Russians invaded, he enlisted.

He had requested to be placed as close to the front as possible. The soldiers going toe-to-toe with the Russians were the ones he wanted to support. He had never been in a dismounted firefight until this afternoon. It was the first time he had ever fired his personal weapon in combat.

"How did it feel?" Harvath asked him.

The Ukrainian answered honestly, "Terrifying."

"It gets easier."

"I don't know that I want it to. Shooting other human beings, even Russians, should always be difficult. It shouldn't be like a video game.

You should have to think about what you're doing. You should have to weigh every life you take."

It was a deep, rather philosophical statement, especially coming from a truck driver who admitted to having dropped out of school before the seventh grade. But while traits like morality, dignity, and integrity could be incubated in a classroom, they weren't dependent upon how many years you spent in one. Life offered plenty of experiences through which a person could develop their character. Harvath could only imagine how much Givi, as an over-the-road trucker, had seen.

They continued to make small talk until they reached the hills. At that point, the Ukrainian needed to fully focus. Not only were the roads tricky, but the occasional remains of ruined military vehicles were a reminder that they were getting ever closer to the front. Harvath kept his weapon tight to his chest.

Fifteen minutes into the hills, he saw a flash of light up ahead. "What was that?"

Givi brought the UAZ to a stop and peered through the night-vision device. "Looks like a checkpoint."

"Ukrainian?"

"I can't tell."

Using his red light to illuminate the map, Harvath pointed at it and said, "This is where we are. According to what we were told, there isn't a checkpoint until here, in ten klicks."

"It could be Russians. They have been known to set up fake checkpoints. Sometimes it's to interdict troops or supplies. Other times to collect intelligence. Sometimes both."

"Call it in. Let's see if we can verify what's going on."

Givi picked up his radio and tried to reach the element expecting them up at the front. No matter how many times he tried, nor how he angled the radio's antenna out the window, all he could hear was static.

"Bad terrain," he said. "I can't get a clear signal. What do you want to do?"

Explaining his plan, Harvath traced the road in front of them with his finger and picked the spot he wanted to be dropped. Givi nodded and got the UAZ moving.

Four minutes later, the two vehicles blocking the road ahead of him flipped on their high beams and a pair of soldiers ordered him to stop and exit his vehicle without his weapon. The Ukrainian did as he was ordered.

When the soldiers got close enough, the first thing he noticed was that they were wearing the same uniform he was. While one kept him covered, the other went to investigate his UAZ. Holding his hand up against the glare of the headlights, he could make out at least four other figures, all holding rifles, spaced a good distance apart from each other.

"Who else are you traveling with?" the soldier asked.

"No one else," Givi replied. "This is a medical transport. I am going to pick up wounded men from the front."

The soldier searching the UAZ touched one of the freshly painted crosses and held up his gloved hand to show his colleague the paint that had come off.

"Where did this vehicle come from?" the soldier continued.

Givi shrugged and replied, "Russia?"

"Where did *you* get it?"

"We found it."

"Found it where?"

"About fifty kilometers back. Near the spot where our APC broke down. What's the problem?" asked the Ukrainian, who then raised his voice as if he was getting frustrated. "No one told you I was coming?"

"Calm down," the soldier said.

"Calm down? There are wounded men at the front. Men who need to be evacuated. Every second we waste is a second off their lives. *Fucking shit.*"

From his position in the trees behind the checkpoint, Harvath had heard the conversation, but hadn't been able to understand it. At least not until Givi had used the code words at the end—*Suka blyat.* These were not Ukrainians. They were Russians and the checkpoint was bogus.

Slinging his rifle over his back, Harvath drew his knife and crept toward the nearest soldier.

Approaching him from behind, he covered the man's mouth with his left hand and used his right to press his blade against his throat. Then, very quietly, he whispered in the man's ear the phrase that Zira had taught him: "Say *palianytsia*."

Partially uncovering the man's mouth, he listened, but instead of saying the passphrase in Ukrainian, the man began to babble in Russian. Harvath sliced his throat and dropped him to the ground.

With the soldiers focused on what was happening in the headlights of their vehicles, they paid no attention to other threats that might be lurking in the dark.

Harvath's task for now was to eliminate the rest of the Russians without letting any harm come to Givi.

If he'd had a suppressed .22 pistol with subsonic ammunition, he might have risked putting bullets in the three remaining soldiers behind the checkpoint vehicles. The two Russians with Givi probably wouldn't have heard a thing. But as it was, even his suppressed Galil made a distinct crack when fired. The moment that Russians heard it, it would have been like a starting pistol going off. The race for cover, and maybe even to put a bullet in Givi, would have been on. Harvath would have to stick with his knife.

The sloppiness of the Russian soldiers was another testament to the poorly trained fodder that Peshkov was feeding into the maw of the war.

Harvath grabbed the next soldier from behind and plunged his blade into the notch at the base of the man's skull, the foramen magnum, and twisted his knife like a corkscrew, severing his spinal cord and, with a slap to the pommel of the blade, turning out his lights for good.

He took the next soldier out by coming over the top of the man's right shoulder, plunging his blade through the base of his neck, and executing a flick of his wrist that sliced fully through the man's throat, severing both his arteries. Lowering him to the ground, Harvath left him to silently bleed out in the road while he stalked his final Russian soldier.

This man was a challenge. He seemed nervous. He was pacing—two feet forward, two feet back. Making him an even more difficult target was the fact that he kept changing his orientation. One moment he was watching the interrogation taking place in the headlights, the next he was looking off into the woods on his side of the road. Getting the drop on this Russian pinball might not be possible. There was, however, something else Harvath could try, but his timing would have to be perfect. Givi's life depended on it.

The best way to kill three birds was to have more than one stone. In Harvath's case, the best way was to have plenty of stones and a frag grenade.

Staying out of sight, he leaned against one of the checkpoint vehicles and prepared his rifle. Normally, a shot like this, out in the middle of nowhere without a night-vision scope, would be next to impossible. But thanks to the Russians having left their high beams on, he liked his odds.

Reaching into his pouch, he pulled out a frag. Peering behind the vehicle, he saw the nervous Russian soldier still pacing nearby—two feet forward, two feet back; facing the interrogation, turning to look off into the woods.

Resetting himself, Harvath steadied his breathing. If there was one thing he had learned, it was that once the pin was out of the grenade, the sooner you got it away from you, the better. He was about to violate that lesson—big-time.

To be clear, pulling the pin didn't initiate the fuse inside the grenade. The pin was merely a safety device. Releasing the lever—the concave handle on the side of the grenade—that had been previously held in place by the pin was what got the party started. Its biggest drawback, though, was its unpredictability.

Once the lever had been released, the time to detonation could be anywhere from two to six seconds. That was why there had been so many movie and TV scenes depicting a grenade landing in a foxhole, only to have soldiers pick it up and throw it back at an enemy position, where it then detonated. That was what could happen if you had a slow burner.

If you had a fast burner and let go of the lever without immediately tossing it, you could lose your hand, your arm, half your body, or even your life. The bottom line was that it was a crapshoot; totally uncertain. There was only one way to find out.

He pulled the pin, released the lever, and counted. *One. Two. Three.* Then he lobbed the grenade through the air at the pacing Russian.

The device made a perfect arc and detonated just as it was about to hit the ground in front of him, killing him instantly.

Before the other two Russians could figure out what had happened, Harvath was on his rifle, pressing his trigger.

He took out the soldier who was interrogating Givi first. The round went right through the man's right eye. The second soldier, the one who had been examining the UAZ, was harder to hit because the moment the grenade had detonated, he dove for cover behind the vehicle.

Harvath hammered the UAZ with rounds of 7.62 from his Galil, allowing Givi a chance to escape.

The Ukrainian ran toward him and didn't stop running until he was behind the checkpoint vehicle next to him.

Picking up an AK-47 from one of the dead Russians, Givi then took over laying down withering cover fire on the UAZ. As he did, Harvath pulled the last two fragmentation grenades from his pouch, pulled their pins, and sent them hurtling in the direction of the last Russian soldier.

The added distance meant that Harvath didn't have to worry about how long they would take to detonate. And while he was no Tom Brady, the throws were pretty damn good.

One of the frags landed right behind the vehicle, and the other landed atop the soft canvas roof. Both detonated at the same moment, shredding the Russian with shrapnel and taking him out of the fight.

It was also the final nail in the coffin for the UAZ, which had already taken heavy damage from their rifle rounds.

As it burned, Givi said to Harvath, "That's the second vehicle of mine you have destroyed."

"In all fairness," Harvath replied, inserting a fresh magazine into his Galil, "I think the Russians should get the blame for this one, too."

The Ukrainian took a step back and looked at the two checkpoint vehicles. One was a Polish armored personnel carrier known as an AMZ Dzik, capable of carrying eight people. The other was a Ukrainian light armored vehicle known as a Novator. It was based on the Ford F-550 chassis and could carry five. Both had been clearly marked as Ukrainian military.

There was no telling where the Russians had gotten them, but as the men inspected the vehicles, it was obvious that they had seen heavy fighting. The dried blood inside and outside both left little to the imagination as to what had become of their crews.

Needing a similar vehicle to replace his ruined APC, Givi opted for the Dzik, while Harvath took the Novator. They divided the supplies, including the extra jerry cans of diesel fuel the Russians had been carrying, and then fired up their rides and headed for the front.

Finally, Harvath would be linking up with his team. He just hoped he wasn't too late.

# CHAPTER 21

Ten kilometers later, Givi, in the lead vehicle, navigated them through the legitimate Ukrainian checkpoint.

He had to spend a few minutes explaining what had happened and why they weren't driving the Russian UAZ with white crosses. After the soldiers searched both vehicles and confirmed with their superiors that everything was okay, they allowed the men to pass.

After two more kilometers, they arrived at a long strip of forest that ran just behind the front line. Bringing the Novator to a stop, Harvath killed the engine and climbed out.

The farther up into the hills they had climbed, the cooler the air had gotten. It was now downright cold. Though it was dark and most of the fighting had fallen off for the night, random exchanges of gunfire, back and forth across the line, could still be heard.

The air was heavy with the smell of pine. In any other situation, after the day he'd had, Harvath would have sat down, closed his eyes, and breathed it in. But this was a war zone, not a camping trip. He remained alert, his hands on the rifle slung in front of him.

Givi had parked nearby and was met by a small team of infantry. Their commander wanted to debrief over what had happened down in the village, as well as what had happened at the fake checkpoint. That much Russian activity on this side of the line was an issue that needed to be dealt with.

Before leaving, the man came over to say good-bye. "Thank you," said Givi, extending his hand.

Harvath shook it. "You're welcome. Thank you for getting me here. I'm sorry about blowing up your APC *and* the UAZ."

"You didn't blow them up," the man replied with a smile. "Technically, it was the Russians."

Harvath smiled back. "Stay safe, Givi."

"You too, Captain."

Harvath watched as the truck driver-cum-soldier rejoined the infantry troops and headed off toward a makeshift observation post. He silently wished the best for Givi. He was a good man pursuing a just and noble cause. He prayed that the guy would be successful. For his part, all that was left for Harvath now was to wait for his men to arrive.

He had been in contact via radio. The men had been in a rough stretch of trench where the fighting had been intense. Though things had died down, they didn't want to leave their comrades until it was safe to do so.

Harvath understood where the men were coming from. In addition, Givi had made some inquiries and had explained that fresh troops were already being sent up to that position. It wouldn't be too long. He decided to take advantage of the situation.

Fishing out one of the Ukrainian MREs, or meals ready to eat, from the truck, he sliced open the top of the pouch with his knife and tried to figure out what was inside.

It was a twenty-four-hour field ration, which meant that it contained three meals, plus powdered beverages and snacks meant to get a combat soldier through a full day. It came in a hefty, waterproof green pouch that weighed about five pounds.

He found three smaller pouches inside—one for each meal—along with a pouch containing flameless ration heaters that allowed you to warm things up without exposing yourself to the enemy via an open flame.

His appetite, due to having pushed so much adrenaline through his system, wasn't that big. He knew, though, that he needed to eat something and opened the smallest of the pouches, which was the breakfast meal.

Setting the main course aside, he pulled out two snacks—a small dark chocolate bar and a pack of dried apricots. They were exactly what he needed. He washed down his bites with water from a large plastic bottle, all the while keeping his eyes and ears on the trees. He was on his last piece of apricot when he saw his men appear.

They looked much different than their service photos. They were dirty and tired. They were also leaner than when they had signed up and joined the fight.

The war had taken its toll—even on them, volunteers who had willingly chosen to be here and who could walk away at any point and return to the safety of their respective countries and homes. Harvath couldn't help but wonder if there wasn't something extra the war took out of people like them.

Jacks, the thirty-eight-year-old ex–British Army Second Lieutenant who resembled a rugby player, was first, followed by Krueger, the very fit, thirty-four-year-old, no-longer-active U.S. Marine Corps Lance Corporal. Next was the far-too-skinny, twenty-seven-year-old ex–Canadian Army Corporal who went by the call sign Biscuit. Bringing up the rear was Hookah, the forty-two-year-old former U.S. Army Staff Sergeant with the big ears and the boxer's nose.

All the men knew better than to salute him. Had an opportunistic Russian sniper been in range, it would have identified Harvath as an officer and made him an instant target.

"Good to meet you, Captain," said Jacks as he flipped up his night-vision goggles, stepped forward, and shook hands with Harvath. He then quickly introduced the three other men.

"What's this mission of yours?" Hookah asked. "Why are we getting pulled?"

"No one has told you anything?" Harvath replied.

"Zip. Zilch. Zero."

"It's a hostage rescue. American civilian. Female. Twenty-five years old. She was volunteering at an orphanage east of Kharkiv."

"How long ago was she taken?" Krueger asked.

"Four days ago."

"Do you know where she's being held?"

"We do not."

"With all due respect," said Hookah, "I didn't come here to do hostage rescue. I came here to kill Orcs."

Orcs were a hideous, humanoid monster popularized in J. R. R. Tolkien's *The Lord of the Rings* and a popular pejorative adopted by the Ukrainians for Russian soldiers.

"Do you know who has her?" Jacks asked, pivoting away from his colleague's borderline insubordination.

"We believe it's a unit from the Wagner Group. They call themselves the Ravens."

Biscuit let out a low whistle. "That's the Bags detachment."

Harvath was unfamiliar with the term. "'Bags'?" he repeated.

"Yeah. Shitbags, douche bags, scumbags, and nut bags."

"Rest assured that when we get done with them, the only bags that'll be left are going to be body bags."

"Ooh-rah," Krueger replied, employing the Marines' battle cry.

"How many of these Ravens are there?" Hookah asked, still not sold.

"Based on the reports I've seen," Harvath replied, "anywhere from twenty to thirty."

Jacks looked at Hookah and said, "That's a lot of Orcs."

"Where's the rest of the team?" the man asked.

"This is it," Harvath stated. "This is all the Ukrainians could spare."

Hookah shook his head. "I don't like this. It sounds like a suicide operation to me."

"I can't force you to come. But what I can do is take you off the line for a night, offer you a hot meal, and give you a full debrief on everything the Ravens have done. After that, it's up to you. Either you join me, and we go after them, or you go right back to whatever you were doing before I got here. Sound fair?"

"Throw in a hot shower," quipped Biscuit, "and I'm all in."

"I'm hoping they've got hot water where we're going, but I can't promise anything."

"We're not going back to the FOB at Staryi Saltiv?"

"No, we're going to a village, about thirty klicks from here, called Kolodyazne."

"What's in Kolodyazne?" asked Jacks.

"It's the last place the Ravens are known to have struck."

"If they've already been and gone," replied Hookah, "what's the point of us going?"

"I'll explain once we get there. So, if you're coming, toss your gear in the truck and let's mount up. If not, good luck with the war."

As Hookah, Krueger, and Biscuit conferred, Harvath pulled Jacks aside. He assumed that, as a fellow officer, he could speak frankly with him.

"Obviously, there was a breakdown in communication somewhere. You guys were *never* briefed?"

Jacks shook his head. "All we were told was that we'd be assisting a Special Services Group operation. We figured it might be some hit-and-run thing behind enemy lines. Some sabotage or something like that."

"And you weren't given a list of gear and equipment to stockpile?"

"No. We were not."

"What can we get our hands on?"

"Ammo," Jacks responded, "grenades, maybe some medical supplies."

"What about Javelins?"

"That kind of request happens back at the FOB and has to be put through by—"

"A company commander," said Harvath, repeating back what the Supply Sergeant had originally told him. "What about night vision? I lost my goggles in an attack this morning, along with my thermal scope."

"Krueger has a thermal scope in his pack he'd probably lend you. As far as NVGs are concerned, though, I don't know what to tell you. Next to body armor and high-end rifle optics, night-vision goggles are a hot commodity over here."

"If he's in, I'll ask him. Thank you."

"We're in," said Krueger as he walked back over with the other two men.

"At least as far as Kolodyazne," stated Hookah.

"Then it's unanimous," Jacks confirmed. "Mount up."

•     •     •

After a resupply of ammo and grenades, they headed downhill, past the checkpoint, and back into farmland. Harvath kept his headlights off and piloted the vehicle via the Novator's onboard night-vision cameras. Jacks sat next to him riding shotgun and the rest of the team sat in the backseat. Everyone kept their weapons close at hand, ready to go if the enemy made contact.

The men were exhausted, yet too wired from the stress of combat to sleep. Unlike Givi, none of them wanted to talk. They rode in silence, save for occasional words from Jacks, who was helping Harvath navigate.

Despite heavy shelling, the road was in relatively decent shape and Harvath was able to make good time.

When they arrived in Kolodyazne, he knew exactly what building he was looking for. Even though the buildings around it had sustained serious damage, the Ukrainian Baroque architecture of the Mother of God Convent had been left completely unscathed. To the nuns who comprised its inhabitants, it must have seemed like a miracle; that they had been blessed by the Holy Mother herself, at least right up until the moment the Ravens had arrived.

Harvath pulled through the once ornate, wrought-iron gates, which had been ripped from their hinges, and parked on the convent grounds, nearest to the main building with its blue, onion-shaped domes.

Bundled up against the night air, a pair of old men with sawed-off shotguns in their laps sat guard outside the convent's large double doors.

"Wait here," Harvath told his team. "I'll be back in a minute."

Leaving his rifle, he exited the truck and cautiously approached the men. In broken Russian, he explained who he was and pointed to the patch on his uniform. It was the logo for the GUR and depicted an Owl with outstretched wings dangling a sword over a map of Russia. On multiple levels, not the least of which being that Russia's military intelligence unit, the GRU, employed a logo of a bat, and owls eat bats, the logo had been called an epic troll of the Kremlin by the Ukrainians.

Harvath told the old villagers that he was very sorry about what had happened at the convent. He and his team were here to pay their respects and gather evidence in order to bring the perpetrators to justice.

"Give them Ukrainian justice," one of the men said, hefting his shotgun.

The other man just looked at Harvath and concurred by drawing his thumb across his throat like a knife.

Harvath nodded. These men didn't want justice. Not in the conventional sense. They wanted revenge. The more painful for the evildoers, the better.

After the men pointed out the small support building that had been prepared for him, he returned to the vehicle to get the team.

"This is where we're spending our night off?" asked Krueger.

Harvath nodded. "But first I need to show you something."

"I sure hope it's a shower," replied Biscuit.

Reading the solemnity on Harvath's face, Hookah said, "It's not a shower, is it?"

"No," Harvath answered as he retrieved his rifle. "It isn't."

"What is it, then?" asked Jacks. "What are we supposed to see in there?"

"A war crime."

# CHAPTER 22

I t was a scene of abject horror. The screams of the nuns, though now silent, seemed to echo psychically throughout the structure. It was something so malevolent that even Dante himself would have rejected it for *Inferno*.

From the moment the two old men opened the doors and stood aside, the blood was everywhere—on the stone floors, the plastered walls, even some of the arched ceilings. There had been a great, splashing orgy of barbarity and terror here. The Ravens had unleashed hell on earth and had chosen a place of solitude and worship in which to do it.

Scattered braziers loaded with coal that had been used to heat fireplace tools as instruments of torture were still warm to the touch. According to the evidence shown to Harvath on the train from Poland, the attack had happened only two nights ago. After a local Ukrainian Army unit on its way to the front had confirmed the depraved attack, the convent had been sealed and a local guard posted. This was the first time it had been opened since.

The Army unit had transmitted their photographs back to its headquarters and those photos, along with the unit's report, had made it to the GUR. That was a big piece of what the man with the briefcase had shared with him.

But even having viewed the photographs, Harvath knew he wasn't fully prepared for the actual scene.

As they moved toward the expansive chapel, he steeled himself. No matter how much unspeakable violence he had seen over his career, when it was visited upon the innocent and most defenseless—especially women and children—it still had a profound impact on him.

The team stepped through the wide entrance and into the chapel together. To a man, no one spoke. No one could speak. Not even Harvath. They had been rendered fully speechless. They could do nothing but gawk at the carnage.

It was Biscuit, the youngest in their group, who finally broke the spell. Rushing back out into the hallway, he puked his guts out in a corner.

The others stood transfixed—not just by the amount of blood, but by the bodies of twelve naked nuns who had been slaughtered and hung upside down from the ceiling.

Their bodies showed significant forms of trauma, including burns akin to branding marks, as well as different types of welts resulting from lashes, indicating that they had been beaten with objects such as belts and electrical cords. Many had had large pieces of scalp torn out. Some had been disemboweled. All showed signs of severe sexual abuse.

Though a majority appeared to have suffered blunt-force trauma to the head or facial area, it was hard to say what the precise cause of death was, as each of the corpses had also had its throat slashed.

The floor of the chapel was slick with blood. How additional blood could be found all the way up to the front doors of the convent was unknowable. If Harvath had to guess, his money would have been on the Ravens having chased their petrified victims throughout the building—torturing and then killing them before dragging their bodies back to the chapel.

While Biscuit was still retching out in the hall, Hookah was the first to actually speak. "What kind of sick motherfucker does something like this? This isn't even human. This is straight-up, straight-out-of-hell evil."

"Why this place?" asked Jacks. "Of all places. Why here? Why nuns?"

"Because they're Orcs," said Krueger. "It's what they do. And whoever these Ravens are, they're the worst of all the Orcs."

"You're right," Harvath replied. "They are Orcs and the Ravens *are* the worst of them. But there's another reason they were here. They chose this place because the nuns had a secret. They were hiding something."

"What the fuck could they have been hiding that warranted all of this?" Hookah asked, looking up at the suspended bodies.

"Nothing warrants any of this," Harvath responded. "Nothing at all. But they weren't here by coincidence. They were here looking for something and they were prepared to do whatever needed to be done to get it."

"So, what the hell was it?"

Backing out of the chapel, Harvath motioned for the men to follow him.

They waited a moment for Biscuit, who, no longer throwing up, was resting his head against the cold stone wall. Helping him to the front door, they left him with the guards outside to take in some fresh air.

It didn't take Harvath long to find the entrance to the basement, its heavy lock blown to bits.

They followed the stairs down and felt the temperature change as they descended into the bowels of the earth beneath the convent.

Multiple side rooms lined the low, hand-carved hall. All their doors had been left open and the contents of each room had been violently upended. Someone had definitely been searching for something down here.

The final room on the right-hand side was the ultimate target. Inside, a false wall had been breached, revealing a small chamber just beyond. Harvath stepped inside and swept his light from side to side.

Bare wooden pallets, placed along the floor, were all that the chamber now contained.

Jacks looked around. "What's this?"

"It was supposed to be a safe haven."

"A safe haven for what?" he asked as Hookah and Krueger joined them.

"When it became obvious that Russia intended to invade, Ukraine set up a very special type of resistance—an underground railroad of sorts, but for art.

"Museum directors, gallery owners, even private collectors all wanted to make sure that the country's soul, its artistic and cultural heritage, wouldn't be plundered and wiped out by the Russians. To make sure, they arranged for the nation's most important and valuable pieces to be hidden away.

"Across the country, they identified what needed to be saved—

illuminated manuscripts, sacred icons, even pieces of modern art—then appointed citizens to help smuggle and protect those pieces. The Mother of God Convent was one of the secret repositories."

"What, specifically, were they hiding?" asked Krueger.

Harvath removed the list entrusted to him by the man with the briefcase. Cross-referencing the location with the specific item or items it was supposed to house, he replied, "A section of the Bohorodchany Iconostasis—a very big, very elaborate altarpiece."

"How big?"

"When fully assembled, forty-two feet high by thirty-six feet wide. It was created in the late 1600s by an artist named Kondzelevych along with twenty carpenters, joiners, goldsmiths, and other artisans. It took seven years to create and is considered the pinnacle of Ukrainian art and the key to the country's identity."

"How did the Ravens know it was here?"

"I have no idea," Harvath responded. "This has been a tightly held national security secret from the beginning."

"Well, obviously somebody talked."

Harvath nodded. "The French faced a similar problem in World War II. The Nazis were ravenous looters, especially when it came to art. From Paris alone, they spirited away countless boxcars full of priceless treasures. Remarkably, the Louvre Museum had acted early and had managed to get their most important pieces packed up and hidden before the Nazis took the city."

"So, the Ravens are a marauding band of psychopathic art thieves?" asked Hookah, trying to piece it together.

"In a way, yeah."

"But what's any of this got to do with your hostage?" asked Krueger. "Was her orphanage a stop on the underground railroad?"

"No," Harvath replied. "To be honest, we have no idea why they were there. According to the list, no art was being stored in that town. The orphanage was maybe just in the wrong place at the wrong time and everyone inside paid a horrible price."

Hookah looked at him. "How horrible?"

"Picture the barbarity you saw upstairs but with children as the victims."

"Jesus."

Harvath nodded. "Now you know why I took this assignment. And why I'm going to see it through; even if I have to do it alone."

"You're not going to have to do it alone," said Hookah. "We're going to help you kill these Orcs. Every last one of them."

"Amen," Jacks replied.

"Ooh-rah," said Krueger.

.     .     .

They found Biscuit standing alone outside smoking a cigarette. "You all right?" Hookah asked.

The young Canadian responded slowly. "This *fucking* war," he said.

They all felt the same way. There was nothing more to say. It was time to shed their equipment, stand down, and rest for a little while.

The small building that had been prepared for them turned out to be an empty garage with a small, rustic guest accommodation above.

After Harvath had moved the Novator inside, they unloaded their gear and carried what they needed upstairs.

A fire had been lit in the fireplace and a pile of split wood stacked next to it. On the stove, a large pot of stew, probably rabbit, sat simmering.

"Holy shit," Biscuit said from the bathroom. "A shower. And the water's hot."

"Don't use it all," Hookah warned, removing his battle belt and setting it in the corner next to his rifle. "Or else."

A large glass bottle filled with cloudy liquid and stopped with a nicked-up cork sat in the middle of the dining table. In front of it were several glasses, as well as plates with pickles, cured pork, cheese, and pieces of dark rye bread.

Jacks uncorked the bottle and took a whiff. "*Samohon*," he declared. "Ukrainian moonshine. Anyone interested?"

All the men, including Harvath, raised their hands. After what they'd seen inside the convent, they could each use a good, stiff drink.

Jacks lined the glasses up and poured.

While he did, the men peeled off their plate carriers, kicked off their boots, and made themselves comfortable.

Leaning back on the couch, drink in hand, Krueger said, "I forgot how good this feels."

Removing some pain pills from his IFAK, Harvath sat down at the table, popped them in his mouth, and washed them down with a big swig of moonshine.

"Can you spare a couple of those?" asked Hookah.

Harvath tossed him the bottle of pills. The man shook some into the palm of his hand and then tossed the bottle back. "Thanks," he said.

"Don't mention it."

The team was wiped out and they soon fell into a fatigued silence with nothing but the fireplace crackling in the background.

When Biscuit emerged from his shower, Krueger went next, followed by Hookah and then Jacks. Harvath volunteered to go last. With the burn he had suffered to his back, he'd be taking the world's shortest shower and really didn't care how much hot water was left at that point. He just wanted to get clean and apply some of the salve they'd given him at the hospital.

Finally showered, shaved, and with a couple of shots of moonshine in them, the men's appetites began to return, and they helped themselves to food.

After they had eaten, Jacks said, "So what's the plan?"

Harvath motioned for the team to move their plates and glasses. Once the table was clear, he spread out his map.

On it, he marked every location known to have been associated with the Ravens. He walked the men through everything he had learned.

"Let me get this straight," said Krueger. "Up until three weeks ago, the Ravens were the 'Murder, Inc.' wing of the Wagner Group. Rape, murder, torture—the worst of the worst stuff we've been hearing about. Then, all of a sudden, they're stealing the most precious works of art in the entire country. Works of art that have been very carefully and very quietly hidden. Do I have that about right?"

Harvath nodded.

"What happened three weeks ago that set them on this new and, presumably, highly lucrative path? Did Wagner HQ stumble onto some intel, pull these guys out of their combat role, and retask them?"

"I don't think so," Harvath replied.

"Why not?"

"First, nobody in their right mind would trust a group of criminals with that kind of assignment. Second, there've been rumors that Wagner lost contact with one of its units in Kharkiv Oblast. We think it was the Ravens."

"Lost contact when?" Hookah asked.

"Just over three weeks ago."

"Anything about where this unit was before it disappeared?"

"During the heavy fighting they were in this area," said Harvath as he circled part of the map.

Hookah then pointed at a village due south and made eye contact with his teammates.

Harvath looked at him. "Do you know this area?"

"We were in that fight," the man replied. "It was intense."

"What happened in that village you just pointed to?"

"We came across a Russian unit that had been machine-gunned. Completely slaughtered. It was like they hadn't even seen it coming. Most of their weapons still had the safeties engaged."

"And that wasn't all," said Biscuit. "There was some bizarre trash left at the scene—almost like someone *really* wanted it to look like Ukrainian soldiers had committed the attack. Pieces of yellow-and-blue tape that they use for armbands, empty Ukrainian cigarette and MRE packages— as if they had slaughtered the Russians and then had sat down for lunch and a smoke. It just felt weird."

"Weirder still," Jacks added, "the engagement hadn't been reported up the chain. We were the first ones to call it in."

"That is weird," Harvath agreed. "What about the unit itself?"

"I think what we found most remarkable was how clean they were— their uniforms, their boots . . ."

"And especially their hands," Krueger hopped in to clarify. "Softest hands I've ever seen. Those were not soldiers; at least, not all of them."

"What do you mean 'not all of them'?"

"The bodies of the guys who did manage to flick off their safeties and, who knows, maybe even got off a couple of shots—*those* guys had hands like soldiers. Rough, nicked up with cuts, and more than a couple of scars here and there."

*A security detail*, Harvath thought to himself. "Anything else?"

"A couple were really pushing it age-wise. Lots of eyeglasses, too. One guy was even carrying a pipe," Biscuit added. "We joked that the Russians must be so desperate that they had begun recruiting in libraries and faculty lounges."

"Bottom line," said Jacks, "they didn't strike us as a combat unit."

Harvath agreed. "What about vehicles?"

"There weren't any. Whoever wiped them out had probably taken them."

"Along with all the moving blankets, empty crates, and packing materials that were inside," said Hookah.

"Exactly," Harvath replied.

"You think the dead Russians were also art thieves?" asked Biscuit.

"I think they were the *original* thieves—experts and muscle sent from Moscow. Who knows how they crossed paths with the Ravens. Maybe it was just dumb luck or maybe the Ravens had gotten wind of what they were up to and had been following them. It doesn't matter. Eventually, it happened. And because they were fellow Russians, the Ravens were able to get in close enough to take them out, which is what they did."

"Leaving them free to take over their art racket," stated Hookah. "The Ravens went AWOL from the Wagner Group and have been under their own management ever since."

Harvath nodded. "A bunch of criminals alert to criminal opportunities. In a war zone no less. Go figure."

"How do we catch them?" asked Jacks. "You've got more targets on your list than we can possibly cover."

"We know where they've been, so the key for us is to uncover any type of pattern."

Hookah walked over to his chest rig, pulled out his land nav kit, and, removing the protractor, returned to the table.

Borrowing Harvath's grease pencil, he began marking off distances and making notes on the border of the map.

"Look at you go, Grandpa," said Biscuit. "Old-school. How many cubits?"

"Just one," Hookah replied without looking up as he gave the young Canadian the finger.

The rest of the team chuckled.

Harvath watched as the man continued to work. Soon enough, he set the pencil down, visibly frustrated.

"What is it?"

"Stolen anything," said Hookah, "is a very specific kind of game."

"Meaning?"

"Until you're ready to get rid of it, you've got to have a safe place to keep it. Ditto for a hostage."

Harvath nodded. "Keep going."

"The Ravens, it's safe to assume, are also on *everybody's* shit list. You want them. The Ukrainians want them. The Wagner Group wants them. And if they haven't already, once the Russians figure out what they've done, they're going to want them as well."

"Which means what?"

"I'm guessing that there's a limit to how far away from . . . let's call it their safe house that they're willing to conduct operations," Hookah said. "Easy out, easy back. That'd be the smart play."

Harvath looked at the map, specifically all the locations the Ravens had already hit. "Then the key is to figure out what that distance is and try to determine their base of operations."

The man nodded. "The front lines have moved back and forth. If these guys leaned more toward greed than they did smarts, I think they'd be hitting some of the locations farther out—at least while there wasn't any fighting there. But they're not doing that. They're avoiding getting too close to the front, which tells me they're disciplined."

"Or scared," stated Harvath. "Having gone AWOL from Wagner, they've cut themselves off from any battlefield intel. They're blind, which makes them vulnerable across the board."

"Agreed. They no longer have a full view of what's happening. Even better, with everyone looking to kill them, there's no cavalry coming to rescue them if they get in trouble. That bodes very well for us. *If* we can find them."

Draining the last drop of moonshine from his small glass, Harvath dried the inside with his napkin, turned it upside down on the map, and motioned for Hookah to hand him the pencil.

"Based on the scale of the map, what's the diameter of my glass?"

Hookah laid his protractor across it. "Twenty-two klicks."

Centering the glass over each of the spots the Ravens had hit, Harvath traced a circle around it and then moved on to the next.

Once he was finished, he removed the glass and looked. The map was a mess. The circles were all over the place. Too few of them intersected in any way that might have provided useful information.

"Well, that was a total waste of wax," said Harvath.

"Maybe not," Hookah responded, placing his protractor back down and adjusting it.

As the man started drawing lines again, Harvath saw something—an actual *pattern*.

But to fully make sense of it, they were going to need one more piece of data. He hoped that Nicholas would be able to fill in the blank. Which brought him to the method of communication.

When operating inside, or very close to, enemy territory, the goal was to position yourself as a needle in a stack of needles. If everyone else was using a specific encrypted messaging app, that was the one you should be using. Standing out, being different, was not a good thing. It only attracted attention, usually undue attention.

The only problem with free, encrypted apps was that eventually they would be broken—usually by the Israelis, though the Chinese had been right on their heels lately. So had the Russians.

If Moscow could crack the popular messaging apps being used by the Ukrainians, it would be like the Allies breaking the Nazis' Enigma machine—a complete and total game-changer.

Harvath's transmissions were too sensitive to risk being intercepted. Pulling out his phone, he powered it up but placed it into airplane mode. He then opened the proprietary, encrypted app his organization used and wrote up an overdue situation report. There was a lot to fill Nicholas in on. There was also that missing piece of data he needed.

Once his SITREP was ready, he clicked out of airplane mode and tried to see if there was any cell service.

It took a few moments, but eventually he was able to lock onto a weak signal that bounced between one and two bars on his phone.

He hit send and waited for confirmation that his message had been received on the other end. When he saw the confirmation, he put his phone back into airplane mode and powered it down.

There was no sense in leaving it on. It would probably take Nicholas a while to get back to him. He wanted to grab a good chunk of uninterrupted sleep before it was his turn to take watch. He also knew that a live phone could be a beacon for the enemy, like striking a match at night and lighting a cigarette at the front lines. It was much better to be safe than sorry.

Tucking his phone in the pocket of his fatigues, Harvath bedded down for the night. It took a moment for the tension of the day to leave his body and for his brain to lower its alert level, but soon enough he had stepped off the edge of consciousness into a deep well of dreamless sleep.

• • •

Three villages over, a Russian Leer-4 electronic warfare system—capable of picking up more than two thousand cell phones within a ten-mile range—sat beneath a high-tech web of advance camouflage netting.

Inside the command truck, a signals specialist beckoned his commander over to look at his screen.

"What do you have?" the commander asked.

"A handful of cell phones. Each has been turned on and then back off. They seem to be exhibiting a level of operational security."

"Where are they?"

The specialist overlaid a digital map. "They look to be somewhere on the grounds of the Mother of God Convent."

"A convent? Why the hell would a bunch of nuns be concerned with operational security?" It was a rhetorical question. The commander didn't expect an answer and pressed on, asking, "Were you able to intercept any of their communications?"

"Negative," the specialist replied. "It's encrypted. It appears that all but one of the phones are using the Telegram app."

"Ukrainian soldiers?"

"That'd be my guess."

"What about the phone that's not using Telegram?"

"It's using a type of encryption I've never seen before. From what I can see, it looks to be light-years ahead of Telegram. Whoever's using it is probably high value. Maybe a military or intelligence officer."

The commander thought about their options. "Do we have any reconnaissance teams in the area?"

The specialist consulted a list. "No, but we do have a four-man assault team. Spetsnaz soldiers. They can be on target within the hour."

"If possible, I want the high-value target captured and brought back for interrogation. If not, take them all out. No survivors. Just make sure that the team brings back that phone. Moscow will be very interested in getting their hands on such new technology."

# CHAPTER 23

K ozar, the Ukrainian Intelligence official who had accompanied them on the overnight train from Poland, had done Nicholas a huge favor. In addition to getting him set up in his own accessible office, he had teamed him with one of the brightest stars in their agency. He assumed her job was to keep an eye on him, but he liked having her around.

She was a twenty-one-year-old hacker extraordinaire named Yulia. Behind the keyboard, she went by the nom de guerre Valkyrie.

Yulia was fast and unbelievably intelligent. She spoke three languages—Ukrainian, Russian, and English. She wanted to learn anything Nicholas was willing to teach her; anything at all that would help her better serve her country.

His small stature wasn't off-putting to her. Neither was his rather checkered past. And like Kozar, she loved dogs. In a word, she was perfect.

They got along instantly, and their bond was only deepened when, worried about the comfort of Argos and Draco, who were relegated to the cold concrete floor, she sourced two foam mats and brought them into the office.

"I'm sorry," she said as she entered the office and handed Nicholas a bowl and spoon. "This was all they had. Beef borscht. A Ukrainian classic."

"Don't apologize," Nicholas replied. He had just fed the dogs and was looking forward to getting some food himself. "Borscht reminds me of my youth. Besides, how many soldiers at the front tonight won't get a hot meal at all?"

"You are right. I need to practice more gratitude."

He smiled. "It's all about perspective. Did you hear the one about the Ukrainian soldier who was being interrogated by a Russian officer?"

She shook her head.

"The Ukrainian looks down and sees that the officer has only one boot. He asks, 'Did you lose a boot?' 'Nyet,' the Russian replies. 'I *found* a boot.' "

The young woman laughed. "Perspective."

"It is the key to everything."

"Speaking of which," she said, changing the subject, "am I going to get a preview of your presentation? I know our digital team is looking forward to it."

"You do," he answered, holding up two fortune-cookie-sized pieces of paper. "There are the two case studies. Which one do you want to tackle first?"

On one, he had written the provocative words *Naked Pictures (of my wife)*. On the other *Come Fly with Me*.

The way he was holding them, only he could see what he had written.

Yulia reached out and took one.

"I already regret this," she said. "No, I don't want to see any naked pictures of your wife."

Nicholas chuckled. "Don't worry. A, I'm not married. B, we're using someone else's wife. In fact, several others."

"I am not following you."

"Blackmail is especially powerful because it plays upon a person's shame and embarrassment. As you know, part of the reason I am here is to teach you and your colleagues how to uncover and leverage blackmail material against the Russians. Tonight, however, I'm going to show you how to put a different twist on it. This operation exploits a different, albeit adjacent emotion: humiliation. And humiliation is as corrosive as acid when it comes to morale."

Yulia placed her own soup on the desk and pulled over a chair. "This sounds fantastic. What's the other surprise?"

The little man smiled. "We'll get to that. First the humiliation."

They both paused to take a couple of bites of soup, which was quite good, before Nicholas continued. "As you know, the moment Russia invaded Ukraine, I began crafting several different digital operations. The first one we dubbed Operation Pinup."

"'We'?" she asked.

"I came up with the idea and got it rolling, but the Ukrainian Cyber Resistance deserves the credit for being so successful with it."

"When did you team up with the Cyber Resistance?"

"Almost as soon as the war broke out," he replied.

"So, what's Operation Pinup?"

"We tricked a dozen Russian military wives into slowly giving away personal information about their husbands. We made them believe that they would be helping boost morale among officers by posing for a pinup calendar.

"We had them strike sexy poses while dressed in their husbands' uniforms, which helped us uncover even more information about the men. The more biographical nuggets we were able to mine, the more targeted our hacking was able to become. We not only were able to locate where the officers lived and what they were paid, but where they had served, where they were currently serving, their cell phone numbers, operational orders, email accounts and passwords, et cetera. It is an absolute treasure trove of information, which we'll be handing over to Ukrainian Intelligence in the coming days, and none of it would have been possible without the participation of the men's wives."

"And the humiliation component? Are they humiliated because they didn't realize they were assisting our side?" she asked.

"There's that," Nicholas conceded. "Also, we couldn't let those sexy pictures go to waste."

Her eyes widened. "You actually created a calendar?"

"Absolutely. In fact, the Cyber Resistance had insisted. Some of the photos the women provided were quite revealing. And, as it turned out, multiple women had posed for even racier pictures, something the Cyber Resistance uncovered as they hacked into their phones and email accounts."

"Did the calendar get distributed to the husbands' fellow officers?"

"It was posted on the internet and emails were sent to everyone in each of their divisions."

"That *is* humiliating," she stated.

"And corrosive," Nicholas added. "From the top down and the bottom up. It erodes confidence in the husbands—both from the troops they're in charge of leading and from the leaders higher up the chain who now question whether those officers are competent and can be trusted."

"What about the second surprise?"

The little man handed her the other piece of paper.

" 'Come Fly with Me,' " she read aloud. "Like the Frank Sinatra song?"

"Exactly. In fact, the second operation I'm going to share with you was named Operation Acapulco, after one of the lyrics in the song."

"And is this another operation meant to humiliate the Russians?"

Nicholas smiled. "Anytime one of our operations is successful, I hope the Russians feel humiliated, but to answer your question, no. The goal here is not humiliation. Our goal is to get Russia to help in the war effort by giving their best airplanes to Ukraine."

Yulia guffawed. "You have got to be joking."

"I'm totally serious."

"Why would Russia give Ukraine anything, but especially aircraft?"

"You're right," said the little man. "I should have said they're going to let us buy them for a fraction of what they're worth."

The young woman took another spoonful of borscht and encouraged Nicholas to keep talking.

"The plan for Operation Acapulco is simple. We convince three Russian pilots to defect to three different Ukrainian air bases with their aircraft. When they land, each pilot receives Ukrainian citizenship, one million dollars cash, and assistance smuggling their family members out of Russia for resettlement anywhere in Europe they choose."

"Wow. Has this happened? Because if it has, this is the first time I am hearing about it."

"It's not complete. Not yet. It's still an ongoing operation."

"How far along are you?" she asked.

"We've established contact with three pilots. All have agreed. One has offered to drug his copilot. One has offered to claim a technical malfunction that will force him to land. And the third is still working on what he thinks his best course of action will be."

"I can't believe it."

Nicholas smiled. "Neither could the pilots. They thought it was a scam at first; that we were Russian Intelligence trying to test their loyalty and entrap them."

"Of course they did. They're not stupid. They're pilots, after all. How did you get to them?"

"Two months after the war started, Ukraine created a law that said that any Russian who voluntarily surrendered high-end military equipment would be generously compensated. In particular, helicopters were worth five hundred thousand dollars and bombers, fighter jets, and fixed-wing attack aircraft were worth one million. We made sure that those bounties were well publicized inside Russia.

"We needed to get a database of Russian pilots and tried several different hacks. Eventually, we managed to access a server that had a list of pilots, right down to who was the flight commander and who was the navigator. This gave us names, but we had to keep digging to get contact info.

"Pilot number one, Igor Tveritin, is the oldest and most experienced on our list. He's trained on the Tupolev Tu-160 strategic bomber, which is a supersonic aircraft that can be outfitted with nuclear missiles. He was actually born in Ukraine, in Melitopol, back when it was part of the Soviet Union. He has a wife, three kids, and they all live on the air base together and his kids go to school there. He's very worried about the logistics of getting everyone out. He took a five percent down payment in crypto.

"Pilot number two, Andrei Maslov, is an Su-24 tactical bomber pilot. He's married, has no kids, and wants his mistress, a fitness instructor, smuggled out. He insisted on cash, and we have delivered two down payments to him of four thousand dollars each. But we think he may have been compromised."

Yulia looked up from her dinner. "Compromised how?"

"We asked him to send us a copy of the mistress's Russian identity documents so that we could begin putting a passport together for her. It just came through two days ago. The minute we saw her photo, we were fairly certain that Maslov had been burned. She is *way* too hot for him. We're still working on it, but it's not looking good. All her friends are hookers, and she has been placing a lot of calls to a man we think is an FSB asset. We may have to cut our losses with Maslov.

"Pilot number three, Roman Nosenko, flies the Su-34 Fullback and the Su-24 Fencer bombers. Like the others, we asked him for proof and he sent back pictures of his aircraft with a piece of paper in the foreground with a three-digit number we asked him to write on it. Nosenko has been the most standoffish, the toughest pilot to recruit.

"His wife is also going to be tough to extract because she's a military psychologist. He doesn't know if he can convince her to defect and he doesn't want to go without her. He's also worried that we're just trying to lure him into our airspace so we can shoot him down. He's heard that Ukrainian antiaircraft teams get paid big bonuses for shoot-downs.

"Our plan, if we can, is to get all the family members to safe houses in Belarus. Once there, they can be given their new passports and cash. At which point, they can use a prearranged code, over an encrypted app, to let the pilots know they made it out safely. Then all that's left is for the pilots to fly their planes into Ukrainian airspace, where they'll be met by Ukrainian interceptors and guided to their respective landing strips."

"Pretty amazing plan," said Yulia. "It sounds like you've invested some money in this. Did you get anything beyond just pictures of their aircraft?"

Nicholas nodded. "We also got photos from inside their aircraft, photos of technical manuals, information about their units, their air bases, how they have been flying their routes, targeting intelligence, and what kinds of munitions they have been using. Even if the entire op had to be shut down tomorrow, it has already been quite valuable."

"Once you were able to surmount their initial skepticism, once they were confident that it wasn't a scam, you've found them to be cooperative?"

"For the most part, yes."

"Why do you think that is?" she asked.

"It's simple. They don't believe in the war. They think Peshkov is a petty tyrant. They may have believed in Russia at one point, but they don't believe in him. Not anymore."

"I can understand that. So, what else do you have for me? Tell me about the other ops."

Nicholas looked down as his phone chimed. It was a SITREP from Harvath. He needed to handle this in private. "I'm happy to chat some more," he said. "But first I need to deal with something. How about if I come find you when I'm done? Would that be okay?"

"Of course," said Yulia as she stood and picked up her bowl. "If I'm not in my office, check the conference room."

"Will do."

"May I say good-bye to the dogs?"

Nicholas nodded and she walked over to give each of them a pat. She then smiled and exited his office, politely closing the door behind her.

Pulling up Harvath's situation report, he read through the whole thing as he ate his borscht. It was unbelievable what that man had been through.

He then arrived at Harvath's request. It was relatively straightforward. He only hoped he'd be able to get his friend the answers he needed.

Picking up the landline phone on his desk, he dialed Kozar's extension. When the Ukrainian Intelligence officer answered, Nicholas said, "I have to ask you for a favor, but I need you to keep it between us."

"Of course," the man replied. "What is it?"

"I'd rather not ask over the phone—even via an internal line. Can you come down to my office?"

"No problem. Give me five minutes."

"Thank you," Nicholas replied as he hung up the phone.

Now all he had to do was figure out how to phrase his request in such a way that Kozar would give him what he wanted, rather than putting him on the first train back to Poland.

# CHAPTER 24

Leonid Grechko was a man who kept his passions under control. He ruled over them and not vice versa.

As such, he felt he had earned the right to indulge himself when he was off the clock. His personal time was just that, *personal*. How he spent it was no one's business but his.

The typical trappings of male adulthood—a wife, a family, a bustling household—had never appealed to him. Part of it was because of the job. Intelligence operatives, at least those working out of embassies with official cover, were forced to move every few years. It was how the game was played and not conducive to that style of life.

The other part was that he could count on one hand the people he knew who were happy in their marriages. When you threw children into the equation, he didn't even need all five fingers to count the people he knew who were honestly happy. Perhaps it was a Russian attitude, a tilt toward the nihilism so prevalent in their culture. Regardless, he was the envy of his male friends.

In his opinion, relationships, by their very nature, were transactional. Sex was no different. When he wanted it, he paid for it, and treated the women quite well.

He didn't buy them expensive gifts or take them on vacations, but as someone who loved good food and exceptional wines, he included them in sumptuous meals.

There was often some form of entertainment—ballet or the

theater, after which they would spend the night in a luxury hotel room. He always paid for them to stay the night, though he was always gone before they awoke. He would leave a note, encouraging the young lady to enjoy breakfast from room service and thanking her for the evening.

He had only one rule. He never slept with the same woman twice. It didn't matter how beautiful she was. It didn't matter how skilled she was. Repeat visits could lead to foolish attachments, which could make him vulnerable to his enemies. The rule made sense and had served him well. He had only broken it once, but it had been worth it.

Inessa was the closest he had ever been to falling in love. In fact, if he were to be honest with himself, he *had* fallen in love with her. That was why he had broken his rule and had agreed to see her a second time and then a third and a fourth. It was a white-hot, passionate affair that had lasted for weeks.

She was a woman of flawless beauty who possessed a deep appreciation for all things cultural. She was well read, well traveled, and well trained in the erotic arts. Had he not been so drawn to her, so absolutely susceptible to her spell, he might have recruited her and molded her into one of the best female agents the world had ever seen.

But he had known that was impossible. The idea of not being able to have her, fully, to himself would have driven him mad. The mere thought of her being with other men was enough to poison him with jealousy and to torment him beyond all reason. He had never, not even as a child, wanted anything as badly as he had wanted her.

She was his Helen of Troy. Hers was the face that could launch a thousand ships and send millions of men into battle. She was a drug more potent than any narcotic. His only guard against losing his mind, and himself, was to end it, to go cold turkey and cut off contact with her. And, for the most part, it had worked.

Because he couldn't help himself, he had kept tabs on her from afar. He had watched as she became the mistress of a mining oligarch named Tsybulsky, who had relocated her to the South of France.

From that point on, he had spent many nights alone in his bed, wondering what might have been. It was a needless, self-inflicted pain that picked at a deep and very tender wound, which he never allowed to fully heal.

In retrospect, it was good that she had moved away to France. It was also good that she wasn't on any social media platforms. Having to see photos as her life unfolded would have been too much.

It had been five years since he had last seen her. Then, this very morning, he had bumped into her coming out of a boutique on Tverskaya Street. She was even more radiant than he remembered.

Ever the fashion plate, she was dressed in designer brands from head to toe and was dripping with diamonds. Her thick, dark hair was pulled back, accentuating her high cheekbones and sleek jawline.

He felt his heart catch in his throat. He was angry with himself for being so overwhelmed by his emotions.

They made small talk. She was in town, only briefly, with her "boyfriend." He had business to attend to and then they'd be flying off to Switzerland.

She asked him how he had been. He lied, said he was fine, and that work was keeping him busy.

She then asked if he ever thought of her. This time, he didn't lie. He told her the truth.

She told him she thought about him quite often; that her feelings for him had not lessened since leaving Moscow. She had a good life, a comfortable life, but it wasn't the life she dreamed of. He could feel his heart catch in his throat once more.

She asked if he was available for dinner. There was nothing wrong with that, was there? Two old friends could have a meal and catch up, couldn't they?

When he asked about her boyfriend, she explained that he would be in meetings for most of the evening. As long as she was home early, there was no reason for it to be a problem.

Grechko didn't even think. He said yes immediately. No matter what had been on his schedule, he would have canceled it for her.

She wanted to go back to the restaurant they'd had so many wonderful evenings together in. Could he get them a reservation at the White Rabbit on short notice? He told her not to worry and that he would see her there at seven.

They said good-bye and as they did, Inessa leaned in and kissed his cheek. She still wore the same heady perfume. She still pressed the palm of her hand against his chest the way she used to. She still drove him crazy. It was like being hit by a lightning bolt.

He walked the rest of the way home thinking about nothing but her. Back at his apartment, after he called the manager of the White Rabbit and reserved their most romantic table, he poured himself a drink, put on the music they used to listen to together—Dinah Washington and Billie Holiday—and tackled a stack of reports he had to finish from the office. It was difficult to keep his focus, but he pushed through it.

When the time came, he put together what he was going to wear—a bespoke, dark gray Henry Poole & Co. suit with an open-collared black shirt—then showered and shaved.

He no longer wore the same cologne he used to wear when they had been together—even that was too much of a reminder of her—but he had something similar that he had picked up abroad, less pepper, more tobacco.

After polishing a pair of Bruno Magli monk strap loafers, he selected his favorite wristwatch, a Patek Philippe Calatrava in white gold with a black alligator strap. He carefully folded an extra handkerchief, just in case she might need it, and placed it inside his left breast pocket.

Checking himself one last time in the full-length mirror, he was pleased with how he looked. He had maintained the same diet and exercise regimen over the years and still clocked in at the very same weight. *Clothes may make the man*, he thought, *but it doesn't hurt to start with a solid frame.*

With a smile on his face as he anticipated the night to come, he reached for the closet door and removed his coat. He wanted to get to the restaurant a few minutes before her. It was the gentlemanly thing to do. He also wanted to make sure everything was perfect.

He hesitated for a moment, wondering if he should bring a bottle of his own wine, as he had some exceptional vintages in a locked storage room down in the basement, but decided against it. Even while Moscow was suffering under the crush of international sanctions, the White Rabbit maintained an impressive selection. He also knew that there were some very special bottles not on the wine list that the manager and sommelier had hidden away.

Certain that he hadn't overlooked anything, he gathered up his wallet, keys, and money clip and exited his apartment.

The evening air was chilly, which was probably a good thing, as he had been perspiring.

He walked a couple of blocks and hailed a taxi. Climbing in, he told the driver to take him to Smolenskaya Square. Halfway there, his phone rang.

Removing the device from his pocket, he looked at the caller ID. It was from a blocked number. Immediately, he thought it must be Inessa, calling from the oligarch's residence, canceling their date because Tsybulsky's plans had changed. Taking a deep breath, he answered his phone.

It was not Inessa. It was Beglov, President Peshkov's advisor.

"He wants to see you," said the advisor.

"Who?"

"You know who."

*Peshkov? On a Saturday night?* Grechko thought. This was the last thing he needed. Even so, he maintained his professionalism. This was the President of Russia, after all. "When would he like to get together?" he asked, hoping Beglov would suggest a time for tomorrow or maybe the day after.

"Now. Tonight. How soon can you get to the Kremlin?"

He wanted to say, "Not for several hours," but, continuing to maintain his professionalism, replied, "Fifteen minutes."

"Excellent," the advisor replied. After telling him which gate to use, he was about to end the call when Grechko spoke back up.

"I am not wearing a tie," the intelligence officer admitted.

There was a pause as Beglov covered the phone's mouthpiece, presumably to speak to someone else in the room, and then uncovering it, said, "It's your lucky day. The firing squad has the night off. Hurry up and get over here."

*What a prick*, Grechko thought as he ended the call and gave the cab-driver his new destination.

The advisor was a prick not just for making such a tasteless joke—from inside the Kremlin no less—but for even calling him in the first place. Based on Beglov's jocular attitude, it didn't sound like there was a national emergency that required Grechko, of all people, to drop every-thing and hotfoot it over to the Kremlin. What's more, it sounded like the advisor might have been drinking. *What a night.*

*How the hell is this happening?* Inessa had one night—*tonight*—available for him. And it wasn't even the whole night. She had to be back before her "boyfriend" returned from whatever meetings he was having.

Grechko looked at his watch. There was no way he was going to make it to the White Rabbit in time for their seven o'clock reservation. He hated the idea of leaving her alone at the table, not knowing when he would arrive.

Opening his messaging app, he sent her a text: **I am so very sorry. Something has come up. I cannot make our seven o'clock. Not sure how long it will take. May I text you as soon as I am out of my meeting?**

He watched until he saw the bubbling dots at the bottom of his screen, indicating that she was composing her response. It didn't take long. **I un-derstand,** she replied. **I will wait to hear from you. Good luck with your meeting.**

Though she hadn't said it, he knew she must have been as disap-pointed as he was. Being called to a meeting at the Kremlin was a pretty good excuse for missing dinner, but he had never revealed to her what he did for a living. As far as she knew, he was a banker. Though what kind of banker would have an emergency meeting on a Saturday night was some-thing else altogether. He needed to get this meeting with Peshkov and Beglov over with as quickly as possible.

Arriving at the Kremlin, he was put through primary and secondary security screening. With the war going so poorly, Peshkov continued to be vigilant about assassination attempts. There were very few people who were able to get close to him.

Grechko was accompanied by a security team up to the lavish

presidential office, where, after being announced by intercom, the doors were opened and he was shown inside.

Three men sat in a seating area near the fireplace—President Peshkov, his advisor Oleg Beglov, and Inessa's "boyfriend," mining oligarch Arkady Tsybulsky.

*What the hell is he doing here?* Grechko wondered.

"Leo," Beglov said as he stood to greet him. "Thank you for coming. Mr. President, here he is, Leonid Grechko."

There was a half-empty bottle of vodka on the table as well as food. Judging by the flush in the men's cheeks and the unsteadiness with which the President now stood, the intelligence operative figured this probably wasn't their first bottle.

Walking over to Peshkov, Grechko shook the leader's hand. "It is a pleasure to see you again, sir."

"And you, Mr. Grechko. Do you know my old friend, Arkady Tsybulsky?"

"I only know of him," the intelligence operative replied. Maintaining his poker face, he shook the jowly oligarch's meaty hand. "It is an honor to meet you."

"Something to drink?" Beglov asked as he pointed to the chair he wanted him to take.

"I am okay. Thank you."

Peshkov smiled. "Nonsense. He'll take a vodka."

Grechko knew better than to refuse the President's hospitality.

Once each of the men had a fresh glass, they toasted to Russia and knocked back their shots.

The President insisted Beglov refill the glasses but urged temperance. "This one," Peshkov said, "we sip."

The intelligence operative had no idea what was going on. A direct meeting with the President and one of his advisors was rare, but not unusual. To have a mining magnate in the room, however, made no sense at all. What possible reason could require him to be there?

Further, this was a side of Peshkov he hadn't seen before. He was used to the stern, serious leader he had seen in meetings and on TV. This after-hours, slightly drunk version was something he was quite unprepared for.

"I hope we didn't interrupt your Saturday night," the President said, eyeing his intelligence operative's crisp suit and polished shoes.

"No, sir. Not at all," Grechko lied. "I am at your service twenty-four hours a day, seven days a week."

"That's a very good answer," Peshkov responded. "The *correct* answer."

"That's why he's one of our best men," Beglov added. "Totally dedicated."

Grechko looked to see if the advisor was still wearing his wedding band, which he was. And as far as he could tell, he hadn't suffered any scratching or bruising at the hands of his wife. There was no telling if she had noticed the lipstick on the man's collar from the night before or not. Perhaps someone had tipped him off before she'd seen it.

The intelligence operative didn't really care. All he knew was that at this moment, he disliked Beglov even more and he downright hated Tsybulsky. The thought of that corpulent man having his way with Inessa was burning him up inside. He wanted to wrap his hands around the man's fleshy throat and choke the life out of him.

There were no bodyguards in the room; they were seated just behind a false door, watching everything via closed-circuit TV. He guessed that if he really wanted to do it, he had a thirty percent chance of success before the security men were on top of him and pulling him away. He'd be better off improvising something with a cocktail pick or one of the shrimp forks sitting on the coffee table in front of them.

"I saw you looking at Mr. Tsybulsky," Peshkov said, "and I can read your mind."

Grechko doubted it, *big-time*, but he was polite enough not to say so. "What am I thinking, sir?"

"You are thinking, *What the fuck is he doing here?*" the President said, laughing, as the other two men joined in.

The intelligence operative smiled and waited for the laughter to die down. "It's always good to see old friends, Mr. President."

"Yes, this is true. It is even nicer when the friend doesn't want something from you."

Tsybulsky raised his glass in tribute to his host and took a long sip of vodka. As he did, Grechko fantasized about driving the glass down the fleshy man's esophagus and finishing him off with a throat punch. But it was just that, a fantasy.

Peshkov, after helping himself to a long sip of vodka, finally got around to the point. "Arkady," he continued, "tell us again about your great idea, the one we were discussing before Mr. Grechko arrived."

"How I avoided sanctions by putting many of my assets in my mistress's name?" the fat man asked, laughing again.

"No," the President replied, shaking his head. "Tell us about your idea for an intelligence operation against the Americans."

Grechko couldn't believe his ears. Peshkov was soliciting espionage advice from one of his drinking buddies? Tsybulsky no less? This night really couldn't get any worse.

The obese oligarch shifted his girth so he could address the intelligence operative head-on and asked, "What do you know about Turkey?"

It was all Grechko could do not to roll his eyes. "Second-largest army in NATO and host of the Allied Land Command headquarters. Turkey is one of our top three trading partners and last year more than doubled its trade with the Russian Federation. Energy and tourism are key markets. Turkey has an embassy here in Moscow and consulates-general in St. Petersburg, Kazan, and Novorossiysk, as well as an honorary consulate in Ekaterinburg, while we have an embassy in Ankara and consulates-general in Istanbul, Antalya, and Trabzon, as well as an honorary consulate in Izmir.

"Over the objections of the United States, Turkey is an adopter of our S-400 missile system and has expressed interest in us helping their air force develop next-generation fighters. The Turkish drone program has—"

Peshkov held up his hand to stop him. "You are obviously well versed in all things Turkish." Turning to Tsybulsky, he said, "Tell him your idea."

"Three NATO member states abut the Black Sea—Turkey, Bulgaria, and Romania—along with two non-NATO members, Russia and Ukraine. Control over the Black Sea is a key Russian objective. Interestingly enough, the Black Sea happens to be one of NATO's most underdeveloped strategies. The Americans realize this and are pushing to reposition the Black Sea as the center of NATO's focus. There are rumors that they even want to increase the U.S. military footprint and economic engagement in the region."

Grechko had heard similar rumblings, but military strategy was neither his area of focus nor of expertise. He didn't quite grasp why he was being subjected to this lecture. Nevertheless, he remained quiet and allowed the President's chum to hold forth.

"The Black Sea is NATO's Achilles' heel. Their influence over Europe's southeastern flank depends on them controlling it. It's like they have suddenly woken up to a huge gap in their planning. There's just one problem—Turkey.

"Turkey is the Black Sea's gatekeeper. They control the Dardanelles and Bosporus straits—the only way into the Mediterranean—and they have no desire to cede even a modicum of that control to NATO.

"When our special military operation in Ukraine began, Turkey exercised its legal powers under the 1936 Montreux Convention to close the straits and lock the Black Sea down. Only Russian warships returning to their home ports have been allowed through. No NATO warships have been permitted entry. As I suggested to the President, this policy works to our benefit and, for the foreseeable future, should be encouraged."

Grechko didn't disagree. There was no telling what kind of trouble could be created by NATO warships steaming into the Black Sea and providing assistance to Ukraine from off the coast. He still, however, had no idea what this had to do with him.

Tsybulsky stared at him as if a big, obvious lightbulb should be going off in his head. It wasn't.

After a long and uncomfortable pause, Grechko replied, "How can I be of service?"

"You should create a psychological campaign," the oligarch said, karate-chopping his hands in the air, "rallying American citizens against involvement in the Black Sea."

The intelligence officer wasn't happy and shot Beglov a look.

"I have several ideas for you," Tsybulsky continued. "But first, more vodka."

At that moment, Grechko knew he was stuck. There was no way he was getting out of there anytime soon.

It was unfathomable what the war had reduced Peshkov to. Taking operational "pitches" from one of the President's pals was an incredible indignity. At least when James Bond author Ian Fleming had given JFK ideas for dealing with Cuba, they had been coherent and somewhat creative.

Tsybulsky, on the other hand, was a complete moron. His ideas were terrible. But for the vodka, Grechko wondered if President Peshkov would have made him sit there and listen to the man babble on for half the night.

As soon as he was allowed to leave the Kremlin, he hurried outside and texted Inessa.

She apologized, but it was too late for her to meet with him—even for a nightcap. She didn't know when she would be back in Moscow. Hopefully, they would see each other again soon. She wished him well and told him to take care. Russia was headed in a bad direction, and she feared for his safety.

That was the second time tonight someone had shared a geopolitical opinion that he didn't disagree with.

As much as he detested Tsybulsky, supporting Turkey's control over entry to the Black Sea *was* in Russia's interest. It required, however, a prolonged, comprehensive strategy, not just a dumb, one-off psy ops campaign against the United States.

Then there was Inessa. She was right to be worried for Russia. He was worried for Russia as well. Things were not going well. Peshkov's continued tightening of his inner circle, so that he was taking counsel from men like Tsybulsky, was extremely troubling. He wasn't Hitler, but only Hitler could be Hitler. As the old saying went, history doesn't repeat, but it does rhyme.

There was enough to be concerned about that Grechko began to ponder something he hadn't pondered before—*getting out*.

# CHAPTER 25

J acks woke Harvath up. "We've got company," he said.

Harvath had no idea how long he'd been out, only that it felt like just a couple of minutes.

All the lights in the guest quarters remained out. Someone had cracked a few chem lights and tossed them in the corners so that there was just enough light to see by.

Harvath kitted up as fast as he could—plate carrier, battle belt, all of it. Thanks to Krueger, his helmet now sported a flip-up/flip-down, thermal imaging monocular. Securing his helmet, he powered up the device, grabbed his rifle, and mustered at the stairs with the other men who were already geared up and had their night-vision goggles on.

"Hookah and Biscuit are outside, on the far end of this building, facing the front doors of the convent," said Jacks. "We have four armed hostiles who came over the back wall and are moving in this direction."

"A little late for villagers to be paying a visit," Krueger replied.

Harvath shook his head. "These aren't villagers. They're Russians."

"Agreed," said Jacks. "Someone in the village must be on their payroll and ratted us out."

"Or the Ravens are returning to the scene of the crime," Krueger stated.

"We'll know soon enough," Harvath said. As he took the lead, he told the men, "On me."

His plan was to get away from the structure. He wanted to set up in a different, more secure position where they could still create interlocking fields of fire with Hookah and Biscuit. Though it had been a smart decision to stash the Novator in the garage, it sure would have been nice to have it outside to hide behind.

Instead, he made a beeline for a small, open-air chapel. It was constructed from stacked, interlocking logs about four feet high, which supported a corrugated, teepee-like metal roof with a gilded dome about the size of a beach ball on top. It was the best cover they were going to be able to get.

Once they were in position, they radioed Hookah and Biscuit for a SITREP. The men could still see the enemy team approaching and stated that Harvath and his men should see them any moment.

The one upside to all of this was that the two old Ukrainians who had been guarding the front doors of the convent had gone home. There was no need to stay. The Americans were here, they had seen what they needed to see, and so the old guardians had locked everything up. As Harvath was unloading his gear, they had told him they'd be back in the morning. That act had probably saved their lives. At least Harvath and his guys didn't have to worry about collateral damage. It was a small consolation.

As the enemy team approached, the first thing Harvath noticed was how well they moved. They were practiced, and extremely precise, with each man and his weapon covering a different angle. They moved as one; as an experienced unit. Everything about them radiated professionalism. These weren't random soldiers. This was a Special Operations team.

Keeping his eyes focused on the threat, Harvath listened for any sound of a drone overhead. It was quiet, which meant that so far, they had dodged a particularly nasty bullet. Not only could drones use night vision to pinpoint you and alert the enemy to your position, but they could also drop a multitude of deadly munitions right on top of you.

The picture Harvath was seeing through his thermal monocular was different from what his colleagues were seeing through their night-vision goggles. His device was designed to detect heat, while theirs was designed to detect ambient light. And even though they had a much crisper picture than he did, one thing was obvious—the Russians had very sophisticated gear and had come loaded for bear.

Their rifles were outfitted with chunky, high-end night-vision scopes. Two of the men had bandoliers with 40mm grenades strapped across their chests, and launchers hanging from their backs. This was no ordinary fireteam. These were straight-up headhunters. Assaulters like this only got dispatched when a high-value target was in the offing.

Harvath was beginning to doubt that some random village spy had given them up. There had to be another reason why the Russians had sent such a crack team. Now wasn't the time to figure that out. Now it was time to fight.

Over the radio he whispered, "Hookah, how's your line of sight?"

"Gooder than good," the man replied.

"Good copy," said Harvath. "Get ready to shred these guys. On my mark."

He watched out of the corner of his eye as Krueger and Jacks—like a perfectly trained pair of attack dogs—responded to his command. Adjusting their grips on their rifles, the men crouched even lower and prepared to pop up above the logs and begin firing.

Harvath gave the countdown. "Three. Two. One. *Now*."

Jacks was unbelievably fast. He had leapt up and had his rifle barrel over the top of the log wall before Harvath or Krueger. But when he acquired his target and pressed his trigger, he didn't get a *bang*, he got a shit-your-pants *click*. For some reason, the round didn't fire.

To their credit, instead of acting like a pack of rabid dogs and rushing toward Jacks, the Russians relied on their teammate, who already had his weapon trained in that direction. The man put down a withering and extremely accurate barrage of fire.

A round skipped off the top of Jacks's Kevlar helmet as he dropped to the ground. Had he hesitated even a fraction of a second, he would have been dead.

Aborting their attack, Harvath and Krueger had also dropped to the ground as logs splintered all around them.

From their position, Hookah and Biscuit opened up and began shooting. The Russian at the front of the team instantly returned fire.

Seeing that Jacks had cycled his weapon and had purged the bad round, Harvath nodded to him and Krueger. They needed to get their guns in the fight, especially before one of those Russians could transition to their launcher and let loose with a grenade.

In unison, the men jumped up, pressed their triggers the moment their barrels had cleared the wall, and sent a wave of high-speed lead toward the enemy.

The two Russians closest were cut down like someone had gone through them with a lightsaber.

The remaining two were focused on the fire they were taking from Hookah and Biscuit, who had a much harder time with their accuracy, as they were farther away.

Nevertheless, they were able to put multiple rounds on the point man, sending him down into the dirt. Which left only one.

The man got all four blades of the blender as Harvath and his team lit him up. Once the last Russian had collapsed to the ground, Harvath ordered his men to cease fire.

The cloud of weapons' smoke blew slowly off the convent grounds. None of the Russians were moving. That didn't mean that they could be ruled out as a threat. Not yet.

Harvath warned his team over the radio to move cautiously and to keep an eye out for a second wave. Slowly, they approached the bodies.

The first thing that became apparent was that these were definitely not run-of-the-mill soldiers. They were, as Harvath had assumed and the insignia on their uniforms confirmed, Special Forces; Spetsnaz to be exact. And one of them, it turned out, was still alive.

Always conscious of their proclivity for hugging live grenades as they died—in the hopes of taking out a few more of the enemy when they were moved or rolled over—Harvath proceeded with caution. Both of the man's hands were visible and there were no loose grenades evident.

Separating the soldier from his weapons, Harvath did a quick assessment of the man's injuries. He'd been shot in the abdomen and was in a tremendous amount of pain. It looked bad and there was a good chance the soldier had internal bleeding. Harvath had seen enough gunshot wounds to know that if this guy didn't get treatment soon, he probably wasn't going to make it.

He located the man's IFAK and opened it up. The paucity of medical supplies, especially for a high-end Spetsnaz soldier, was ridiculous. Opening his own IFAK, he pulled out what he needed, began packing the wound with sterile gauze, and applied pressure.

"Your injury is bad," he said in Russian. "You need a doctor."

The man writhed in pain.

"I am going to try to help you," Harvath continued, "but first, you need to help me. Who sent you?"

He waited but the man did not reply. "Who. Sent. You?" he repeated in Russian, but still nothing. The soldier just looked at him defiantly.

As this was happening, the two older villagers, drawn by the sound of gunfire, returned.

"Russians," one of the men said in Ukrainian, spitting to get the taste of the word out of his mouth.

"Is he going to live?" the other asked in Russian.

Releasing pressure on the wound, Harvath stood. "No, he's going to die."

Harvath was under no obligation to save the Spetsnaz soldier. If the man wasn't going to cooperate, Harvath wasn't going to waste an additional ounce of energy on him. Reaching down, he unplugged the man's microphone and turned off his radio. He then motioned for the two old Ukrainians to come with him.

As the blood began soaking through his bandage, the Russian tried to apply pressure himself to the wound, only to realize how much trouble he was in. "Zhdat!" he shouted in Russian. *Wait!*

•   •   •

Harvath very quickly hit the ceiling on his Russian language capability and assigned the villagers to take the soldier's rapid, difficult-to-understand confession.

The team had been sent in search of an unknown, high-value target who was using some form of advanced encryption on his phone. Their assignment was to bring the phone and its owner back for interrogation.

When Harvath asked, "Back where?" the villagers pulled a map off one of the other soldiers and had the Russian identify where the command truck for the Leer-4 electronic warfare system was located.

Once the Russian did, Harvath had a decision to make. The soldier had lived up to his end of the bargain.

After speaking with his team, he turned his phone back on, dictated a rapid situation report, and transmitted it to Nicholas before turning his phone back off.

The convent had been exposed and was no longer safe for them. There was no telling if the Russians would send a second team or not. They would have to find someplace else to hole up. He was glad they had all gotten a shower and a hot meal when they had.

According to the Russian, his team was driving a 4x4 Škoda that they had parked nearby. Harvath sent Hookah and Biscuit to go get it.

While they were gone, he had Krueger and Jacks retrieve all of the Russians' radios and cell phones. After pulling their batteries, he wrapped them in a Mylar space blanket and enclosed them in an empty ammo can he had retrieved from the Novator in the garage.

It didn't make for a perfect Faraday cage, but it was better than nothing. Ukrainian intelligence might find the equipment useful, and he didn't want the Russians tracking any latent signal.

He also didn't want them tracking the elderly villagers who had selflessly offered to drive the injured soldier back to the front, where he could be transported to a Ukrainian field hospital.

Harvath explained the importance of keeping pressure on the wound and put together some extra gauze and bandages for the trip.

When Hookah and Biscuit arrived with the Škoda, Harvath and Jacks helped load the injured soldier and then told the villagers to get going. Whether he lived or died depended on how fast they moved.

As the Škoda exited the convent grounds, Krueger looked at the three Spetsnaz corpses and asked, "What should we do with them?"

"Gather up all their weapons and ammunition and throw it in our truck," said Harvath. "Beyond that, I don't care what happens."

"Roger that," the man replied.

•     •     •

As the team loaded their gear, Harvath studied his map, which he had unrolled across the hood of their armored vehicle.

"Where are we headed?" Hookah asked as he threw his pack in the back and came around to join him.

"I'm torn between the Ritz-Carlton here," said Harvath, pointing at one of the villages he had circled, attempting a little levity, "and a pretty nice Four Seasons over here."

"I'm more a boutique hotel man myself," he replied. "Craft cocktails. Themed rooms . . ."

"Heart-shaped bathtubs," Krueger interjected, "vibrating beds, hourly rates. You know, classy."

Harvath smiled as Hookah gave his colleague the finger.

"All kidding aside," stated Jacks, "even though you guys think you've narrowed it down, we still don't know where the Ravens are going to be next."

The Brit was right. It was a coin toss. Without the added piece he needed from Nicholas, there was no way to be certain. He only had his gut to go on. That meant he was going to have to take a guess. "We're going to the Four Seasons," he said, tapping the village on the map.

"I hope they've got a breakfast buffet," replied Krueger.

"With an omelet station," added Biscuit. "I haven't had a good omelet in a long time."

Harvath appreciated the esprit de corps. The truth was that they'd be lucky to find anything resembling a single creature comfort once they got out on the road. He had a very bad feeling that it was going to be *Mad Max* from here to the end of their assignment.

Firing up the Novator, he pulled out of the garage, pausing only long enough for Hookah to close the doors and hop back in the truck. Then, with the night-vision cameras activated, they headed north.

Based on the pattern he and Hookah had discerned, there were three locations Harvath believed were the most likely for the Ravens to target next.

He felt certain that their base of operations—or their safe house, as Hookah had called it—was close. *Close*, however, was a relative term. In essence, the Ravens—no matter how messed up and evil—were like any army. They were reliant upon logistics. How much fuel did they have access to? How far and over what kind of terrain could their vehicles travel? Did they have sufficient stocks of food and water, or did a chunk of their day need to be spent in finding and replenishing their supplies? What physical condition were they in? Were any of the Ravens sick or injured? Did they have access to enough manpower to capably carry out their assignments?

If the atrocity at the convent was any indication of their ability, they definitely weren't suffering in the labor department, which remained one of the biggest problems in Harvath's mind.

Hookah hadn't been wrong when he had expressed his concern about potentially being outgunned by five or six to one. It was absolutely something to be troubled by. The only thing worse than those kinds of odds was having to do battle with a foe of that size while they were entrenched in a fortified position. If that came to pass, Harvath and his guys would be raising up some big prayers to the tactical gods.

Their best hope was to catch the Ravens out in the open; take them by surprise in an ambush of some sort and cut them all down. But as Harvath had found in almost every assignment in his career, Murphy—of Murphy's Law fame—was going to want to have a say, especially as the battlefield was his playground.

There was also the issue of Anna Royko. Harvath knew close-quarters battle like the back of his hand. He had undergone so much hostage rescue training that he could do it in his sleep. But what about Jacks? Could he slice the pie and clear rooms at a level that wouldn't get himself, or the rest of them, killed? What about Biscuit? Or Krueger? Or Hookah?

He was 99.9 percent certain that they weren't going to find Anna tied to a tree in the middle of a field of flowers. She was going to be in the interior of a structure somewhere and that interior was going to very likely be hardened against attack. If the Ravens were halfway near as psychotic as they were made out to be, the booby traps at their lair were going to be a big problem. Was Harvath's team up to the challenge?

Or was it going to come down to him, slipping in like the fog, killing everyone in sight, and slipping back out with Anna over his shoulder? There simply was no way of knowing. Not, at least, until they found her and could put together a full plan. For the moment, he needed to put it out of his mind. Jacks helped him refocus.

"Up ahead, in seven hundred meters," said the Brit, who once again was riding shotgun and studying the map, "and we need to go right."

"Seven hundred meters," replied Harvath, "fork in the road. We go right. Roger that."

Jacks helped count down the distance until they arrived at the fork and Harvath took it.

There were a bunch of dilapidated signs, all in Ukrainian, which Harvath couldn't read. Some were road signs. Most were for businesses in the village up ahead.

One of the signs was bracketed with bunches of grapes. Its first four letters were the same as the word in Russian—*winery*.

"Look alive, everybody," said Harvath. "We're approaching our destination."

# CHAPTER 26

Harvath had no interest in driving through the center of town only to be met with an ambush. He'd taken that ride in the M113 on his way to the front lines and had no desire for a repeat.

Pulling off to the side of the road, on a high piece of ground, he decided that they'd take a nice, long, slow look around.

The Novator's forward-looking night-vision camera hadn't seen any movement. It was late. Any people still living down in the village would be asleep.

"Jacks and I are going to dismount for a quick reconnaissance," said Harvath.

There was a chorus of acknowledgments as the two men checked their rifles and then quietly exited the vehicle.

Stepping outside, he felt the wind and was reminded of how brisk it was. If they didn't find a decent place to camp tonight, they would have to sleep in the truck.

Besides the temperature, the other thing that was remarkable was the quiet. No dogs barking, no radios, nothing. It was eerie. Powering up his thermal device, he flipped the monocular down and scanned the village. There was not a single heat signature to be found—not even so much as a warm chimney or stovepipe. The entire town appeared deserted.

Turning to Jacks, he asked, "See anything?"

The Brit, who had put on his night-vision goggles, shook his head. "From here, nothing. Maybe if we get in closer."

"Agreed," said Harvath.

Once he and Jacks were back in the truck and had closed their doors, he put the Novator in gear and headed down into the village.

He drove through the empty streets. Unlike many villages he had seen, this one hadn't been ravaged by bombs and bullets. It was pretty much intact. So where was everyone?

As they continued, he noticed that most of the doors stood open and that people's personal property was scattered about. In his mind, that meant one thing—looting. Someone had recently been through here. Either Russian soldiers or the Ravens. He feared it was the latter.

They soon arrived at the end of the village, where he slowed the truck to a stop and took a final look around. There was another sign for the winery, informing would-be visitors that it was only two kilometers away.

"Everybody stay frosty," he advised.

He wanted the men to remain on heightened alert. They weren't out of the woods yet. In fact, there was every possibility that danger was waiting for them just up ahead.

The winery was fronted by a short, dirt road with rows and rows of what looked like overgrown, untended vines on each side.

As they neared the main building—a long, brick structure with terra-cotta roofing tiles—the dirt road turned into a paved drive.

Harvath kept going. His plan was to do a full loop of the property, to get a feel for who and what was there, before coming to a stop and getting out.

There were multiple support buildings as well as a wine garden with picnic benches and strings of overhead party lights. In any other situation, it probably would have been quite festive, especially on the weekends. Right now, however, it was as somber as a graveyard. There wasn't another living soul to be found.

They parked the Novator around back, out of sight from anyone who might be entering from the main road, and climbed out. It was now time to see if these guys had what it took when it came to room clearing.

They would tackle one building at a time. He'd leave a two-man team outside to stand guard while he took the other two inside with him. He'd then switch it up at the next building.

Explaining his plan, he, Hookah, and Krueger then made entry into the first building while Jacks and Biscuit took up positions outside.

The majority of the ground floor was a tasting room with benches and long wooden tables. There was broken glass and puddles of wine all over the place. Bottles had been smashed against the walls.

They cleared the tasting room, as well as two bathrooms, a small kitchen, an office, and a storage area—all of which had been ransacked. Upstairs were several more storage areas that had also been turned upside down. Hookah and Krueger had done plenty of house-to-house urban combat in Iraq and knew what they were doing.

Harvath switched it up for the wine-making building, taking Jacks and Biscuit inside with him while Hookah and Krueger stood guard. From the crush and fermentation areas to the lab, bottling, and casing departments, the Brit and the Canadian did a good job. And while Biscuit wasn't as experienced as his teammates, his basic skills were solid.

Once he had a feel for what they could do, he kept switching the room-clearing teams up—Hookah and Jacks, Biscuit and Krueger, et cetera—as they moved through the rest of the buildings.

One of the last structures they tackled was the vintner's residence. It was a modest, traditional Ukrainian structure, with a feature they had been seeing across the property—a ramp.

Inside was a table full of family photographs. The house appeared to belong to a family of four—a mom, a dad, and two twin daughters about four or five years old. The father was in a wheelchair.

They did a quick sweep of the house. Everything had been ransacked—drawers pulled out of dressers, chests upended, even the medicine cabinet had been hit.

Exiting the house, Harvath pulled the list of hidden Ukrainian art from the pocket in his chest rig.

"What kind of art were these guys protecting?" asked Krueger as he saw him reading.

"Three oil paintings," he replied, showing him pictures. "Landscapes by artists named Ivan Pokhitonov, Georgy Kurnakov, and Pyotr Sokolov."

"There's only one place we haven't cleared," said Biscuit.

Harvath nodded. "The cellars. That's our next stop."

. . .

The entrance was marked by a pair of large wooden doors with thick bands of metal and knobby metal rivets. They were set into the side of a hill behind the vintner's house and looked like they were a thousand years old.

With Biscuit on one door and Jacks on the other, Harvath, Hookah, and Krueger steadied their weapons and prepared to make entry. When Harvath nodded, the men pulled back the doors.

A tunnel, carved out of the rock, led down beneath the hill. Cautiously, they made their way inside.

It appeared to be a limestone cave system of some sort that had been enlarged and improved over the years. A sensor picked up their presence and automatically switched the lights on.

Harvath hated tunnels. They were bullet funnels, often with no place to hide or take cover. Picking up the pace, he moved as rapidly as good tactical procedure would allow.

The tunnel bent to the left and opened into a large cavern stacked with wine barrels. Up ahead, beyond the barrels, Harvath could see a body.

They worked quickly but methodically toward it, making sure it hadn't been placed there as bait and that no one was hiding in the barrels along their path.

When they got to the body, Harvath saw the wheelchair close by and knew who the deceased was. Someone had stuck a shotgun in the man's mouth and had pulled the trigger.

On the other side of the room was the naked corpse of the man's wife. She had been tied between two barrels and her throat had been sliced. He had no doubt that she had been sexually violated. And when he saw the empty, specially insulated barrels that had been used to hide the paintings, he knew who had done it.

Being underground, the cellar maintained a constant temperature. Harvath removed his glove and touched the woman's skin. It was cool, practically cold. He checked for rigor mortis, which had already begun to set in. She could have been dead for a good three to six hours. Maybe even more.

All he knew was that had he and his team arrived sooner, they might
have been able to stop this, and that pissed Harvath off. Orphans, nuns,
and a man in a wheelchair: the Ravens were absolute animals.

Harvath had no idea of the whereabouts of the couple's twin daughters, seen in the photos back at the house. He prayed to God that they
hadn't been present for their parents' brutal murders.

The men spent several minutes sweeping the various subterranean
side rooms but found nothing. The Ravens had come, they had gone, and
there was no telling where they would appear next. Nothing of any value
had been left behind.

Walking back up the tunnel, they exited the double doors and took a
deep, pained breath of fresh air.

Jacks and Biscuit could read the expression on their colleagues' faces.

"How bad was it?" the young Canadian asked.

"Terrible," replied Krueger.

"They killed the husband *and* the wife," Hookah stated. "The guy was
in a wheelchair, and they fucking killed him."

Jacks looked at Harvath, who shook his head and said, "It's a horror
show down there. Not sure how quickly they ended it for the husband,
but they definitely made the wife suffer. I've seen a lot of gruesome things
in my time, but what the Ravens are doing is . . ." His voice trailed off as
he sensed something to their left.

"Movement left," he stated, raising his rifle and turning in the direction of the threat. "Ten o'clock."

As the men all took cover and adjusted their weapons, Harvath flipped
down his thermal vision and powered it up.

When the image came on line, he could see the heat signature of a
lone figure attempting to use the brush for cover. The figure did not appear to be armed.

"I count one person," he said. "Doesn't appear to be armed—at least,
not with a long gun. I don't think it's a hostile."

"Could it be a local?" asked Jacks. "Someone from the village?"

"Let's find out," Harvath replied. Raising his voice so it could be
heard by the person in the trees, he called out using the term for bread,
"Palianytsia!"

A few moments later, a shout came back. It was a woman's voice. "Pa-lianytsia!" she replied. "Khto ty?"

She was speaking Ukrainian, but the phrase sounded almost identical to *Kto ty?*—the Russian words for *Who are you?*

"Amerikantsy," Harvath shouted back. "Mezhdunarodny Legion." *Americans. International Legion.*

"Ne strelyayte," she said, now in Russian, as she headed in his direction with her hands raised. *Don't shoot.*

"Dvigat'sya medlenno," Harvath cautioned her. *Move slowly.*

When the woman got close enough, Harvath let his weapon hang from its sling and quickly patted her down while his men kept her in their sights.

Whisps of white hair protruded from beneath her babushka. She was seventy years old if she was a day. Her body was bent and her deeply creased face was worn and weather-beaten. She had a million questions for Harvath, and they all came tumbling out at once.

Despite speaking in Russian, she was upset and talking too fast. He had to ask her to not only slow down, but also to simplify her questions and make them easier for him to understand.

The first question was about the family who lived at the winery. *Where were they?* He told her that the man and the woman had been killed.

Once again, she grew upset and very agitated. *What about the twins? The little girls? What happened to them?*

Harvath shook his head and told her he didn't know. They hadn't seen any sign of anyone else. The thought that the Ravens might have taken the two little girls and might have been doing God knows what to them made bile rise in his throat.

The old woman was also distraught and Harvath guided her toward a bench and helped her sit down.

After giving her a moment to collect herself, he asked her to tell him what had taken place. As she spoke, he did his best to translate for the team.

"Bad men came. Painted devils. Those who could escape came to the hills. There are lots of caves here. This is where she and a handful of others have been hiding."

"Painted devils?" Hookah repeated.

Harvath asked the old woman to explain. When she was done speaking, he said to his team, "Several of the men had their faces painted to look like skulls."

Hookah looked at him. "Are you serious?"

"Are you surprised?" Biscuit broke in. "Those Ravens are sick fucks."

Harvath agreed. "You're not wrong," he said as he turned back to the old woman, and they continued speaking.

As she laid out what had happened, he translated: "They came through this afternoon. Many trucks. Another villager, who had seen them coming, had sent a warning.

"When the men arrived, half went toward the winery, while the other half started looting homes. The villagers who had escaped to the caves barely made it out in time.

"Most of those who remained behind—friends, family, and neighbors—had been taken to the far end of the village and shot. ·

"A few, who had enclosed themselves in hidden spaces inside their homes, had described how the painted devils had gone through kitchens, dining rooms, and bathrooms looking for alcohol and medicines."

When Harvath pressed the old woman on any identifying characteristics, beyond the painted faces, she said there was one item all of the men had in common.

"On each of their uniforms, there was a patch," Harvath translated. "The head of a large, black bird—a raven."

"Did anyone notice anything else?" asked Krueger. "Maybe which direction they went when they left?"

Harvath asked, but the woman shook her head.

"Is she sure?" Krueger pressed. "Someone must have seen something. Maybe someone overheard a Raven talking. Ask her again. Better yet, let's get the rest of them out here and we can ask them one by one."

"You're pissing up a rope," said Hookah, exasperated and wanting his colleague to drop it. "They were terrified. All they cared about was staying alive. If they had any actionable intelligence, they would have given it to us."

The man was right. They had been terrified and their number one focus had been on staying alive, but Harvath realized that the woman had indeed given them a piece of actionable intelligence.

Removing his map again, he illuminated it with his flashlight and asked her to point out the village that had alerted them that the Ravens were headed their way. She did.

He then asked her how they had communicated. *Via cell phone*, she informed him. *And, before that, had another village warned them?* he asked. *Probably*, the woman replied. *We all stay in touch to help each other*. At that point, he only had one more question.

When she answered *yes*, he offered her his arm, helped her up, and began to lead her back to the vintner's residence.

"What's going on?" Jacks asked. "Did she come up with something?"

Harvath nodded. "It turns out, she's got access to a very special and very valuable piece of technology."

"What kind of technology?"

"A bush telegraph."

# CHAPTER 27

The Speaker of the House was hard enough to get on a weekday. On the weekends, it was practically impossible, which was why Greg Wilson had to put an incredible piece of bait on the hook. Actually, *two* pieces.

To get the Speaker to cancel his Saturday evening plans, Wilson had needed to offer him something better. That something was dinner at D.C.'s hottest and most difficult to get into restaurant—Minibar. And Wilson hadn't just gotten them *a* table at the two-Michelin-starred avant-garde eatery, he had gotten *the* table.

The private dining room just off the kitchen would allow them to speak freely while also enjoying a one-of-a-kind, experimental tasting menu that was renowned for fusing art and science.

The fact that they would be eating kitty-corner to the FBI's headquarters and only a couple of doors down from Ford's Theatre—where Abraham Lincoln had been shot—amused Wilson.

At one point, he had held both Lincoln and the Bureau in the highest regard. But that was the old Greg. The new Greg Wilson was post-American.

He had severed all emotional and psychological ties with the United States. It was just another country to him now; a means to a ten-million-dollar nest egg and a new passport.

To that end, his handler had offered him a sweetener—a bonus of sorts, to help get him to his goal even faster.

Before parting ways in Boston, Nistal had given him a new set of instructions. It was coming from the top and his bosses wanted to see results quickly. If Wilson could make things happen, he'd receive an additional $500,000, deposited into the bank account of his choice, anywhere in the world.

It was a generous incentive and one that Wilson intended to collect on as quickly as possible. He had no intention of spending another winter in D.C., or America for that matter. When he closed his eyes, he could almost taste the frothy blender drinks, smell the tanning oil, and see all the lithe female bodies along the beach. There had only been one hitch.

The Speaker wanted to bring his second-in-command, the House Majority Leader, who was responsible for helping set the legislative agenda and implementing policy. The man was an equally craven politician, so Wilson hadn't been averse to it. Then, because of how hot the restaurant was, the men had insisted on bringing their wives. It put Wilson in a tough spot.

Ever the negotiator, he amiably encouraged the women's attendance, with the caveat that after dinner they would retire next door to the restaurant's cocktail lounge, at which point the men could be left to talk business.

With the terms agreed to, the attendees met and had a fabulous meal. From the caviar-infused wagyu tartare to the steamed mussels, complete with shells made from frozen squid ink, which were designed to be eaten whole, the experience not only lived up to the restaurant's reputation but exceeded their expectations.

Once the wives had adjourned for their nightcaps, the men ordered digestifs and the conversation shifted.

"I've got to be honest," said the Majority Leader, taking in the expensive restaurant and glasses of Hennessy Paradis cognac that had been placed on the table in front of them, "I really felt for you when you lost your primary, Greg. But you totally landed on your feet. This is not a bad way to be living."

The Speaker agreed. "Yup. You got hit by a bus, but it was a twenty-four-karat-gold bus."

Wilson forced a smile. "I'm doing all right. But don't fool yourselves.

You guys, up on the Hill, are where the action is. That's the center of the universe."

"Six more months would have changed everything for you," the Majority Leader stated. "Hell, three months and the voters' opinions would have changed. Nobody cares about sex scandals anymore. You were the last casualty of that war."

"Now," the Speaker said with a laugh, "all that matters is how hard you pound the other side. All our constituents care about is that we're fighting. They want it nonstop, twenty-four/seven."

"And if we don't have anything to fight about, then we need to create something," the Majority Leader added. "We expanded our entire communications department to bring on savvier, more aggressive social media warriors. As we like to say, 'If you can't meme, there's no space on the team.'"

Wilson wasn't surprised to hear that Congress had devolved into an even worse form of theater since he had lost his seat.

"There is one thing that has really surprised me," the Speaker stated. "You have no idea how much the small-dollar donations have exploded. I mean, they've gone absolutely *stratospheric*.

"It used to be that you could really only count on small donations from voters in your district. But now, if you have a good fight with a witness during a hearing, or a good fight with an opposing member on your committee, and it goes viral, the donations pour in from across the country.

"We actually bring in media trainers to teach our freshman members how to ID these moments and maximize them. It's a license to print the easiest money you have ever seen in your life."

This also didn't surprise Wilson. In fact, it was one of the least shocking things he'd heard in a long time. The other side did the same thing with their voters. It all came down to one simple political maxim—*the base makes the case*.

Districts these days looked like they were drawn by someone having a seizure while holding a broken crayon. They were gerrymandered so that the party in control of that district remained in control. That meant that if your party was in charge, you had to appeal to those people who voted in the primaries, which was the base. If you won your primary, you were all but guaranteed to win the general election. It was, however, a deal with the devil.

Once you were in power, you had to continue to serve that base—no matter what it wanted—if you wanted to be reelected.

It could be unreasonable fiscal policies, outlandish environmental policies, or absolutely insane conspiracy theories—once you bought the ticket, you had no choice but to take the ride.

And if you ran afoul of the base—for example, by trying to demonstrate to them why a policy was better for the country in the long run, even if it meant giving up an opportunity to score points against the opposing political team—you were toast.

The base makes the case. What they want goes. As French politician Ledru-Rollin once said, "There go the people. I must follow them, for I am their leader."

It was, of course, corrosive for the body politic and a recipe for unmitigated disaster. If your immune system was constantly at war with itself, there was no way it would ever be able to fight off a hostile foreign invader. Wilson chalked it up as yet another reason he was glad to be getting out.

Steering the conversation to why he had shelled out several thousand dollars for this dinner, he said, "What's the next session shaping up to look like? Or is that going to depend upon what memes are trending?"

Both men chuckled.

Swirling the cognac in his glass, the Speaker replied, "I refer to it as our three-legged stool. Subpoenas. Investigations. And wall-to-wall media coverage."

"All circuses and no bread?"

"We're also working on the bread part, but that's not why you booked us the hottest table in town. What can we do for you? Or should I say, what can we do for the Paulsen Family Foundation?"

Wilson smiled, as did the Speaker and the Majority Leader. They could talk about small-dollar donations all day long, and they were substantial, but the real power still resided with the wealthy megadonors.

"It's funny you should mention them," said Wilson. "I was just up in Maine visiting with Mr. and Mrs. Paulsen this morning."

"I bet *that* house is amazing," the Majority Leader stated.

"If it's half as nice as their ranch in Jackson Hole," the Speaker replied, "it would put all of Georgetown to shame."

"It's impressive," the ex-Senator said. "The views alone are worth the trip. But I'm glad you mentioned the ranch."

"Yes. They were very kind to let us use it for our retreat. That place is like a world-class resort. Please thank them again for all of us."

"Mr. and Mrs. Paulsen were glad to make it available. In fact, the Paulsen Family Foundation wants to make it permanently available to you."

The Speaker's eyes widened. "What does that mean?"

"They're setting up a trust with the ranch as its centerpiece. They're getting older and they want to see their values, their *American* values, continued. They see the ranch as the perfect place from which to teach and promote those values. They envision leadership conferences, lectures, a thought leaders' festival, those kinds of things.

"Because you are a member of Congress, Mr. and Mrs. Paulsen understand that you couldn't be directly involved, but once you retire, they've prepared a very handsome offer for you to consider as president and CEO of the organization.

"In the meantime, the ranch is yours to use however and whenever you want—both in your professional and your personal capacities. Mr. and Mrs. Paulsen wanted me to suggest that you bring your family out for Christmas break. You can ski, snowmobile, snowshoe, the works. Just say the word. Their jet is available to you as well and it goes without saying that they're happy to color this however you want for disclosure purposes."

Looking at the Majority Leader, Wilson added, "And I know the Paulsens would consider it an honor to have the Majority Leader and his family as guests as well."

"Well, Mr. and Mrs. Paulsen continue to be extremely generous," said the Speaker. "Their support is much appreciated. They're incredible Americans. And, as I expect that you'll be billing them for this dinner, let me ask again, what's on their minds?"

The ex-Senator took a sip of cognac and replied, "Ukraine."

"That's a subject on a lot of people's minds."

"The Paulsens have specific thoughts."

"Such as?"

"Big picture—we should disengage, fully. No money, no weapons, no training, nothing. The sooner we're out, the better."

The Majority Leader looked at him. "The bulk of the American people wouldn't agree with you on that one."

"No," said Wilson, "but your base would. They don't want us anywhere near this war."

"We've got a general election coming up," said the Speaker. "If we want full control in Washington, which we do, we have to thread this needle *very* carefully. We can't play exclusively to the base, because we'll turn off key swing voters."

"But," the Majority Leader stated, "if we go too moderate, we risk the base staying home because they're pissed off."

"I get it," said Wilson. "And the Paulsens understand it, too. With control of the House, the Senate, and the Oval Office, you can do whatever you want. That's why I said cutting Ukraine loose was big picture. That's the long-term goal. In the short term, can you at least slow things down? Can you reduce the aid they're receiving? Tie up the weapons and ammunition flowing to them?"

"There's already a supplemental appropriation in place. That's going to keep money flowing for the rest of the fiscal year," the Speaker replied. "The Department of Defense sends older equipment to Ukraine and is able to use those funds to buy new equipment. As long as the defense industry keeps up, the United States doesn't have any readiness issues."

"And if it doesn't?" asked Wilson. "What happens if defense contractors fall behind—weapons systems going out the front door and nothing coming in to replace them?"

"Then we've got a problem."

Wilson thought for a moment. "It sounds to me like a strategic pause, long enough to audit supply chains and conduct a thorough review of America's military readiness, might be quite prudent. An investigation of this sort would not only please the base, but would also demonstrate that, under your leadership, you and the party take America's defense seriously."

The Speaker took a moment to reflect on what he had just heard. "Every business keeps one eye on the books, right? If the books don't balance, that can spell disaster. Which in this case could impact the performance of our own armed forces."

"I'm not saying *don't* arm the Ukrainians," Wilson clarified. "I'm just saying that, in all good faith, they shouldn't get so much as an additional bullet until we know that our service members, if called to battle, would have every single thing that they need."

"Hard to argue with that kind of logic."

"Agreed," replied the Majority Leader. "And anyone who does argue with it is not only being unreasonable, but they're also placing the safety and effectiveness of Ukrainian troops over America's sons and daughters."

The ex-Senator was very pleased with how the Speaker and Majority Leader were positioning themselves on this.

"Attacking the other side for prioritizing the national security of another nation over our own is a good fight," said the Speaker. "Let us kick it around internally a little bit. I'd like to get a poll in the field first thing on Monday morning. Let's see how people respond."

"Thank you," Wilson responded.

"You're welcome. Is there anything else you wanted to discuss? If not, I think we're going to go join our wives before they get in any trouble."

"Just one additional item. I want to suggest a piece of legislation."

"What's that?" the Majority Leader asked as he drained the last of his cognac.

"The Paulsens would like to see a bill introduced that prohibits Americans, particularly veterans, from going over and fighting for the Ukrainians."

"Not sure how much support you'd be able to get for that in the House. We might not be able to whip enough votes for it to pass."

"It doesn't need to pass," said Wilson, "not right away at least."

"I'm not sure I follow."

"What matters most is that the bill is introduced. You don't need to bring it up for a vote immediately. You can drag it out in committee. What's important is that the bill is a topic of conversation. If Americans know that their involvement with Ukraine might be criminalized at any moment, they'll think twice about going over. It'll have a chilling effect."

The Majority Leader nodded. "I see."

Finishing his cognac, the Speaker said, "Just thinking out loud, but we could assign something like that to one of our edgier freshmen. A rep from a rabid district where this kind of red meat would play well."

"But not a rep who's a kook," Wilson stated. "I don't care what their district looks like. Whoever is quarterbacking this should be good on TV, not too much of a bomb thrower. It helps if this issue, just like the military readiness review, becomes a mainstream topic of conversation."

"Got it," said the Speaker, setting down his snifter. "We'll get working on this right away. In the meantime, thank you for dinner and thank you for letting us bring our brides."

The ex-Senator stood and shook hands with his former colleagues. "You're welcome. And thank *you*. Mr. and Mrs. Paulsen are going to be pleased to get my report."

As he watched them leave the private dining room, he couldn't believe how easy that had been. It almost made him sorry he was getting out of the lobbying business. *Almost.*

After signing the check, he took a final sip of cognac and pushed himself away from the table. It had been a busy day. Juggling the Paulsens, the Russians, and the FBI was a bit like juggling chain saws, but as long as he paid attention, he was confident he was going to get out of this with his hands, fingers, feet, and toes intact.

The key to successfully walking away was not to prolong it. The people who got addicted—whether it was to the money, the proximity to power, or the excitement of it all—were the ones who ended up getting hurt.

Beyond the pain of a sunburn or the occasional hangover from too much rum, Greg Wilson had no intention of getting hurt. In his mind, he was already packing his bags. There was no one who'd be able to stop him.

# CHAPTER 28

Joe Carolan was standing in the FBI's underground garage. "Do me a favor," he said to the technician. "Check it again."

"What if there's no tracking device on your car?" Fields asked as he came back over to join her.

"There's a tracking device. Believe me."

"How do you know that your phone isn't hacked?"

"Because I already had it checked," the senior FBI agent replied. "And based on Carolan's razor, a tracker is the most likely answer."

"You mean Occam's razor. The simplest answer is usually the best answer."

"No, I do in fact mean Carolan's razor, which holds that the Russians, though never to be underestimated, are usually lazy and therefore strive to achieve their objectives by the easiest means possible."

Fields laughed. "You named a razor after yourself?"

"You go as long in the game as I have, grapple with as many Russians, I believe you earn that right. But you can take it or leave it."

"In other words," she replied, "it's a disposable razor."

The FBI man rolled his eyes and tried to get them to focus. "Let's replay what we learned from Mike Taylor, our conspiracy blogger and photographer. He's never met his 'Florida' employer. All his communications are via a messaging app. He was dispatched to the crime scene outside Burman's apartment and told to get as many photographs as possible. He was additionally told to keep an eye peeled for anyone who looked like federal law enforcement, specifically FBI. Whoever sent him assumed that the Bureau would be responding. That person wanted our photographs. They wanted to know who was working this case.

"And there I was, trying to spot Russians in the smattering of bystanders. Why get your own guys out of bed, why risk them being spotted, when you can just send a photographer? It's like the old joke about the dog that was so lazy, he didn't chase cars, he simply sat on the curb and wrote down license plate numbers."

Fields smiled. "Okay, but you haven't gamed this all the way out."

"What am I missing?"

"You originally thought that our conspiracy kid might be tailing the detective from D.C. Metro and, if so, that he had a source inside the PD. But when we interrogated him at his apartment, he told us that wasn't the case. He said he'd been told that you were headed toward the yacht club and he should get over there to take pictures."

"Exactly. That's how I know he's got a tracking device somewhere on my car."

"As far as Taylor told us, he was only at Burman's taking pictures. He didn't mess with anyone's car. He violated the restraining order at his ex-fiancée's place and then went home and uploaded his photos to a Dropbox page set up by his employer. If there's a tracking device on your vehicle, who put it there?"

It was a totally reasonable question and one that Carolan had been trying to figure out.

"I reviewed the CCTV footage from Burman's building, but based on where I parked, you couldn't see my vehicle. I couldn't see yours, either."

"You think my vehicle has a tracker on it, too?" Fields asked.

"Think about it. Just because you were the first FBI agent to show up doesn't mean there were going to be more. If we suspend Carolan's razor for a moment, maybe the Russians weren't that lazy. Maybe they had Taylor there taking pictures while somebody else had the job of placing devices."

"Right under the noses of all those cops?"

Carolan laughed. "How many cops do you know who even lock their cars when they pull up to a scene?"

"None."

"Exactly. You'd have to be insane to mess with a cop car; at least, that's what most people would think. With everyone focused on Burman's body and looking for evidence, no one was focused on the cars. Especially not those belonging to two FBI agents."

"Fair point," said Fields. "If they wanted to access either of our vehicles, they'd have to do it somewhere out on the street."

"Which, if they did do it while we were at Burman's, means they know we paid the conspiracy kid a visit."

Fields thought about that for a moment. "Only after he plastered your photo all over *The Public Truth* site. Even the Russians should have anticipated a knock-and-talk coming. Hell, if the situation was reversed, they probably would have hauled him off to a gulag."

"True," the FBI man agreed. "But regardless of what the Russians might think, we should consider him burned. Whoever was tasking him, they'd already placed a decent firewall around him. We'll have our cyber people continue to chip away at the Dropbox account, the messaging app, et cetera. Maybe we'll get lucky. In the meantime, I've got something else to show you."

Carolan reached into the bag at his feet and pulled out a manila envelope. Opening it, he withdrew a stack of surveillance photos and handed them over.

"Where'd these come from?" she asked.

"They were taken earlier today by agents from the Boston field office."

"You put a surveillance team on former Senator Greg Wilson?" she asked, a bit incredulous. "How did you even know he was going to be in Boston?"

"I've been watching his bank accounts and may have flagged his credit cards."

"Again with the extrajudicial actions? Jesus, Joe."

Carolan ignored her distaste for his behavior. "I thought the trip to Maine, right when we needed to speak with him about a murder, was highly suspect."

"But his assistant had told you that the trip had been on the books for weeks."

"Assistants lie for their bosses all the time."

"So, you took it upon yourself to look into his banking records and flag his credit cards?"

"Not all his banking records," the FBI man admitted. "He's got some high-level things going with some private banks that'll require serious legal paper to puncture. But the lower-level stuff, his mortgage, his credit cards, yes. I wanted to confirm that the Maine trip had indeed been preplanned."

"And had it?"

Carolan nodded. "Yes, the assistant was telling the truth."

"Then why place the flags?"

"You know why. You've been at this long enough. When the law starts closing in, some people panic. They run. I wanted to make sure that Wilson didn't take off."

"Seeing as how he was in Maine and could have hopped over the border into Canada," said Fields, "maybe you should have also flagged his passport."

"I did."

"Of course you did."

The FBI man kept going. "When I saw that he changed his airline ticket home to include a stop in Boston, I reached out to the field office and asked them to keep their eyes and ears open.

"They had a surveillance team working a separate case in the North End, which is Boston's version of Little Italy. They saw Wilson leaving one of the restaurants there. He walked out alone. Then a few minutes later, the next guy in the photos walked out. Alone.

"When the surveillance team wrapped their shift and returned to the office, they heard about my request regarding Wilson and sent the photos down."

Fields studied the photos again. "Do we have any idea who this second person is? Or if he and Wilson are even connected?"

"Yes and no," said Carolan. "After receiving the photos, I sent another request. The Boston field office then sent agents by the restaurant. Those agents confirmed that Wilson did in fact meet and have lunch with the other man. The other man paid for their lunch in cash. We don't yet know who that other man is."

"Or what they were there to talk about. It could be nothing. You could be violating not just Greg Wilson's civil liberties, but also those of the man he was having lunch with."

He shook his head. "That's not what my gut tells me."

"More of Carolan's razor?"

"Think about it. Wilson is one of the last people to have seen Burman alive. Burman is thrown off his roof and now not only are the police involved, but also the FBI. We try to talk with Wilson, but he puts us off because he's got a trip on the books. Yet instead of returning straight to D.C. to sit down with us, he changes his plans and flies to Boston for lunch. Kind of weird, isn't it?"

"That's the thing, though. 'Kind of weird' isn't against the law. This could be some new client that just popped up. It could be an old friend. Who knows? The point being, we don't get to color outside the lines. You've got to knock this the fuck off. And yes, I said *fuck*. Deal with it."

Carolan was about to reply when the tech called out to him from the other side of the garage.

When he and Fields walked over, the tech said, "You're never going to believe this."

"Try me," Carolan replied.

"There's a frequency range that we normally sweep for. About ninety-nine percent of what we look for falls within that range. Then people started using Apple AirTags to track vehicles and we had to adjust the range.

"I swept your car for everything we know of. There was nothing to be found. On a lark, I decided to drop the frequency. And I mean *really* drop it. All of a sudden, bingo. I got a hit."

"What did you find?"

"I want to film this," the tech said as he handed Carolan his scanner and pulled out his phone to take a video. "We may end up teaching classes on this."

Once the man began recording, he had Carolan sweep the scanner back and forth over the left rear quarter panel. The beeping increased whenever the scanner got close to the tire.

Bending down, the tech filmed inside the wheel well and then felt along it with his bare hand. Moments later, he found something.

Pulling a folding knife from his pocket, he flicked it open and removed what looked like a blackened piece of gum, or even road tar, with a hair sticking out of it.

"What is that?" Carolan asked.

The tech stood up and took the scanner back. After powering it off, he set it on the trunk and then examined what he had pulled from the wheel well.

"I've never seen anything like it," he said. "It's so small. The signal has got to be next to nothing. Unless . . ."

"Unless *what?*" Fields asked as the man's voice trailed off.

"Unless it's specifically meant for a high-density, urban environment."

Carolan looked at him. "Meaning?"

"It could be much smaller than an AirTag but work similarly, hopping from one Wi-Fi network to another. The trail would be spotty, depending upon the coverage, but the trade-off, in my opinion, is totally worth it. This thing is practically invisible."

Fields pulled her keys out, chirped the alarm on her vehicle, and handed the fob to the tech. "Please check my car right now."

The tech took it from her and headed toward her vehicle.

As he walked away, she said to her boss, "If this happened while we were at Burman's, they know where we live. You and I have both been home since then."

Carolan's mind was already several steps ahead. "I'm going to call Margaret and tell her to pack a bag. She's overdue for a visit with her sister. Do you have someplace else you can stay for a while?"

Fields nodded. "I've got a couple of options. What about you?"

"I'll probably use the couch in my office. At least for tonight. After that, we'll see."

"Found another one!" the tech yelled out from Fields's vehicle.

"That was fast," Carolan replied as they walked over to him.

"Now that I know what I'm looking for, they're actually pretty easy to find."

Reaching into the wheel well, he pulled out an identical tracking device and held it up for them to see.

"Any other vehicles you want me to check?" the tech asked.

"Yes," he responded as he pulled out his phone. "Stand by."

Walking a few feet away, Carolan brought up his address book and selected the entry for his predecessor—the woman who had headed the Quick Silver operation and had suffered a series of massive, still-unexplained heart attacks—and placed a call to her cell.

"Nancy," he said when she answered, "it's Joe Carolan. I'm sorry to bother you, but I want to have someone inspect your Bureau vehicle. Is it at your house? May I send one of the countersurveillance people out right now?"

As soon as the call was finished, he walked back over to the tech. They traded cell phone numbers and Carolan texted him Nancy's contact information.

"Let me know as soon as you're done. Okay?"

"Will do," said the tech as he placed the devices in Faraday pouches, gathered up the rest of his gear, and headed off to his car to drive out to Bethesda, Maryland, to make a house call.

Fields waited for the tech to be out of earshot and then asked, "Do you think whoever planted these trackers was also behind what happened to Nancy?"

"I don't know yet," Carolan replied. "But I think it's worth looking into."

"So where does that leave us? What's our next step?"

He gestured at the photos still in her hand and said, "Short of any new leads, I think there's only one road available to us, and that road points right to Greg Wilson."

# CHAPTER 29

Harvath was exhausted. His entire team was exhausted. But they couldn't let their guard down. Not now. Not with danger so close.

As Hookah and Biscuit had been standing guard at the convent and hadn't had any sleep, he ordered them to turn in. He placed Jacks and Krueger on watch and stepped inside the vintner's residence with the old woman.

She stopped at the table full of photographs, picked up one of the family, and clasped it to her chest.

As she did, tears began to roll down her cheeks. "Druz'ya," she said in Russian. *Friends.*

Harvath had her sit down in the dining room while he stepped into the kitchen and began looking through the cupboards. They had been cleaned out. The Ravens had taken everything.

He told her to wait and then hustled outside to their truck, where he gathered up a couple of Ukrainian MREs and brought them back inside.

"Chay ili kofe?" he asked her. *Tea or coffee?*

"Chay, pozhaluysta," she replied. *Tea, please.*

As he started boiling water in the kitchen, he opened a fresh MRE and offered her an assortment of snacks—biscuits, some more dark chocolate, cheese, as well as another pouch of dried apricots.

"Nyet," she said. "Dlya detey." *For the children.*

He pointed at the MREs and told her not to worry. There were more in his vehicle.

He knew she must be hungry and encouraged her to eat. Slowly, she thanked him and accepted a sleeve of biscuits.

When the water had come to a boil, he found two glasses and prepared a tea for her and a coffee for himself. The MRE came with a packet of sugar as well as creamer, which he handed to her along with a spoon.

"Spasiba," she responded. *Thank you.*

He gave her a moment of peace, perhaps the first she'd had all day, and allowed her to drink her tea undisturbed. Faceup on the table in front of her was the picture of the vintner and his family. "Druz'ya," she said again, lovingly touching it.

"Druz'ya," Harvath repeated.

Once he felt that a long enough respectful silence had passed between them, he removed his map and laid it across the table. The old woman nodded and set the photo off to the side, out of the way. She understood that work needed to be done.

Harvath asked her to confirm their position on the map and then asked her to show him again which village had alerted them that the Ravens were coming. She pointed to the same village as before. That was good. The old woman hadn't struck him as someone with cognitive difficulties, but this was critical intelligence they were gathering, and he had to be positive that she was fully with it.

With that out of the way, he wanted to reverse engineer the bush telegraph. They would do that by contacting the person who had let them know that the Ravens were coming. Kind of like Paul Revere's midnight ride, but backward.

He asked the old woman if it had been via text or a voice call. Her response surprised him. She said that she didn't know. When he pressed her for more information, she explained that she didn't have a cell phone. Someone else had received the warning. She had merely helped pass it along and had guided everyone to the caves.

Harvath was frustrated, but he maintained his composure and smiled. If his Russian had been better, perhaps this fact would have been clear from the jump.

He followed up by asking if the person who had received the warning was in the caves. The woman shook her head. His heart was ready to drop into his stomach. Was this person still alive? Or had they lost a crucial link, perhaps *the* crucial link, in the bush telegraph?

He asked where the person could be found now. She informed him that the woman with the phone was in the woods keeping watch. He asked if she could take him to her. The old woman agreed.

Stepping out of the vintner's residence, Harvath let Jacks and Krueger know what he was up to. They offered to come along with him, but he told them it wouldn't be necessary and that they should remain in place.

Powering up his thermal device, Harvath followed the old woman up into the hills above the cellar.

Despite her age and crooked posture, she moved at a good clip. Soon they were stepping into the trees at the edge of the woods. Twice, the old woman looked over her shoulder and asked if Harvath needed a rest. He did, a nice long one, preferably on a warm beach somewhere with Sølvi and a bottomless bucket of ice-cold beers. Right now, however, he would have settled for forty-five minutes sitting upright in a chair or laid out in the back of the truck.

Repeatedly running, gunning, and trying not to die—all while on little to no sleep—reminded him of Hell Week as he fought to become a SEAL. He was a lot younger then, but the lesson had been seared into his mind. Sleep was a luxury. When pushed, there was a tremendous amount he could still do without it.

Deeper into the woods, the old woman began calling out for her friend with the phone. Seconds later, Harvath picked up her heat signature on his thermal.

The old woman introduced her as Vesna. After a quick discussion, they led Harvath to the cave where the others were hiding.

It was a mix of women and children, about fifteen in total. He invited them to come down to the winery, get something to eat, and spend the night there. When they agreed, he radioed Jacks and Krueger to let them know.

The vintner's residence was too small to cram fifteen additional people into. Hookah and Biscuit were already bedded down there. Dragging in a crowd would make it impossible for them to sleep. And there was also only one bathroom. The best option was the tasting room in the main building.

By the time Harvath arrived with the villagers, Krueger had already gone through with a large push broom and had swept up most of the glass. He had also found a mop and a bucket, which he had filled with soapy water. When he reached for it, the old woman insisted that she be allowed to do it. Politely, he stood back.

As the women and children used the washrooms, Harvath went out to the truck and grabbed a stack of MREs, as well as bottles of water.

Bringing them back to the tasting room, he opened them up, distributed the snacks to the kids, and explained to a couple of the ladies how the flameless ration heaters worked. They smiled nicely, set the heaters aside, and took the pouches of food into the kitchen to warm the meals up the old-fashioned way—on the stove.

Sitting Vesna down at the far end of the room, Harvath removed his map and spread it across the table. The old woman had already explained to her what he needed.

Her phone was almost out of power, but she had been smart enough to bring her charger when she fled the village. Plugging it into a nearby outlet, she moved her chair closer to the wall and sent her first text message. They waited, but there was no immediate response.

It probably had to do with the hour—it was late and the person she was attempting to reach was likely asleep. Taking the initiative, she gave up on texting and placed a call. She was a self-starter. Harvath liked that.

She was also smart and had understood, right down to the minutiae, what he needed.

He had told her to ask questions like a journalist or a police detective. It wasn't just which direction the Ravens had been seen traveling in that he wanted. He also wanted to know how many men and what types of vehicles they had been driving. What kind of weapons did they have? Had they stopped to loot any other towns? What did they steal? Did they post guards on the road? Every single piece of information was critical.

While she continued working the phone, one of the ladies brought Vesna a mug of tea and something to eat.

With each contact she made, the woman identified the town or village on Harvath's map and slowly explained for him what had happened. Slowly, rung by rung, they were working their way up the ladder.

Everyone she spoke with had been horrified to hear what had happened in her village and out at the winery. Several had their own terrible tales of wanton slaughter. The Ravens had been blazing a trail of savagery across the region. There was almost no one anywhere in the area who had been untouched.

After fixing himself a cup of coffee, Harvath returned to the table and went back to making notes and circling places on the map. He couldn't have asked for a better intelligence network. The bush telegraph was helping him close in on the Ravens.

He was also developing a picture of their strength and how they operated. Their hits weren't simply pell-mell, anything-goes free-for-alls. There was, at least on a small level, a little bit of tactical thinking going on.

The men with their faces painted to resemble skulls were part of every raid. Their war paint and violent behavior appeared to be meant as a form of shock and awe, a way by which to cow villagers and townspeople into submission.

Harvath was also open to the possibility that the "painted devils," as the old woman had called them, were recruits from Russian insane asylums who either didn't know any better or didn't care about charging headlong into potentially deadly situations.

For the more mentally balanced members of the unit, the painted devils might have been nothing more than cannon fodder—bullet sponges, sent in first to see what happens.

Regardless of how they deployed their forces, the mercenaries were ruthless and showed no concern for life or limb. In keeping with earlier reports, eyewitness accounts continued to place their strength somewhere between twenty and thirty soldiers.

Harvath still wasn't crazy about taking on that many and he knew his team wouldn't be, either. Their best bet was to try to thin the Ravens' ranks before engaging in a head-on fight. Based upon the developments he was seeing on his map, he was beginning to think that he might have identified an opportunity.

When Vesna had completed her last call, he listened to the facts she had gathered, made a few additional notes, and thanked her. She, and the people in the other villages, had been an incredible help. It was now time for him to get some rest.

After making sure everyone in the tasting room had everything they needed, he checked in with Jacks and Krueger before returning to the vintner's residence to grab a little shut-eye.

As Hookah and Biscuit had set themselves up in the home's two bedrooms, Harvath took the couch in the living room.

With his rifle leaned against the coffee table, he set his plate carrier on the floor and stretched out. He was so tired that he didn't even bother taking his boots off.

He was glad to be bringing this horrific day to a close. He hoped that tomorrow would be considerably less gruesome, but he doubted it.

Unrolling his sleeping bag, he draped it over himself and closed his eyes. Within seconds, he was asleep.

# CHAPTER 30

The next morning, Harvath pulled his equipment together and walked over to the main building.

Hookah and Biscuit were seated at a table outside, their rifles at the ready, eating.

"Are those omelets?" asked Harvath.

Biscuit nodded. "You definitely picked the right hotel."

"Where'd you get those?"

His mouth full, Hookah pointed toward the tasting room with his fork.

Harvath stepped inside and saw a hive of activity. The kids, having slept and eaten, were running around, while several of the ladies were chatting, and two more were in the kitchen cooking.

Upon seeing him, the old woman came over, told him to sit down, and asked if he wanted tea or coffee. He chose coffee. Jacks and Krueger were sitting nearby, almost done with their food.

"Where'd the eggs come from?" he asked.

"One of the villagers walked back to town to get them," said Krueger.

"Got to hand it to Biscuit," Jacks stated. "First, he asks for hot showers, then an omelet station. We're trying to decide what to have him ask for next."

"How about the safe return of a twenty-five-year-old American aid worker and two little Ukrainian girls?" Harvath answered.

The two soldiers sat in stunned silence. It was an unnecessarily sharp reply and Harvath knew it. Though he had slept, he hadn't slept well. Compounding matters, he had risked switching his phone on to see if he had any messages from Nicholas. He did, but it wasn't good news. The little man had been unable to get him what he had asked for. None of this, however, was an excuse for Harvath to be a dick to his men.

Softening his tone, he asked, "You guys want some more coffee?"

The men nodded.

"Why don't you finish your breakfast and let's meet outside. I'll bring a pot out with me."

Jacks and Krueger chowed down their last couple of bites, took their dishes into the kitchen, and, carrying their cups, exited the building.

The old woman reappeared at the table and set Harvath's breakfast in front of him.

"Spasiba," he said to her. *Thank you*.

"Pozhaluysta," she replied. "Segodnya vy naydete detey." *You are welcome. Today you find the children*.

He knew exactly what children she was referring to. They were the daughters of the vintner and his wife, the little twins.

There was no telling if they were alive or where they might even be. Nevertheless, he nodded his head. If they were out there and he could bring them back, he would do it, along with Anna Royko.

As he took a sip of coffee, he asked the old woman if she had enough to make a pot that he could take out to his men. She told him to eat his breakfast and she would check.

As he was finishing his omelet, she returned and set a pot of hot coffee on the table. He thanked her again and she took his plate back to the kitchen. He then went outside to join his men.

Filling their cups, he asked, "Everyone get enough to eat?"

They all nodded and, setting the pot down, he retrieved his map and spread it out on the picnic table where Hookah and Biscuit had been eating.

"I've got good news," he said. "And I've got bad news."

"Bad news first," Biscuit replied.

"Okay, bad news, then. I was unable to get any information on troop movements and where the next push might come on the front lines."

"Can you blame them?" Krueger asked. "That's some of the most closely guarded information the Ukrainians have."

Harvath nodded. "Knowing that the Ravens shift as the front lines shift, it could have helped us get ahead of them, but I don't blame the Ukrainians for not sharing."

"What's the good news?" asked Jacks.

"The good news," he replied, straightening the map, "is that we've narrowed down where we think the Ravens' base of operation is. We've also learned a little bit more about how they operate.

"They like to hit their ultimate target around nightfall. Along the way, they're opportunistic. Sometimes, they'll pass through towns and villages without stopping. More often than not, however, they'll pick them clean as they go.

"And if they have too much time on their hands, that's when things really get brutal. The unlucky locals who haven't hidden or fled get rounded up, tortured, and exterminated. Their depravity knows no limits.

"They move in a six-vehicle convoy. One Humvee in front and one in back, both with what sounds like .50-cal machine guns. In between are two four-by-fours, as well as two large cargo trucks capable of carrying additional men, as well as whatever art and other items they're looting.

"The four-by-fours are outriders, like motorcycle cops blocking traffic for a motorcade. One secures the entrance to the village while the other handles the exit. As the rest of the phalanx rolls in, the gunners in the Humvees put rounds on anything that moves.

"In the towns or villages where there has been art to recover, one Humvee will accompany one cargo truck to the target. The remaining Humvee and cargo truck will pillage shops and houses. In other locations where there isn't a predetermined target, it's a mad dash to grab whatever they can."

"These guys really are animals," said Hookah.

Harvath nodded. "Animals, with just a little bit of training, which makes them all the more dangerous."

"Are we sure they actually have training, or are they just being told what to do by somebody who has experience?" asked Jacks.

"Good point," replied Harvath. "We actually don't know. In fact, once unleashed, they show a lot of indiscipline. Which brings us to their leader. According to witnesses, there's always the same guy in charge. Some big, muscle-bound, baldheaded asshole. He barks out the orders and everyone reports to him."

"How many is 'everyone'?" Krueger asked. "Any further clarity on their troop strength?"

Harvath shook his head. "By all accounts, the number hasn't changed. Still somewhere between twenty and thirty." Tracing his finger along the map, he added, "As far as I can tell, these are the routes they've taken over the last several days."

"Which means," said Hookah, drawing a circle with his own finger, "they're likely to be based somewhere in this area."

"Agreed," Harvath replied. "Our question now, *very* specifically, is where?"

"What's left on the list?"

Harvath pointed to three spots on the map.

"Is there anything unique about them?" Hookah continued. "Anything that might suggest who's next to get hit?"

"We don't know who's next or even when," said Harvath. "But we've got a network of informants now."

"Which will only tell us when they see these motherfuckers roll by," said Krueger. "We'll still be playing catch-up. We won't be out in front of them, prepping the battlefield, and tilting the situation to our advantage."

"Unless," Harvath replied with a smile, "we turn chasing them to our advantage."

"How would that work to our advantage?" Jacks asked.

"When they have an objective, they break into separate teams. If we arrive on scene and take out one of the outriders on either end of the village, we've already reduced their strength. We may even gain an additional vehicle and God only knows what gear inside."

"And if one of those outriders, before we can snuff him out, calls all of his buddies back to fight us? Then what?"

"Then we run, or even better, we fight."

Biscuit shook his head. "I don't know if I like this plan."

"You got a better one?" said Hookah.

"He doesn't need one," said Harvath. "We actually may be able to tilt the scales a little bit further in our favor."

"How?"

"We can't afford to split up, so that means we need to be able to respond as a group as quickly as possible wherever the Ravens strike next. Based on how they've been moving," said Harvath as he pointed to different spots on the map, "we need to place ourselves just outside their area of operations.

"If their sphere of influence is like a watch face, we want to be hovering right near nine o'clock. This side holds the remaining targets they haven't hit yet. We may not be able to beat them to the next one, but the roads to the west are better and have sustained less damage. At the very least, when we receive a tip, we can get to the next village at the same time or just behind them."

"And then what? We gun it out with twenty to thirty Ravens?" asked Biscuit.

"Maybe we don't have to," Harvath replied. "All we need is one to tell us where they're keeping Anna Royko."

"So you want to grab one of the Ravens as a hostage?" said Krueger.

Harvath nodded. "Truth be told, I'd like to grab a couple of them. Just to make sure that what we're being told is accurate."

"Where do you plan to interrogate your hostages?" Hookah asked. "Right there in the street? Or do we need to set up a safe house in the area where you can have a waterboard ready to go?"

"I'm confident I can get an answer right in the middle of the road. Especially if I have more than one Raven to work with."

"What are you going to do? Shoot one of them to make the others talk?"

"Don't worry about what I'm going to do," he replied. "I've got my orders and you've got yours. As long as you follow my lead, everything'll be fine."

"I hate to sound like a broken record," Jacks interjected, "but I want to bring it up again—what happens if we accidentally tip our hand and all the Ravens come crashing down on top of us? What's that fight look like?

And more important, how the hell do we win it? We've got rifles and grenades. They've got .50-cals on at least two vehicles and God knows what else inside."

"Listen," said Harvath. "There's a lot of intel that I'd love for us to have, which we're not going to. Improvisation is key. We'll have to formulate our plan on the go. The situation on the ground will dictate everything. That's just the way it has to be."

"So we're just going to wing it?" asked Hookah.

"You saw what they did at the convent. You saw what they did here. I told you about the orphanage and countless other atrocities these guys have perpetrated. I wish we had more support. Hell, I'd give a month's pay for a little, off-the-shelf drone at this point. But we're not going to get any of that.

"We're going to war with the army we have—*us*. It's either me and you four, or, like I said before, it's just me. Each of you came here to make a difference. *This* is how you do it. This is how you have the biggest impact and make life better for these people.

"I'm packing up the truck and I'm leaving in thirty minutes. Whoever wants to come, I'll see you in a half hour."

With that, Harvath collected his map, picked up his coffee cup, and headed back to the vintner's residence.

•   •   •

Thirty minutes wasn't a ton of time to get ready. After doing a quick field strip and a cleaning of his rifle, he cleaned himself up and put some more burn cream on his back. He was tempted to pop a pain pill, but he was going to be driving into who-knew-what and didn't want anything in his system that might dull his reflexes. Packing up his gear, he took everything outside and loaded it into the truck.

After attaching a spout to one of the jerry cans and topping off the Novator with diesel, he returned to the tasting room to have a final chat with Vesna. Everything depended on her staying in touch with the other villages and getting him information as quickly as possible. She promised to keep her phone charged and to reach out to him as soon as she heard something. He thanked her for all her help.

He had hoped to say good-bye to the old woman too but couldn't find her. Then, as he left the main building, he saw her headed toward him.

She stopped, wished him well, and then pressed something into his hand.

Walking away, she switched to Ukrainian and left him with the words "Slava Ukraïni." *Glory to Ukraine*. It was the national battle cry and a testament to the resistance of the Ukrainian people against the Russian invasion and all the horrors the Russians had perpetrated.

Opening his hand, he unfolded the photograph she had placed in his palm. It was the one from the frame, the one she had picked up from the table, showing the vintner, his wife, and their twin daughters.

He looked at it for a moment and then tucked it into his pocket.

When he arrived back at the truck, Biscuit, Jacks, Krueger, and Hookah were all standing there, gear packed, ready to go.

"This looks like a good sign," said Harvath.

"Biscuit finally knows what he wants to ask for," said Jacks.

Harvath glanced at the young Canadian. "I don't know how you top hot showers, followed by an omelet station, but go ahead. Let's manifest our next amenity."

"It's not an amenity," the young man replied. "I want to recover the hostages and for all of us to get out safely."

"And if there are no hostages?" Harvath asked, preparing his team for that eventuality.

"Then we do what we came here to do. We kill as many fucking Orcs as possible."

"Ooh-rah," Krueger replied.

"Slava Ukraïni!" said Jacks, adding the popular second phrase, "Heroiam slava!" *Glory to the heroes*.

The men returned the battle cry and climbed into the truck.

Sliding behind the wheel, Harvath removed the picture of the vintner and his family.

As he fired up the engine, he affixed the photo to the dashboard and said, "Time to clip some wings."

# CHAPTER 31

They had been on the road for a couple of hours when they finally reached their destination. It was a crossroads where they would await confirmation that the Ravens had been spotted. Nearby was a stream and an old, abandoned mill.

The mill, though infested with pigeons, was perfect. It was just large enough to get the Novator inside, close the doors, and allow them to remain out of sight.

"I'll take first watch," said Harvath. "The rest of you guys can get some sleep, eat, kick back, whatever you want to do."

His was the only cell phone that was allowed to be on. If the Russians had another electronic warfare system anywhere in the area, he didn't want it to pick up a cluster of phones all in one location. They would be begging to get shelled.

He had also completely closed the encrypted app he used with Nicholas. The only app he had open was Signal, which was popular with Ukrainians and Russians alike. If and when Vesna had intel for him, that was how she was going to make contact.

Picking a spot with the best view of the road outside, Harvath got comfortable. A few minutes later, Hookah came over and joined him.

"Smoke?" he asked, offering one of his cigarettes.

"No, thanks," said Harvath. "I don't smoke."

Hookah had found an old coffee can, added some stream water to ash into, and set it on the ground between them.

Lighting his cigarette, he took a long drag and held the smoke deep in his lungs. After exhaling, he asked, "How long have you been with the legion?"

His eyes still on the road, Harvath replied, "Less than two days."

"And already a captain on special assignment," the man said with a laugh as he took another puff. "I don't think lightning even moves that fast in Ukraine."

"Wars can be funny."

Hookah exhaled. "Not that funny."

"What about you?" Harvath asked, changing the subject.

"I signed up about eight months ago. Jacks and Krueger got in about six months ago and Biscuit four."

"Interesting. What about your call signs? Did you guys pick your own or were they given to you?"

"It's a camaraderie thing," said the man. "You get a call sign from fellow soldiers within the first couple of days."

"How'd you get yours?"

Hookah held up his cigarette. "I guess my guys thought I smoked too much."

Harvath smiled, remembering what he would have called the man. "Could have been worse. What about the rest of the team?"

"Jacks had a bunch of Union Jack patches on all his shit, so that's where his call sign comes from. Krueger arrived with something like eight knives and got named after Freddy Krueger from the slasher movies."

"And Biscuit?"

"He grew to be a fat motherfucker after getting out of the Canadian Army. I mean *morbidly* obese. Nobody believed him until he popped a picture up on his phone of what he used to look like. He wasn't three hundred pounds, but he was close. One of the guys said he was just a biscuit under and the call sign stuck. The doctors had told him that if he didn't get his act together, he was going to die. So what did he do? He dedicated himself to getting back into fighting shape and then rewarded himself with coming to Ukraine and joining the legion."

"That's some interesting psychology," Harvath replied.

Hookah shrugged and took another pull off his cigarette. "People have all sorts of reasons for doing what they do. I think Biscuit had a hard time readjusting to civilian life. A lot of guys are in the legion because they believe in the mission, but there are those who also just miss the action. Probably a bit of both for many. What about you?"

"Me?"

"Yeah, you. Why are you here? Miss the action? Believe in the mission?"

"I definitely believe in the mission," said Harvath. "I also think that I'd probably go crazy without the action."

Hookah nodded as he blew a cloud of smoke into the air. "I hear you. Nothing worse than being a *former* action guy. It's certainly a lifestyle that's hard to walk away from."

"Agreed."

"How'd you get your call sign? When the legion told us we'd be linking up with you, they said it's Norseman?"

Harvath smiled again. "I got it back when I was a SEAL. I dated a few Scandinavian flight attendants and it stuck."

"So you're one of those guys."

"What guys?"

"You brought your own call sign with you."

"And?" asked Harvath. "Is there a problem with that?"

"There's no *I* in *team*, but there is *me*, right?"

Harvath chuckled. "Are you going to bust my balls because I didn't get a call sign here?"

"No, sir, Captain. I wouldn't dream of it."

"Sure you wouldn't."

"Even if we wanted to give you a new call sign, it takes a couple of days to get to know you, so . . ."

"I'm safe."

"And you're Norseman. For now."

"Good," said Harvath. "That's one less thing for me to worry about."

Hookah flicked some ash into his coffee can and changed the subject. "You're not over here just fighting the good fight. What are you? One of the alphabets in the soup? Wait, don't answer that. Let me guess. CIA?"

Harvath shook his head. "I'm just a guy here to do a job."

Hookah laughed. *"Just* a guy. Okay, I won't push it. Your secret's safe with me."

"There's no secret."

Hookah took another drag and gave Harvath an exaggerated wink. "Right. No secret. I got it."

Harvath nodded and let it drop.

They sat for several moments with neither man speaking. Up above, you could hear the occasional pigeon. Outside, the stream rippled as it moved past the mill and its old wooden wheel.

Hookah exhaled a curl of blue smoke and asked, "Any new thoughts on how we might handle the Ravens?"

"I spent a good chunk of the drive here thinking about it," said Harvath. "But I'm not sure how good any of the ideas are."

"I'm all ears," the man responded.

"The Ravens have been conducting their assaults completely unopposed. They post security at each end of a village because it's good tactics, not because they're expecting any trouble. If I had to guess, I'd say those guys are the least switched on.

"Pulling security is likely the most boring assignment the Ravens hand out. It's also one of their weakest links—four men at each end, normally with no line of sight to any of their teammates, and only connected via radio."

"Agreed."

"The security unit at the back of the convoy already knows what's behind them. That's not where the mystery is. The mystery is what's at the other end of the village and what might be headed their way. That security team is going to be playing things tighter. All things being equal, I'd want to take on the team covering the rear. I think they're going to be the most relaxed."

"Also agreed," replied Hookah.

"But the minute the bullets start flying, these guys are going to be on the radio alerting their teammates. Even if they were all standing around, leaning on their jeep having a smoke, if we took out three of them and tried to kneecap the fourth, he'd be calling it in, and we're screwed."

"What if we rammed them? What if we came flying out of nowhere, took them completely by surprise, and T-boned their vehicle?"

Harvath shook his head. "They'd have to all be sitting inside of it and you'd have to hope that you hit them so hard, they'd be seeing stars and were too dazed to get on their radios. That's just too much left to chance."

"You got any other ideas?"

"When they loot a village, two guys go into each house while the Humvee with the .50-cal and the cargo truck wait outside. If we could get into one of the houses before them, we might be able to grab one of the guys, spirit him out the back, and take him someplace to interrogate."

"What about his partner?" Hookah asked.

"We'd have to kill that guy and make it look like the house was booby-trapped. There'd have to be a big enough explosion that the Ravens would assume both men had been killed in the blast. That way, they wouldn't be worried that we had snatched the first guy. The minute they suspect we have one of their people, they're going to go into panic mode and lock everything down. The only hope we have of breaching their safe house, once we have it pinpointed, is for them not to know we're coming."

"So, for the moment, this continues to be a goat rodeo."

"Yep," said Harvath, peering back out toward the road.

"Keep your thinking cap on," replied Hookah as he dropped his cigarette butt into the coffee can. "I'm going to get something to eat. You want anything?"

Harvath shook his head. He had grabbed a bottle of water and an MRE before starting his watch. He'd be good until Jacks relieved him.

•     •     •

When Jacks did take over, Harvath was glad to get up and stretch his legs. He mixed up some coffee and used a flameless heater to warm it up. It wasn't piping hot, but it was better than nothing and he was glad to get a boost of caffeine.

As he drank, he did a thorough review of his gear, double-checking that all his magazines were topped up and making sure that everything else on his battle belt and his chest rig were secure.

Once that was complete, he decided to put his feet up for a bit. There was no telling what the night would bring, and the evening would soon be upon them.

Unrolling his sleeping bag in the bed of the truck, he made himself comfortable. He checked to make sure that he was still getting a good cell signal and then shut his eyes. Even with the coffee in his system, he could still slow his breathing down and get himself into a rejuvenating, meditative state. It wasn't the same as a good solid nap, but it did have its advantages—one of them being that sometimes he did fall asleep, which was exactly what happened.

Yesterday had been a hell of a day and he hadn't gotten nearly enough sleep overnight to make up for the beatings he had been through. Oftentimes the body knew best what it needed.

He shouldn't have been surprised and yet, when he woke up to the chime of his cell phone several hours later, he couldn't believe how long he had been out.

Reading the message from Vesna, he hopped out of the back of the truck and said, "Heads up, everyone. The Ravens are on the move. Get your gear together. We're leaving in five minutes."

The good news was that the Ravens were not taking the night off. The bad news was that there had been a cell service interruption and the bush telegraph was behind in warning about the mercenaries' movements.

This time, Harvath put Krueger behind the wheel, and he rode shotgun. He wanted to review the map and study the terrain in order to put together the best plan.

One of the options that he had considered was to simply hang back, let the Ravens strike, and then follow them back to their lair. But having seen the evil they executed when they hit a target, that struck him as morally unacceptable. It was also way too risky.

Not only might the Ravens have night-vision equipment, allowing them to pick up a tail, but they also might have lookouts along the route back, making sure no one was following them at a distance.

Though Harvath had no idea how he was going to do it, he was going to have to figure out a way to thread the needle. He needed to prevent any further loss of life *and* locate the hostages. At this moment, he had no clue how he was going to make that happen.

As soon as the team was loaded, Harvath opened the mill doors, waited for Krueger to pull out, and then, shutting the doors behind them, climbed into the Novator and they headed out.

He plugged his phone into the charging port and kept everyone apprised of Vesna's updates.

His hope that the first village to send in a report might give them a fix on the Ravens' safe house was a bust. From what he was able to gather, the Ravens varied their routes. Villagers never saw them two days in a row.

From a security standpoint, it was smart of them to vary their routes. And from a looting perspective, you'd want to be rolling through fresh towns and villages every time you went out.

The good thing was that by Vesna reaching out, up and down the bush telegraph, the inhabitants in the area knew that as soon as they heard the Ravens were coming, it was imperative they flee. They could not wait. While the Ravens might drive straight through a village without stopping, there was no way to know for certain. The only certainty was that not moving meant death. Harvath instructed Krueger to drive faster.

As the man drove, Harvath used the Signal app to send Nicholas a message. There was no text, just a pin, dropped on a digital map of where he believed the Ravens were headed. Nicholas would know what it meant.

Nobody in the vehicle spoke. All of the men had their game faces on. There was the occasional rattle of equipment as weapons were checked or gear was repositioned, but other than that, silence. The only time any words were exchanged was when Harvath gave driving instructions to Krueger and Krueger confirmed them.

The area was a patchwork of farmers' fields studded with strips of heavily wooded forest. It reminded Harvath of places he had seen in Germany and Switzerland—both rugged and beautiful.

With the purple light of twilight turning into the blue-black sky of evening, Harvath checked his watch. Like vampires descending from the clouds, the Ravens would be entering the village at any moment. He and his team would be at least ten minutes behind. He just prayed that the locals had heeded Vesna's warning.

As the road dipped into a small valley, the ribbon of asphalt began to wind back and forth just like his map showed. What the map hadn't reflected, however, was how thick the trees were. Along with the turns, they made it difficult to see what was up ahead.

Nearing the village, Harvath cautioned Krueger to slow down. There was a dirt road that cut through the forest, and he didn't want to miss it. It would allow them to loop around and come up behind the Ravens. It was also going to be their escape route and it was important to confirm that it was devoid of any obstructions.

When they found the road, they took it and headed into the trees. It was a bit overgrown, but in relatively good shape.

Because the Novator was a diesel, it wasn't the quietest, most stealthy vehicle. They were only going to be able to risk getting so close to the village before having to get out and proceed the rest of the way on foot. Harvath had decided both where the truck would stop, and who would remain behind with it.

Biscuit wasn't crazy about being left behind, but he understood why it was necessary. If the team needed an extraction, he was going to be the one to do it.

As the truck came equipped with night-vision tech, Harvath swapped his thermal device for Biscuit's night-vision goggles.

Once they were mounted to his helmet, the team did a quick radio check and, with Biscuit keeping an eye on the Novator, struck off for the village.

They moved soundlessly through the forest, weapons ready. Just before the end of the road, they stepped fully into the trees and crept to a position where they could get their first look at the village.

It was a mixture of stone buildings and wooden houses organized across a hodgepodge of crooked streets. There was a church with a small, domed steeple, as well as a tiny square built around a communal well. Standing at the entrance to the village was an old Russian 4x4 military jeep known as a Tigr. Four Raven guards leaned against it with their rifles slung over their shoulders. They were smoking and chewing the fat. They were also doing something else—passing a bottle of vodka back and forth. No one was keeping an eye out for trouble. Harvath now knew exactly what he wanted to do and quickly laid out his plan.

From what he could see, the village was empty of inhabitants. There were no lights, and no smoke rose from any of the chimneys. Apparently, they had taken the warning seriously and had gotten out in time. That gave Harvath and his team one less thing to worry about.

Continuing to use the trees to conceal their presence, they moved parallel to the village.

At a narrow strip of farmer's field, they stepped out of the forest and moved as quickly as they could to the closest village building. In the distance, they could hear the other Raven vehicles, the cargo trucks and the Humvees, as they carried out their operation.

Pressing themselves up against the wooden structure, Harvath gave the signal for the team to split up. Hookah and Krueger would continue around the back of the buildings and Harvath and Jacks would go up the front.

It was the one facet of the scenario Harvath hadn't been able to visualize until he was physically on scene. The placement of the guards at each end of the village had been meant to fend off any external threats. None of the Ravens had anticipated trouble from inside—at least not anything they couldn't handle via the .50-cals atop their two Humvees.

Harvath and Jacks covered each other as they scrambled from building to building.

When they were within striking distance of the guards, they took a fraction of a second to catch their breath. Then Harvath double-clicked the transmit button on his radio.

As soon as Hookah double-clicked his in response, Harvath counted down from five and gave the "Go" command.

He and Jacks then crept from their hiding spot and popped up from behind the jeep.

"Ne dvigaysya," he ordered, taking the guards completely by surprise. *Don't move.*

Startled, the men did move and tried to back away from him. That's when Hookah and Krueger appeared around the front of the jeep, their weapons pointed right at the men.

When one of the Ravens reached for his radio, Jacks butt-stroked him with his rifle, knocking him to the ground, unconscious. Slowly, the other three men raised their hands in surrender.

As Jacks stood guard, Hookah and Krueger disarmed and secured the prisoners while Harvath stripped them of their radios and patted them down for any other weapons.

"What are we going to do with them?" asked Krueger.

"Throw them in the back of the jeep," Harvath replied. "We'll drive them out of here and make it look like they went AWOL. I'll let Biscuit know we're headed his way."

Moving back to the rear of the jeep, he dropped the vehicle's tailgate and saw something he hadn't noticed a moment ago when making sure no one else was inside—two RPG-26 antitank shoulder-fired missiles. "Change of plans," he immediately told his team.

Grabbing the RPGs, he handed one to Jacks and helped load the prisoners as he rattled off a quick list of instructions.

"Good copy?" he then asked.

"Good copy," Hookah replied.

"Ooh-rah," said Krueger.

As they fired up the jeep and drove off with the four Ravens, Harvath and Jacks headed back into the village. They had a chance to level the playing field a little bit. It was time to go hunting.

Subtlety was no longer on Harvath's agenda. He wanted to deliver the biggest blow he could. To do that, he needed to take out the Humvees. Because of the crooked streets, they were going to have to get pretty close to do it. They were also going to have to split up.

According to Harvath's list, a home in the village was hiding 2,300-year-old gold artifacts from the Scythian empire, dating back to the fourth century BC. It was one of the reasons he had reached out to Nicholas. In case Vesna's warning didn't make it through, or if the person responsible for safeguarding the items was suspicious, someone in the Ukrainian command structure could warn them.

With the house empty, there was no one to torture into revealing the location of the artifacts. The Ravens would be reduced to tearing the place apart brick by brick. The Humvee pulling security at that location was the one Harvath would take out. Jacks would hit the one covering the Ravens who were looting the other properties in the village. They went as far as they could together and then they split up.

With the RPG slung across his back, Harvath hopped fences and ran through yards, stopping every couple of houses to use his ears to triangulate on his target.

Finally, he found it, and once he did, he radioed the team. "Norseman in position."

Up ahead he could see the Humvee, its gunner standing in the turret, as well as the cargo truck, which, to his delight, was positioned nearby.

A few moments later, Jacks came over the radio with his confirmation: "Jacks in position."

All they were waiting for now was for their other team members to be in position. The Novator and the jeep were key to pulling off the rest of the operation.

The radio squawked, "Hookah en route," followed by "Biscuit en route."

A minute later they heard "Biscuit in position."

Then Hookah's voice came back again: "Hookah, fifteen seconds out. Send it."

"Roger that," said Harvath. "Jacks, you're cleared hot. I'll see you at the pickup."

"Jacks is cleared hot. Roger that. See you on the other side," the Brit replied.

Unslinging the RPG, Harvath prepped the disposable launcher, flipped up the sighting device, and sighted in his target.

He waited until he heard Jacks's RPG launch and then he fired his own. Depressing the firing mechanism, there was a loud bang as the rocket exited the launcher, the switchblade-like fin stabilizers popped out, and it screamed toward the Humvee.

The explosion was the equivalent of being hit by six and a half pounds of TNT. Shrapnel was sent in all directions, including into the cargo truck.

Before the last pieces had hit the ground, Harvath was already up on his feet and running.

He didn't stop until he reached the entrance to the village. There, Hookah had replaced the Russian jeep right where they had found it. The four Ravens were now lying hooded and hog-tied in the bed of the Novator, which was idling in the center of the road, waiting for him.

Jacks, who was right on Harvath's heels, arrived and hopped into the truck. Hookah and Harvath then removed frag grenades, pulled the pins, and pitched them into the jeep.

Whether the rest of the Ravens were going to hang around long enough to investigate what had happened or, believing they were under attack, would take off, Harvath wanted to add as much uncertainty as possible to what had happened to his four prisoners.

He and Hookah made it to the Novator and shut the doors just as the frags detonated.

As the Russian jeep exploded in a massive fireball, Biscuit hit the gas and they disappeared back into the forest.

# CHAPTER 32

Nicholas felt as if he had let Harvath down. No matter how hard he had tried to get Kozar to share the information with him, the Ukrainian Intelligence officer wouldn't budge. "Some things are too precious," the man had said. "Too sensitive."

Of course, the man was correct. In war, intelligence was as indispensable as bombs and bullets. The lengths that the United States and its allies had gone to keep the D-Day invasion secret were extraordinary. The operation itself was shrouded in a thick mist of half-truths and outright lies. In fact, he wouldn't have been surprised to learn that the disinformation campaign had taken almost as much time, money, and manpower as the planning of the actual event.

Great Britain had been shot through with spies. The ability of the enemy to penetrate its intelligence services and other critical wartime efforts was astounding. Nicholas could only imagine how little sleep counterintelligence chiefs got during the war.

But if the Brits knew one thing, it was how to ferret out moles and other enemy operatives. It was often by very clever, yet very simple means. Their record wasn't perfect, but in the end Hitler and the Axis powers had been defeated.

One of his favorite counterintelligence operations was called the Double-Cross System, or the XX System for short. It was a program by which captured Nazi spies, or those who had voluntarily surrendered, were used to transmit false information back to their German handlers. Interdicting fresh spies was made even easier once the Brits had broken the Nazi encryption machine known as Enigma.

The idea of using spies against their controllers appealed to Nicholas. There was something poetic about turning a dagger around and plunging it into the unsuspecting heart of the person who had intended to use it against you.

But in the wilderness of mirrors, as the espionage game had been dubbed, crosses and double crosses could be quite dangerous. In his estimation, the simplest, most straightforward operations were always the best.

Tonight he was going to present to the GUR's digital unit another case study in hacking and utilization of the electronic dark arts against the Russians. Codenamed "Fortitude," this operation had been inspired by the Double-Cross System back in World War II.

As he sat at his desk, preparing the slides for his presentation, he saw the dogs perk up and then heard a knock at his door. It was Yulia.

"Hungry?" she asked, holding a pizza box.

"That's what the cafeteria is serving tonight?" he asked.

She shook her head. "I have to take a break from that food every once in a while. I'm all for patriotism, but it's like being force-fed by my grandmother."

The little man smiled. He had a sophisticated palate and very expensive taste, but anyone who said they didn't like a good slice of pizza every now and again was a liar.

Clearing a space on his desk, he said, "What did you get and where did you get it?"

"It's a place called Napule," she replied, setting the box down and giving the dogs a little attention. "They call this pizza 'a cafona.' It has tuna, onion, tomatoes, mozzarella, and basil."

Tuna on pizza was a *very* European thing. He could remember asking for it at a pizzeria in the United States and how the room had gone absolutely silent. Everyone had looked at him like he was some sort of a monster. They had no idea what they were missing.

"In the middle of a war, I'm stunned that Kyiv has pizza to go."

"Life goes on," she responded, pulling a bottle of Chianti out of her backpack. "Even in the middle of a war."

"Are you allowed to bring alcohol into the office?"

She smiled. "Nope."

Nicholas smiled back. "This is all very nice of you. Thank you."

"Consider it Ukrainian hospitality. Except to exercise the dogs, you never leave the building. You work with our digital people all day and then give an evening lecture. If you're going to keep these hours, this is the least we can do to repay you."

Opening the wine, she produced two paper cups, filled them, and then, raising hers, said, "Cheers."

Nicholas tapped his against hers and replied, "Cheers."

After they had taken a sip and had each helped themselves to a slice of pizza, she asked, "What are we going to learn about tonight?"

The little man closed his eyes and took a moment to savor his first bite. "This is amazing."

She smiled. "Good, right?"

"Incredible."

"How about the wine?"

Nicholas tilted his hand from side to side and said, "Meh."

Yulia laughed. "Pizza is one thing, but do you know how hard it is to get wine in the middle of a war?"

"In that case," he conceded, "it's excellent. Especially for a Chianti. Thank you."

"You're welcome."

He took another bite of pizza and said, "Tonight's presentation is about sowing disinformation."

About to take a drink, she paused. "As in counterespionage?"

Nicholas nodded. "It's based on something the Brits did back in World War II to throw off the Nazis regarding the D-Day invasion. I helped the GUR develop something similar, but in this case it has to do with troop movements.

"You see, the Russians believe they have penetrated Ukrainian Intelligence. What they don't know is that the GUR has identified these operatives and has been allowing them to access false intel, which they are reporting back to their handlers in Moscow."

Yulia smiled once again. "Very clever."

•　　•　　•

In his office, watching via a hidden camera system, Kozar smiled as well.

"Very clever," he said to himself. "Very clever indeed."

# CHAPTER 33

"Got him!" Fields said when her boss, who had stayed up half the night running down leads, had finally answered his phone. "Senator Wilson's lunch partner up in Boston."

"Who is he?" asked Carolan.

"His name is Joseph Nistal. And you're never going to believe this. Want to know where he lives?"

"Go ahead," grunted Carolan as he sat up on his office couch and rubbed the sleep out of his eyes.

"In Dimitri Burman's building. He's Burman's flipping neighbor."

The FBI man was wide-awake now. "You've got to be kidding me."

"I'm as serious as cancer," Fields replied.

"Where are you?"

"At my desk."

"Don't move," ordered Carolan. "I'll be right there."

Exiting his office, the FBI man walked down the hall to Fields's. When he got there, she already had a coffee waiting for him.

"Thank you," he said, removing the lid and taking a sip as he sat down. "Walk me through it. All of it."

"Okay, well, we know that Greg Wilson hadn't intended to go to Boston. He had purchased a round-trip ticket to Maine, which he then changed at the last minute. Based on when he arrived in Boston and when he departed for the final leg of his journey back to D.C., he had only gone to Boston for one reason."

"The lunch."

"Exactly," answered Fields. "It got me wondering if his lunch buddy maybe flew in as well. I passed the photos we received to a friend of mine in the National Joint Terrorism Task Force, and he asked his contact at TSA to run it through their facial recognition system. They got a hit. After wrapping lunch, he also hopped a flight."

"To D.C.?"

"No, but close. He flew to Baltimore."

"How long had he been in Boston?" asked Carolan.

"Only a few hours. He'd flown out that morning."

"These guys could have just met in D.C. or Maryland."

Fields nodded. "Seems odd, right? He didn't change his plans until we reached out to his office and requested an interview. I couldn't help but wonder if the lunch might have had something to do with Burman's death. Maybe he was worried we'd be waiting for him at the airport when he got back."

"Possible. How'd you get the name?"

"The TSA guy gave my guy the manifests for the Baltimore-to-Boston and Boston-to-Baltimore flights. Only one passenger appears on both flights—Joseph Nistal. Out of an abundance of caution, I asked a contact at the Maryland State Police to run Nistal and see if they had a file on him."

"Did they?"

"Nope. The guy is clean. I did, however, get a copy of his driver's license," she stated, pulling it up on her monitor and showing it to him.

"What else do we know about him? Any social media presence, dating apps?"

"Zero. The guy is nowhere to be found on the open internet."

"How about on the not-so-open internet?"

Fields smiled. "When I visited some of the data broker sites we subscribe to, a bigger picture started to emerge. Mr. Nistal does own a house in Frederick, Maryland, which matches the address on his driver's license, but several months ago he used the address of a Frederick self-storage unit on a rental application."

"And the rental was for a unit in Burman's swanky building?"

"Correct. Which got me to thinking. What if the reason we couldn't capture our killer on video was because he'd never left the building? What if he'd been in there the whole time?"

"Jesus," Carolan exclaimed.

"And taking out the backdoor camera? How smart would that have been? It's the ultimate red herring. Precisely what a hit man or a wet-work team would do, right?"

"This is excellent work, but we're going to need more than just a rental application to nail this guy."

"I'm not done yet," said Fields.

Carolan took another sip of coffee and let her continue.

"In addition to confirming Nistal's house in Maryland, I was also able to pull information about his car—a late-model, white Nissan Sentra. The color made me think about Burman's sneakers and how you pointed out how the toes were scuffed. If he was dragged across the terrace and tossed over the side, the marks suggested a two-person job. So I went back to the CCTV footage from the building looking for Nistal and any-one I might be able to connect him to."

"And?"

"Nothing. At least not coming or going from the lobby. But the day of Burman's death, there's video of Nistal's car pulling into the garage."

"Could you see anybody else in there with him?"

Fields shook her head. "Looks like it was just him. But something piqued my interest, so I reached out to the building manager and asked if she'd be kind enough to upload some additional footage."

"What kind of additional footage?"

"I asked for everything she had since we'd been there. I wanted to see what had been taking place."

"Tell me you found something."

"I did," said Fields. "A day after Burman's death, Nistal drives out of the garage and then returns about a half hour later. Take a look at these three screenshots. This first is the vehicle driving in on the day Burman dies and then driving out and returning the day after. What do you see?"

Carolan leaned over her desk to get a better look at the screen captures. "They all look the same to me—Nistal in his white Sentra coming and going. It doesn't look like anyone else is in the car with him."

"Look closer," she instructed as she picked up a pen and pointed to where she wanted him to focus. "Specifically at the rear tires."

It took the FBI man a moment, but then he saw it, too. "Coming in, on the day Burman dies and then going back out again the next day, he's got something heavy, *really* heavy, in the trunk."

"Bingo. Then when he comes back, in the third shot, the car is riding much higher above the rear tires."

"He dumped whatever, or whoever, he was carrying."

"That's what we need to figure out."

Carolan stood up and headed for the door. "Get a hold of Detective Greer at D.C. Metro. Tell him we need to see him right away, in his office."

"Where are you going?"

"I'm going to shave and put on a clean shirt. Be ready to roll in ten minutes."

•    •    •

Because it was a Sunday, it took less time to drive from FBI headquarters to Greer's office than it did for Carolan to shave, change, and get his car out of the garage.

When they arrived, the detective was waiting for them. Fields had given him the broad brushstrokes on Joe Nistal, his vehicle, and what they were looking for.

Offering the FBI agents a seat in his conference room, he attached his laptop to a cable and a series of traffic camera feeds from across D.C. appeared on the monitor at the front of the room. Next, he picked up the phone and told his tech to start rolling the footage.

The ALPR, or automated license plate reader, was a computer-controlled system of cameras mounted on streetlights, on traffic lights, on overpasses, and at other locations throughout D.C. that automatically captured each license plate as it drove past. A picture of the vehicle and the driver was also taken as the time, date, and geolocation of the plate was entered into a central database.

Within seconds, Metro PD had not only found Nistal's car, but had tracked its route.

"It looks like your suspect was looking to get right with the Lord," said Greer.

Carolan peered at the screen. "What are you talking about?"

"He drove into the garage at the Washington National Cathedral. That's the feed in the upper left-hand corner."

The two FBI agents watched and moments later Nistal exited the garage and headed back toward Burman's building.

"Can you back it up?" asked Fields.

"Sure," Greer answered. "How far?"

"Just so we can get a profile of the vehicle."

The detective relayed the request to his tech, who not only backed the footage up but increased the size of the image to fit full screen.

"Look, now he's riding higher," Fields stated. "He emptied his trunk in the garage."

"You want to track his return trip?" Greer asked.

Carolan shook his head. "Go back to the camera covering the garage. Let's see who comes out."

They didn't have to wait long. Soon, a black Toyota Camry exited the garage, turned in the opposite direction Nistal had, and drove off. There was a driver and a passenger. Both males.

"Can you track that vehicle to its destination?" Carolan asked. "Also, can we get the best possible still shot of the occupants?"

Greer nodded and once again relayed the request to his tech.

They watched as the system followed the vehicle. When it got to where it was going, the detective said, "I guess I owe you an apology. You were right. This really is about national security."

The final piece of footage showed the car pulling up to the gates of the Russian Embassy and, despite it not bearing diplomatic plates, being waved straight through by security.

•     •     •

"No, this can't wait until tomorrow," said Carolan as Fields drove and he spoke on the phone. "We have to move now."

By the time they made it back to the office, a secure conference room had been all set up.

"This better be airtight," a Bureau lawyer said as he squeezed past and grabbed a seat at the table.

On a suite of monitors at the front of the room, top brass appeared via secure video links. It was a sea of button-down shirts and V-neck sweaters.

Last to activate his camera was the FBI Director, who was wearing a coat and tie. He handed things right over to Carolan's boss. After a couple of brief remarks, Carolan was given the floor.

He kept the briefing exactly as he would have expected one of his people to give it. He stuck to the facts, spoke clearly, and did not embellish. When he was finished, he took questions. As would be expected, there were lots of them.

If Burman had been murdered by the Russians, it would require a very serious response. That, however, would ultimately fall to the President and was beyond the scope of the moment. What mattered now was who did it and whether it could be proven.

There was also concern over the tracking devices that had been found. The fact that another one had been discovered on the vehicle of Carolan's predecessor only raised further concerns that her health had been purposely targeted. Once again, if the Russians had been involved, it would only deepen the severity of the situation.

After all of their questions had been answered, the top brass adjourned to a private chat to discuss what should be done.

Not knowing how long it would take for them to reappear, or if they could be heard, none of the people in the conference room spoke.

When the feeds went live again, the Director sided with Carolan. If Nistal had been behind Burman's death, he needed to be stopped before he killed, or caused someone to be killed, again. Warrants would be expedited. Carolan was given the green light to proceed.

It made sense to hit all three addresses—the D.C. apartment, the

Frederick, Maryland, house, and the Frederick self-storage facility—all at the same time.

After the Frederick PD sent an unmarked car past Nistal's home and confirmed that his Sentra was in the driveway, Carolan decided he and Fields would accompany that raid team.

A helicopter picked them up on the roof of the headquarters building and flew them to Fort Detrick, where they met up with agents from the Baltimore field office and proceeded to the target.

Nistal lived in a quiet subdivision that backed up onto a large, wooded area. As the FBI agents drove past in a nondescript van, children rode their bikes and played outside, neighbors chatted, and dogs darted back and forth in yards. It was the quintessential American neighborhood— the perfect place for a Russian operative to blend in and disappear.

With their weapons ready, the van pulled into Nistal's driveway and a stream of agents in blue windbreakers piled out.

They formed a stack outside the split-level ranch with Fields in the lead. Conferring with the team leaders at the other locations, she gave the command to execute their coordinated raids.

Pounding on the home's double front doors, she yelled, "FBI! Search warrant!"

Immediately, she stood back and let her breacher bash the doors in with his battering ram. Then, retaking the lead position, she led her team inside and began to clear the house.

When she got to the kitchen, she saw the back door was open and caught a flash of someone in the woods.

"Runner! Runner! Runner!" she announced over her radio. "He went out the back door. Headed southwest into the woods." With Carolan right next to her, she took off after him.

The ground was rough, uneven, and uphill. Carolan started feeling the effects almost instantly. He was in no condition to handle a difficult foot chase.

Flushed and breathing heavily, he began to fall behind.

When Fields looked over her shoulder to see what was the matter, Carolan was bent over wheezing. "Go!" he yelled.

Refocusing on Nistal, she kicked in the afterburners. There was no way she was going to let this guy escape.

Thundering up the hill, she was almost at the top when she heard a gunshot and a bullet went whizzing by her face. Instinctively, she dropped to the ground.

There were two more shots. One hit just to her right and another landed only a couple of feet in front of her. Steadying her Glock, she fired off several shots of her own and scrambled to find cover.

Seconds passed. There was no additional gunfire. She risked a quick peek out from behind her position and when no one engaged her, she got back on her feet and moved carefully but quickly to the top of the hill.

Nistal started shooting at her again and once more she was forced to dive for cover. This guy was pissing her off.

"Joseph Nistal," she shouted. "You're under arrest. Anything you say can and will—"

Before she could finish, she was drowned out by another barrage of gunfire. None of these rounds, however, struck anywhere near her. Either this guy didn't know where she was, or there was too much distance for him to effectively strike his target. Fields feared it was the latter.

Leaping to her feet, she charged back after him, zigzagging through the trees so as not to give him a clean shot.

When she finally caught sight of him again, he was already far downhill from her position. Taking a deep breath, she steadied her pistol, exhaled, and pressed the trigger.

The weapon bucked in her hands and, just like she had learned training with her friends on the FBI's Hostage Rescue Team, she followed up, pressing her trigger four more times until she saw him fall.

Conducting a tactical reload, she drove a fresh magazine into her pistol and closed in on Nistal, who was lying facedown at the bottom of the hill. "Suspect down," she said over her radio.

"Hands out where I can see them!" she ordered.

Nistal didn't respond.

"Stretch your hands out in front of you where I can see them!" she ordered him again.

Nothing.

"Subject has been shot," she transmitted over the radio. "Dispatch EMS."

Addressing Nistal once more, she warned him, "If you move, I *will* shoot you!"

He wasn't moving. It looked like he wasn't even breathing.

As she got closer, she saw a 9mm Beretta lying on the ground, likely having been dropped when he tumbled the rest of the way down the hill. Mentally marking where it was so she could come back and get it, she kept going.

When she reached him, she gave him a final warning: "You so much as twitch and you're a dead man."

She then kicked both of his legs but received no response.

Nothing would have made her happier than to let this scumbag bleed out, but there was untold intel they might be able to extract from him. If he needed immediate medical assistance, she was going to have to be the one to deliver it.

With pressure on her trigger and her pistol pointed right at him, she bent down to roll him over. That's when he sprang his trap.

Swinging his legs like a couple of bullwhips, he took her legs out from under her and twisted his body to avoid being shot.

As Fields fell to the ground, Nistal pulled a snubnose .357 and shot her four times in the chest.

He would have shot her a fifth time, probably in the face, had not another shot rung out and knocked him over backward.

Carolan, pistol in hand, had come charging through the woods just in time.

He wanted to help Fields, but first he needed to make sure Nistal was no longer a threat.

Kicking the man's weapon away, he rolled him over, patted him down, and restrained him with flex-cuffs. Then he rushed to Fields.

She was struggling to breathe.

"Easy," he told her as he ripped off the Velcro flaps of her Kevlar vest. "You're going to be okay."

Peeling off her vest, he checked to make sure there'd been no penetration. At any distance, much less point-blank, .357 rounds were like getting hit by a truck. She was going to be bruised. She might even have cracked or broken ribs, but the integrity of the vest had held.

"There's no penetration," he said, tightly clasping her hand. "You just got the wind knocked out of you. I'm going to find you some dirt, you're going to rub it on your wounds, and then we're going to get a coffee."

As the air returned to her lungs, she was in too much pain to laugh. Instead, she motioned for him to come closer and when he leaned in, she said, "Fuck you."

In this situation, Carolan didn't mind the foul language. In fact, he was about to give her a funny, somewhat salty reply when he heard FBI agents up above cresting the hill.

"Here!" he yelled. "Suspect in custody. Agent down."

# CHAPTER 34

To be rock-solid certain that he was being told the truth, Harvath isolated each of the four Ravens and interrogated them individually. Simultaneously, he streamed the interrogations to Nicholas, a native Russian speaker, to ensure that nothing was being lost in translation. The information he gleaned from the mercenaries wasn't good.

The Ravens' safe house, their base of operations, was an old stone fortress less than thirty klicks away. Their commanding officer, a man they referred to as the "Colonel," was obsessed with security—and for good reason. The Ukrainians, the Russian military, and the Wagner Group all wanted him and his Ravens dead.

The grounds surrounding the property were dotted with mines and antipersonnel devices. Machine-gun positions were set up inside the fortress, which would allow the Ravens to combat attacks from any direction. They had a stockpile of RPGs, small arms, and ammunition. In Harvath's opinion, the only thing they were missing was a moat filled with alligators.

According to the four prisoners, Anna Royko was indeed being held there and she was still alive, but just barely. If Harvath hoped to save her life, he was going to have to move fast.

In any other scenario, he would have assembled a highly skilled and highly experienced team, they would have dropped in via helicopter, and, having had sufficient intel and time to rehearse, they would have carried out a precisely choreographed operation.

With Anna Royko in such bad shape, none of that was going to happen. He was going to have to go in tonight—with the team, the intelligence, and the equipment he had at hand. He couldn't afford to wait.

The one item he had angled for was additional troops. He didn't care if they were Ukrainian or International Legion. The Ravens still comprised a significant force. In addition to the two dozen that went out on raids, a contingent of ten more was always left behind to guard the fortress. Yes, Harvath and his team had captured four and had likely killed several more in the ambush on the Humvees, but they were still seriously outgunned.

Nicholas spoke to Kozar on Harvath's behalf, but the situation hadn't changed. Troops couldn't be pulled from the front. They were on their own.

Harvath did, though, have a potential ace up his sleeve. The Colonel hadn't completely boxed the Ravens into a corner. They came and went via the main gate, but the man had preserved a back door, an emergency escape from the fortress, should they ever need it.

Hundreds of years ago, when the fortress had been constructed, a series of tunnels had been built underneath. They had been used to store everything from gold and gunpowder to food and enemy soldiers. The tunnels ended at a thick, iron gate, which opened out onto a narrow footpath. It was the only part of the property that wasn't embedded with mines.

While all the Raven prisoners had confirmed this, there was only one way to be sure. They would take one along to act as their personal mine "magnet." The other three would be secured and left behind in the mill.

Hog-tying those men once again, Harvath used an additional length of rope to secure them to a post and each other. If they tried to move or slip free of their bonds, the knots only grew tighter.

He then put Nicholas on speakerphone to push, in Russian, for any final pieces of information the men might have held back. Nicholas explained that if it were to be discovered that the men hadn't been completely forthright, they would be delivered back to the Wagner Group, who had become notorious for executing deserters with a sledgehammer. Harvath had also taken the men's cell phones and Nicholas assured them that their families would be tracked down and punished as well.

The only additional piece of information handed over was that the main drive up to the fortress was flanked with hidden MON-200s, Soviet-era antipersonnel devices similar to U.S. claymore mines.

Based on what one of the prisoners recounted, it sounded like the Ravens had created a kill box similar to the one Harvath had set up for the Iranian drone instructors and their Russian FSB handlers in Belarus. Anyone foolish enough to come up that driveway uninvited would be in for a very deadly surprise.

Once the man had explained how the MON-200s were triggered, Harvath gagged and hooded him, as well as his two compatriots. He also took their boots. The likelihood of them escaping was next to nil, but just in case, he wanted to make it as difficult as possible for them.

With that taken care of, they pulled their gear together, loaded the mine magnet into the truck, and got on the road.

Normally, Harvath would have conducted a detailed mission brief. In this case, however, they didn't have a lot of details. The tunnel system they would use to access the fortress was different from the below-grade area where Anna Royko was being kept. They would have to come up in the main building and go down another set of stairs to find her.

There was also the issue of the little twin girls the Ravens had abducted. Harvath was determined to get them out as well. His prisoners, though, were fuzzy on where they were being kept. They had heard the Colonel claim that he was going to "make women out of them" and had assumed that they were being kept in his quarters.

It was an absolutely repellent declaration. Of all the monsters Harvath had hunted in his career, the Ravens were the most abhorrent. His only regret was that he would not be able to visit upon them the equivalent amount of suffering that they had visited upon their victims. But that didn't mean he wasn't going to try.

They drove in silence, the men keeping their own counsel as they thought about the serious operation that lay ahead.

Before leaving the mill, Harvath had offered them, for the third and final time, one last chance to bow out. No one had taken him up on the offer. They all intended to see this through with him. They were good and decent men. True warriors.

As the Novator, its headlights off, sliced through the darkness, Harvath was preoccupied with a very particular piece of the night's puzzle. After being attacked in the village, what was the Ravens' tactical posture? Were they all hopped up, expecting to get hit again? Had they doubled down on their defense of the fortress? Had they hung around long enough for the flames to die down in the jeep, only to see there were no bodies inside? And if they had figured that out, did they suspect that their teammates had been taken prisoner and might have given up their location?

The Colonel had exhibited enough tactical fluency to expect that the answer to most of those questions would be yes. Even if the Ravens had fled before knowing if there were any bodies inside the burning jeep, they would have been jumpy and on edge. That energy was best channeled into fortifying their defenses. They would have been foolish not to assume something else could be headed their way.

For his part, Harvath was most concerned with getting through the gate and into the tunnels. According to the prisoners, the gate, of course, was locked.

Harvath and his team didn't have any breaching tools, they didn't have any C4, they didn't have any of the standard items an operator might use to make entry. If they couldn't get through that gate, he didn't know what their next move would be. There was no Plan B. But as an old SEAL pal used to say, they'd have to burn that bridge once they got to it.

·    ·    ·

When they neared the fortress, the men prepped their weapons and double-checked all their equipment. Things were about to go next level.

"Any special rules we need to be aware of here?" asked Hookah, flipping down his night-vision goggles and powering them up.

Harvath shook his head. "Our American woman and the two little girls are all that matter. Anyone else you see is a legitimate target. Weapons free."

"Roger that."

They pulled the Novator off the road and into the trees, southwest of the property. This was where the footpath was supposed to be.

Yanking the prisoner out of the truck, Harvath placed a piece of duct tape across the man's mouth to keep him quiet and then tied a long piece of rope to the flex-cuffs binding his wrists behind his back. He then handed the rope to Biscuit. "If he does anything stupid, kill him. But do it quietly."

"Where are you going?"

"We need to find the trailhead," he replied, activating his night-vision goggles. "We'll be back as soon as we've ID'd it."

After twenty minutes of careful searching, it was Krueger who finally found the footpath.

Returning to the Novator, Harvath donned a lightweight, collapsible medevac rescue stretcher that could be worn like a backpack.

Then, taking the rope from Biscuit, he instructed their Raven prisoner to walk toward the fortress. If the Russian was lying about mines on the path, he'd end up being the one who paid the ultimate price.

Per their training, and out of an abundance of caution, Harvath and each of his men stayed directly in the footsteps of the man in front of him.

He wasn't crazy about having to hold his rifle *and* a rope, but at this point, Harvath didn't have a choice. Things could have been a lot worse and he took a moment to remind himself how fortunate they were that there were no cameras or other electronic sensors on the property.

Up ahead, he could see the hulking shadow of the old, abandoned fortress. According to Nicholas, who had been able to pull up some information online, it had been built in the 1600s and starting in the 1800s had steadily fallen into a state of disrepair. It had been revived as a military academy in the early 1900s but left to rot after World War II.

Other than a quick stint as a folk museum in the 1970s, there had been no money to do anything with it and it had been completely surrendered to nature. Drug addicts, teenagers, and the occasional outlaw or ghost-hunting YouTuber were the only human life the place had seen in decades, until the Ravens had come along.

From what the prisoners had said, the Colonel had recognized the strategic value of the property instantly upon seeing it. There was no electricity or running water, but it checked so many other important boxes, he had decided to make it their home.

To illuminate their nights, the Ravens were dependent upon lanterns, candles, and flashlights. In many respects, they were as backward as the Taliban. Harvath loved that. He had killed a lot of Taliban, especially at night, and especially in the darkness of their own homes. What he loved even more was that, unlike the Taliban, the Ravens didn't have dogs. Nothing could screw up an operation faster.

Arriving at the gate, he handed the rope off to Biscuit and stepped forward. With Jacks, Krueger, and Hookah scanning for threats, he let his rifle hang from its sling and gave the gate a tug.

Nothing happened.

He pushed in on it, but still nothing happened. *Fuck*.

Running his hand along the contours of the entrance, he felt the gate, its hinges, and the stone surrounding it. These people didn't have proper medicine or flush toilets in their day, but they could design a lock that would survive hundreds of years.

Frustrated, Harvath grabbed the gate with both hands and jerked it back and forth. As he did, he heard the metal groan and noticed some of the mortar around the hinges begin to chip off.

Leaving Krueger to stand guard, he called Hookah and Jacks over to help. Together they used brute force to rock the iron gate, pushing and pulling until the first hinge snapped, then the second, and then finally the third.

Carrying the gate inside, they gently set it against the wall. But before they could go any farther, something had to be done about their prisoner.

Harvath was about to have him lie down so they could hog-tie him when Jacks raised the butt of his weapon and struck the man across the back of his head, knocking him unconscious.

"Problem solved," the Brit said.

Even though the man was out, there was no telling how long he would stay out. Harvath hog-tied him anyway and left him there.

With their Raven out of commission, they prepared to push into the compound. Harvath took point, followed by Krueger, Biscuit, Jacks, and Hookah. The sooner they were out of the tunnel, the happier Harvath would be.

Allegedly, the tunnel ended in a large mechanical room. Beyond that was an exterior courtyard followed by the main building. Pressing the stock of his Galil into his shoulder, Harvath led the way.

Following the tunnel, they eventually arrived at a room with two old, enormous furnaces, rusted pipes, and scrambles of frayed wiring. Ahead of them was a large, metal door. Harvath signaled for Biscuit to pull it open but cautioned him to do it slowly.

The moment the Canadian began to draw the door back, it started to make a loud, metallic squeal. As soon as that happened, Biscuit stopped what he was doing and froze in place.

*Were any of the Ravens close enough to have heard that?* Harvath strained his ears but couldn't pick up anything that would suggest that they'd been blown.

He motioned to Biscuit to pull up the handle in order to help lessen the weight on the hinges and cut down on the noise. The young man did as he'd been instructed, and the door swung open soundlessly.

Harvath poked the tip of his suppressor out, applied pressure to his trigger, and leaned his head to the side, ready to engage, but the courtyard was empty.

Calling up Krueger, he sent him outside, followed by Jacks, Hookah, and then Biscuit. Harvath was just about to join them when the courtyard erupted in gunfire and out of the corner of his eye, he saw Biscuit go down.

There were multiple shooters along a rampart, about fifty meters from their position. Harvath joined his teammates in subjecting their attackers to a withering barrage of fire.

Krueger was the first to yell, "Reloading!" soon followed by Jacks and then Hookah.

As they slammed home fresh magazines and continued the fight, Harvath flipped down the magnifier on his rifle, gave it a quick adjustment, and began picking off the shooters one by one.

Only when the shooters were neutralized did he look back down at Biscuit. He was slumped on the ground, exsanguinating, the blood spurting from the right side of his neck. Grabbing Biscuit by his collar, Harvath dragged him back into the mechanical room.

"Tangos inbound!" Hookah yelled, having spotted more Ravens pouring into the courtyard.

Ripping open Biscuit's IFAK, Harvath snatched a package of gauze, as well as a bandage, and dressed the wound as quickly as he could.

By the time he raised the Canadian's hand to guide it to the spot where he should apply pressure, the bandage was soaked through with blood and the young man was pale and unresponsive. He wasn't going to make it.

"Contact front!" Krueger yelled as a new wave of gunfire broke out.

"Everything's going to be okay," Harvath told Biscuit. "You hold here. Cover our six. We got this."

Standing up, he readied his weapon, popped around the doorframe, and got back in the fight.

Hookah, Jacks, and Krueger had already moved to cover. There were too many bullets flying for Harvath to join them, so he returned fire from where he was.

"Frag out!" Hookah yelled as he sent a grenade hurtling toward their assailants.

Harvath and the rest of his team crouched down behind their various pieces of cover and waited for the detonation. Once the explosion happened, they got back up and started firing.

Harvath used the opportunity to run toward Krueger's position. When he got there, he changed magazines and announced to the team, "Reloading!"

Jacks and Hookah laid down cover fire for each other as they charged over to where Harvath and Krueger were.

"Biscuit?" Jacks asked as he changed magazines.

Harvath shook his head.

Hookah closed his eyes for a brief second as he swapped magazines. "Motherfuckers," he said. "What's the plan?"

Harvath didn't hesitate. He knew that every second wasted was a minute of a hostage's life. "We push. Right now."

"Ooh-rah," Krueger stated.

Hookah and Jacks nodded.

"On me," Harvath ordered. "Let's go."

Peeking out from behind their cover, he saw another wave of Ravens pouring into the courtyard—the biggest one yet. Before he even realized that he had applied pressure to his trigger, he was firing.

As the Ravens dropped, he was joined by the rest of his team, all of them sending rounds across the courtyard and ripping the enemy to pieces.

Leaping to his feet, Harvath charged forward, leading his men deeper into the fight.

Without even needing to be told, the men contracted into a tight tactical formation, delivering controlled bursts of deadly fire at anything that moved. Within seconds, they had reached the main building.

As Krueger and Hookah took up covering positions and Jacks watched the courtyard behind them, Harvath removed a frag, pulled the pin, and tossed it inside the main building.

"Frag out!" he yelled as he and his teammates turned away from the explosion.

The moment it detonated, they regrouped and rushed inside. Harvath now had a horrible decision to make. Go find Anna Royko first, go find the little twin girls first, or split the team in half and do both at the same time.

He hated situations like this. But this was why he had been trained the way he had. The core mission took precedence. Anna Royko came first. That's why they were here.

As Harvath and his team crossed the polished vestibule floor, they continued to fire tight bursts. Waves of Ravens kept flooding in.

Using the room's massive staircase for cover, they pushed the Ravens back and chased their retreat with another frag grenade, felling even more of the Russian mercenaries.

In a gunfight, there were only three things you should be doing—shooting, moving, or reloading. Harvath's team knew this all too well and were executing a perfectly orchestrated, bloody ballet without even thinking.

Crossing into a large reception hall, they pushed fast toward the doorway at the other end. They needed to get downstairs and get to Anna Royko before any of the Ravens decided to kill her.

They were almost at the door when it burst open and a trio of Russians leapt out. Harvath drilled all three of them.

The darkness was working to their advantage. Few if any of the Ravens were using night vision.

With Harvath on point, they stepped over the bodies and moved quickly but quietly down the stairs.

The basement was cluttered with all sorts of art and artifacts—gilded paintings, altarpieces, crates filled with rare books and manuscripts. It was ground zero for all the cultural treasure the Ravens had stolen.

There were also multiple little rooms off to each side that they didn't have time to fully clear. Popping open each door with their guns up, they did a quick peek and moved on. The priority wasn't finding and eliminating bad guys, it was finding and rescuing Anna Royko.

As Harvath and Krueger pushed forward, Jacks and Hookah kept their focus on the team's six—just in case a threat came down the hall from upstairs or out of one of the rooms they had just looked into.

Finally, Harvath arrived at the last door, this one with a padlock on it. Using the butt of his rifle, he broke the lock off with one blow and pushed the door open. A figure was chained to a bed inside.

Scanning for threats, Harvath stepped into the room and approached the bed. The figure didn't move.

Carefully, Harvath brushed the hair back from the woman's face and identified her.

"Anna Royko," he said. "My name is Scot Harvath. We're here to get you out."

Krueger entered and helped assemble the stretcher as Harvath did a quick assessment of Anna's injuries. She was in rough shape.

Snapping the lock that secured her to the bed, they moved her as delicately as they could to the stretcher and then covered her with a Mylar blanket.

He quickly explained to her what was going to happen next.

When he asked if she understood, she nodded. Then, her voice barely above a whisper, she said, "There are two other hostages. Two little girls."

"Have you seen them?"

Once more, she nodded. "He brought them to show me. To torment me."

"Who's 'he'? The Colonel?"

"Yes," Anna rasped, the children even more important in her mind than rescuing the art. "They're babies. You have to find them."

"My job is to get you out of here."

"*Please*," she insisted.

Waving Jacks in to help Krueger carry the stretcher, Harvath asked her, "Do you know where the girls are being kept?"

Anna shook her head. "Find him and you'll find them."

Stepping out of the room and into the hallway, Harvath inserted a fresh magazine into his rifle and took point. Jacks and Krueger emerged with the litter carrying Anna, and Hookah positioned himself to bring up the rear. They would have to fight their way back to the mechanical room and freedom.

At the top of the stairs, Harvath peered over the three Russian bodies into the reception hall. So far, the coast was clear. He gave the command to move.

They crossed the hall and crept along its long, north side. They passed alcove after alcove where statuary or suits of armor must have once stood. The emptiness of the space only contributed to its evil eeriness.

Pausing at the main doorway, Harvath listened for any sound of the enemy. It was all quiet, but that didn't mean they weren't close. He risked a peek into the vestibule.

As he did, he heard a thud and a roll as something was dropped from someone on the stairs.

"Grenade!" Harvath yelled as he jumped back into the reception hall.

There was a huge explosion as the device detonated and sent shrapnel flying in all directions.

Thankfully, Harvath was able to get out of the way and escape harm, as was the rest of the team, who were farther back in the hall.

Getting to his feet, he crept back over to the doorway and pounded the staircase with rounds of 7.62 from his Galil.

Ducking back into the hall, he swapped out magazines, called Hookah up, and told the team to get ready to move.

On Harvath's signal, he and Hookah lunged into the vestibule and began shooting. As they did, Krueger and Jacks rushed Anna toward the front door.

With a pile of dead Ravens on the staircase, Hookah watched for any additional threats from behind, while Harvath once again took point. All they needed now was to just make it across the courtyard.

The moment Harvath opened the front door to take a look outside, it was riddled with heavy automatic weapons fire. The Ravens had moved one of their general-purpose machine guns, probably a PKM, onto the rampart over the courtyard. They had the high ground and they had them cut off. There was no way they could make it across the courtyard as long as that machine gun was live. They needed to take it out.

Off the vestibule was another, deeper alcove fronted by a large stone counter. Harvath had Krueger and Jacks place Anna behind it. Then, with Jacks keeping guard over her, he had Krueger take up position near the front door.

Once everyone was in place, he and Hookah readied their weapons and, climbing over the dead Ravens, charged up the stairs.

Reaching the top, they turned right and proceeded cautiously down a long, wood-paneled hallway. Like the basement, it had a ton of doors. At the moment, however, there was only one door they were interested in—the one all the way at the end that led to an anteroom attached to the rampart.

There was no time to check each room for threats. There were simply too many and they had absolutely no time. Keeping their heads on swivels, the pair moved as quickly as they could.

When they got to the end of the hall, Harvath signaled to Hookah what he wanted to do. The man flashed him the thumbs-up, removed a frag grenade, and pulled the pin.

Harvath tried the door. It was unlocked. Looking at Hookah, he mouthed a silent countdown. *Three. Two. One.*

As Harvath slid the door open and Hookah cocked his arm to throw, they were met by a fusillade of bullets. One of them caught Hookah in the shoulder and he fumbled the grenade, dropping it to the ground.

Despite the gunfire, he went to lunge for it, but Harvath knocked him out of the deadly line of fire.

As Hookah tumbled into the hallway, Harvath kicked the grenade into the room and dove out of the way, landing on top of him. The grenade detonated before it even had a chance to stop rolling. It was one of the shortest fuses Harvath had ever experienced.

Leaping off Hookah, he brought his rifle up and, approaching the shattered doorframe, began firing into the room. The two Ravens inside were already dead.

Without waiting, Harvath approached the door that led to the rampart. Over the radio, he told Krueger to begin firing at the rampart.

As soon as the shooting began and he heard the machine gun open up, Harvath pulled open the door and lit up the man out on the rampart.

"Tango down," Harvath radioed. "Cease fire. Prepare to move."

While Krueger went to help Jacks carry Anna's stretcher, Harvath carefully exited the anteroom. Scanning every rooftop and every window for threats, he put two more rounds into the machine gunner, just to be safe.

Moments later, Krueger's voice came over the radio. "Ready to move," he said.

"Copy that," Harvath replied. "Overwatch secure. Move now."

Guarding the two men as they exited the front door with the litter, Harvath watched as they safely crossed the courtyard and disappeared into the mechanical room.

That task complete, he exited the rampart, stepped back inside, and went to check on Hookah.

"You good?" Harvath asked, seeing him in the anteroom. He had let his rifle hang from its sling and was trying to pull an Israeli bandage from his IFAK.

"Bullet's in pretty deep. Hurts like hell. Feels like it's against the bone. I can't move my arm."

"Can you handle your pistol with your opposite hand?"

Hookah nodded and Harvath helped to pull it from his holster and handed it to him. As the man kept watch, Harvath tore open the Israeli bandage as well as a package of gauze. After packing the wound, he did the world's fastest wrap, using the bandage to create a makeshift sling that would keep Hookah's useless arm pressed against his chest.

Transitioning back to his rifle, Harvath said, "Let's get the fuck out of here."

Hookah nodded and once Harvath made sure that it was clear, they both stepped into the hall.

Harvath had lost track of how many Ravens they had killed. The only thing he was certain of was that they hadn't killed all of them. How many were left, and where they were, was anyone's guess. The situation was still very hot and still very dangerous. The sooner they got out of there, the better.

His senses hyperalert for any sign of danger, they were creeping past one of the final doorways on the opposite side of the hall when he heard something that caused him to freeze in his tracks—a child crying.

Harvath looked at Hookah. He had heard it, too.

Blading his body so as to present the narrowest target possible, Hookah raised his pistol with his good arm and, pointing it at the door, nodded to Harvath.

Harvath tried the knob. It was locked.

Standing back, he raised his boot and kicked the door in.

As he and Hookah charged through the splintered wood, two Ravens, their faces painted like skulls, began firing at them.

Harvath dispatched the first with two rounds through his head, but Hookah's shots were going wide of his target. Adjusting his aim, he double-tapped skull face number two, killing him dead.

They were in a large bedroom. In the corner, locked in a dog kennel, was the source of the crying—the vintner's two little twins.

"Watch the door," Harvath ordered as he cleared the rest of the room, the closets, and the bathroom.

The little girls were beyond terrified.

Approaching them, Harvath removed their family picture, which he had taken off the Novator's dashboard and carried with him.

"Druz'ya," he said, pointing at himself and Hookah as he unfolded the photo and showed it to them. *Friends*.

Sliding it through the wire, he encouraged the girls to take it. One of them tentatively reached out and did so.

A length of knotted cord had been used to secure the kennel door. As he spoke softly to the girls in Russian, explaining that he was an American here to help them and take them back to their village, he let his rifle hang from its sling and removed his knife.

He was slicing through the cord when he suddenly heard gunshots behind and practically right on top of him.

As Hookah went down, a gigantic, baldheaded monster of a man came barreling into the room. It was the man the Ravens called the Colonel. He had been shot several times, yet, undeterred, was charging right at him.

Harvath didn't have time to gain control of his rifle or draw his Glock. The man was almost on top of him.

Adjusting his knife, he leapt up and drove the blade as far as he could into the monster's stomach. Then, with all his strength, he ripped the blade as far as he could to the left.

The gash was enormous, and the man's blood and bowels began pouring out of his body.

He must have been hopped up on some sort of drugs, as the damage didn't seem to affect him at all.

Landing on top of Harvath, he rained down blows—his massive fists crashing into Harvath's helmet like sledgehammers.

Harvath tried to get out from under the man, but it was nearly impossible. He must have weighed more than three hundred pounds, all of it muscle.

Reaching up with his free hand, Harvath punched the man over and over again in the face, breaking his nose and shattering one of his orbital sockets.

When the man shifted to readjust his attack, Harvath kneed him as hard as he could in the groin.

It seemed to catch the monster off guard, some modicum of pain finally registering in his brain, but as he bent forward, he brought his massive fist crashing into Harvath's jaw.

He felt the blow from his teeth all the way down to his toenails. He also saw stars—and it wasn't just because his night-vision goggles had taken such a beating. One more solid hit like that and Harvath was done for.

Planting his feet, Harvath surged with all his strength, trying to roll or throw the ogre to the side. No dice. The guy was just too big.

As the man drew back his fist for another strike, Harvath plunged the knife and his entire forearm into the giant's gut and drove the tip of the blade straight up into his heart. Confident he had found his mark, he twisted the blade, ripping it through the rest of the organ, causing as much damage as possible.

When the monster's fist dropped, Harvath once again planted his boots, and this time successfully knocked him over.

The Colonel landed with a wall-shaking thud and his head slammed against the floor.

His hand slick with blood, Harvath pulled his Glock, rolled over, and placed it beneath the man's chin. He felt for a pulse, but the man was dead.

Getting to his feet, he went to check on Hookah. Miraculously, he was still alive. He had taken one round, maybe more, to the head and face, but his helmet and shattered night-vision goggles had saved him. It had been enough to knock him over, and he was bleeding, but he was going to make it.

Harvath was about to help him to his feet when Krueger's voice came over the radio.

"The Ravens are getting in their vehicles," he said. "I think they're about to abandon ship."

"Roger that," said Harvath. "Stay with the package."

He didn't want anything happening to Anna Royko. But by the same token, he would be damned if he was going to let the rest of the Russians escape.

Handing Hookah his Glock, he told him to keep an eye on the little girls and that he would be right back.

Stepping over the gun the Colonel must have dropped when he got shot, Harvath slipped into the hallway and, weapon up, headed for the stairs.

"Coming out," he radioed when he got to the main front door.

When Krueger had confirmed the message, Harvath stepped into the courtyard and ran toward the main gate of the fortress.

Breaking a pane of glass on the locked gatehouse door, he stuck his arm through and opened it from the inside.

Once he'd gained access, he ran his hand beneath the counter until he found what he was looking for.

Out the window, he could see the remaining Ravens, their headlights full and bright, as they fled.

Flipping up the safety covers of the detonators, he then activated the chains of MON-200 antipersonnel devices running up and down both sides of the road, barbecuing the last of the mercenaries.

As the thunderous roar of the explosions drifted away and the charred vehicles burned, Harvath had done his job. Anna Royko had been rescued and the Ravens were no more.

# CHAPTER 35

The Russian border guard studied Leonid Grechko's paperwork. "What's your purpose in going to Norway? Business or pleasure?"

"That depends," the intelligence operative replied. "If your wife sent you to do her shopping, what would you call it?"

Since the beginning of the war, most countries had shut their borders to Russia. One of the few passages to the west that remained open was above the Arctic Circle in Storskog, Norway. From there, Russians were allowed to travel to Kirkenes to go shopping for things like diapers, cigarettes, coffee, alcohol, and chocolate.

"Open your trunk," the guard ordered.

Grechko depressed the button for the trunk release and the guard searched it. There was nothing to see. Anything he intended to carry into his new life was already on his person.

Closing the trunk, the border guard returned his paperwork and waved him through the checkpoint.

Once he had made the decision to defect, everything else was simply a formality. Setting up some routine meetings with intelligence colleagues in Murmansk, he had flown up from Moscow, rented a car, and taken a hotel room.

After checking in, he had left his suitcase in his room and had made the short drive to the border. Many Russians crossed over to do their shopping. The prices were good, the Norwegians tended to have a much better selection, and the quality of the items was much higher than what was available in Russia.

The Norwegian border guards were extremely efficient and moved him quickly through their checkpoint. Grechko had almost made it.

It was only a couple of miles from the crossing to SPAR, a large Norwegian supermarket popular with Russian shoppers. Parking his car in the lot, he left his fob in the cup holder and headed inside.

He moved slowly up and down the aisles, reading labels and placing items in his cart. In front of the smoked fish, he studied all the different versions of salmon that were available.

As he did, a store employee, in a long white butcher's coat, approached him and asked, "Are you interested in any fresh Norwegian caviar? The catch was especially good this weekend."

Grechko smiled and replied, "Yes, I would. In Russia, Moscow especially, good caviar has been very difficult to find."

The employee pointed to a set of double doors and said, "Our supplier just pulled up. You should come taste some."

The intelligence operative nodded and then followed as the employee led him through the back and to the loading dock.

There, a team from the Norwegian Intelligence Service was waiting for him. After patting him down and placing his watch, phone, and other personal items into a large Faraday pouch, a very attractive blond woman stepped forward and introduced herself.

"Mr. Grechko," she stated, extending her hand. "My name is Sølvi Kolstad. I am a Deputy Director at NIS. Welcome to Norway."

# CHAPTER 36

KYIV

Cleaned up and dressed in civilian clothes, Harvath gave Argos and Draco a bunch of extra attention before dropping into a chair in front of Nicholas's desk.

"How do you feel?" the little man asked.

"I feel like I need a vacation."

Nicholas fished a bottle and two glasses out of his drawer. "I'm not surprised."

"How are my guys?"

"The Canadian, Biscuit," he said as he poured, "is lucky to be alive. Five minutes more and he would have been dead."

"I've got to be honest," Harvath replied, accepting his glass. "I thought he was dead. He'd lost so much blood. If you and Kozar hadn't gotten us that helicopter when you did, he wouldn't have made it. Thank you."

"You're welcome," the little man said, raising his shot. "To the heroes."

"Slava Ukraïni," he toasted, clinking glasses. "Heroiam slava."

Nicholas savored the flavor. "That's not bad."

"What is it?"

"Varenukha. Vodka with spices."

Harvath held his glass out for a refill and asked, "How's my man Hookah?"

"He's good. He'll get full use of his arm back, but he's got a lot of physical therapy in front of him."

"What about Anna? How's she?"

Nicholas poured them each a fresh shot and replied, "They've already transferred her to Landstuhl Regional Medical Center in Germany. Her family's en route to meet her there. Physically, they expect her to make a full recovery. Emotionally and psychologically, after everything she's been through? That's up to her. She's got a long and difficult road ahead."

"Here's to another hero," said Harvath, raising his glass. "To Anna Royko."

"To Anna Royko," Nicholas replied, clinking glasses.

"And the little girls? The twins. What about them?"

"They've been taken in by a family in their village, but, like Anna, they're going to need a lot of help."

"If there's anything I can do . . ." said Harvath, setting his glass on the desk.

"You're a good man. I'm going to help keep an eye on them and will let you know."

"Please do," he said, nodding when his friend offered him one more drink.

"You know, the Ukrainians want to give you a medal for taking out the Ravens and recovering all of that stolen art. They'd like you to hang around for a while."

Harvath smiled. "I'm honored, but they should give it to the guys. Besides, I'm not hanging around. There's a train back to Poland tonight. We both should be on it."

Nicholas filled his friend's glass and slid it across the table to him. "I'm going to stay for a little bit."

"You are?"

"There's still some more I can teach them. Plus, there's been a development."

"What development?" Harvath asked, pausing mid-sip.

Nicholas looked up to where Kozar had indicated one of the hidden cameras were. All of the surveillance equipment in the office could be turned on and off via a fingerprint reader under Nicholas's desk. "The GUR has been dealing with a mole who has been feeding all sorts of sensitive information to the Russians."

Harvath wasn't surprised, but it was still a shock. "Do they have any idea who it is?"

Nicholas nodded.

"What kind of intelligence have they been leaking?"

"For starters," the little man said, "the classified list of Ukrainian cultural artifacts and where they were hidden."

"And the Ravens lucked onto it when they slaughtered the team the Kremlin had sent to do the initial looting."

"Bingo," said Nicholas. "That's why Kozar wouldn't put troop movements on the table and give you what you were asking for. I'm going to stay to help feed bad intel back to the Russians through the mole."

Harvath held his glass up "Here's to leveraging the mole."

"To leveraging the mole," responded Nicholas, raising his glass.

As the men knocked back their shots, there was a knock at the door.

"Come in," said the little man.

Yulia stuck her head in, holding a takeout bag of some sort. Smiling her big, bright smile, she asked, "Who's hungry?"

Reaching his hand under his desk, Nicholas placed his finger against the biometric sensor and activated the surveillance system. The mole had entered the room.

# CHAPTER 37

Greg Wilson knew what was in the FedEx package, but he opened it anyway. He wanted to make sure that the boots were absolutely perfect. After all, his Russian handler, in a manner of speaking, was paying well over half a million dollars for them.

Nobody made boots like his guy. Pulling each of them out, he marveled at the quality, the incredible craftsmanship. That was something he was going to miss living in the Caribbean. The only things they were good at were cocktails and sunsets—neither of which required much effort.

Running his hand along the supple leather, he wondered if he'd ever see a new pair of boots again. Once he was gone from the United States, he had no intention of ever returning. Whether it was a birthday, funeral, wedding, or retirement, he'd just send flowers. He planned to put the "ex" fully in "expatriate."

"Senator Wilson?" his receptionist said over the intercom. "They're here."

"Have them hold," he replied.

Carefully repackaging the boots, he put the FedEx box in his office closet and poured a stiff bourbon.

*Everything's going to be okay*, he told himself. *Stay calm. You had dinner and drinks. That's it. Nothing else can be connected to you.*

Gulping down the bourbon, he wiped the empty glass with a towel and set it back down with the others.

On his desk was a tin of Altoids. Opening it, he popped three of the mints into his mouth and, as he chewed them up, paged his receptionist to tell her to send the FBI agents in.

When his office doors opened, he could see a lot of agents in the reception area. All of them were wearing the blue FBI windbreakers. This was not a good sign. In fact, it was a very, very bad sign.

The two agents his receptionist showed into his office were the only two not wearing windbreakers. Though they both wore blazers, their badges and guns were clearly visible. Wilson had seen enough federal drama during his time in politics to recognize a stage-managed law enforcement production when it was happening.

"Special Agent Carolan," he said, meeting the man halfway across the floor of his large and intentionally opulent office. "Good to meet you."

The FBI man was all business as he shook hands and then introduced his colleague. "This is my deputy, Special Agent Fields."

"Nice to meet you," the former Senator replied, shaking her hand. "Shall we sit?"

He directed them to a plush seating area where coffee, water, and snacks had already been laid out.

Once they were all seated, Carolan, using the man's honorific to put him at ease, said, "Thank you for taking the time to meet with us, Senator."

"Of course," Wilson replied, smiling like the politician he still was. "What can I do for the FBI?"

"Certainly, you're well aware of the death of Dimitri Burman."

Wilson reached for a bottle of San Pellegrino. "Terrible," he said. "We'd had dinner that night. It was a lot of fun. We drank some terrific wines."

Fields knew he was guilty of something, but she also knew she needed to tread lightly. "Any idea who may have killed him?"

Wilson shook his head. "Nope." Then, after thinking about it a moment, he collected himself and said, "Wait. Was he murdered? Or did he die by suicide? I heard it was suicide."

"Interesting. Who told you that?"

"Ah, I—" he began, but Carolan cut him off.

"How'd your trip to Maine go?" the FBI man asked.

"Good. Good," he stammered. "I was there to meet with the Paulsen family. They'll back that up."

Fields shot him a very icy look. "Why would you need them to back you up?"

"I, um, I don't know. I assume we're here to talk about Dimitri's death, so anyone you're talking to needs an alibi."

Carolan smiled and removed a folder from his briefcase.

"We're well beyond alibis, Senator," said Fields as she leaned in. "We're just here as a courtesy to assess how fucked you really are."

"Wait. What?" Wilson replied. "I don't like this. I think we need to stop."

"Your friend told us that you would say that."

"My friend?"

Carolan pulled a photo out of his folder and held it up for Wilson to see. In it, Joe Nistal was in a hospital bed, flanked by the two FBI agents who now stood in Wilson's office. In his hands, whether it was photoshopped or not, Nistal held a piece of paper with the words *We're fucked. Don't be stupid. Cooperate,* written on it.

"Senator Wilson," Carolan asked, "did you know that Joe Nistal is an agent of the Russian government?"

"I, uh. No, I didn't know."

"Well, did you know that he was amassing tracking devices in his storage unit in Frederick, Maryland, which he subsequently placed, or caused to be placed, on multiple FBI vehicles?"

"Of course not. I had no idea."

Fields looked right at him. "Did you know that he had Dimitri Burman thrown to his death off his terrace and that he used you to further a conspiracy about the Commodore Yacht Club?"

Wilson was visibly shaken. "Of course not," he replied, fearful of what was coming next. "What the hell is going on here?"

"Senator Wilson," said Carolan, "you have the right to remain silent."

# CHAPTER 38

Harvath had learned his lesson the hard way. From the moment the GUR agents had met him at the station in Kyiv to take him to Nicholas until he had crossed the border back into Poland, he had kept his phone off just in case the Russians were targeting unusual encryption apps.

It turned out to be doubly smart, since the overnight train he was riding on also included the Ukrainian President.

When his people learned that Harvath was on board, they invited him to have dinner with the President. They were also able to present him with his medal.

Harvath accepted their kind hospitality and their grateful accolades with humility. Truth be told, he had never been comfortable with praise of any kind. It wasn't why he did what he did.

After dinner and a short ceremony, he reluctantly agreed to join the President for cigars in his private compartment. While not a soldier, the man was a leader of soldiers and was eager to learn from Harvath's experience.

Though Harvath tried to dissuade the man from a full and unvarnished debrief, the President had insisted. And so, pulling out all the stops, Harvath had given it to him.

The two men stayed up all night talking. Most of it wasn't pretty. Yet the pair pressed on. Harvath gave him the truth, exactly as he had observed it. Then, when the President asked for his opinion, Harvath didn't hold back.

This was war. Freedom was at stake and the Ukrainian people wanted nothing more than the ability to preserve their sovereignty and decide their own future.

•        •        •

When the train quietly rolled across the Polish border and pulled into the station the next morning, passengers were told to remain in their cabins.

Harvath knew why. It was for security purposes. It was to allow the Ukrainian President to disembark first and head off to wherever in the world he was going in order to make the case for Ukraine.

Then there was a knock on Harvath's door.

Before he could respond, an exceedingly fit protective agent slid the door open, peered inside, and stood back.

Seconds later, the Ukrainian President stuck his head inside.

"Thank you," he said. "For everything. We were right to put our trust in you. You did an amazing job. I don't know how you did it."

"I don't know, either, sir," Harvath replied, smiling. "I had about ten percent of what I needed to get the job done."

The President smiled. "Now you know what it means to be Ukrainian. Slava Ukraïni!"

Harvath smiled back and declared, "Heroiam slava!"

Once the President and his detail had disembarked, the rest of the passengers were allowed to gather their things and step off the train.

Harvath had no clue what he was going to do next. There was no private jet waiting for him at the airport and even if he wanted to hop a train back up to Warsaw, he had no idea when the next one was scheduled to leave. All he knew was that he was grateful to be back in NATO territory.

What he wanted most now was that beach, that bucket of ice-cold beers, and Sølvi.

Pulling out his phone, he texted her, but she didn't reply.

Figuring that she must be busy, he found an open café, ordered the world's biggest breakfast, and finally allowed himself to breathe.

An hour later, as he was savoring the last sip of orange juice from his glass, he paid his bill and exited the café.

The sun had risen and all around him, despite the war, life continued.

Crossing the square, he walked into the train station and studied the schedule. He needed to pick a destination, someplace to go.

As he studied his options, his phone rang. It was Sølvi.

"Hey," he answered. "Did you get my text?"

"I did."

"So, what do you think?"

"Are you kidding me?" she replied. "A beach vacation sounds wonderful. But I just had something major drop in my lap."

"How major?"

"Between us, I now have a high-ranking Russian Intelligence officer on my plate."

"That's major," Harvath replied. "How about if I come up to Oslo?"

"Can you do that? Can you get the time off?"

Selecting the train to the nearest airport, he replied, "Let them try to stop me."

# ACKNOWLEDGMENTS

This has been one of the most intense novels I have ever written.

As someone who enjoys books and movies about World War II, I have always wanted to write a thriller set in a similar conflict. The more I read about what was happening in Ukraine—especially the atrocities committed by Russia and the Wagner Group—I knew this was the background I wanted to use.

What was amazing, and often quite disturbing, was how quickly reality was outpacing fiction. To that end, I have gathered my research, as well as some additional, fascinating information for you, at my website: BradThor.com. Please feel free to swing by and take a look.

At this point in the writing process, it feels terrific to be composing the acknowledgments. Yes, it's wonderful to know that the project I have been pouring myself into for a year plus is now complete, but it's also where I get to thank the many wonderful people who were so helpful.

First and foremost, I always begin by thanking you, my wonderful **readers**. This is my twenty-second Scot Harvath novel and my twenty-third novel overall. Thank you for all of your support, your reviews, your word of mouth, and the enjoyable interactions we have online. I work as hard as I do because you are my employers and I want to consistently surprise you, entertain you, and raise the bar. Thank you.

Without the marvelous **booksellers** around the world who sell my thrillers, I wouldn't be connected with so many readers. You are the wheels that make this operation run. Thank you for everything you have done and continue to do for me and my books.

Once again, I have to thank one of my oldest and dearest friends,

**Sean Fontaine**, for all of his help on this one. Thank you, Sean, for everything, but especially for your unwavering dedication to our nation.

The outstanding **Jon Karp**, president and CEO of Simon & Schuster, continues to have my deepest gratitude for everything he does, not only for me as an author but also for furthering the art (and business) of books and publishing. All of us at S&S are very lucky to have you. Thank you, Jon.

There are many moments when I pause and reflect upon how lucky I am to have been with my sensational editor and publisher, **Emily Bestler,** for over two decades. It has been an incredible journey and I couldn't have done it without you, Emily. You really are the *best* in the business. Thank you.

**Lara Jones**, **Hydia Scott-Riley**, and the rest of the superb **Emily Bestler Books** team are absolutely invaluable. They do the real heavy lifting, keep the trains running on time, and allow me to focus on my love of writing books. I do not know what I would do without them. Thank you, team.

My fabulous Atria publisher, **Libby McGuire**, and associate publisher, **Dana Trocker**, continue to knock it out of the park for me. I appreciate them more than I think they will ever know. Here's hoping 2023 will be our best year ever. Thank you both.

For almost twenty years, I have used this space to rave about what an awesome publicist **David Brown** is. And he is. But he's an even better friend. That's why I decided to dedicate this book to him. When I reflect upon all of the many wonderful things that have come out of my career as an author, my friendship with David is one of the things I value the most. Thank you, D . . . for everything.

I joked last year that I was WAY overdue for a visit over cocktails with my good pal (and the remarkable senior VP of sales for Simon & Schuster) **Gary Urda**. Hopefully this is our year. Thank you, Gary, for all that you and your outstanding **team** do for me each and every day.

And while we're on the subject of outstanding, I want to give a shoutout to **Jen Long** and her team at **Pocket Books**, all of whom are absolutely exceptional. Thank you for pushing to get my thrillers in all the best places with all the best placement.

I cannot express how much I value the magnificent **Al Madocs**, **Christine Masters**, and the entirety of the **Atria/Emily Bestler Books production department**, including my eagle-eyed copy editor, **Tom Pitoniak**. They work *tirelessly* to make me look good and I appreciate them to no end. Thank you.

In addition to owing Gary Urda a bourbon or two, there is a whole team of fantastic people I miss and am overdue to spend time with. I hope all of you know that I appreciate so much what you do for me every single day. I'm looking at you, **John Hardy**, **Colin Shields**, **Suzanne Donahue**, **Janice Fryer**, **Liz Perl**, **Karlyn Hixson**, and **Gregory Hruska**. Thank you.

Another massive thank-you goes out to the extraordinary **Atria/Emily Bestler Books** and **Pocket Books sales teams**. Having been in sales, I know what a hard job theirs is. It is because of them that I can focus solely on writing the books that they sell. You all are terrific. Thank you very much.

Once again this year, I sat down early with the wickedly gifted **Jimmy Iacobelli** of the Atria/Emily Bestler Books art department. When Nicholas sees the raven alight on the gilded wings of the statue in Kyiv, that was inspired by Jimmy's gorgeous cover. Thank you, Jimmy.

The spectacular team at the **Simon & Schuster audio division**, including **Chris Lynch**, **Tom Spain**, **Sarah Lieberman**, **Desiree Vecchio**, and my longtime friend and narrator, **Armand Schultz**, have continued to create audio editions of my thrillers that are out of this world. You are an unrivaled team of artists and professionals. Thank you.

My astounding agent and dear friend, **Heide Lange** of **Sanford J. Greenburger Associates**, has helped shape another wonderful year for me. Words cannot express how grateful I am for both my personal and professional relationship with her. Heide has been with me from the very beginning and I wouldn't change a single moment of it. Thank you for your sage counsel and great sense of humor.

I also want to thank the incomparable **Iwalani Kim**, **Madeline Wallace**, **Charles Loffredo**, and the rest of the terrific SJGA team. The business of being an author has so many moving parts, and I thank all of you for keeping such a close eye on them. I couldn't do this without your help.

The marvelous **Yvonne Ralsky** has proven once again why she is so indispensable to the writing and publishing of my novels. Thank you, YBR, for everything, but most of all your friendship, which I treasure above all else.

To my friend and amazing entertainment attorney, **Scott Schwimer**, I want to extend my heartfelt thanks for another incredible year. Through the wilds of Hollywood, you continue to be my steadfast guide and one of the best friends a person could ever ask for. Thank you for everything you have done for me.

Finally, I want to thank my beautiful **wife and children**. Nothing is possible for me without them. Year after year, no matter how much time a book requires, you are always there with your love, your support, and your understanding. You are the secret ingredient in everything I do, and you are the reason I do it. I love you all tons and tons. Thank you for being the best support team any author could ever ask for. Let's pop some champagne!